Readers lo

'Packed with tension, intri
folklore, the quaintness (an   .. and
hidden truths. I can't r(.. this book enough!'

The Australian Bookshelf, www.australianbookshelf.wordpress.com

'An impressive debut from Anna Romer . . .
I will definitely be picking up her next book.'

Book'd Out Blog, www.bookdout.wordpress.com

'A truly captivating and haunting read, *Thornwood House*
made me dig out one of my favourites, *Rebecca* by Daphne
Du Maurier, another gothic tale of obsession and secrets . . . It
made me want to read another book by Anna Romer. Soon.'

Write Note Reviews, www.writenotereviews.com

'a beautiful yet tragic tale which brings to life the fascination
that can be found in old letters and diaries . . .
and the beauty of the Australian countryside and the
fierce way in which it can be transformed into something
dark and dangerous. An exceptional debut . . . romance,
history, mystery and suspense. I will certainly be
keeping my eye out for more of Romer's work'

Beauty and Lace Blog, www.bookgirl.beautyandlace.net

'Romer resists the temptation to race ahead, allowing
the reader to appreciate the hours of research and writing
that she's put into it. I recommend it to any who
want to read a novel exploring family history, suspicious
circumstances, and the beautiful Australian outback.'

The Australian Review, www.theaureview.com

THORNWOOD
HOUSE

THORNWOOD HOUSE

Anna Romer

**SIMON &
SCHUSTER**

London · New York · Sydney · Toronto · New Delhi

A CBS COMPANY

THORNWOOD HOUSE
First published in Australia in 2013 by
Simon & Schuster (Australia) Pty Limited
Suite 19A, Level 1, 450 Miller Street, Cammeray, NSW 2062
This edition published in 2016

10 9 8 7 6 5 4 3 2 1

A CBS Company
Sydney New York London Toronto New Delhi
Visit our website at www.simonandschuster.com.au

National Library of Australia Cataloguing-in-Publication entry
Author: Romer, Anna, author.
Title: Thornwood House/Anna Romer.
ISBN: 9781925456257 (paperback)
               9781922052414 (ebook)
Subjects: Family secrets – Fiction.
               Country life – Queensland – Fiction.
               Inheritance and succession – Queensland – Fiction.
Dewey Number: A823.4

Cover design: Christabella Designs
Cover image: Mark Owen/Trevillion Images
Internal design and typesetting: Midland Typesetters, Australia
Printed in Australia by McPherson's Printing Group

The paper this book is printed on is certified against the
Forest Stewardship Council® Standards. FSC® promotes
environmentally responsible, socially beneficial and
economically viable management of the world's forests.

To Sarah
For a lifetime of love, friendship and faith . . .
I'm so glad you're my sister!

If you reveal your secrets to the wind,
you should not blame the wind
for revealing them to the trees.

KHALIL GIBRAN

THORNWOOD
HOUSE

Prologue

On a sunny afternoon, the clearing at the edge of the gully resembles a fairytale glade. Ribbons of golden light flutter through the treetops and bellbirds fill the air with chiming calls. The spicy scent of wildflowers drifts on a warm breeze, and deep in the shady belly of the ravine a creek whispers along its ancient course.

But then, come dusk, the sky darkens quickly. Shadows swarm among the trees, chasing the light. Sunbeams vanish. Birds retreat into thickets of acacia and blackthorn as, overhead, a host of violet-black clouds roll in from the west, bringing rain.

Here now, in the bright moonlight, it's a different place again. Nightmarish. Otherworldly. The open expanse of silvery poa grass is hemmed in by black-trunked ironbarks, while at the centre stands a tall, fin-shaped boulder.

I'm drawn towards the boulder. It seems to whisper, shadows appear to gather at its base. I go nearer. Shivers fly across my skin. I stumble in the dark and pause to listen, straining to hear the sound of a voice, of a muffled cry or sob – but there's only the tick of rain in the leaves and the ragged rasp of my breathing. Further down the slope wallabies thump unseen through the bush, and something meows overhead, probably a boobook owl.

'Bron . . . are you here?'

I don't expect an answer, but when none comes my sense of panic sharpens. I cast about for a broken bough, a trail of flattened grass, a familiar scrap of clothing abandoned on the ground . . . but there's nothing of my daughter here, nothing of the man who took her.

I search the shadows, trying to see beyond the tree-silhouettes that shift and sway around me. Lightning illuminates a dirt trail that cuts uphill through the undergrowth. I edge towards it, then stop. A chill skates up the back of my neck, I sense I'm not alone. Someone's near, it must be him. Hiding in the trees. Watching. I imagine his gaze crawling over me as he speculates how best to strike.

When he does, I'll be ready.

At least, that's what I keep telling myself. In truth, I feel as though I've relived this scenario a thousand times, hovering in this desolate glade waiting for death to find me, but each time floundering at the critical moment.

The air is suddenly cold. Rain trickles off my face. The trees bow sideways in a damp gust and gumnut flowers spin from high branches, carrying forth the sharp scent of eucalyptus.

A twig cracks, loud despite the rain; a violent sound like a small bone being broken. I whirl towards it. Lightning threads through the clouds, brightening the glade. A solitary shadow catches my eye on the other side of the clearing. It breaks from the greater darkness and moves towards me.

I recognise him instantly.

He's a big man, his features a pale blur in the dimness. His skin shines wet, and something about the sight of his face makes my blood run thin.

'Hello, Audrey.'

And it's only now that I see the axe handle grasped in his hand.

1

The sky over the cemetery was bruised by stormclouds. It was only mid-afternoon, but already dark. A large group of mourners stood on the grassy hillside, sheltering beneath the outstretched arms of an old elm. In the branches overhead, a congregation of blackbirds shuffled restlessly, their cries punctuating the stillness.

Crows. Darkness. Death.

Tony would have loved that.

I swallowed hard, wishing I was anywhere but here; anywhere but standing in the rain, shivering in a borrowed black suit, silently saying goodbye to the man I once thought I'd loved.

Bronwyn stood beside me, her dark blue dress making her fair hair and complexion all the more stark. She was eleven, tall for her age and strikingly pretty. She held an umbrella over our heads, her thin fingers bloodless around the handle.

Despite the rain, despite the glances and hushed talk behind our backs, I was glad we'd come. No matter what anyone said, I knew Tony would have wanted us here.

The coffin hovered over the grave, suspended from a steel frame by discreet cables. Nearby, a blanket of fake grass was draped over a mound of dirt that would later fill the hole. Huge wreaths of white lilies and scarlet anthuriums carpeted the ground. They looked expensive, and my handpicked roses seemed out of place among them.

Everything glistened in the rain: the coffin's brass handles, the garlands of lilies, the clustered umbrellas. Even the minister's bald head gleamed as he intoned the scripture. 'Deep from the earth shall you speak, from low in the dust your words shall come forth. Your voice shall rise from the ground like the voice of a ghost.'

The ancient words were muffled by the rain, spoken with such solemnity that they seemed to drift from another time. If only they were true. If only Tony could speak to me now, tell me what had driven him in those last desperate days.

Lightning flickered, and thunder rumbled behind the clouds. The crows lifted from their perch and flapped away.

Bronwyn shuffled closer. 'Mum?' There was panic in her voice.

The pulleys suspending the casket started to move. The long black box began its descent. I grabbed Bronwyn's hand and we clung together.

'It'll be okay, Bron.' I'd meant to offer comfort, but the falseness of my words was jarring. How could anything ever be okay again?

I grasped for a memory to latch on to: Tony's face as I most wanted to remember it – his cheeks ruddy, his dark hair on end, his sapphire eyes alight as he stared at the tiny bundle of his newborn daughter cradled in his arms.

'She's so beautiful,' he'd muttered. 'So beautiful it scares me to look away from her.'

Bronwyn tugged me closer to the edge of the grave and together we stared down at the coffin. It seemed impossible that a man who had once embraced life with such gusto now lay in the boggy ground beneath a mantle of rain. Impossible that he of all people had given up so easily.

Bronwyn kissed the parcel she'd made for her father and let it drop onto the coffin lid. It held a letter she'd written to him, a package of his favourite liquorice and the scarf she'd been knitting for his birthday. I heard her whispering, but her words were lost in the rain. When her shoulders began to quiver, I knew tears were brewing.

'Come on.' We turned away and started down the slope to where I'd parked my old Celica. Heads pivoted as we passed, their faces pale against the cemetery's grey backdrop.

Ignoring them, I slid my arm around Bronwyn and kept walking. Her sleeve was damp, and through the fabric I could feel the coldness of her flesh. She needed to be at home, cocooned in the warmth and safety of familiar territory; she needed soup and toast, pyjamas, fluffy slippers . . .

'Audrey – ?'

I looked up and a thrill of shock made me release Bronwyn. My nerves turned to water, my mouth went dry. Silly, such fear. I took a breath and summoned my voice.

'Hello, Carol.'

She was stony-faced, the strain showing around her eyes. Her hair was coiled at the nape of her neck, and as usual I was struck by her beauty.

'I'm pleased you came,' she said quietly. 'Tony would have wanted you both here. Hello Bronwyn, dear . . . how are you holding up?'

'Good thanks,' Bronwyn answered dully, her eyes on the ground.

I rattled out my car keys. 'Bron, would you wait in the car?'

She took the keys and plodded off down the wet slope, the umbrella bobbing over her head. At the bottom of the hill, she wove through a line of parked cars until she reached the Celica. A moment later she disappeared inside.

'How is she really?' Carol asked.

'She's coping,' I said, not entirely sure it was true.

We were alone on the slope. Mourners were hurrying out of the wet, back to their cars. The cemetery was nearly deserted. Carol was gazing down the hill, so I stole a closer look – marvelling at her perfect face, her expensive clothes, the way she held herself. She wore a black dress, fitted and elegant, and at her throat was a chip of ice. A diamond, probably. Fine lines gathered at the edges of her eyes, but they only seemed to intensify her loveliness. No wonder Tony had given up everything to be with her.

Carol caught me looking and frowned. 'I know what you're thinking. The same thing everyone else is thinking ... But you're wrong. Tony and I were getting along fine, our marriage – ' She drew a shaky breath. 'Our marriage was as strong as ever. Things were good between us, they had been for a long time.'

'You weren't to know, Carol.'

She shook her head, her eyes glassy. 'But that's just it, isn't it, Audrey? ... Of all people, I *should* have known.'

'What Tony did was no one's fault. You can't blame yourself.'

'I just keep thinking if I'd done more ... noticed more. Been more attentive. You see, the night he left, I knew something wasn't right.'

I frowned. 'How do you mean?'

'Well ... we were in the lounge room at home. I was watching TV and Tony was flipping through the paper. For some reason I looked over at him and he was staring into space ... All the colour had drained out of his face. He got up, folded the newspaper and went to the door. He kept saying "They found him. They found him." Then he went out. I heard the car start up, heard the wheels crunching over the gravel in the drive. And that was the last time I saw him.'

'What did he mean? Found who?'

Carol shook her head. 'I don't know. Later I scanned the paper he'd been reading, hoping for a clue ... but there was nothing. Nothing that made any sense to me – as you can imagine, I was distraught.'

'Didn't he call?'

'No, but the police did, ten days later.' Carol shifted closer, her eyes searching mine. 'I'll tell you now it was the worst shock of my life. Tony was dead, just like that. When they told me his body had been found in Queensland outside a little town called Magpie Creek, I thought they were talking about someone else. But he . . . he – God, it was so sudden, so unexpected. I never even knew he owned a gun – '

I flinched, and Carol's eyes went wide. A single tear trembled on her lash.

'I'm sorry,' she said, 'it was a horrid thing to say . . . but that's the most confusing part of all. Tony was terrified of guns – he hated any sort of violence, didn't he?'

Since hearing about Tony's death from a mutual friend, I'd been wondering the same thing. Wondering why Tony – ever the advocate for peace, love and goodwill to all – had chosen to end his life so viciously and leave a legacy of devastation to those of us who'd loved him.

To my surprise, Carol grasped my wrist. 'Why would he do that, Audrey? How could he have been so selfish?'

The sudden fervour of her words shocked me. I groped for something reassuring to say – as much for myself as for Carol – but she rushed on, digging her fingers into my arm.

'You were always so close to him – early on, anyway. Did he ever tell you anything – a childhood trauma, something that might have come back to haunt him? Had he ever been ill when you were together? He wasn't taking anything, not that I know of . . . but he might have been trying to protect me. Unless there was another woman? Oh Audrey, no matter which way I look at it, I can't make any sense of what he did.'

Her eyes were haunted, rimmed by delicate rabbit-pink, the skin around her mouth blanched white. I understood what she was saying – outwardly, Tony had appeared to be too level-headed to ever succumb to depression or self-pity. Yet I couldn't help remembering our years together – the happy days so often overshadowed by his recurring nightmares, his abrupt mood swings, his episodes of broody silence. His almost phobic horror of violence, blood. And his passionate hatred of firearms of any kind.

'Tony never talked about his past,' I said. 'Whatever secrets he had, he kept them from me, too.'

Carol looked away. 'You know, Audrey, if we'd met under different circumstances, you and I might have been friends.'

I dredged up a smile, knowing it was her grief talking. Carol Jarman and I were just too different to be anything other than strangers to one another. We moved in different circles, came from different worlds. She was poised, elegant, beautiful, and enjoyed the sort of lifestyle I'd only ever dreamed about. If it hadn't been for Tony, our paths would never have crossed.

Carol slid her hand into her shoulder bag and withdrew a small parcel wrapped in fabric. 'I found this in his belongings. I thought it was something you might like to have.'

I recognised the fabric at once – it was a scarf Tony had brought back from a trip to Italy, the first year he'd flown over for the Venice Biennale. Wrapped inside was a Murano glass paperweight with an electric-blue butterfly preserved at its centre.

'Thank you.' A buzz of warmth. I locked my fingers around the object's cool hardness, flashing back to the days when Tony and I had been happy.

'I might not see you again,' Carol said, 'so I should tell you now, rather than let you hear from the lawyer.'

I looked up from the paperweight, still aglow with bittersweet memories. 'Tell me . . . ?'

'Tony left instructions for the Albert Park house to be sold. I hate having to ask this of you, Audrey, but you'll need to vacate within twenty-eight days. I won't kick you out if you need longer . . . but I'd like to start renovating as soon as possible so I can put it on the market.'

I could only stare at her. 'Twenty-eight days?'

'Don't worry. Tony wouldn't have dreamt of leaving you homeless. You and Bronwyn will be well provided for,' she added cryptically. She seemed about to say something more, but instead gave my arm a quick squeeze – gently, this time – then turned abruptly and hurried away.

I watched her glide down the hill. Her friends gathered around her; a couple of them shot me furtive glances. Then they bundled her off towards the line of waiting cars, where she ducked into a glittering Mercedes and was whisked away.

Twenty-eight days.

I clutched the paperweight tight. Tony had never actually lied to me about his past, but his stubborn refusal to talk about it had always been hurtful, as if he didn't consider me worthy of his trust. Now, as I glared up the slope, I felt the burden of his silence shift around me, stirring up all my old doubts and inse-curities. In that moment I wanted nothing more than to climb back up the hill and hurl the paperweight into the grave as a final, bitter farewell. But it was raining again. The ground was sodden and the slope looked slippery.

I shoved the parcel into my pocket. Alive, Tony had brought me nothing but trouble; now he was dead, I refused to allow him the same opportunity. With that promise firmly planted in my mind, I picked my way back down the hill to the Celica and my waiting daughter.

In other parts of the country, September heralded the begin-ning of spring. Here in Melbourne it still felt like the tail-end of winter. Weeks of rain, chilly nights and mornings. Endless grey skies. There were days – like today – when it seemed as though this drab, gloomy purgatory would never end.

Albert Park, the sought-after heritage suburb where we lived, seemed even colder and drearier than everywhere else.

Tony's funeral had left us in a low mood. We were shivering as we pushed through the front gate and unlocked the house. It was dark inside. I stalked through, cranking up the heat and switching on the lights until the place glowed like a furnace. Bronwyn refused soup and toast, but hovered in the kitchen while I made her a mug of hot Milo. Then she fled to the haven of her room.

My own bedroom was icy. I buried the Venetian paperweight under a pile of clothes in a bottom drawer, then threw my damp suit into the washing basket. Dragging on soft jeans and an old T-shirt, I wandered out to the lounge room and stood gazing through the window.

Silvery raindrops cascaded across neighbouring rooftops, making haloes around the streetlamps. Lights shone like beacons from nearby houses, but out over the bay the water was lost beneath a shroud of premature darkness.

Drawing the curtains, I stood in the centre of the room, hugging my arms. Getting my head around Tony being gone. Wondering, for the millionth time, what had possessed him to load up a gun and end his life in such a violent way. Tony had been many things: a charming and wildly successful artist, a brilliant father to Bronwyn, a sufferer of nightmares . . . and in the end, a selfish two-timing bastard; but I'd never pegged him as a man who'd willingly devastate the people he cared about.

I wandered out to the dining room. He was gone, I reminded myself. No amount of speculation was going to bring him back. And there was no point feeling abandoned by a man who'd already deserted me years ago. Even so, I could feel my old resentments creeping back. Bronwyn and I were about to be torn from our home, a home that Tony had promised would be ours as long as we wanted. He'd bought it in the early days, after a string of sell-out overseas exhibitions. Later, I hadn't bothered to argue when he'd suggested it remain in his name. I was just glad to continue living in it rent-free. I'd been young, full of pride. Angry at Tony, and stubbornly opposed to feeling indebted to him.

But now I ached ... ached for my daughter and the grief she would carry with her for life. Ached for Tony, whose suffering must have run deep; and for Carol, whose world had revolved around him. Ached for my own selfish longings that sometimes whispered in lonely unguarded moments that perhaps – by a miraculous twist of fate – he might one day come back to me. And I ached with the burden of questions he'd left behind. Why had he rushed out that night, then driven for days to some little backwater? What had finally pushed him over the edge?

Carol said she'd checked the paper, but had been too distraught to properly focus. I remembered that Tony had subscribed religiously to the *Courier-Mail*. He'd grown up outside Brisbane – one of the few morsels of background info I'd managed to prise from him – and had liked to stay abreast of Queensland news.

I booted my laptop and went online.

It took a while to sift through the search results for the *Courier-Mail* dated just before Tony's death. Nothing leapt out. My neck started cramping from peering at the screen and I was about to log off, but as a last resort I punched in the name of the town where they'd found Tony's body, 'Magpie Creek'.

A single search result filled the screen.

DROUGHT SOLVES TWENTY-YEAR-OLD MYSTERY
BRISBANE, Fri. – For most people, Australia's current drought – called the worst in a thousand years – has been the cause of deep concern. For the small community of Magpie Creek in south-east Queensland, it has brought an unexpected solution to a mystery that has baffled the town for twenty years.

On Wednesday last, a group of conservationists were taking water samples from the near-dry Lake Brigalow Dam, 24 kilometres from the town, when they discovered a vehicle submerged in the mud. Fire and Rescue Services retrieved the car, only to discover inside it the remains of a human body.

Magpie Creek Police have linked the car to a local man who was reported missing by his family in November 1986. Positive identification of the remains will necessarily await the results of forensic examinations and post-mortem.

I sat back and stared at the screen until my eyes blurred. Maybe I was clutching at straws, but I couldn't help wondering. Had Tony known the missing man, been close to him? Had the man been a one-time friend, a relative? Someone whose death had mattered enough for Tony to walk out on his wife with barely a word and travel 1600 kilometres into a past he'd so obviously put behind him?

In 1986, Tony would have been fourteen. His father, then? Reported missing by his family; by Tony's family. A family that Tony had – in the twelve years I'd known him – steadfastly refused to acknowledge. Shutting my eyes, I tried to restrain my rampaging thoughts. It was unlikely, probably just coincidence. Probably nothing more than connections made by a brain fuelled with exhaustion and grief.

Logging off, I went out to the kitchen and looked in the fridge. It was crammed with food, but my hand reached robotically for a Crown Lager. The beer was icy, deliciously wet on my grief-tightened throat. While I drank, I stared at the black square of window. In it I saw the woman the past five years had caused me to become: hollow-eyed and gaunt, with shadows beneath the pallid skin where there should have been a healthy flush. I would be thirty this year, but my face wore the grey resignation of someone much older.

I rubbed my palms over my cheeks, then smoothed my hair. It had escaped the neat ponytail I'd forced it into for the funeral, and reverted into a shaggy seventies-style bob. I recalled Carol's restrained elegance, and grimaced at the small, boyish person reflected in the window. The pinched little face stared sullenly back at me, silently accusing: You see why he left? You see why he wanted her and not you?

Turning from the window, I went along the hall to Bronwyn's room and knocked lightly. There was no response, so I cracked open the door. Her lamp was on. She'd fallen asleep on top of the bedcovers – her fair hair fanned over the pillow, her face was blotchy from crying. She was wearing the pyjamas her father had given her a year ago, too tight now, and faded from overuse.

'Bronny?' I whispered, stroking her hair. 'Let's get you under the covers, sweetheart.'

Up until six months ago, she'd seen Tony every Sunday without fail. Just as the church bells began to chime across the waking city, Tony would pull his dazzling black Porsche into the driveway, honking the horn as Bronwyn ran down the path to greet him. Meanwhile, I lurked in the front room, my lips pinched tight, spying on them through the shutters. Six or seven hours later I'd hear the familiar honking, and Bronwyn would rush in brimming with news of what a fabulous time they'd had, cooing over the presents he'd bought her, eyes aglow and cheeks flushed pink with joy.

Then, six months ago, the visits ground to a halt.

Tony stopped showing up for their Sunday outings. He forgot to ring, sending expensive gifts in lieu of a visit. Without explanation, he disengaged himself from her life. I watched helplessly as the sorrow grew in her like a sickness, turning my bright little girl into a forlorn shadow-faced creature who moped around the house as though, rather than living in it, she was haunting it.

Bronwyn sighed and rolled over. Tucking the blanket around her, I laid a whisper of a kiss on her brow. She smelled of honey and chocolate, of fresh washed laundry and lemon shampoo. Safe, familiar smells. I was about to tiptoe out when I caught sight of a photo propped against her night lamp. I hadn't seen it for years, and it brought back the past with a pang of sadness.

Tony sat on a low concrete wall, the National Gallery's water-curtain doors in the background. His eyes glinted behind his glasses and he was smiling his famous heart-stopping smile. He wasn't traditionally handsome – his face was too bony, his nose too large, his teeth a fraction crooked – but he had a compelling quality, an intensity that was both guarded and beguiling.

I switched off the bedside lamp and took the photo out to the kitchen, leaning it against a jar of peanuts on the bench so I could study it in full light. It felt good to look at his face, to pretend he was still out there somewhere, moving through life, perhaps taking a moment to gaze up at the stars and think of me.

It almost worked.

Then I remembered the coffin. The boggy slope, the yawning grave beneath the elm. By now the cemetery would be dark, its poplars and cypresses sagging beneath the weight of rain, the sky raked by fingers of lightning.

Though I hadn't seen Tony for months, suddenly I missed him unbearably. With him, I'd been different – strong, capable. I'd laughed more, worried less, opened up and found pleasure in unexpected places. When he left I pulled back into my shell – escaping into my work, neglecting my friends, desperate to lose myself. Tormented by the knowledge that the man I loved no longer loved me.

The only light in that dark time had been Bronwyn. Despite her own confusion over Tony's leaving, she'd been a chirpy little girl, seemingly wise beyond her six years. I'd thrown myself into mothering her, and been rewarded by moments of closeness we'd rarely shared before. Even as a baby, Bronwyn had gravitated to her father – she was the tiny moon that orbited Planet Tony, worshipful and constant. She'd run to me for scraped knees, for a bandaid and a pat . . . but afterwards she'd always hobble off to Tony, knowing he was the only one able to kiss away her pain, calm her vexation, tease a laugh from her baby lips.

But then, after Tony left, we connected. Bronwyn would giggle madly and fling her arms around my waist, insisting that I was the prettiest, the best, the nicest mummy in the whole entire world . . . and those moments had saved me.

I sighed. 'Dammit, Tony. Why did you have to go and die?'

I'd met him at art school. At seventeen I'd been critically shy, but determined to establish myself as a photographer. I'd grown up with my Aunt Morag, and after she died I'd found a Box Brownie camera in her belongings. I quickly became obsessed, and when I realised there were people who made a living by taking pictures, I was determined to count myself among them. Not knowing where else to start, I enrolled at the Victorian College of the Arts.

Tony was in the painting department, and a few years ahead of me. He was talented, mysterious, popular, funny . . . yet oddly – and enticingly – vulnerable. We'd been rubbing shoulders at the local watering hole for nearly six months before I drummed up the courage to speak to him. To my baffled delight we hooked up quickly. Within a year I was pregnant. I deferred my studies, unable to think of anything but Tony and the baby. As our child grew within me, so did my confidence. Tony loved me, and the world was a happy place to be. Commissions for photographic work trickled in, and for the first time in my life I felt as though I belonged somewhere – truly belonged.

Tony's success came swiftly. He began selling his paintings through a top-notch gallery, building a name for himself, working harder than ever. He got invited to the Venice Biennale, a career highlight for him at the time, and also a memorable milestone in our life together. Bronwyn was born soon after his return, and it seemed that life couldn't get any better. It was so dreamily good, so fairytale perfect, that it made me nervous. That was when the decay set in. Slowly, so slowly at first that I barely noticed.

Tony began spending more time away. He was working at the studio, he said, preparing for a big group show at the National Gallery. Over the next few years a pattern developed. The more Tony withdrew into his career, the tighter I clung to him . . . and the tighter I clung, the further he withdrew.

I chewed my fingernails to the quick, spent nights prowling the house, unable to sleep. My photos became dark and somehow disturbed: hollow-eyed children; solitary old people feeding pigeons or gazing out to sea. Bare trees, derelict buildings, empty playgrounds. Fear nibbled at my happiness, creating holes I could find no way to fill. On the surface, life went on as usual. We took Bronwyn to the beach, or for long country drives; we helped organise school concerts, attended ballet then netball like the doting parents we were . . . But privately, we were both wretched.

We argued all the time. Money became an issue. We stopped making love. So when Tony started coming home later and later – and then not at all – I knew the end was near.

How wrong I was. Unknown to me, the end had already been and gone.

The phone shrilled on the kitchen bench, jolting me from my thoughts. I allowed it to ring, waiting for the answering machine to splutter awake. An entire evening of wallowing lay ahead and I intended to make the most of it. But then, at the last minute, I panicked and made a lunge for the handset.

'Hello?'

'Ms Kepler, it's Margot Fraser here, Tony's lawyer. Sorry to call so late in the day, but there's a pressing matter I need to discuss with you. Are you free tomorrow?'

I stiffened. Tony's lawyer? My mind began to scramble, stirring up a muddy froth of guilt and alarm. My long-dormant survival instinct bubbled forth. Say anything, it warned; blurt any excuse to buy more time.

'Tomorrow's Saturday,' I informed her lamely.

'It's regarding Tony's will,' the woman explained, 'and rather urgent. I'll be in the office tomorrow until four o'clock, but I can drop by your house if that's more convenient?'

Fear laced through my stomach and tied itself in a knot. The last thing I wanted was anyone on official business coming here. Crazily, I had the urge to tell her about the spare room – all the boxes of books I'd stored there, Bronwyn's old bike and the piles of untouched sewing that had been gathering dust for years. Surely she wasn't going to insist we vacate the house immediately?

'Ms Kepler, are you there?'

'Yes, tomorrow will be fine. I'll pop into the office.'

She gave me the address, then said, 'Sometime after lunch, let's say two o'clock? It won't take long, but if you've got any questions it'll give us time to be thorough.'

'Great,' I said hurriedly, ever the chicken-hearted. 'See you then.'

'Here's one.'

Saturday morning, the kitchen smelled of toast and fresh coffee. Rain bucketed down outside. The windows were fogged, cutting us off from the rest of the world. Usually I loved hearing rain hammer the roof and hiss along the guttering. Today the sound was unsettling, a reminder that the secure little world we'd created here was about to end.

Bronwyn elbowed me, tapping her finger on the rental section of the newspaper she'd spread across the table in front of her. 'What do you think?'

I blinked at the sea of print. Sleep had foxed me again last night, luring me to the brink of much-needed unconsciousness, only to skitter away the moment I began to drift. I kept seeing Tony's grave, surrounded by sodden flowers and fast filling with water . . . and I kept hearing Carol's fretful words: 'Why would he do that, Audrey. Why – ?'

I took a gulp of coffee. 'How much?'

Bronwyn made an approving sound. 'Three-ninety a week. Second bathroom. Looks nice.'

The coffee burned my throat and I let out a weak little cough. A second bathroom was all very well, but three-ninety? Our rambling old house had its drawbacks, but it was rent-free. Tony had never paid child support; I'd refused him that satisfaction. Instead, I'd agreed to stay on at the old house after he moved in with Carol. In the five years that Bronwyn and I had lived here alone, I'd saved a substantial nest egg that would go towards buying a home of our own one day. All I needed was a few more years . . .

'Is there anything cheaper?'

'That's about the cheapest, Mum. Unless we cram into a bedsit.'

I rubbed my eyes, seeing my nest egg swiftly sucked into the vortex of someone else's mortgage. 'Maybe there'll be something in tomorrow's paper.'

'Tomorrow's Sunday.' Bronwyn's finger moved expertly down the page as she continued to scan. 'They don't do real estate on a Sunday.'

I gazed at her, wondering how an eleven-year-old knew these things. Wondering how she managed to stay so calm, while my stomach was twisting itself into knots. I checked the clock above the fridge. Only a few more hours of torture to go. The muscles in the back of my head were as tight as rubber bands. I rolled my shoulders to ease the strain, then tried to focus on my daughter's finger as it snailed through the maze of potential new homes.

The finger stopped abruptly. Bronwyn peered into my face. 'You keep checking the clock. Are we going somewhere?'

'Your father's lawyer wants to see me this afternoon. It won't take long. I'll drop you at netball and be back in plenty of time to pick you up.'

Bronwyn's eyes widened. 'He's left us something?'

I shrugged, not wanting to get her hopes up. 'Carol might've changed her mind about the twenty-eight days. She could want us out of the house sooner.'

'I'm coming with you.'

I hesitated. The Sundays Bronwyn had once spent with her father were now passed in her bedroom – the door locked while she pored over photos of the two of them, shuffling through her mementoes, refusing to eat anything until early evening when she'd re-emerge red-eyed and solemn as a priestess. She'd been grieving for him long before his death, I realised.

'Please, Mum?' She gazed up at me, her eyes blue as spring-water.

'It'll be boring.'

'Please?'

I sighed. Carol had hinted that Bronwyn would be well provided for. Whatever Tony had left her, it wasn't going to repair the damage he'd done by withdrawing from her life. On the other hand, it might offer a welcome reassurance. I prayed that he'd left her something wonderful, so she'd know he really had cared.

'All right,' I conceded. 'Just don't get your hopes up.'

'Magpie Creek?'

My heart kicked over. Tony had died there, and I knew with a sudden pinch of apprehension that the little town must have meant more to him than a random port of call. I remembered the *Courier-Mail* article about the man's remains found in the dam ... and wondered if I'd dismissed the connection too hastily.

I cleared my dry throat. 'That's in Queensland, isn't it?'

The woman sitting behind the vast oak desk – Margot – smiled warmly. 'It's an hour or so south-west of Brisbane. Quite pretty, I'm told. Mostly farmland, but it boasts spectacular volcanic remnants that draw a lot of tourist interest. The town is small, but there's a thriving art community and several award-winning cafes, as well as the usual amenities.'

Bronwyn sat on a leather chair beside me, perched forward, gazing raptly into the lawyer's face. She looked older than her eleven years: maybe it was the dark blue dress and smart black sandals she'd insisted on wearing. Then again, perhaps it was simply that she'd brightened on hearing the news of her father's bequest. A considerable trust fund accessible when she turned twenty-one, and a huge delicate watercolour of a robin that she'd long admired.

Most astonishing was what Tony had left for me.

'A house,' I marvelled, shifting awkwardly. I couldn't help wondering if there was a catch. 'What about Tony's wife?'

Margot nodded. 'Carol is satisfied with Tony's decision; she's informed us that she won't be contesting the will. Now . . . Tony left keys in security with our office. The probate process should take about a month, after which time the keys and all documentation will pass into your hands. In the meantime, perhaps you'd like to hear a little more about the property?'

'Sure.'

Margot opened a folder. 'Thornwood originally belonged to Tony's grandfather, but I expect you already know that?'

I shook my head. 'This is the first I've heard of it.'

'Well, you're in for a treat,' she said, drawing out a large colour photo and placing it on the desk before us. 'That's the homestead – gorgeous, isn't it? It was built in 1936, a classic old Queenslander with four bedrooms. It's fully furnished – I'm assuming Tony decided to keep the place intact for sentimental reasons. There's a vegie garden, orchard, creek access . . . Also, hidden up in the hills surrounding the property, there's a small dwelling that was probably the original settlers' cabin, most likely built sometime in the late 1800s.'

The photo showed a magnificent residence skirted by a shady wraparound verandah. Stained-glass panels curved out from twin bay windows, and iron lacework festooned the eaves. The garden surrounding it was a maze of hydrangeas and lavender hedges, with a brick path meandering up the grassy slope towards wide welcoming stairs. Dappled sunlight danced across the lawn, where a magnificent old rose arbour sat smothered in crimson blooms.

'The house itself is quite a feature,' Margot went on, 'but as with any property, the true value is in the land. The total land size is 2500 acres – that's just over a thousand hectares. The property adjoins two other large farms, but most of it backs onto the Gower National Park. You have 200 acres of grazing pasture, with rich dark soil, dams, fencing, a permanent creek . . . and according to the report, the views are stunning.'

Bronwyn sighed. 'Mum, it's perfect.'

'We're not going to live there,' I said hastily.

'But Mum – '

'We'll sell it and buy a place of our own here in Melbourne.'

Bronwyn gave me a mournful look, but I ignored her and resumed my inspection of the photo. After Tony's death I'd vowed to forget him . . . for Bronwyn's sake as well as my own; how could I do that if we were living in his grandfather's house? The old homestead looked huge and rambling and mysterious. Probably full of secrets, riddled with ghosts, haunted by other people's memories.

Tony's memories.

Margot drew out another photo: an aerial view that showed the property as heart-shaped and densely forested. A section of cleared grazing land rolled along the southernmost quarter, a verdant patchwork stitched with fences and dotted with brown dams. Central to the photo was the homestead – a rectangular patch of iron roof, surrounded by sprawling gardens that rambled uphill and vanished into bushland. A ridge of hills swept to the north-west, mostly heavily treed, but there were curiously bald areas where stone formations pushed through the rust-red earth.

'If you did change your mind and decide to live at Thornwood,' Margot told us, 'there's really not a lot to do. The paddocks are mostly in agistment, which means you'll have additional income from farmers grazing stock on your land. The rest is natural bushland, so aside from general maintenance near the house, it's the sort of property you can simply sit back and enjoy.'

She collected the photos and slid them back into the property file. 'Now, I expect you're keen to know how much it's worth.'

Shadows were creeping across the room; the light filtering through the window had taken on a grey tinge. My chair creaked as I shifted my weight. A rundown old house on a chunk of wilderness, miles from anywhere; a few grazing paddocks, some muddy dams. Nothing to get too keyed up about, surely?

I nodded.

Margot wrote on a notepad and tore off the top leaf, then placed it reverently on the desk in front of us.

Bronwyn gasped.

The lawyer smiled approvingly. 'Certainly worth the trouble of a quick look, wouldn't you say?'

2

In early October we disembarked at Brisbane airport. As we walked across the shimmering asphalt, the winter greyness thawed from my bones. Under my heavy cardigan, I began to sweat. Bronwyn was already peeling out of her tracksuit top, baring her lily arms to the sun. I knew that within minutes she'd be a lobster, but the warmth was so delicious after months of cold that I decided to let her enjoy it while it lasted.

After all, we were only here for the day.

My mission: To inspect the old homestead Tony had left me and make a note of any maintenance it must certainly need. Then I'd enlist a local real estate agent to sell it. According to Tony's lawyer, Thornwood was worth more money than I could reasonably comprehend . . . but that wasn't why I was keen to offload it. Of course, the money would be a life-changing boon. My income as a freelance photographer was often patchy; as it was, I'd dipped into my nest egg to get us here. My qualms were hard to put into words, but I knew what lay at their heart: Tony had caused my daughter a great deal of joy in her short life . . . and also a great deal of grief. For Bronwyn's sake – and my own – I knew it was time to shake free of Tony's shadow and move on.

By mid-afternoon we'd escaped the city traffic and were cruising along wide country roads, cocooned in a bubble of aircon. The gleaming late-model hire car flew over the tarmac like a bird, barely registering the potholes and gravel traps as it sped us south-west in the direction of Magpie Creek.

Bronwyn had chattered all the way from the airport, but the moment we left behind the bleak flatness of the city outskirts she'd fallen silent. Now she sat staring fixedly through the windscreen, as though willing the car to eat up the road and get us there faster.

She wore her customary jeans and tank top, and restrained her pale hair beneath a polka dot headscarf that her father had given her last birthday. The gesture wasn't lost on me. She'd worn it for him, and just the sight of it framing her flushed face made me uneasy. I wondered what she was hoping to find at Thornwood. Relics of her father's childhood, or perhaps clues as to why he'd withdrawn from her life in the last six months. Or maybe, like me, she was curious about the world Tony had kept hidden from us for so long.

The road climbed steep hills, then nosedived along the rim of sprawling valleys. We passed a few scrubby patches of bushland – but the countryside was mostly farms. Paddocks of freshly ploughed rust-brown soil, or green pastures colonised by herds of sleepy cattle, were offset against a backdrop of sharply peaked hills and craggy mountains. My modicum of pre-travel research had revealed that the formations surrounding Magpie Creek had once been part of an active volcano, now dead for over twenty-five million years. When the early settlers arrived in the 1870s they'd harvested the surrounding brigalow scrub to build their cabins and then their towns. Logging became a major industry – forests of pine, red cedar, rosewood, and eucalypt were culled and hauled away, and the land sown with grass to accommo-date dairy cattle. Now, the hills stood mostly naked, their volcanic origins jutting from the velvety mantle of pasture, as though the giants who slept beneath were all bony knees and elbows.

'Why didn't Dad ever talk about where he grew up?' Bronwyn asked suddenly.

'Maybe he wanted to forget his old life and move on.'

'Why?'

'Sometimes people outgrow the place they come from. As they get older they start to feel cramped, so they go in search of a home that fits them better.'

'You mean like a hermit crab? When it gets too big for its shell?'

'Something like that.'

'But he didn't really move on, though, did he, Mum?'

'How's that, honey?'

'All this . . .' She waved at the windscreen. 'The pointy hills and grey old trees, the big wide sky. It's like we're driving through one of his paintings.'

She fell silent, and I found myself viewing the passing landscape with fresh eyes. Suddenly, everything I saw reflected Tony's familiar palette: dusty-lavender hills, earth-red verges, ash-white tree trunks, lime-tipped leaves, a cloudless cerulean sky.

Tony must have loved this place. The volcanic remnants, the spiky grasstrees; the bushland dotted with palms and soaring river gums, the rolling green paddocks. And yet he'd never spoken of his home, his family, his schooldays, his friends, or the land that had so obviously inspired his life's work. I couldn't begin to guess why, but one thing was clear – bad memories lurked in Tony's unspoken childhood, memories which he'd found too painful to face, even as an adult.

I recalled the *Courier-Mail* article I'd found: Human remains discovered in a muddy dam, presumably those of a man who'd gone missing twenty years ago. Back in Melbourne it'd been easy enough to dismiss it as coincidence, but driving through this vibrant landscape so reminiscent of Tony's paintings, I had to wonder. *They found him*, Tony had said. *They found him*. Had he known the man in the dam, after all?

Unclamping my fingers from the steering wheel, I patted my jeans pocket. The big iron key I'd stowed there was a solid reminder that we were driving straight into the past. Tony's past. Suddenly it didn't seem like such a brilliant idea, and if it hadn't been for Bronwyn I might have turned the car around and gone home.

Just after two o'clock we entered the wide dusty streets of Magpie Creek. Passing a huge wirework sculpture of a horse, we hooked through a roundabout and entered a tree-lined avenue. An elderly couple sat on the verandah of a classic old pub, but otherwise the town appeared deserted. I counted two bottle shops, a BP service station, a Caltex service station, four tiny cafes, and a quaint little post office. There was even a historic-looking cinema complete with a billboard of curling movie posters and a mangy dog sniffing in the doorway. Flocks of pink rosellas swarmed in the upper branches of an enormous fig tree, their piercing calls the only intrusion in the stillness.

'It's a ghost town,' Bronwyn said.

'It's just too hot for people to be outside,' I reasoned. 'They'll probably come out in droves when the sun goes down.'

'Yeah, like blood-sucking zombies.'

I smiled. 'There's a fish and chip shop over there. Do you want to stop for lunch?'

'I'm not hungry.' She was staring through the windscreen with obvious impatience, her eyes aglow. I guessed that, hungry or not, she had no intention of delaying our journey with something as non-essential as food.

Soon the town receded behind us. The map Tony's lawyer had given me was clearly marked with the name of the road we wanted, but nearly five minutes passed before I spotted the buckled old signpost. It was leaning dangerously low to the roadside, pockmarked with bullet holes, its chipped lettering almost unreadable.

'This is it,' Bronwyn said excitedly, 'Briarfield Road.'

We sped past green paddocks and corridors of thick bush, manoeuvring swayback curves and bouncing over bone-rattling bridges and cattle grids. At one point we passed a large timber gate – behind it, a gravel track wound up the hillside to a dilapidated dwelling. I drove on, but saw nothing resembling Tony's old homestead. After a mile or so, the bitumen road turned to dirt, then ended abruptly at a wall of bush.

Pulling over, I examined the map. Then I twisted in my seat to squint back the way we'd come.

Trees loomed at the roadside, sparse shade cowering at their feet. Beyond the heat haze stretched a horizon of prehistoric hills. I saw nothing I recognised. No buildings, no familiar rock formations. We might as well have just landed on the moon.

Bronwyn narrowed her eyes at me. 'Mum, are we lost?'

'Of course not.'

'Then where are we?'

I crumpled the map back in my tote, then revved the motor and cut a U-turn into the gravel.

'We'll head back to the main road,' I decided. 'This time keep your eyes peeled. We probably drove straight past it.'

I sped back along the dirt track, churning up a universe of dust in my haste to encounter something I recognised. Then, to my relief, I spied the hilltop dwelling we'd passed earlier.

Pulling over, I buzzed open the window and looked up the hill. The little weatherboard bungalow looked abandoned, but I noticed potential signs of life: two cars parked out front, and droopy singlets flapping on a clothesline.

I got out and dragged aside the gate, drinking in the wildflower-scented air. Cicadas screamed in the roadside grass, bullfrogs chorused in the distance. The only other sounds were the tick of the car's overheated motor and the whisper of wind-blown leaves.

I drove up the track, pulling in behind the other vehicles. One of the cars was an immaculately restored vintage peacock-blue

Valiant. The car next to it was an ancient Holden ute with bald tyres and cracked windscreen, its battered body half-eaten by rust.

I made a beeline for the bungalow. Paint peeled from its battered flanks. None of the windows wore curtains. The roofing iron had buckled up on one side like a sardine tin. Only the rampant grapevine shading the front door saved it from being a total loss; the broad leaves drank in the intense sunlight, swamping the entryway in cool green shadows.

As I climbed the stairs, a dog barked somewhere inside.

'Pipe down, Alma,' growled a voice, and the barking stopped.

The screen door clattered open. A tall scarecrow-like man stepped onto the verandah. He was perhaps sixty, with a halo of receding snow-white hair. His shabby workpants were stained black, his flannelette shirt threadbare. One lens of his glasses was patched with duct tape.

'Sorry to intrude,' I said, 'but we've gotten ourselves a bit lost.'

'What're you after?' the man asked.

'I'm looking for a property called Thornwood. The address says it's on Briarfield Road, but I've driven back and forth and can't seem to find it.'

While I spoke, the screen door creaked again and a second man peered out. He was nearly identical to the other man, only taller, thinner. His jeans were rolled to the knee over skinny legs and bony bare feet. His sparse white hair stood on end, and his face was frozen into an expression of bewilderment. He studied me uncertainly.

'What's going on?' he rasped, and I recognised the voice that had quieted the dog.

'It's all right, old mate,' the first man said. 'She's lost.'

'What's she after?

A pause. 'Thornwood.'

The taller man flinched and shot me a startled look. Without another word, he jerked back into the shadowy doorway and vanished inside.

'No one lives at Thornwood,' the first man told me. His tone had changed, his words more clipped. 'The house has been empty for years. You sure you got the right property?'

'Yes.'

The man regarded me with narrowed eyes, perhaps hoping for further explanation. When none was forthcoming, he stepped closer, peering down his nose with evident suspicion.

'You've come too far. Thornwood's on Old Briarfield Road, but that's not on any of the maps. You see that hill up there?' He pointed to a steep knoll behind the house, its base crowded with ironbark trees, its bare peak a mass of boulders. 'Thornwood's on the other side. Y'see that glint in the distance through the trees? That'll be the homestead's roof.'

I squinted, but saw only endless grey trunks and glittering, sun-spangled leaves. I looked back at the man. He was still frowning at the hillside, which gave me the chance to observe him at close range. His features were sharp, his skin leathery; his wispy ash-white hair seemed to have a mind of its own. It might once have been a friendly face, but time had soured it; frown lines bracketed his mouth and his cheeks were creviced. From behind the tape on his glasses peeped a ridge of scar tissue.

'It's only a half-hour walk from here,' he was saying, 'but a couple of miles by road. Just head back towards town. Old Briarfield Road'll be the first on your left.'

I thanked him and headed back to the car. Behind me, I heard the screen door bang shut . . . then, in the airy stillness that followed, two hushed voices drifted from the other side of the flywire. I couldn't make out what they were saying, but the muffled words sounded urgent, on the edge of panic.

I reached the car and got in.

'Are we badly lost?' Bronwyn wanted to know.

'Not lost at all,' I told her. 'We're only a few minutes away.'

She released a stifled shriek, hugged herself deeper into the passenger seat, drumming her heels excitedly on the floor.

The car tyres crunched over the gravel. At the bottom of the hill, I got out and hauled shut the gate. As I secured the post chain, I glanced up at the dilapidated bungalow, but there was no sign of the two men. Behind the dwelling, a bloom of ink-black shadows infested the hillside, painting the bald outcrops of stone in shades of purple-grey.

Bronwyn was chattering. Happily, impatiently. Something about a family of black wallabies crouched at the roadside watching us drive past – but her words sailed right over my head. I felt suddenly out of my depth, an intruder in a world I had no right to be in. A city girl in an expanse of country that, though not exactly hostile, was making me feel distinctly edgy.

The car bumped along the dusty bitumen, its wheels jolting over potholes and cattle grids. I gripped the steering wheel so tightly my knuckles throbbed. It would be a relief to sell the old house, I told myself; to finally let go of Tony and move on. Yet I couldn't shake the notion that fate had taken control . . . and – despite my efforts to pull free – was speeding me towards something I didn't feel entirely ready to meet.

'It's a dump!'

Bronwyn flung open the car door even before I'd cut the engine. Dashing across the verge towards the old homestead, she ran along a brick pathway and up the front stairs. I heard her hammer on the door, then a moment later she vanished into the deep shadows of the verandah.

Climbing from the car, I stood on the springy grass and stared at the house Tony had left me. Perched at the top of a rise, glowing faintly in the brilliant sunlight, it was resplendent in all its shabby, rundown, neglected glory. Its paint was peeling, some of the guttering hung loose, and the verandah was choked by flowering vines which rampaged up the walls and escaped across the roof. More creepers and weeds overran the garden, and the lovely old rose arbour was derelict, its roses long dead. Thornwood was a far cry from the well-tended mansion in the lawyer's files, and would need more than a few days of cursory maintenance to ready it for market.

Yet it was beautiful. Wrought-iron lacework fringed the eaves, and etched glass panels framed the front door. The stairs were wide and welcoming, and huge leadlight windows winked red and blue and amber in the sun, enticing me closer.

As I walked along the crooked brick path, dandelion heads popped against my legs and I had the curious sensation of sliding backwards in time. I felt a glimmer of that childish Christmas-morning feeling, bubbling with a mixture of anticipation and longing.

Climbing the stairs, I went along the verandah to the front door and took out the key. As I jammed it in the lock, I noticed my fingers were trembling. The door crunched open, and the smell of mildew enveloped me. Drawing on my dwindling reserve of courage, I swept aside the cobwebs and went in.

A narrow entryway led into a massive lounge room. The high ceiling was strung with spiderwebs, many of them still inhabited. Sunbeams struggled through the grimy windows, splashing eerie streaks of light across a threadbare Persian rug. Around the rug's perimeter, the floorboards were dull with dust and littered with dead insects and dry leaves, and big drifty balls of what looked like cat hair.

The furniture was mostly antique, but colonial rather than overstuffed English parlour, and would have looked at home in our Albert Park house. There were blackwood sideboards with curvy legs, leadlight china cabinets, and immense leather armchairs which, despite their mantle of dust, made me want to curl immediately among their generous cushions and lose myself in a good book.

An ornate fretwork archway opened into an airy kitchen. Above the sink was a panelled window that cast oblongs of golden light across the floorboards. The cupboards were wood, and there was a square table with chairs arranged precisely around it. At the sink I twisted on a tap, cupped my hand under the flow. Sniffed the water, took a careful sip. It was cool and sweet.

I peered out the window, saw the curve of an old corrugated iron water tank mostly covered by creepers. Beyond it was a jungle of fruit trees and grevillea. Another brick path forged through banks of out-of-control nasturtiums then disappeared beneath a dense overhang of shadowy trees.

'Nice backyard,' I said, as Bronwyn clattered into the kitchen.

She joined me at the window and we stood looking out. The Albert Park house had a cramped concrete courtyard where even weeds struggled to take hold. Slivers of Port Phillip Bay had compensated for the indignity of living in a rundown old renovator, but I hadn't realised until now how much I'd been craving the sight of some greenery.

Off the kitchen I found a huge bathroom, complete with roomy old clawfoot tub. Dried flowers littered the floor beneath the window, where sprays of wild jasmine poked their tendrils through a broken pane. I caught Bronwyn's eye in the vanity mirror.

'It needs work – cleaning, a few repairs. But it's a lovely old house, isn't it?'

Bronwyn scowled, elbowing past me. Mystified, I followed her back out to the lounge room. A narrow hallway branched off into another wing of the house. An ancient carpet runner sank beneath my shoes, and along one wall hung a line of black and white photos. I paused to study them: stark images of windswept trees, a tiny weatherboard chapel, and what looked to be an old schoolhouse. Bronwyn made a bored sound and stomped off.

I found her clattering around in the first bedroom. The room was sparsely furnished – a bed, a dressing table, a colossal wardrobe. Bronwyn was fussing about as if in search of hidden treasure – sliding open the dressing table drawers, sticking her head into the wardrobe as though expecting an enchanted doorway to appear in the back panel.

'What are you looking for?'

She glared at me and hurried back into the hall without a word. I was puzzled. For a girl who'd been so eager to get here, she was acting as if she couldn't wait to leave.

The next two rooms were the same – sparse decor, simply furnished. The smallest bedroom overlooking the front garden had a bay window inbuilt with a day seat.

'Oh, how lovely,' I said, turning to Bronwyn. 'It'd be great with comfy cushions, you could sit here and read. Just look at that view!'

'I won't be sitting there,' Bronwyn pointed out, 'because I won't be living here. If anyone sits there to read, it'll be the people who buy the place off us.' Before I could reply, she'd turned on her heel and stalked off.

I stared after her, baffled. For weeks, she'd chattered non-stop about Thornwood, bubbling over with eagerness to see it, even nagging me to move up here . . . which was out of the question, because our lives were too deeply entrenched in Melbourne. The nagging had finally stopped, and I assumed she'd resigned herself to the fact we'd be selling the old place . . . but clearly I was wrong.

I looked around, seeing the house through Bronwyn's eyes: A spacious old mansion with lots of secret nooks and crannies, big airy rooms, and a wonderful garden to explore. More intriguingly, her father had probably spent much time here as a boy. It was easy to see why Thornwood might appeal to her . . . but could she really want to live here?

I followed her along the hall, down another passageway lit by more tall windows. At the end of the passage we found a fourth bedroom. It was more cluttered than the other rooms, full of personal belongings, as if someone was still living there.

An antique sleigh bed was pushed against the far wall, its mattress sunken, its head and footboards woolly with dust.

Opposite crouched a wardrobe with curved doors, and near the window sat an old-fashioned dressing table backed by an oval mirror. My reflection rippled in the glass as I approached. On top of the dresser was a collection of objects: brush and comb, a dusty little book that on closer inspection turned out to be an old Bible; cufflinks in a dish – once opulent, now dull with tarnish, forgotten.

I was about to turn away when a framed photograph on the wall near the window caught my eye. It was a portrait of a man standing in the rose arbour in the front garden. The roses had been in bloom when the picture was taken – large dark-hearted flowers that seemed too heavy for the leafy brackets they sprouted from.

The photo was rectangular, the size of a paperback, and sat crookedly inside its silver frame. Its edges were ragged, as though they'd been cut hastily with a pair of scissors. A little brown huntsman had made its home in a corner of the frame, and a couple of ancient fly carcasses dangled from the base like pom-poms.

I peered closer. The man had to be Tony's grandfather, though there was no way of knowing for certain. He was nothing like Tony . . . and yet I had the oddest feeling I'd seen him before – which was impossible, because Tony had never even spoken about his family history, let alone produced any photo albums for us to pore over. Even so, there was something about the intense eyes, the stern fullness of his mouth, the strikingly handsome face, that rang a chord with me . . . as if somewhere, a long time ago, I'd known him –

'Mum?'

'Hmmm?'

'Can we go now?'

I tore my attention from the photo and looked around. Bronwyn stood at the end of the bed, carving her initials in the dust.

'Honey, we just got here.'

'I don't care. I want to go.'

'But you haven't even poked about in the garden.'

'It's just old trees and stuff. Bor-ing.'

I sighed. 'Bronny, we travelled all this way . . . You were so looking forward to exploring the old house. Why do you want to leave all of a sudden?'

'What's the point in exploring? We're only going to sell it, so someone else can live here.'

'Oh, Bron,' I said, crossing to put my arm around her shoulders. 'We've talked about all this before. We can't move up here. What about our life in Melbourne? What about your friends, and school . . . and my work contacts? We'd be crazy to give all that away to come and live in an old house in the middle of nowhere – '

Bronwyn shrugged me off and stalked to the door. As she disappeared back into the passageway I heard her mutter, 'Whatever.'

After locking the house, I went down the stairs and along the brick path. The grass was thigh-high and thick with weeds, but it smelled of sunlight and the seed heads were alive with butterflies.

I detoured over to the rose arbour. It looked ancient, buckled in parts and eaten by rust in others, with gnarled remnants of vine still clinging to its wrought-iron supports. I recalled the man in the photo. Tony's grandfather. He'd been standing in this very archway, where I now stood, his face and shoulders dappled by sunlight, his dark eyes fixed on the photographer. Again I caught myself wondering why he seemed familiar. Perhaps he bore a fleeting resemblance to Tony, after all – ?

A horn blared, nipping short my musings.

Back at the car I found Bronwyn already belted up in the passenger seat. She was glowering through the window, arms crossed, cheeks hot-pink, sweat blistering her hairline. I could tell an argument was brewing, possibly a tantrum.

I looked back at the house.

It hovered in the blazing afternoon light, a pale island in a sea of gently rippling grass, ghostly and silent. It seemed anchored to another time, a solitary remnant of an era that had long ago ceased to exist. Even the insects buzzing in the grass and the crows cawing mournfully overhead seemed to belong to a place that wasn't quite real.

If anyone had asked me to put into words what I was feeling at that moment, I'd have been unable to say. I tried to recall another instance when my arms had rippled with tingles, when the same delicious stillness of heart had rendered me incapable of speech . . . but in truth, I'd never before felt such a sense of belonging.

I wanted to run back along the brick pathway, hurry through the clumps of dandelion and seeding weed-heads, through the bobbing swarms of bees and butterflies, and fling myself back into the old house's shadowy embrace. I was itching to roll up my sleeves and start clearing cobwebs and dust, spend the afternoon fossicking among the treasures that I knew must be hidden within those forgotten nooks and cubbyholes. I wanted to lose myself in the labyrinth of rooms, get covered in ancient dust, soak up memories that weren't mine . . . and only surface once my desire to know the place more intimately had been satisfied. I was already fantasising about the renovation: who I'd call, what jobs I could do myself –

Bronwyn honked the horn again. 'Hurry up, Mum.'

My pleasure-glow winked out. Reality crashed back. I had job contacts in Melbourne that I'd spent a decade developing; Bronwyn had school. Not to mention our various networks of friends, and the comfortable monotony of our city environment. Moving to another state, to a remote old house, making a clean break and starting our lives over . . . Well, even the idea of it was intimidating.

I flopped into the driver's seat and slammed the door. Dug the key into the ignition. The motor rumbled, then idled quietly while I sat rock-still, frowning at the windscreen.

Aunt Morag had always insisted she had restless blood. That was why we never stayed long in any one place. She'd earned a modest living as an artist's model, which allowed her the freedom to relocate whenever the whim took her ... which was often. When I was a child, we lived in a never-ending succession of basements, warehouses, ramshackle shacks on the outskirts of dusty suburbs; tiny, musty apartments, or stately old mansions fallen to disrepair and rented for a song. We even spent a year in a sculptor's studio, bedding down among an assortment of plaster busts and huge blocks of powdery marble, surrounded by treelike flower arrangements and podiums topped with plastic-enshrouded clay. We stayed until Aunty and the sculptor had a falling out, and then we moved on.

It wasn't until my teens that I learned the truth about my aunt's restless blood. After an overheard phone-call, the dots had joined. My mother was a drug addict who pestered Morag for money. Our frequent moves from place to place, it seemed, were less about Aunt Morag's arty whims, and more about avoiding her sister-in-law's teary confrontations.

When Morag died a few weeks shy of my seventeenth birthday, I fell into the only pattern I knew. I began to drift from place to place, making temporary homes in shared houses, squats, dubious one-room rentals. I slept on couches, bunked down on floors and, for several weeks one summer, even camped on a leafy inner city rooftop.

When I met Tony, all that changed. He took a mortgage on the old bluestone terrace in Albert Park, and then Bronwyn came along. For the first time in my life I had a real anchor, a family; a reason to settle in one place long enough to discover that I liked it. Not just liked it; *needed* it –

'Mum?' Bronwyn was peering across at me. Sweat beaded her brow, tendrils of hair clung to her face. 'We'd better get going.'

I made a show of glancing at my wrist, although my watch was lying at the bottom of my tote with a broken strap. 'There's plenty of time,' I told her. 'Why the hurry?'

'I'm not in a hurry. I'm just bored.'

I searched her profile, worried by the wall of resistance she was putting up, wondering how much of it had to do with Tony.

'You're allowed to speak about your father,' I ventured. 'You know – ask questions, that sort of thing. I won't mind.'

A sigh from the seat beside me. 'Mum, I'm all right.'

'If you ever want to – ' Talk, I'd been about to say. If you ever want to talk about him, I'm here. But then I noticed her hunched shoulders, her fingers curled into protective fists, the pallor of her face – and decided I'd said enough.

Gravel popped under the tyres as we swung a U-turn and eased down the access road in a cloud of red dust. To our left, the garden receded into a forest of eucalypt saplings. On the right the hill dropped steeply away, plunging into a bowl-like valley where gumtrees cast long shadows across the paddocks. Sheltering in the patchy shade were white specks, probably cattle.

The valley vanished as the road was engulfed on either side by tall ironbarks and thickets of bottlebrush and acacia and prickly hedges of blackthorn. As the way grew dark, my thoughts returned to Aunt Morag: her pudgy, waxy face framed by a fuzz of henna-red hair, her twinkling hazel eyes that somehow outshone the diamond ring she wore on her small freckled hand. She'd been always on the move, chattering nonstop, rushing through life like a purple-clad tornado.

Aunt Morag had believed that the human heart was a sort of barometer. Only rather than measuring atmospheric pressure, it allowed a person to more easily navigate their life's convoluted path. 'You'll get that ache,' she used to say, tapping her fingers in the hollow of my bony ten-year-old ribcage, 'a sort of tightness in the middle of your chest, just behind your breast-bone. Don't go fobbing it off as indigestion, my girl – it's your internal barometer warning you that you're about to make a dingo's breakfast out of your life.'

I stepped on the brake pedal and killed the ignition. Keeping my eyes on the track ahead, I groped around inside myself. Sure enough, I had the symptoms: An ache in my chest. An edgy throb of foreboding. A shortness of breath as I realised that something special was about to slip through my fingers. My barometer reading was loud and clear: You want this, so go for it. But how could I violate the resolutions I'd made in Melbourne? Rather than consigning Tony to the ancient history basket and moving on with my life, I was seriously considering thrusting myself – and my daughter – into a past that even Tony had fled.

And yet . . .

In my mind I saw the back bedroom with its rosewood dresser and sunken sleigh bed, and the photograph in its dusty silver frame. The man in the picture regarded me from the rose arbour, his expression seductive, his dark eyes commanding, almost hypnotic, as if willing me back to him –

'I've made a decision.'

Bronwyn's head snapped towards me, a frown puckering her forehead. In that instant she looked uncannily like her father. Of course, she was fair-haired while he was dark, but the high cheekbones, the wide-spaced sapphire eyes, the bony features that made her so striking to look at, were all distinctively his.

I gave a little cough, strangely nervous. 'What if we were to move here . . . ?'

'Move here?' Bronwyn echoed incredulously.

I saw hope flit into her eyes, but it was quickly hidden. I realised she'd been protecting herself, and my heart wrenched. I stole a look in the rear-view mirror. Somewhere behind us, the old homestead slumbered in its timeless sea of grass. I imagined unpacking my boxes in its cavernous lounge room, crowding the empty spaces with my own belongings. I pictured myself waking in the darkest hour of the night, listening to the old house creak and sigh around me. I remembered the taste of rainwater from the kitchen tap, surprisingly cold and sweet. The giant bathtub, the jasmine poking through the broken window. The sun-drenched rooms with their elegant hand-carved furniture, the stillness that lay over the place like a gently held breath . . . and – dreamlike in its intensity – the image of a dark-haired man smiling from an old black and white photograph.

A powerful yearning gripped me.

I looked at my daughter. 'The old house might take ages to sell,' I reasoned. 'It needs painting and heaps of repairs. If we moved in we could clean it up ourselves, make it exactly how we want. We do need a home, after all . . . and think of all that country air – no more traffic fumes or nosy neighbours, no more peak-hour holdups. We'd have room to breathe here, it'd be like a fresh start, a whole new life . . .'

Bronwyn stared at me wide-eyed. 'Really, Mum? You want us to live here?'

Tingles went up my spine. I nodded.

Bronwyn let out a shriek of unrestrained joy. Suddenly she was in my arms, all pointy elbows and skinny shoulders and giggles, hugging me tighter than she had in years.

'You'd have to go to a new school,' I warned.

She pulled away and buckled back into her seat, laughing happily. 'Whatever.'

'You'd be leaving behind all your friends.'

'I'll make new ones.'

'What about netball?'

She gave me a quizzical look. 'They'll have netball up here.'

'What about – ?'

She dazzled me with a two-thousand-watt smile and rapped her knuckles on the dashboard. 'Come on, Mum. Let's go. The sooner we're back in Melbourne packing our things, the sooner we can get back here.'

3

By early December, we'd wound up our life in Melbourne: cancelled subscriptions and utilities, packed a cargo of boxes and organised the removals, filled out Bronwyn's emancipation papers from one school and enrolled her in another for the new year, attended our going-away parties, and eaten farewell lunches in all our favourite cafes.

I'd expected to be overwhelmed with regret over leaving Albert Park, but as we crammed the last of our belongings into the old Celica and backed out of the drive, all I felt was relief . . . and a thrill of anticipation that rivalled my daughter's.

For three days we drove. The Newell Highway ran mostly straight, like a tattered black ribbon with no beginning and no end. Summer heat billowed through the windows; the atmosphere seemed ablaze, but we barely noticed. As we sped northwards, the landscape morphed from lush farms and sparse bushland to desiccated flat wastelands, and then to rolling haze-blue hills and thickly treed eucalypt forests. We navigated through dusty towns, bunking down at night in caravan park cabins, then setting out again at dawn.

When we finally crossed the Queensland border, Bronwyn let out a whoop of joy. At Goondiwindi we joined the Cunningham Highway and veered north-east across the Great Dividing Range. Soon we were surrounded by thick forests where tropical

palm trees swayed among the red gums and ironbarks, and huge
bracken ferns ran amok in the understorey. The road climbed
one dizzying hairpin bend after another. When we passed
through the Main Range National Park we wound down the
windows, delighting in the chiming song of a million bellbirds.

We arrived at Thornwood hot and dusty and wilted, but
the sight of our new home was like a blood transfusion. We
screamed, we danced, we cavorted through the airy rooms like
a pair of mad things. It was simply too good to be true. After
a lifetime of squats and rentals and wishful daydreaming, we
were finally home.

We spent the following weeks restoring the old house to its
former glory, vacuuming dust, swirling up cobwebs, washing
the floorboards, scouring bathroom tiles, buffing the lovely old
brass taps back to a golden shine, and polishing the windows
with vinegar and newsprint until they sparkled. Once our
belongings arrived from Melbourne, we set about unpacking.
I couldn't decide what to do with the existing furniture – it was
far too beautiful to sell or give away – so I simply crammed my
own art deco pieces in around it.

We celebrated a traditionally Aunt Morag-style Christmas
– presents in the morning, then a huge lunch. Crispy baked
potatoes, honey-glazed onions and carrots, roast chicken with
herb seasoning, beer gravy, green salad . . . Followed by plum
pudding complete with embedded sixpence, and lashings of
vanilla ice-cream topped with cream. Afterwards we blobbed
out on the lounge, reading magazines and nibbling chocolates,
then later enjoyed a leisurely walk through the garden.

We barely noticed the new year drift in. Bronwyn was
counting the days of freedom left to her before school began
– twenty-one – while I had started putting my feelers out for
freelance photographic work. We were happy to float along,
clearing away the empty packing cartons, picnicking on the
lawn, and finding perfect places for our eclectic treasures.

The final effect was – for us, at least – dazzling. The tribal masks Aunt Morag had acquired during her childhood in New Guinea hung on the walls beside Bronwyn's exuberant butter-fly paintings. Her miscellany of birds' nests, shells, crystal geodes, and tall Vacola jars crammed with deceased beetles were all somehow jostled among my rainbow-hued art-glass vases, brightly woven dilly-bags, historic teacups, and antique camera paraphernalia. Vintage patchwork cushions brightened the deep leather armchairs, and I replaced the moth-eaten floor rug with a vibrant kilim. By the first weekend in January, the sad old house was transformed into a home; our home.

There was only one small fly in the ointment of my other-wise considerable pleasure: since arriving at Thornwood four weeks ago, sleep had eluded me. Each night, while my daughter slumbered peacefully in her bed, I stalked the house like a poltergeist – opening drawers, peering into cupboards, digging through dusty cartons as if searching for something – what, exactly, I had no idea.

As my state of weariness grew, I became forgetful, absent-minded. Clumsy, too – knocking into furniture until my arms and legs were blotched with bruises. I fumbled constantly, causing accidental breakages, and – weirdest of all – I began to catch glimpses of strange shadows from the corner of my eye. Birds, lizards. And once, a willowy dark-haired girl. In the larger scheme of things, this was no big deal; probably just a stress-response to the upheaval of the move. So I pumped my system full of caffeine to get through the day, and tried to convince myself it would pass.

One sleepless night in early January I lingered in the doorway of the back bedroom, swallowing a yawn.

Despite my careful cleaning, the room had the atmosphere of a time capsule. I'd swept the floor, replaced the bed sheets and washed the old quilt, and carefully wiped away the gritty detritus of neglect from all the furniture – but otherwise the room was just as Tony's grandfather had left it.

The yawn finally got me and I stepped blearily into the room. The sleigh bed looked inviting, despite the sunken mattress and faded old patchwork quilt. A full moon shone through the windows, throwing gauzy curtains of light over the walls. The old homestead creaked and groaned in its sleep, and outside in the garden an owl hooted a love-song to its mate.

Going over to the elegant old rosewood dressing table, I ran my fingers across its arrangement of objects – the brush and comb set, the little Bible still flocked with ancient dust, the silver tray containing cufflinks, and a gold signet ring inscribed with the initials S.R.

Tony's grandfather, Samuel Riordan. I'd seen his name on the deed of the house and until now it had been just that, a name. But now, as I stood in his room in the moonlight, I felt his presence brush against me, every bit as tangible as that of a flesh and blood man. A shiver sped across my skin, but it wasn't from fear; more, a sense of expectancy – though for what exactly, I had no idea.

The dressing table had only one drawer. I tugged on the knob but the drawer refused to budge. Thinking it jammed, I gave it a sharp jiggle but only succeeded in making the cufflinks rattle in their silver dish, and the mirror lurch wildly, throwing demented shards of moonlight over the walls.

Then I saw the keyhole. For a while I searched, running my fingers under the mirror, examining the floor around the dresser's legs – but failed to turn up a key. I pondered grabbing a screwdriver and forcing the drawer open, but that seemed too destructive . . . Besides, it was probably just full of moth-eaten old socks and undies. They could wait.

When I could put it off no longer, I went to the bedside and switched on the lamp, then stood in front of the photo.

On another sleepless night I'd spent an hour obsessively polishing the tarnished frame, buffing the glass. The better to see him, I suppose.

Samuel would have been in his mid-twenties when the snap was taken. His close-cropped dark hair accentuated a high forehead and winged brows that swooped over intense eyes. His shirt strained across a broad chest, the sleeves snug around muscular arms. He was gazing intently at the camera, a smouldering half-smile touching his lips, his eyes curiously alight. Again, I had the niggling sense that I knew him.

I searched his features for echoes of Tony – but Tony's face had been bony and angular, open and amiable – vastly different to the brooding dark-eyed man staring out of the photo.

I went over to the window.

The sky had lightened. Dawn was less than an hour away. Once again I'd spent a sleepless night, and the cobwebby mechanisms of my brain had wound down to a sluggish torpor. My eyelids kept drifting shut, I felt drugged. I pondered the sunken mattress with its lovely old quilt. Surely a quick snooze wouldn't hurt? Five minutes, just until I mustered enough energy to go back to my own room.

Flicking off the lamp, I settled on the bed. My limbs grew heavy. Tension melted away. After a while, the room around me receded into the gloom and my thoughts began to unravel.

Samuel. I rolled the name around my mind. As though responding to my summons, he appeared in the darkness behind my eyes, an apparition of such lifelike detail – his rumpled white shirt, his spectacular face with those brooding green eyes, that seductive smile – so vibrant it took my breath away. Nearer he came, so close now I could reach out and touch him. His skin was warm from standing in the sunny arbour, lightly freckled and velvety soft, the muscles firm beneath. If I stretched out on the bed, he might hold me while I slept, and I would dream of sunshine and newly planted rose trees, and a lilting voice whispering close to my ear, a single word, over and over, a word that sounded like . . .

Eyelash –

I snapped awake and shot to my feet. Swayed there as my pulse tripped erratically, my head reeling as if I'd just stepped off a roller-coaster. Sleep was way overdue, I realised. When my imagination went haywire like that, tripping out, scaring me, I knew it was time to stop dallying around in the dark and go back to bed.

But my own room seemed very far. I sat down again. Wriggling back, I leaned my shoulders against the headboard, then somehow sank down onto the pillow.

My eyes drifted half-mast.

The rafters creaked. A family of bats twittered in the trees outside. Leaves scratched the windowpane. Somewhere in the distance, a lonely dog was barking. The night settled like a heavy blanket and the darkness tucked me in.

Then somehow, I found sleep.

I woke a while later. At least, it felt like waking. Tangy sweetness drifted in the air: eucalyptus leaves, stringybark blossoms. From somewhere overhead came the cry of a tawny frogmouth, then the soft flurry of wings as it took flight. The outside world seemed very close. I tried to recall if I'd fallen asleep directly beneath the window – but as my vision adjusted, lofty treelike shadows emerged around me and I understood that I was lying on damp ground out in the open.

Something was wrong.

Stones dug into my spine, my bones screamed in pain; my head was thrown back at an unnatural angle and my lungs felt unyielding, the air solidified in them. I tried to call out, but my mouth was full of warm wetness.

A heavy feeling of foreboding throbbed in me. Had I fallen, hurt myself? I couldn't quite remember –

Dim shapes and jumbled sensations flitted through my mind. There'd been shouting. An arm had raised up, then came down again and again. Something hard struck my shoulder, my upthrust hands, my head. There was the ugly sound of cracking bone.

Blinking, I tried to struggle awake. The darkness shifted. Far above me, between the leaves, the sky was growing lighter. I wanted to move, but my arms and legs refused to obey; they were skewed under me, useless. A funny smell lifted off my skin, a repulsive coppery odour that frightened me . . . and somehow I knew I had good cause to be afraid.

I pricked my ears. There was the trickling murmur of a creek, the chirp of frogs, the soft groan of wind in the branches.

And then, footsteps.

A voice began to cry through the gloom.

Eyelash . . . Eyelash.

I tried to cringe away, fearing that my attacker had returned to finish me, but no more able to move than I had been before; all I could do was lie helpless on the damp gravel and wait . . . wait for death or oblivion – whichever came first – to find me.

I woke again, this time for real. The acid glow of moonlight filtered into the room, and as I sat up and gazed about, formless shapes became apparent, materialising slowly from the dimness. The rosewood dressing table, the bulging armoire, the dark doorway, and the faintly luminous window.

It was not yet dawn, the sky outside still mostly black. The only trees I could see now were those in the garden – fig and mango, avocado and poinciana, all of them muted in the setting moonlight, hazy as ghosts.

I'd been dreaming, but couldn't remember why my dream had made me feel so heartsick. I only recalled shadows swaying and bowing above me – a windblown tree one moment, a murderous apparition the next.

I swung my legs over the side of the bed and toed my feet into my slippers. Shuffling to the door, I hovered a moment, trying to rationalise. *The fear you feel right now is nothing more than the residue of a nightmare . . . For heaven's sake, forget it and go back to sleep.*

But old habits die hard. Tiptoeing down the hall to my daughter's room, I pushed open the door and went in. Her cheeks were overly flushed in sleep from the stifling heat, and her eyes twitched beneath their diaphanous lids – but she was breathing, alive. Safe. Unable to help myself, I smoothed an invisible lock of hair off her brow and stooped to plant a kiss on her damp scalp. Then, satisfied, I wandered half-unconsciously back to my own bed.

4

'I don't want to wait in the car,' Bronwyn grumbled.

She was slouched against the kitchen sink, mopping raspberry jam off her plate with a corner of toast, washing down mouthfuls with chocolate milk from a carton. She wore her regular uniform of cut-off jeans and tank top, and her hair hung over her shoulders in twin braids.

'The flight won't last long,' I reassured her. 'Thirty minutes at most. We can do something fun afterwards if you like . . . Go into town for ice-cream?'

Placing the coffeepot on the stove, I raced around collecting my camera bag and spare lenses. A few days ago I'd secured some freelance photographic work with a local real estate agent – my first assignment was to take aerial shots of newly listed farm holdings. The flight was scheduled for ten-thirty that morning.

Cramming my telephoto lens into its case, I zipped up – then noticed the silence. I looked at Bronwyn. She was frowning down at her unfinished crusts of toast, a pink smear of jam on her chin. The countdown to school had reached the four-day mark, and I knew she was getting edgy.

'Aren't you scared of going up?' she asked.

'I've done dozens of flyovers. I might get little queasy sometimes, but never scared.'

The coffeepot began to gurgle. I filled my cup, dumped in two sugars and a squirt of milk, winced as it scalded my tongue on the way down.

'But Mum, it's different this time.' Bronwyn abandoned her plate on the sink and tossed her carton in the recycle bin. Then she went to the window and peered worriedly out at the sky. 'We're in a new place, you don't know the pilot. He might be careless. He might not check his equipment properly. Something might go wrong.'

'Nothing'll go wrong. I've been up so many times I reckon I could fly a Cessna myself.'

'I want to come with you,' she blurted. 'Up in the plane, I mean.'

'It'll be boring.'

'You always say that.'

'Bronny, you can't come up – the insurance doesn't cover passengers. Besides, I feel happier knowing you're safe on the ground.'

Her head whipped around. Suddenly she was all eyes. 'It's *not* safe, then, is it?'

'I didn't mean – '

'Mum, what if something happens? What if the plane crashes? What if the pilot flies into a mountain? What if he turns out to be a crackpot, like those ones in America?'

'The plane won't crash. Flying in a small aircraft is safer than travelling by car, even safer than crossing a city street.'

I had wanted to sound reassuring, but there was a catch in my voice. Dream images flashed through my mind. Dim shapes and tree-shadows, someone shouting. A hazy figure with its arm raised up. Darkness and fear, pain. And a sense that unseen danger lurked just ahead . . .

I shook off the irrational feelings. 'Nothing's going to happen, Bron. I promise.'

Bronwyn fixed me with a worried look. 'If you died,' she said at last, her voice high and quivery, 'what would happen to me? There's just the two of us now, Mum. If one of us died, the other one would be alone. I don't have an Aunty Morag to fall back on, like you did. I'd have no one.'

My head reeled from coffee overkill, and maybe just a little from the sudden pang of concern her words had inspired. Soon after Tony died I'd spoken to the counsellor at Bronwyn's old school, who said to expect anxiety, tears, tantrums and atypical behaviour. Children's grief responses were varied and unpredictable. The only remedy was lots of reassurance . . . and time.

'Oh, Bron,' I said gently. 'No one's going to die.' I went over and thumbed the smear of jam off her chin, then moved to give her a hug, but she dodged me and escaped to the lounge room. Slinging my camera case over my shoulder, I followed her, deciding not to force the issue. Instead, I got busy collecting the rest of my equipment: Lenses, extra photo-cards, shutter release cable. Lens cloth, spare battery. I glanced at my wrist, then looked around for the wall clock I couldn't remember unpacking.

'Honey, what's the time?'

Bronwyn lifted her forearm ridiculously close to her face and squinted at her watch.

'Ten-oh-five. In the *morning.*'

I grabbed an apple from the bowl to eat on the way, another for Bronwyn. 'Come on, I'm not going to be late on my first day.'

'Why can't I stay here?'

'Just because.'

'But I don't want to wait in the car.'

A twinge of annoyance. 'Too bad.'

'I'll be all right, Mum. I won't open the door.' She was standing tall, hands on hips, which meant she was marshalling forces to dig in her heels and argue.

I sighed. From past experience I knew that if I was late for an aerial shoot, I'd be flustered. If I was flustered, my hands would shake. If my hands shook, the photos would be useless. Worse, I'd be unfocused and miss all the good angles. In a plane you have to be quick – not just with your fingers, not just with your eyes, but quick of mind. You become the camera, dislocate yourself from everything but the images fleeing past the lens. You forget your flesh-and-bone body and attune to the nuances: form, space, colour – and most importantly, light. Everything depends on judging the precise instant to release the shutter.

'Bron, we have to go.'

'You won't be gone long, you said so yourself. I'll be fine here. I can read, make my lists. Get ready for school next week.'

'You know I don't like leaving you by yourself. It makes me nervous.'

'Mum, I'm eleven. I'll be all right.'

I hesitated. It was tempting. It was easier. Best of all it meant avoiding an argument. I calculated that with travel time to and from the airfield, flight time, plus mucking around with forms, I'd probably be back here in less than two hours.

'Mum, you once said you spent heaps of time alone as a kid.'

'Life was different back then.'

She pulled a face. 'All the way back in the dark ages?'

'Bronwyn, I don't have time to stand here arguing.'

'Then go.'

She was doing it deliberately. Punishing me. Getting even for all the slights and misdemeanours that I had committed as a mother in the eleven-year history of our association. I let out a defeated sigh.

'All right! On one condition. You have to stay inside the house.'

'But Mum . . . !'

'Then grab your things and hop in the car.'

'Okay, okay. I'll stay inside.'

'Keep the door locked.'

She grumbled under her breath. 'Whatever.'

'Bronwyn?'

'Mum, if a burglar wants to break in they'd only have to climb through the broken bathroom window. That bit of card-board you tacked over it isn't going to fool anyone.'

I jangled the car keys threateningly.

She sighed. 'All right, I'll lock the stupid door.'

'Make sure you do.' I hovered, still reluctant to leave her. 'It's only for two hours, hopefully less. *And stay inside!*'

Ignoring me, Bronwyn flopped on the nearest lounge chair, snatched up the remote, and flicked on the TV. Crossing her arms defiantly over her bony ribcage, she glared at the screen. When I called goodbye from the entryway, her only response was to creep up the volume.

Twenty minutes later I was pulling the Celica into the car park at Magpie Creek Airfield.

It was a typical small aircraft operation. Lots of wide-open space, windsocks fluttering half-heartedly from their poles at the far end of the runway. Miles of airstrip and brown grass, several sheds clustered around a huge corrugated iron hangar, and a flat-roofed bungalow serving as headquarters.

A shrill caterwauling accompanied me along the narrow concrete gangway that led to the office. As I approached, the noise gathered itself into a more restrained shape, and I was able to identify the recorded voice of a woman singing opera. The orchestra thrashed out the closing bars, then succumbed to silence.

Inside the office, a tall red-haired woman stood at a cluttered workbench, removing a record from an ancient gramophone.

'Right on time,' she boomed cheerfully, offering her large hand. 'You must be Audrey. Hello there, I'm Corey Weingarten.'

She wore a beat-up leather bomber jacket, snug jeans, dusty work boots. A glorious spray of honey-red curls framed her tanned face and cascaded out of sight over her shoulders.

'Here, sign this will you?' She placed a flight form on a bare corner of desk and handed me a pen. 'It's all filled out. Run your eye over the charges, let me know if anything's amiss.'

'All looks fine,' I told her, scribbling on the dotted line.

Without further fuss, we made our way back along the concrete path in the direction of the runway.

'So,' she called over her shoulder, 'you're Cossart's new shooter? Hope they're paying you enough?'

'Pretty fair,' I admitted.

Corey hummed under her breath as she led me out to the plane. We passed several tidy maintenance sheds, and the yawning iron whale-body that served as a hangar. The plane waited on a concrete strip, adjacent to the causeway. It was a gleaming Cessna, three seater, probably about thirty years old.

We buckled in, and the engine gave a wheezy roar as it sputtered to life. Corey scanned the instrument panel, her fingers flying delicately over the knobs and dials as though reading them by touch alone. She twisted her hair out of her face so that it sat octopus-like across her shoulders, then she began to coast the plane in a wide arc. A moment later we were trundling towards the runway. The windows rattled in their casings and the wings groaned as though impatient to take flight.

Corey smiled. 'Been taking photos long?'

'As long as I can remember. My aunt left me an old Brownie camera when she died,' I explained. 'At the start, I was just curious. The first few photos I took were horrendous – people's heads cut off, blurred mystery objects, total black. But I was hooked. From then on all I wanted to do was go around snapping pictures. I spent solid chunks of my life in darkrooms, until everything went digital. I still wake up in the middle of the night thinking I can smell developer.' I looked at Corey. 'What about you? Been flying long?'

'Same as you.' She grinned at me and her cheeks dimpled. 'Dad used to keep an old crop duster on our farm when I was a kid. It'd gone to rust, abandoned since Dad went organic in the seventies. I was intrigued by the old plane, used to play under it, draw it, tell stories about it until I sent the whole family around the twist. Finally, Dad let me sit in the cockpit and pretend to steer the column. I had lessons when I was seventeen – worked every weekend at the Swan for two years to pay for them. I was a hopeless waitress, but once I got in the air . . .' She beamed. 'Well then, let's get going, shall we?'

She twiddled more dials, then adjusted the steering column. The Cessna lurched into speed, rattling and groaning as the tarmac fled away beneath us. The little aircraft nosed the sky, gave a brief shudder as its wheels retracted, then lifted into the air. An icy breeze whined through the open passenger window, smelling of grass and diesel.

'You're new to Magpie Creek, aren't you?' Corey yelled. She peered over and delivered another broad smile. Her teeth were movie-star white, the corners of her eyes crinkled with interest.

I had to shout to be heard over the engine noise. 'My daughter and I moved up six weeks ago from Melbourne.'

'So you're the one who bought Thornwood?' She laughed at my surprise. 'Nothing escapes the bush telegraph, Audrey. You'll find out soon enough. What made you come to Magpie Creek, anyway? It's a bit off the beaten track for most people. I expect you got wind of our scintillating nightlife?'

I locked the heavy telephoto lens onto the body of my camera, enjoying her good-natured curiosity. I wished I could spin an amusing tale about how fate, or whimsy, or just plain fluky happenstance had led me here. I could have lied, of course. Made things easier. But I liked Corey, found myself wanting to trust her.

'I'd never heard of Magpie Creek until a few months ago,' I admitted. 'Thornwood came to me as an inheritance. I flew up here to put it on the market, but took one look and fell in love with the place.'

Corey's smile faltered. 'Inherited? Then you . . . you knew Tony?'

'We were together for a while. Before he got married.'

'And he left you Thornwood?'

I nodded. Cold air and noise rushed through the window. The collar of my thin jacket flapped against my neck. I knew

Corey was waiting for me to elaborate but I was lost for words. How to explain the tangled nest of lies and broken promises that had constituted my years with Tony? How to describe an obsession that was fuelled more by loneliness than by true affection? How to admit to a stranger that I had once made a mistake, and that my fear of being alone had made me keep making it . . . and that the one good thing to come of it was my daughter?

Corey saved me the trouble. 'No one's lived at Thornwood for twenty-five years,' she shouted over the Cessna's grumbling drone. She wriggled in her seat, made fractional adjustments to a dial on the instrument panel, then shot a curious look in my direction. 'I expect you had quite a mess to clean up before you moved in?'

I eased my throttlehold from the neck of the telephoto lens. 'Well, the dust and cobwebs had gone berserk, and a few of the old windowpanes were broken, but otherwise the house was in surprisingly good nick. It took a few weeks of dusting and mopping and polishing but it's lovely now. I could use the services of a handyman around the place, though . . . No one I've called so far can spare the time. I don't suppose you know anyone – ?'

Corey was already patting her pockets. With a magician's flourish she produced a dog-eared business card.

'Hobart Miller,' I read. 'Farm maintenance, tree lopping, general repairs, no job too small.'

'I can recommend him personally,' Corey called over the noise. 'He's trustworthy, punctual, and does a thorough job. He's not a glazier, but knowing old Hobe he'll insist on fixing your windows himself . . . and anything else you might want doing. He cuts grass, traps possums, builds the sturdiest chook pens this side of the black stump. Last year one of my gum trees split down the middle after a storm – Hobe drilled a coach bolt through the divide and winched the trunk back together. You can't even see the bolt now, the bark grew back over it. He's a treasure. I'll give him advance warning if you like, I'm seeing him this afternoon.'

'He's a friend of yours?'

'You might say that. He's lived in Magpie Creek forever. An eccentric old fella, but don't let his scruffy appearance put you off. He's smart, knows everything there is to know about anything. A walking encyclopaedia, Dad calls him.'

That got my attention. 'I wonder how much he knows about Thornwood?'

'Probably its entire history, right down to the type of timber used in the house construction.'

I tucked the card into my pocket, thoughtful. 'Corey, how did you know Tony?'

She looked wary. 'We grew up together – we used to hang out after school, muck about on holidays, that sort of thing.'

'Did you see him before he died?'

'No –' She looked across at me. 'Gosh, Audrey, losing him must have been dreadful for you . . . It was bad enough for me, and I hadn't seen him since we were kids.'

'It was a shock. Tony and I were together for eight years. Then he married someone else . . . but we have a daughter, Bronwyn. She's only eleven, his death hit her pretty hard.'

Corey did a double-take, her freckles dancing like golden tealeaves on her tanned skin. 'Poor kid,' she said. 'She must be devastated.'

'She misses him,' I agreed. 'She was six when Tony left, but they stayed close. Every Sunday they went on outings together, and he always made a fuss over birthdays and Christmas. He was a great dad. Until recently,' I amended.

Corey raised a brow. 'Oh?'

'About nine months ago he went cold. Started phoning to cancel outings, or just not showing up, that sort of thing. I got the impression he was avoiding Bronwyn.'

'Did he ever say why?'

'That's the sad part. Every time I confronted him about it, he shut me out. Refused to listen. Just carried on talking over me, as if he hadn't heard. Bronwyn put on a brave face, but I knew she was hurt.'

Corey muttered something that might have been 'bloody Tony', but her words were eaten by the Cessna's rowdy engine. Gathering her hair, she twisted it distractedly into a knot at the nape of her neck and stared out at the sky. The hair sat restlessly on her shoulders for a few seconds then, strand by strand, began to reach out exploring tentacles and resume its forward migration.

'She's lucky to have you,' she said at last. 'A girl needs her mum, there's no better shoulder to cry on. I don't know how I'd have gotten through adolescence without my mum, bless her.'

It was a kind thing to say, but it stirred a rush of guilt. I tried to smile, but my face felt stiff and masklike.

'Things are a bit strained between us at the moment,' I said over the engine. 'Bronwyn rarely cries about her father – not in front of me, anyway. She hides in her room, as if grieving is something to be ashamed of. Some days I think she's okay, then other times I worry.'

'We all grieve in our own way,' Corey said, with a sideways glance. 'I don't have kids of my own, not yet anyway, so I'm no authority – but give her time, Audrey . . . my guess is she'll be fine.'

Far below, the Cessna's shadow raced beneath us, a small dart-like ghost rippling over hills and valleys, jumping brown dams, and weaving across a patchwork of green and gold paddocks sewn together by post-and-wire fencing. It skipped across yellow dots of baled hay, teasing the cattle that browsed in their quiet fields.

Corey tapped the windscreen.

'First property's coming up on the right. We're approaching from the south-west, that line of trees marks the northern boundary. In a moment, we'll swing east, then hook back around and approach from the north-east boundary so the sun's at our back. I can make a second pass if you want.'

I leaned on the passenger door, balancing the base of the camera against the outer window rim, cushioning it with the heel of my hand as I squinted into the viewfinder.

Rust-coloured soil showed beneath a worn carpet of golden grass, and the corrugated farmhouse roof tossed up shards of fractured sunlight.

Steadying the camera, I switched to manual focus and began shooting before the property had filled my lens. Distractedly, I thought: Corey's a good pilot. These'll be first-rate shots. We're riding smooth despite the hard wind I can feel buffeting my face from below.

We progressed over the heart of the property, the Cessna's groaning engine keeping pace with the metronome whirr of my camera. The farm's gravel driveway looped back on itself and then shot eastwards, towards a stretch of tarmac that joined the highway. A heartbeat later, the property slid away and we were coasting over a darkly treed mountain ridge.

'You need a second pass?' Corey yelled above the din.

'No, that was great.'

'All right, we'll go north-west now. The second property's not far.'

Somehow Corey managed to keep the sun at my back, which made my job a breeze. It seemed no time passed before all four of Cossart's farm holdings lay behind us.

As Corey manoeuvred the Cessna into a wide turn, I began snapping random shots. A ragged circle of peaked hills curved beneath us, green and lush, crosshatched by gullies and shadowy ravines. It was unlike anything I'd ever seen. From up here the world looked peaceful, and yet it was easy to imagine this colossal ring of extinct volcanic remnants as a one-time chaotic furnace of ash and lava.

'Look down there,' Corey called, pointing to my window.

As the plane swung westward, the pilot-side wing tilted straight up while mine dipped almost vertically beneath me. The ground rose sharply and for one dizzying moment I imagined reaching out my hand to touch the treetops.

Then I realised what Corey was doing.

'That's Thornwood.' I couldn't keep the laugh out of my voice. 'I recognise that hill at the back of the homestead, and that crescent-shaped rock-face. It's all so leafy, so beautiful . . .'

I twisted off my lens cap and began shooting again, feeling a thrill as I reminded myself that the rolling landscape below belonged to me. My camera captured the forested hills and valley pastures, the rocky outcrops and steep-walled gullies. It caught the darker green of the garden, and the silver rooftop beneath which my daughter was enjoying her me-time unawares.

The icy gale roaring through the tiny window had frozen my face and fingers and the first threads of airsickness were climbing the base of my spine. My throat was raw from shouting, and my hearing was dulled by the engine's constant hammering . . . yet I couldn't remember the last time I'd felt this happy.

'It's a magnificent property,' Corey shouted. 'I'm glad it went to someone who values it. There's nothing sadder than seeing a place like that fall apart from neglect.'

'Do you know the property well?'

'I grew up on one of the adjoining farms, but my parents sold up in the early nineties. See that green swathe of hills down there? That's our old boundary.'

We peered down at the rugged landscape where the Cessna's shadow bumped over hills and dipped into verdant valleys.

'I have fond memories of Thornwood,' Corey yelled above the engine. 'We used to play there as kids. It was wild and over-grown – infinitely more magical than the Weingarten organic fruit and vegetable farm. Bunyips in the creek, trolls under every hill, that sort of thing. We had a blast – feasting on limes, bananas, mangoes . . . cracking open macadamias, hiding in tree branches, skinny-dipping in the creek. Even after the old man died, no amount of warnings would keep us away.'

I wasn't sure I'd heard correctly over the noise. 'Warnings?'

Corey reached back and slid her window shut, then indicated I do the same. I'd finished shooting, so it was a relief to stop the rush of freezing wind. The noise dimmed dramatically too. The Cessna's roar was muted now, the cockpit a bubble of calm.

'What do you mean, warnings?' I prompted.

Corey gazed into the horizon of blue nothingness. 'Our parents didn't want us going there, I suppose because of how Tony's grandfather died. Anyway, it only made the place more attractive. We pretended it was a haunted house, and made up stories about a secret room full of human skeletons. We used to dare each other to spend a night there, but none of us ever did.' She cast me a sideways look. 'Don't worry, Audrey, the stories aren't true.'

'How did he die?'

She frowned. 'Tony never told you?'

I shook my head.

She studied the controls. 'Some bushwalkers wandered into Thornwood from the national park. They found him under a tree, stone cold dead. His body had been mauled by animals. Apparently he'd been stalking around up there one night and fallen, broken his hip. Poor old guy, they reckon he must've starved to death.'

'How awful.'

'Yeah, it was. But it gives you an idea of the vastness of the place. Thornwood's a huge property – you could walk for days and never see a soul. There are quite a few properties like that around here, up in the hills – especially bordering the national park. It's beautiful,' she added wistfully, 'but you need to watch your step.'

'Didn't anyone miss him?'

'Old Samuel kept to himself. Never even saw much of his family, as far as I recall. I supposed he preferred his own company, seeing as he wasn't all that popular.'

'Why wasn't he popular?'

Another puzzled glance. 'Tony never told you that, either?'

'He never spoke about his family. It upset him too much, so in the end I stopped asking.'

Corey looked uneasy. 'Well . . . I don't know if should break it to you or not . . . after all, you've just moved there and you seem to like the place. I don't want to give you nightmares.'

I stared, waiting.

She sighed. 'He was accused of murdering someone.'

'Who?'

'A young woman . . . Tony's grandmother. Poor thing,' she rushed on, 'it was back in the forties, just after the end of the war. There was a trial. Samuel walked free, but the damage was done. Rumours went around that he was guilty, that the case was discharged because his father knew the judge. Afterwards, the whole town went into shock. Everyone was related to everyone else in those days – people knew each other, and if tragedy befell one family it had a ripple effect through the district. That's the nature of tight-knit communities like Magpie Creek. People know each other's business, and they have long memories.' She looked at me. 'I'm sorry, I've spooked you, haven't I? You're white as a sheet.'

I shook my head – not spooked. But her revelation had jogged my memory . . . A dream, too hazy to recall, but the gist of it came back. I'd been lying in the shadows in a bush clearing, unable to move, my limbs skewed beneath me, the shadow of something large and heavy crushing me beneath its dark weight –

'Murder,' I said, a little breathlessly. 'It seems so – '

Corey widened her eyes in agreement. 'Dramatic. I know.'

'When we moved in,' I told her, 'the old man's belongings were still in the house. Not just the furniture, but clothes and shoes in the wardrobe, toothbrush and shaving gear in the bathroom cabinet. Old tins of biscuits in the pantry. Nothing had been boxed up or thrown away after he died – it was all just left as it was.'

Corey mimed a shiver. 'Spooky. You must have been totally freaked.'

'This'll sound mad . . . but I wasn't freaked at all. In fact – and here's the crazy part – despite all that, the old place felt lived-in and welcoming. There was a vibe there, you know? Sad, but kind of happy, too. I had this weird feeling I was coming home after a long time away.'

'You mean like a past life thing?'

'Not exactly . . . more like a really strong connection.' I flapped my hand, realising how absurd I must sound. 'Probably just the afterglow of inheriting such an amazing property. It's like stepping back in time to a more tranquil, graceful world. It was as if the house was holding its breath, waiting to come alive again. In a strange way, waiting for me.'

Corey eyed me worriedly. 'So you're not going to dash off home and start packing your bags?'

'No way,' I said with a laugh. Secretly, though, my heart raced. I might not have the urge to rush off and pack any bags, but I felt an irresistible compulsion to . . . Well, to do *something* –

The radio crackled, a sudden intrusion. Corey twiddled a dial and listened as the controller's insect-voice buzzed into the cockpit. She signed off, then made an adjustment to her instrument panel. When she eased the steering column to the fore, the Cessna dipped almost imperceptibly earthwards.

'There's a storm on the way,' she informed me. 'We'll head back now, if you're done?'

'Sure am.'

Positioning my camera lens-down on my lap, I scrolled through the photos I'd taken, using my hands to shelter the viewing screen from the light bouncing off the Cessna's wings. The shots were good: lots of glowing colour, crisp contrast, uniform lighting and clear depth of field.

'How did you go?' Corey asked.

'Great. You fly smooth. It makes a difference.'

She chuckled. 'Flattery will get you everywhere, kiddo. Most of the locals I take up complain that I fly too slow, the dorks. No sense of artistry.'

I found myself giggling along with her, and – as the Cessna rumbled back toward the airstrip – I acknowledged again that I was enjoying myself. Despite the revelation about Tony's grandfather and the shadow it cast over Thornwood, I was buoyant.

My fingers slid into the pocket where I'd stashed the business card Corey had given me. I traced the edge of the card, wondering about the old handyman.

Hobe Miller: tree lopper, possum catcher, chook pen builder, walking encyclopaedia. He'd know all about Thornwood's history, Corey had said. And maybe even something more about Tony's grandfather – the details of his murder trial in the forties, perhaps . . . and how he'd come to be accused of killing Tony's grandmother.

I made a superfast delivery to Cossart's, dropping off my photo-card and hastily filling out a job sheet. Then I tore back to Thornwood, my eyes on the dashboard clock. The morning's adventure had transpired in under two hours.

I expected Bronwyn to be curled up on the couch just as I'd left her, maybe sound asleep in front of a movie. The TV was blaring but the lounge room was empty.

'Bronny?'

I tried her bedroom, then went along the hall and checked the other rooms. They were empty too. She wasn't in the kitchen, and when I paused on the back verandah to examine the yard, there was still no sign of her. My pulse tripped up a notch, my palms were sweaty. Calm down, I told myself, she won't be far. Probably on her bench beneath the jacaranda, or in the vegie patch . . .

The back of the house faced west, with a view across a forested valley to purple ranges. The north side of the yard rose steeply, ending at the foot of a small hill. The base of the hill was crowded with black-trunked ironbarks and thickets of tea-tree, while the peak was an open expanse of balding rocky outcrops. It was only noon but shadows had already engulfed the south face of the hill, while the northern slope was awash in light so stark it picked out every leaf and blade of dry brown grass. No other houses, no trace of civilisation; just hills and trees and endless sky.

On the distant horizon drifted a huge grey flotilla, evidence of the storm Corey had forewarned. The clouds were benign for now, approaching slowly, almost stealthily. The shadows in the garden seemed to sense the impending havoc, shifting between the trees.

Despite the muggy heat, I felt a shivery ripple on the backs of my arms. Had this picturesque place really been the scene of brutal murder? Had Thornwood once been home to a cold-blooded killer? I thought about the big airy rooms, the cosy armchairs, the gleaming furniture that fitted so well among my own. Suddenly the house no longer seemed the safe haven I'd imagined it to be.

'Bron, where are you?'

Thudding down the back steps, I ran along the brick path, past the neglected hydrangeas and through a corridor of overgrown pomegranates and loquats. The bench beneath the jacaranda was empty.

I strained to listen over my crashing pulse.

To my city ears, the booming silence at first seemed absolute. But soon a symphony of noise unravelled around me: cicadas droned, bees mumbled in the flowerbeds, cockatoos screeched and chattered in the treetops. Myriad bird species whistled from unseen hiding places . . . and there beneath it all, like the base note in a complex orchestral movement, came the deep-throated bark of bullfrogs in the creek.

Through the din, I recalled Bronwyn's words.

If one of us died, the other would be alone.

'Bronwyn!'

Still no comeback. I was engulfed entirely by white hot panic. I raced downhill, ducking through a garden arch smothered by a wild wig of jasmine, my feet thumping over ground that was barren and dry. Gnarled trunks of grevillea and bottlebrush were choked by an impenetrable wall of blackberry brambles, and on the other side of the brambles I glimpsed a paddock dotted with citrus trees. From somewhere lower down the slope came the babble of water. Hoisting onto tiptoes, I peered into the paddock. A smudge of white hovered on the dark bank of what must be the creek. Someone was there, seemingly crumpled on the ground, motionless.

A flash of dream. Tree-shadows and swirling, frantic shapes. Shouting, and a hazy figure with its arm raised, the arm lunging down again and again, the darkness disjointed and crackling with fear –

If one of us died . . .

Heart thudding drunkenly, I stumbled downhill, seeking a way through the wall of vines. Each stout blackberry branch sprouted hundreds of sharp thorns, their lethal points tipped scarlet in the sun, barring my way as effectively as a barricade of barbed wire.

I lost sight of the figure. A bolt of panic went through me. Making a hasty decision, I threw myself into the first narrow breach I came to. Long arms of blackberry sprang across my path, their spiky barbs snagging my clothes, clawing my skin, tangling in my hair. I got trapped, felt the red-tipped spines stab into my arms and back. Then just ahead I saw open ground. With one final push, I broke through the vines and staggered into the orchard.

Bronwyn jerked around, her face blotched by the sun, her eyes filled with alarm. I registered only her shock and, driven by primal instinct, I rushed to protect her. With my first step, my foot snagged in a loop of vine. Before I could stop my momentum forward, the ground flew up and slammed into me. The breath left my body with a grunt, and I lay there stunned.

'Mum – ?'

I couldn't move. Couldn't breathe. Then, with a hoarse wheezing gulp, my squashed lungs recovered and the world swam back into focus. Twisting my head around, I squinted into the mottled sky. A face was peering down at me, pale eyebrows furrowed, nose wrinkled.

Disengaging the noose of blackberry vine, I struggled to my feet, brushing at my clothes. The paddock spun, so I rested my hands on my knees and tried to breathe. When my vocal chords regained consciousness, I gasped, 'What in blazes do you think you're doing?'

The eyes – so blue they eclipsed the sky – widened.

'Mum, look at your arms!'

I stood upright, glaring at her. Her cheeks were flushed despite her sunhat, and she was holding a jar of dirty water. The water was swarming with small black wriggling things. Tadpoles.

'I told you to stay inside,' I said hoarsely. 'I've nearly had heart failure.'

She blinked, then gave a quick shrug, feigning indifference. 'There's rain coming, so I brought the washing in,' she said with a vaguely accusing tone, 'and you were gone for ages, I thought you'd forgotten about me . . . Anyway, I didn't go far.'

I hiccupped. 'Bron, you don't know who might be lurking around this place . . . weirdos, or anyone.'

She hooked her neck out and stared around, eyebrows raised, making a performance of it. 'Nope, just us.'

'Next time, please just do as I ask, okay?'

'Mum, you're a mess. Your arms – '

I looked down at myself. Every inch of my skin was filthy, criss-crossed with nasty-looking scratches and trickles of dark blood. My T-shirt was littered with leaves and my favourite jeans were ripped at the knees.

Tears began to leak out of my eyes.

Bronwyn wrinkled her brow. 'Mum?'

I sniffed, wiping my nose on the back of my hand, brushing blackberry dross off my ruined jeans.

Bronwyn took a clean hanky from her pocket and unfolded it. I blew my nose, dabbed my eyes, and gave the hanky back. She was staring at me as if I'd grown horns, and I knew I should at least try to explain myself. But how do you admit to an eleven-year-old that she is all you have, and that the idea of losing her – even just the idea of it – is enough to unhinge you?

It was too big a burden to put on a child, of course, so I held my tongue and stowed my fear back in the shadows where it belonged.

'It's lunch time,' I said instead. 'We can order pizza, if you like. Or fish and chips?'

Bronwyn gazed across the distant hills, avoiding my eyes. She swirled the muddy water in the jar, swilling the tadpoles at breakneck speed around the inside of their glass prison.

'Fish and chips'll be fine.'

'Great,' I said bleakly, and limped back up the hill toward the house, this time taking the scenic route through the jasmine.

Later that night, reeking of Dettol and smothered in bandaids, I paused in the doorway of Samuel's bedroom.

Breathing the scent of rain that hung in the air, I wondered why so many outside noises were rushing in. Water gurgled in the guttering, raindrops drummed the wet leaves. A bullfrog's lonely serenade echoed off the walls.

Then I realised I'd left the window open.

Switching on the light, I cast around for damage. The curtain was sodden, rainwater puddled the floorboards. Everything else appeared intact . . . until I saw the solitary nail on the wall where once a framed photo had hung.

Crazy, the sudden panic. I dashed across the room, my limbs all at once loose and hot with dread. Why hadn't I put the picture somewhere safe, out of harm's way? Why hadn't I remembered to shut the window? I imagined Samuel's portrait buckled by water, the emulsion curling away from the backing paper, the image lost forever because of a stupid oversight . . .

The silver frame lay face down on the floor. Picking it up, I found the glass was smashed, and all that remained was a perimeter of jagged splinters like shark's teeth. The photo was unharmed. Picking out the loose shards, I took the frame over to the bedside lamp and tilted it to the light. Without the glass, details I hadn't noticed before became apparent: shallow creases etched his forehead, laugh lines radiated from his eyes; a light growth of stubble shadowed his jaw, and there was a mark on his cheekbone under his eye – a freckle or mole, maybe a scar.

Turning the frame over, I removed the buckled backing board and peeled away the photo, intending to stow it somewhere safe until I could have it remounted.

That's when I saw the slip of paper.

It had been tucked behind the photo, but the passage of time had bonded it flat against the cardboard backing. As I peeled it free, and – with wobbly fingers – unfolded it on my knees, I saw it was a letter.

Wednesday, 13 March 1946

My Darling Samuel,

For four and a half years I feared that you'd forgotten me, or worse – that you'd died in a distant land. Knowing you're alive is both a prayer and a dream come true. I'm sorry we argued in the street today, please understand it was not my intention – I was overwhelmed to see you alive. Forgive me, darling?

I must see you again soon. I can't wait until tomorrow. I need to speak to you tonight, somewhere where there's no one to pry or judge. I've so much to tell you, and there's so much

I need to hear – your travels, how you fared in the war, your plans now that you're back, and most pressingly – although I'm terrified to ask – if you, after all these silent years, still want me for your bride?

Please agree to meet me, dearest. Tonight at our secret place, nine o'clock? I'll be the one wearing a big happy smile for you. And though I know you hate surprises, prepare yourself, my beloved Samuel. I'm bringing someone to meet you, someone very special.

Yours forever,

Aylish.

The looping copperplate had been dashed off hurriedly. Some of the words ran together, others were so faded against the yellowing notepaper they were nearly unreadable.

Smoothing the letter on my lap, I tried to read between the lines.

Something told me that Aylish was Tony's grandmother . . . the young woman Samuel had been accused of murdering. Of course, I couldn't know this for sure, there was no concrete evidence . . . just the mention of 'someone special' who I guessed had been a child, and Aylish's obvious devotion despite Samuel's years away at war.

What had happened between them, why had they argued? Had they met at their secret place that night, had all been forgiven? Or had Samuel misunderstood the letter and assumed Aylish guilty of a more odious crime? Samuel may have been unable to send or receive mail while he was away, which would explain Aylish's fears that he'd forgotten her or been killed. But I couldn't help wondering if there was more – much more – to their story.

Forgive me, darling?

I read the letter several more times, then drew it close and breathed its scent. Dust and old paper. Bitter ink. And very faintly, a waft of rose. Refolding it, I stowed it in the bedside drawer. Then I looked at the photo again under the lamplight.

Yes, a woman had taken the snapshot, I could see it in Samuel's eyes. His seductive smile had been trained on her, deliberately and fiercely, as though no one else in the world existed.

Once, many years ago, I had been besotted with Tony – but he had never smiled at me that way. I had clung to his affection like a drowning mouse clinging to a stick of driftwood; desperately and fearfully, with all the tenacity of someone who has been lonely before and dreads going back there. Tony had loved me, I knew that. Yet he'd never really *loved* me –

'Samuel,' I breathed, and his name on my lips was both intimate and desolate. I looked closer. His eyes were small and slanted like a cat's, intensely dark, maybe black. The broad cheekbones and strong jaw might have been sculpted from stone, but any ruggedness was softened by the perfect, full-lipped mouth.

I was drunk with looking.

Or maybe it was sleep deprivation. My eyelids kept wanting to close. My sluggish brain teetered on the brink of oblivion, my body was suddenly too heavy to stay upright. The blackberry scratches covering my skin made me burn and ache and I longed to lie down.

A possum growled in the rafters then bumped away to its nest. The bullfrog in the grass outside resumed its lonely song. I switched off the bedside lamp. In the moonlight, the walls and ceiling glowed soft pearly-grey like the inside of a shell, like a dream into which I was already stumbling.

Somehow I was on the bed. Dust tickled my nostrils, making me sneeze. The room tilted, I was lying down. Settling my head on the pillow, I breathed a weary sigh, and let my eyelids droop shut . . .

5

Breathlessly I ran along the shady track, through ferns and moist tangles of wonga vine, dodging the bluebells and wild orchids that sprouted from the shadows. Uphill I ran, plunging through ribbons of late sunlight that streamed through the overhanging canopy, my body light as a bird's, my heart singing.

Samuel, Samuel –

Bursting into a grassy clearing, I paused to catch my breath. At the centre sat a ramshackle cottage. It had been built by the pioneer owners of the property eighty years ago, using timber from the surrounding forest and foundation stones dragged up from the gully. The rough-hewn walls bowed inward, and the ironbark shingles on the roof were blackened with age, but there was a happy, homey look about the little place that drew me nearer.

Wildflowers sprouted through the verandah railings – flannel flowers and purple-pea, wild jasmine and yellow-buttons. There were tall stalks of cherry-pink hippeastrum that waved in the breeze, and roses struck off a cutting from the arbour at Thornwood, reaching leafy tendrils toward the sun-warmed roof, their blood-red blooms scenting the air with perfume.

Dashing up the stairs, I pushed through the door and blinked into the cool dimness. Faint light filtered through the tiny window, illuminating the rough walls, the small table and chairs, the tallboy decorated with a vase of rose sprigs. Jutting from the far wall was the narrow cot with its single pillow and modest grey blanket tucked around the edges.

Samuel sat on the cot's rim. His shirt strained around his arms and chest, and his hands were clenched so tight on his knees that, in the gloom, his knuckles shone bone-white. He rose to his feet, his face betraying both pleasure and – by the knotting of his brows – a degree of anguish.

'Aylish, my butterfly . . . I thought you'd never get here.'

He'd been born across the sea in Ireland and arrived here as a boy, too late to lose the burr that sweetened the shape of his words. My name on his lips always sounded like 'eyelash'.

I took a hesitant step. 'You haven't changed your mind?'

He frowned. 'Have you? I mean . . . it's all right if you have, we don't have to – '

'Of course not.'

Neither of us moved.

Samuel cleared his throat. 'What about Jacob, is he – ?'

'Poppa's gone to Ipswich with Klaus Jarman to collect a box of donated Bibles. He won't be back until tomorrow afternoon.'

'I'll be gone by then.'

'Yes. Although . . .'

Samuel tilted his head, eyeing me intently.

'Although,' I continued, feeling braver yet unable to keep the tremor out of my voice, 'at least you'll be leaving with a sweet memory.'

Samuel's expression melted. The crease between his brows smoothed, his eyes shut briefly . . . then he moved so fast my head whirled. He grabbed my hand and drew me to him, then somehow I was sitting on his lap on the edge of the bed, enveloped by his warmth, overcome by this new – and intimate – proximity.

'Aylish,' he whispered into my hair, 'don't you know that *all* my memories of you are sweet? And one day soon, when the blasted war is over, we'll have no need for memories. We'll be married, and I'll never leave your side again.'

'You won't forget me while you're away?'

'Forget you?' He snorted, then gathered me closer against him, kissing my temple. 'There's a war going on, my butterfly, but do you think a man can turn his mind to it? Oh, love . . . how could I ever forget you? My fool head can think of nothing but a certain smile, a laugh that turns my blood to water, a set of legs that render me deaf, dumb and blind to anything of greater import . . .'

I harrumphed. 'What could possibly be of greater import than my legs?'

'That's the problem, my own. To me there is nothing greater than your legs. Nothing more significant than your fingers, your pretty arms, your succulent mouth. The smallest hair on your head holds more meaning to me than anything in this world or the next. There is nothing in existence that means more than the wonderful, thrilling, intoxicating entirety of you.'

My blood raced at his bold words. His breath was warm on my cheek, I could feel the heat radiating from his skin. I tilted my face, giddy with longing; if I moved just a fraction nearer, our lips would touch –

I pulled back. 'Aren't you afraid?'

He sighed. 'No . . . at least, not for myself. But sweetheart, don't trouble yourself – I'll be back for you, that's my solemn promise. And then we'll be married and embark on our wonderful life together.'

His words were meant to comfort me, but I felt my old darkness bubble up. A clammy sweat broke across my shoulders. My ears began to buzz as though a swarm of bees had risen from some vile hive deep inside to suck dry my heart.

Samuel continued to whisper his reassurances into my hair, but my mind strayed. He was nearing the end of his sixth year of Medicine at Sydney University. He'd spent the last ten months studying in the morning and training in the wards every afternoon at St Vincent's Public Hospital. He came home to Magpie Creek on the train each holiday for a few weeks, assisting at his father's busy surgery, and spending all his free time with me.

Our plans for a future together had been going along swimmingly . . . then, when war was declared two years ago, he and several others in his year had requested that their courses be condensed, enabling them to sit their exams earlier. The very minute Samuel graduated, he'd rushed off and enlisted in the Second Australian Imperial Force. I'd hoped the war would end before his training was complete – we had set our wedding date for December, just six weeks from today – but yesterday he'd received notice that his battalion was deploying immediately.

Samuel must have sensed my wretchedness, because he pulled me near and buried his face against my neck. Whispering, whispering. I couldn't make out the words, but after a moment, his whispering began to tickle. I tried to wriggle away but he held me fast. Soon, on account of all my squirming, he began to laugh, a warm, languid, gravelly sound that raced a shiver of glorious tingles across my skin. Soon I was giggling too. The music of our shared nervousness loosened the tension. I forgot my fears. There was just Samuel – my dear, sweet Samuel – and the delicious private moment we now inhabited.

Winding myself around him like an eager vine, I clung tightly, and tighter still as he tumbled us both onto the bed, crushing me under his weight. My skirt found its way to my waist, then left me altogether. Somehow my blouse joined it on the floor, and then my undergarments along with Samuel's trousers and shirt. His skin was velvety smooth, the muscle beneath like iron.

'What if I'm dreaming?' I murmured. 'What if I wake and find you've already gone?'

Samuel stroked his thumbs against my cheeks and kissed the corners of my mouth. The bed creaked as he shifted his weight and rested himself along my length.

'Is this real enough?' he breathed, sliding his hand to my shoulder, then down over my breast. 'Is this proof that I'm no dream?'

'Oh, you're a dream, all right,' I countered, smiling as I slid my arms about his neck and lifted my hips to meet him. 'A beautiful dream I never want to wake up from.'

'We won't wake, then,' he promised. 'We'll stay here forever, just you and me, as we are now, always together.'

I liked the sound of that, and wanted to bask longer in the glow it gave me . . . but then Samuel's mouth met mine with such hunger that I forgot the things he'd said, forgot his vows, forgot the sweet promise of our future together. For the longest time I was aware only of the sunlight fading from the window, the slow-moving shadows as day became night, the gentle squeak of the cot's rusty springs – and Samuel, my dear Samuel, possessing me in a dream that I wished would never end . . .

Later – much later, it seemed – I lay awake while Samuel slept. Somewhere in the heat of our joining I had felt the old Aylish crumble and fall away, like a snakeskin abandoned in the grass. I'd always been an outsider, trapped midway between my father's world of books, Bible study, and prayer – and the simple mission existence of my mother's people. I was neither light nor dark, but a shadow-girl wedged between the two. Now, though, I belonged to Samuel, and he to me. I smiled to myself, feeling full in my spirit. We would, as he had so often told me in the past, create our own world where a person's differences were cherished, and their skills and talents and heart placed far above such trifles as the colour of their skin –

A flinch at the window.

An owl or nightjar, I thought. Flapping past, disturbing the fragile moonbeams that shone into our haven. I wanted to ignore the disturbance, and for a while I did . . . but then my skin began to prickle as though I'd taken too much sun, and I had the oddest sense that we were no longer alone.

My gaze went across the moonlit jumble of garments strewn on the floor, past the oblong shadow of the door to the tallboy and its vase of rosehips. It slid along the rough-hewn wall until at last it alighted on the pale glow of the window.

A face was peering through the glassless opening. A child's face, hovering with no body, a restless spirit drifting out of the night. It was plump and gleamed white as alabaster, floating like a ghost, peering into the room with large curious eyes. For the briefest instant I met its gaze and terror struck my heart. I was looking into the face of death. My death . . . or maybe Samuel's. I couldn't breathe. I opened my mouth, but couldn't cry out. That face had captured my voice, drowned it in a well of silence and turned me mute.

But only for a moment.

At last I gulped air and screamed.

Samuel lurched upright and found me in the half-light, held me until I calmed. When my wits returned enough to babble, 'There, at the window, a face, it was horrible, Samuel, a horrible ghostly face,' he sprang from the bed and dragged on his trousers. Grabbing a cloth bundle from under the bed, he unrolled a black object and rushed out the door. I heard his footsteps pound down the stairs then around the side of the hut, crunching through the bracken as he moved away. A moment later he returned, thudding back up the steps and across the verandah, bursting through the door with a muttered curse.

'Who was it?' he demanded.

'Don't know.'

He replaced the black object on the floor under the bed and gathered me into his arms.

'Whoever it was, they've gone. I tell you, Aylish,' he said, stroking my hair and pressing his lips along my brow, 'if I get my hands on the mongrel . . .' He pulled back and examined my tear-stained face. 'Did someone follow you here? Are you sure you didn't recognise them?'

'It wasn't a person, Samuel. I've already told you. It was a ghost.'

He sighed and threw a thoughtful look across the room. 'Ghosts don't spy on people through windows, Aylish.'

'This one did.'

Samuel's eyes were full of shadows then, and he pulled me close. Retreating into the bed, we lay without speaking. The disturbance had stolen something; we were no longer alone in the universe, no longer cocooned in our dream. The outside world had crept through our barricade of love and polluted it with uncertainty and doubt. The night drifted by, and we must have dozed because, too soon, the piccaninny light began to blush along the eastern horizon, then dawn stained the hem of the sky first with pale green, then pink, then gold.

I shivered. I'd seen death. Death had seen me. Fear sprouted in my heart like a dark mushroom, pushing and straining until it broke through the surface of my resolve.

'I don't want you to go. I'm afraid you might die over there.'

Samuel folded me closer against him and kissed the top of my head. 'No one's going to die. I'll be back before you know it – we'll be married and never spend another moment apart for the rest of our lives. We'll survive the war and be together again, Aylish, have no fear.'

'Oh, Samuel.' I wanted to snuggle like a kitten and take refuge in his arms, but then he was sitting up, drawing away and reaching for his shirt. With one final firm kiss to the corner of my eye, he clambered out of bed and retrieved his object from the floor.

'Which means that while I'm gone, I want you to be safe. And the only way you'll be safe is if you know how to defend yourself.'

Crossing the room, he paused by the doorway to look back. The light had strengthened, the edges of the sky were tinted deepest blue, the colour of wild violets. Samuel drank in a breath of the moist air and shut his eyes, as though capturing the moment – the sight of me dishevelled and naked on the bed, the yearning that surely radiated from my eyes; the vase of rosehips, our scattered clothes, the scent of bush jasmine; and the dark tree-shadowed hole of the window.

'Samuel – ?'

He blinked, then with a smile that seemed more sad than happy, he beckoned me to follow.

I dressed quickly but then lingered on the verandah. Samuel stood ten paces from the hut, fiddling with the object he'd retrieved from under the bed. There came a click as the weapon broke across the middle, and Samuel loaded six brass cartridges. He motioned me to join him.

'No, Samuel.'

'Come on, Aylish. It won't take long.'

'I can't . . . you know Poppa opposes firearms. The mere idea of me handling a revolver would stop his dear old heart . . . But learning to use one? God help him, Samuel, he'd perish – '

Samuel cocked a brow. 'All the more reason to arm yourself. If Jacob won't defend you, then you must learn how to defend yourself. Besides,' he added with a devilish wink, 'what the old man doesn't know won't hurt him.'

I didn't want this to be my last memory of Samuel. I wanted to cling to those moments of passion we'd shared in the rose-scented darkness . . . but the ghostly face had stolen those memories, somehow claimed them as its own. At that moment, I felt bereft, shaken. Poppa's gentle world of prayer and quiet devotion seemed very distant to me; meanwhile, the world of war and of young men leaving to take up guns and kill each other, and of newspapers full of maps and lists of the dead and missing – that world was suddenly very near.

I joined Samuel in the clearing. Tall ironbarks cast shadows on the grass, their leaves shivering in the morning air, while the birds – whip-birds, whistlers, kookaburras, lorikeets – sang up the sun. I breathed the peppery scent of yellow-buttons, the tangy-green sharpness of eucalyptus, and the sweet full-bodied perfume of roses . . . and decided that Samuel was right.

He placed the revolver in my hand, taking care to point it toward the edge of the clearing. 'Rest your forefinger along the top of the trigger guard, and hold the grip firm. Brace it with your other hand like this, and keep your arms straight.'

The weapon was large and weighty, too cumbersome to hold as he'd shown me. A powdery metallic aroma lifted off it, tinged with cloves and sweat, ugly and out of place in the gentle flower-scented morning. I tried to thrust it back into Samuel's hands, but he shook his head.

'No, no . . . keep it pointed outwards. You see that tree over there?'

'I can't, Samuel.'

'Here – ' He moved behind me and enclosed me in his arms, sliding his fingers over mine. 'You're holding it like a dead rat . . . You need to grip it with confidence, claim it as part of your body. An extension of your arm.'

I shuddered. 'It's too heavy. I can't point it properly.'

Samuel adjusted his position. His body was warm against my back, his chest solid, his arms strong and reassuring.

'Hold it tight with both hands, then pull back the hammer with your thumb . . . here, like so, until it clicks into place.'

The lesson was a waste of time. I knew I'd never point a weapon at another living soul, let alone fire off a deadly shot, not even to save my own life. My father might be elderly and set in his ways, but he was also – apart from Samuel – the wisest man I knew. 'Liebling,' he so often said, 'each time we kill even the smallest of God's creatures, we fray away our own connection to the divine.'

But as I snuggled in the luxury of Samuel's nearness, the merits of such a lesson became clear to me. Samuel's shirt was fragrant with the fresh sweat that clung to his skin, and the scent of his hair pomade obscured the oily reek of the weapon. Being close to him made me feel all tingly and loose-limbed. I peeked at him, admiring his slanted eyes, his high broad cheekbones, his full mouth, intoxicating at close range. I found myself swaying closer, pressing my bottom into him, remembering the sweet softness of his lips –

'Pay attention,' he said gruffly.

I pouted.

That made him sigh, and he shook his head, his brows knotted. 'You do realise who we're at war against, don't you?'

'Of course.'

'Then you know that anyone the government considers a security risk to the country will be interned. It happened in the last war, and my guess is that it will happen again in this one. If your father is put in prison because of his nationality, then you'll be alone. You must know how to protect yourself. So pay attention now. See if you can plant a bullet in the trunk of that old tree over there.'

The weapon bucked in my hands, its deafening whip-crack report making my ears ring. I lowered it, shaking.

I missed, of course. On purpose, because then Samuel must instruct me again how to press back the hammer, take aim, hold my breath and ever so gently squeeze the trigger. I decided to be a hopeless shot, to give Samuel no choice other than to persevere with me. On the third try a spray of bark exploded off the side of the old tree. Samuel whooped. A rush of pleasure went through me, pleasure that I'd made him happy. Then, as I studied the damage I'd inflicted upon the innocent eucalypt, a very different feeling came over me. Pain, so intense it stole my breath. The weapon I held in my hands was a deadly thing, designed and built with the solitary purpose of taking life.

In war, a man's life.

A man just like Samuel.

6

Four days after the blackberry incident, I peeled off the last of my bandaids and surveyed the wreckage. My skin was still crisscrossed by scabby scratches, and I was bruised and sore . . . but I'd learned my lesson. No more getting spooked by crazy dreams.

I showered and dressed and went out to the kitchen. Since my discovery of Aylish's letter on Thursday, my nights had been restless. It probably didn't help that I'd been spending every night curled in Samuel's bed. It seemed somehow perverse of me to find solace in the private spaces of a man who'd been accused of murder. And yet, no matter how I tried, I couldn't stay away.

Loading up the breakfast tray, I went in search of Bronwyn. School started today, and I had a sneaking suspicion that I was more nervous about it than she was. I'd put off telling her about Samuel, reluctant to overburden her before the big day . . . and of course now I was worried I'd left it too late.

Going down the stairs, I followed the path deeper into the garden. The air was warm, the bricks beneath my feet were cool and damp. Last night's storm had left behind a dazzling blue sky dotted with frothy curdled-milk clouds, and there were thousands of dewy spiderwebs speckling the lawn.

It was early, not even seven o'clock. In Melbourne we'd have still been under the covers, hiding from the lingering chill, then running late for the school bus. But dawn came fast at this time of year in Queensland, and the mornings were too gorgeous to waste.

I found Bronwyn sitting on her bench beneath the jacaranda tree, which she'd claimed as her secret bower. She was hunched over a battered biscuit tin, her fingers dug under the lid, her face hidden by the pale curtain of her hair.

Setting down the tray, I adjusted the mug of steaming Milo. 'So, ready for your first day at school?'

'Yep.'

'Have you got your bag packed?'

'Yep.'

'Honey, I have to talk to you about something.'

She didn't look up. 'Sure.'

'It's about your dad's grandfather – the old man who used to own this house? He . . . well, people are saying that many years ago he did something bad.'

That got her. She peered up at me, wide-eyed. 'What?'

'They think he killed someone.'

Her eyes bugged. 'Wow. Was he a bushranger? We did bush-rangers at school, how cool if I was related to one!'

'He wasn't a bushranger.'

Her face fell. 'Oh.'

'They think he killed your great-grandma. I don't believe it, of course . . . and it was such a long time ago, way back before your dad was even born – '

'Ancient history, you mean?'

'Mmmm . . . Well, I just want you to be prepared in case anyone at school says something. You know, kids can be cruel sometimes.'

She shrugged and bent back over her biscuit tin. 'More likely I'll be the envy of the place, Mum. Anyway,' she added, grappling her fingernails under the lid, 'look what I found this morning.'

I blinked, reminding myself for the gazillionth time that Bronwyn's generation was light years ahead of the rest of the planet. I threw my talk about Tony's grandfather into the too-boring basket, and feigned interest in the tin.

'Pretty, isn't it, Mum? The picture on the lid is a little town in the snow, like those postcards Dad used to send us from overseas.'

The tin was rectangular, freckled with rust, dented in places but mostly intact. Painted on the lid was a winter landscape – snowflakes, mountains, a tiny alpine village.

'Where'd you find it?'

'Oh, there's this big tree further up the hill? It's got a hollowed-out trunk, so cool. It was covered in cicada shells – masses of them, they were everywhere, I got a whole bagful – anyway, as I was climbing down – '

'You climbed the tree?' I asked disapprovingly.

'I didn't go too high,' she assured me. 'Anyway, the branches formed a kind of ladder, it was easy. On the way down I discovered a hole, which turned out to be a sort of chimney leading into the empty trunk below. Someone had dug a shelf on one side. Tucked into the shelf right at the back so no one'd find it, was an old canvas haversack full of stuff – clothes, makeup, a hairbrush . . . and this tin. The haversack and everything in it was rotten so I threw it away. But the tin looks okay, doesn't it?'

'It's a bit ratty. What'll you do with it?'

She gripped the tin between her knees, prising her nails under the lid. 'If I can get it open I'll put my cicada shells in it . . . Once it's cleaned up it'll be – oh!' The box clattered from her hands and bounced onto the ground.

I picked it up and turned it over. Something inside gave a dull thump.

'Wonder what's in it?' I said.

'Money?'

'Magic bean seeds?'

'A treasure map?' I smiled.

After half a bottle of sewing machine oil, the lid still wouldn't budge. I tapped around the rim with a hammer, and when that didn't work I knocked it against the cedar bench. In the end I gave up, but Bronwyn dug in her nails and gave it one final wrench. The lid sprang open with a squeal.

Eagerly, we peered in.

'Pooh!' Bronwyn said, disappointed. 'Just a musty old wad of paper.'

In fact it was a book. Not just any book: a diary.

For one electric moment I hoped it was a link to Aylish . . . then reality kicked in. The cover was a recent design, maybe fifteen, twenty years old with a picture of a white kitten sitting near a bowl of roses. I tried to flip through it, but the pages were water-buckled and gummed into an unyielding block.

It might have been fun to read, but I could tell it'd take hours to peel apart the fragile old pages, and hours more to trawl through it. Hours that I couldn't spare – at least, not until I'd driven my daughter to school.

'Use the rest of the oil to clean up the tin,' I told her. 'But don't take all morning . . . you still have to get ready.'

She grunted to let me know she'd heard, but didn't bother replying; she was too engrossed in scrubbing the inside of her new treasure box, dousing the hinges in machine oil, digging the rag into its dirt-clogged corners.

My shadow hovered over the cedar bench. It felt good to be outside, breathing the flower-scented air. It made me happy to see Bronwyn so absorbed. Her skin was creamy and unfreckled, her hair the colour of paper-ash, nearly to her waist. I marvelled for a moment at how pretty she was . . . and how much prettier she would soon become.

She looked up, scowled. 'What?'

'You still need to get changed.'

'I know.'

'I've ironed your uniform, it's hanging on the back of your door.'

'You've told me ten times already.'

I walked a little way along the path, then looked back. 'Don't forget to eat your toast.'

Bronwyn narrowed her eyes at me, then, with a shake of her head and a sigh, turned her attention back to the biscuit tin. 'Mum, stop worrying. It's my first day at school, not yours.'

Magpie Creek Primary was situated on the hilly north side of town, a cluster of weatherboard buildings hidden behind a wall of shady pepper trees. On one side a bitumen playing court was enclosed by a high wire-link fence; on the other side was a grassy playground flanked by benches.

Bronwyn had settled easily into her new class. She hadn't appeared nervous at all – smiling patiently while the teacher introduced her, slipping gracefully into her seat, barely looking at me as I'd paused in the classroom door to wave goodbye.

Leaving the school, I hurried along the dappled footpath in the direction of the main street. The sun warmed my face and arms as I walked, helping to ease the concern I always felt at leaving Bronwyn. Once on the main street I headed for the bakery. In my small universe there was only one known cure for separation anxiety: cake. After much deliberation, I settled for a slice of mud cake and a pecan tart, to which I added a jam lamington for Bronwyn as an after-school reward. Clutching my paper bags, I hurried back along the street in the direction of my Celica. Halfway there, someone called my name.

The first thing I saw was the hair – gold in the morning sunlight, tinged with bronze. Corey Weingarten came striding out of the schoolyard, her broad face flushed from the sun. We beamed at each other, then fell into conversation like a pair of old friends.

'I thought I might see you this morning, Audrey. Did Bronwyn settle in okay?'

'She's fine. What are you doing here?'

'Dropping off my brother's daughter, Jade – she's been staying with me while her dad was up in Townsville. Danny got back this morning, but he had an early emergency callout. He's our local vet, does everything from calving Brahmans to rescuing kittens. He travels a bit because of his job – seminars, that sort of thing – so me and Mum pitch in to look after Jade. She's a great kid, but she mopes a bit when her father's away. Ever since her mum died a few years back, she's been a bit clingy.'

'Poor thing, can't say I blame her.'

'She's resilient. Kids seem so much more together these days.'

'Bronwyn's the same.'

Corey's brown eyes appraised me. 'How did you cope after Tony walked out? Did you share custody?'

'When Tony got married we talked about it, but he was always so busy, preparing exhibitions or heading overseas. In the end it just seemed easier for Bronwyn to live with me.'

A currawong alighted on a branch overhead and began to warble; its gurgling song filled the air, full-throated and beautiful.

'Did you have much help from family?'

I shook my head. 'My father died when I was little, hit by a car. I don't remember him. My mother couldn't look after me, so I went to live with my Aunty Morag.'

'Why couldn't your mum look after you?'

A dull discomfort. My instinct was to lie. Invent a story that cast me in a more favourable light. But there was something about Corey that made me want to open up. She seemed genuinely interested, and her brown eyes were kind and intelligent . . . yet it was more than that. Crazy as it sounded, I felt connected to her – as though we shared a long history rather than just a recent acquaintance.

I took a breath. 'My mother was ... well, she had a lot of problems. Drugs, that sort of thing. I guess she never got over my father's death.'

'Do you ever see her?'

'No ... I don't even know if she's alive. Aunt Morag was my family. I guess she filled the gap my parents left behind. Morag was an amazing woman, I was lucky to have her – but sometimes I wonder if her influence on me was too profound ... that I'm not just like her, but that I've become her.'

'In what way?'

I shrugged, feeling at ease despite my unexpected soul-baring. 'After Tony left, it was always just me and Bronwyn. I had friends, but no one close. Like Aunt Morag, I suppose I've always kept to myself.'

'Aunt Morag never married?'

'Didn't believe in it. She worked as an artist's model, even when she was in her seventies. She used to say a husband would've cramped her style. Her most treasured possession, she once told me, was her independence. She shunned the idea of being tied down to a man.'

'What about you?'

I shrugged. 'After Tony walked out, I adopted the Aunt Morag approach. I saw a lot of sense in being self-reliant – at least, that's what I kept telling myself. In truth, I never met anyone.'

Corey was studying my face. There was no judgement in her eyes, no pity, not even a glimmer of fake sympathy. Just curiosity.

'Is Aunt Morag still alive?'

'She died when I was sixteen.'

'That's a shame. She sounds like someone I'd have enjoyed meeting.'

Corey stood close, but I didn't find her proximity alarming. I liked looking at her – I liked the way her face was open and easy to read. I wondered what particular feature gave this impression – the friendly tea-coloured freckles across the bridge of her nose, the inquisitive brown eyes, the exotic broad cheekbones, or the wide mouth that always seemed on the brink of a smile.

'Did you call Hobe?' she asked suddenly.

'Actually, I thought I might pay him a visit. Introduce myself, maybe ask him about the history of Thornwood. Do you think he'd mind?'

'No, he'd be tickled. Besides, you're neighbours. Hobe's place is only five minutes up the road from Thornwood. It's a little timber bungalow on the hill – you can't miss it. The place is a bit rustic, but Hobe'll insist on inviting you in for a cuppa. He loves a chat, especially with someone new.'

I frowned. 'I think I know the place. I stopped there to ask directions the day I came to look at Thornwood. The man I spoke to had one lens of his glasses taped over.'

'That's Hobe, poor old codger.'

'What happened to his eye?'

'No idea.'

'Hmmm . . . I must confess, after what you told me last week, I'm curious to know more about Tony's grandfather – '

Corey lifted a brow. 'No nightmares, I hope?'

I felt the blood climb to my face, remembering Aylish's letter and the restless night it had inspired. 'Nothing like that,' I assured her. 'But to be honest, Samuel intrigues me.'

We regarded each other solemnly. I sensed we were riding the same thought-wave, our minds racing along parallel streams toward a common conclusion.

Corey spoke first. 'You want to know if he was guilty.'

I nodded.

'I'd better warn you, then. Hobe thinks he was.'

'Did he know Samuel?'

'Yeah, and he hated him with a passion. I'd be fascinated to hear what he says about him – you will report back to me, won't you?'

'With pleasure.'

We chatted amiably for a while longer, then Corey had to go.

'A joy flight,' she explained. 'A man and his elderly father, they won the church raffle, God love 'em. What about you, Audrey, when are you coming up with me again?'

'A week or so. Cossart's loved the last lot of photos, so I expect I'll become one of your regulars.'

'I'd like that.'

The warmth of her smile inspired me, and I had to ask.

'Why don't you and Jade come over to Thornwood one afternoon? We could have a barbie – the girls can lose themselves in the garden, and I'll show you around the place. There's a great view from the back verandah.'

'I remember that view,' Corey said, her eyes sparkling. 'It's a wonderful idea. What about on the weekend?'

'Perfect. Saturday afternoon, say four?'

'Great, see you then!'

She gave my arm a squeeze, and loped away. I waited until her red-gold hair had bobbed around the corner and out of sight. Then I hurried back to the Celica, itching to find out what Hobe Miller knew about Samuel.

The Miller residence was exactly as I remembered – a dilapidated bungalow perched on the hillside above Briarfield Road. In the tranquil morning sun, the house seemed less shabby, more cosily inviting. The ironbark forest surrounding the dwelling was no longer a shadowland of unseen threat; the sea of shimmering grey-green leaves looked almost friendly.

As the Celica jounced up the gravel drive I saw there was a third car parked outside the house. Beside the old ute and the immaculate Valiant, sat a sleek black Toyota truck. I pulled in beside the Toyota, cut the engine and climbed out. The stillness was absolute, interrupted only by the crunch of my sandals on gravel, the cawing of native ravens and the ever-present cicada song. As I approached the house, I became aware of another sound: the melodic gurgle of running water.

Looking across the yard, I saw a water tank. It was half-hidden behind a screen of grevilleas and flowering bottlebrush which cast it into deep shade.

Standing beside the tank was a man.

He was bare-chested, leaning over the tap, using a tin cup to douse his torso with water from a bucket. He slid a bar of soap up his arms and across his chest, lathering his skin with pink foam. I guessed he was in his mid-thirties; dark-haired, nicely muscled. He wore only jeans: ragged at the cuffs, torn at the knees, low-slung beneath a tanned stomach.

I twigged why the soap foam was pink; his chest and forearms were smeared with what appeared to be blood. Was he hurt, I wondered. Was that why he hadn't seen me? Was he so absorbed in what he was doing that he hadn't heard the arrival of my car, or the crunch of my sandals on the gravel? Or was he ignoring me?

I stood motionless. The vague ache in my chest told me I was holding my breath, so I didn't know what made him finally look up. Perhaps it was the soft crack of pebbles underfoot as I shifted my weight, or the quiet tick of the Celica's cooling motor. Perhaps he decided that I'd waited long enough.

Shadows swarmed over him, but there was enough dappled sunlight to see the intense dark eyes, the wide unsmiling mouth.

'Hi,' I said. When he didn't reply, I cleared my throat and tried again. 'I'm looking for Hobe Miller, is he about?'

Grabbing a brown T-shirt from the foot of the water tank, the man began to mop himself dry as he walked toward me.

He took his time, which gave me a moment to sum him up.
The ragged jeans, the dusty work boots – he was country boy
all over. Yet the dark mop of unruly curls and intense emerald
eyes gave him an unfair advantage over the average farmer. He
might have been beautiful had it not been for the scowl he was
wearing.

He slid a small notepad and pencil from his jeans pocket.
After scribbling in the notebook, he tore off the leaf and handed
it to me.

I took the note, mystified . . . until I read what he'd written.

I'm deaf. Can you sign?

I felt my eyes go wide. My gaze flew back to his face. He was
watching me, his brows drawn, his eyes fixed on mine.

'No,' I told him. 'I can't sign.'

He scribbled on another leaf and tore it off.

Good thing I lip read. Speak slower.

In the harsh sunlight I saw the grey rim around his pupils,
the faint pattern of freckles across the bridge of his nose. He
was unshaven, and his hair stuck up in sweaty clumps. Shading
his eyes with one hand, he regarded me with unabashed
curiosity.

'I'm looking for Hobe Miller,' I told him, now horribly
self-conscious as I tried to enunciate clearly. 'I've been trying to
contact him about doing some maintenance and repairs on my
property.'

The man blinked at me, then dashed off another note.

No need to shout. Hobe's inside.

Before I'd finished reading the note he'd stalked off, heading
toward the bungalow. While he walked, he pocketed the notebook and finished drying off with his sodden T-shirt. By the
time I caught up with him he was hammering on the screen
door, making a racket that seemed to echo right across the
hillside and bounce back from the valley.

A shabby figure appeared in the doorway.

I recognised him at once. Hobe Miller's bony face was framed by white hair, and as he frowned through the screen door, the single lens of his duct-taped glasses flared in the light.

'What's going on?' he said, glaring at me with evident suspicion.

Before I could speak, the deaf man's fingers came to life as he signed.

Hobe watched intently, then nodded. Swinging open the screen door, he stepped out onto the verandah. For several tense seconds his blue gaze probed my face as though confused by something he saw there.

'You need repairs?' he asked gruffly. 'At Thornwood?'

'Yes, I – '

'You knew Tony Jarman?'

I nodded, puzzled by his abrupt manner. He was nothing like Corey's description – rather than being pleased by my appearance on his doorstep, he seemed threatened. He was scowling at me as though a cup of tea and a friendly chat couldn't be further from his mind. According to Corey, Hobe had hated Tony's grandfather. Had he hated Tony too? And would that hatred now transfer to me?

'I'm sorry if I've called at a bad time,' I told him, glancing at the deaf man. 'Why don't I come back later . . . that is, if you're not too busy?'

Hobe slumped, shrinking into the shell of his frayed shirt. I noticed stains on the worn fabric; they looked wet, as though he'd recently clutched something bloody to his chest. As I pondered this, a noise erupted from inside the house – it sounded like someone whimpering in pain.

Hobe's head jerked around. He shot a worried look at the deaf man. The man sprang to the door and vanished inside without so much as a farewell glance at me.

Hobe resumed watching me with narrowed eyes.

'There's no hurry,' I said, inching nearer the verandah steps, 'it's just a cracked window and an old tree limb that's hanging too close to the roof, probably not even worth worrying about . . .'

Hobe peered into the darkness that lay on the other side of the screen door. 'What day suits you?'

'Tomorrow?'

He pruned his lips to ponder this. 'Eight o'clock too early?'

'That'd be great.' I muttered goodbye and beat a hasty retreat. My legs wobbled as I bounded down the stairs and tried not to run to the Celica. As I climbed in I couldn't resist looking back at the house. Hobe had watched my escape and now stood at the verandah rail peering down at me.

I gave an erratic little wave, jammed my foot on the accelerator, and sped off down the track in a miasma of dust.

Stripping out of my sweaty clothes, I tossed them in the laundry basket then climbed into the clawfoot tub. The old shower-rose was a relic of the past, big as a dinner plate and perforated with pea-sized holes; the resulting torrent was brisk and deliciously cool.

I hung my head and let the gushing water pound my shoulders, feeling better as the dust and heat and stickiness were washed away. When my fingers and toes wrinkled, I climbed out and scrubbed dry, then got into soft old pyjama shorts and singlet.

In the kitchen I brewed a pot of coffee and stood at the window, picking at my pecan pie while I stared out at the garden. Heat-haze shimmered the trees, and the sky was pure cloudless blue; the only motion was a solitary lorikeet sweeping back and forth, back and forth, as though unable to find a perch.

I knew exactly how it felt.

My thoughts flitted restlessly, trying to make sense of my disastrous visit to the Miller property – but no matter which way I looked, the whole episode remained a mystery. The man at the water tank, his chest a lather of pink foam – blood, I felt certain. But whose blood, Hobe's? Did that explain the red stain on Hobe's tattered flannel shirt; had they been in a fight? And what about the whimpering I'd heard while standing on the verandah, surely the sound of someone in terrible pain?

And Hobe . . . he'd been nothing like Corey's description. No neighbourly chats for him; his reception had been down-right unfriendly. I recalled our first meeting and how he'd seemed troubled when I asked directions to Thornwood. Again I wondered if his dislike of Samuel Riordan had somehow trans-ferred to me, simply because I was now living in Samuel's house.

So much for my plan to pick his brains. After his perfor-mance today, I guessed he wouldn't be thrilled about having me quiz him for information about Samuel. Which meant I'd have to do some digging of my own.

But where to start?

I'd already searched the house soon after moving in. Samuel had been a hoarder, his lovely old cabinets and sideboards well stocked with flotsam from the past. Shoeboxes full of prehistoric dockets, void bank bonds, receipts for maintenance work around the house, typed letters from various medical boards; tins of tarnished coins and belt buckles, wood boxes crammed with yellowing shirt collars, shoelaces, cotton reels, oddment buttons. A comprehensive collection of relics, but nothing that yielded any clues as to what might have driven him to murder.

I went out to the back bedroom.

Thick curtains blocked the intense sunshine, plunging the room into twilight and inviting shadows into the corners. There was a sense of deep tranquillity here, which made me feel – as I so often did in this house – as if I was standing on the threshold of a far earlier time. The past seemed to ooze from the stains on the walls, to seep up through the floorboards, and whisper from the crack in the wardrobe door . . . time meandered backwards, lazily, and yet with such inevitable weight that I found myself drawn right into it.

If I squinted I could almost see Samuel hovering by the window, elegantly attired in black pants and jacket offset by a white linen shirt. In my mind's eye he was no longer the youthful man from the rose arbour, but middle-aged, his hair longer and threaded with grey, his face craggier and etched with sorrow, his large frame thinner. His head was bent, and his lips moved. He was reading from a small book, tilting it into the light from the window the better to see. After a while he patted his pocket and withdrew a small object, which he closed between the book's gilt-edged pages –

A shrill ringing startled me.

I jerked around, heart thudding. The phone.

Running along the hall to the kitchen, I snatched up the receiver and answered. My voice sounded hollow, far away. An echo from another time. The woman on the other end of the line introduced herself as the coordinator of an events agency, and wanted to know if I could do a wedding shoot tomorrow. Their regular photographer had broken his leg and they needed someone at short notice.

'Yes,' I said, jotting the details on the back of an envelope. 'Yes, yes . . . See you then.'

After hanging up I stood for an age, staring at what I'd written. Seeing – not the envelope defaced by my chicken-scrawl notes – but the dusty little Bible which had sat untouched for decades on Samuel's rosewood dressing table.

G⟶

The Bible's leather cover was cracked with age, the corners ragged, its gilt-edged pages faded under years of dust. It was small enough to hold on my outstretched palm, surprisingly heavy. I opened the cover. On the flyleaf was a neat inscription in faded blue ink: 'Awarded to Samuel James Riordan by St

Joseph's Primary School, Dublin, 1925'. As I rifled through the pages, something slid out and clattered onto the floorboards at my feet.

A tiny key.

It was very old, with a hollow post and elaborately wrought heart-shaped head, age-blackened and freckled with rust. I knew immediately where it belonged.

I unlocked the dressing table drawer, half-expecting to find nothing more than a collection of greying underwear and socks.

And stared.

I'd been fourteen when I'd last handled a firearm. An old flame of Aunt Morag's had been a gun enthusiast, a collector of old and rare handguns. His greatest delight was introducing new eyes to his extensive armoury, and I'd spent many hours poring over his exhibits, repulsed by them . . . and yet greatly intrigued.

Reaching into the shadows of the drawer, I withdrew the revolver.

It was large, very heavy. I checked the cylinder. There were no cartridges, not even spent ones. Curling my fingers around the grip, I lined my sights at the window. It was illegal to have it in the house, unlicensed. In Samuel's day, there'd been no regulations about possessing firearms; everyone on properties had them, every farmer or grazier, any landholder. Not now. By law I'd have to surrender this to the police station, or risk a charge.

I tightened my fingers around the grip. Samuel's hands had once been where mine were now. Perhaps traces of his skin – certainly his fingerprints – still clung to the weapon's lacklustre surface. A part of him, here now, in my hands. I raised the handgrip to my nose. It had a dark aroma – sweat and grease, gunpowder and ash, the euphoric sourness of blued metal and cleaning fluid. It smelled as though it had lain a long time underground, buried away from the healing warmth of the sun. It smelled like money, like stories told in sleazy bars, like smoke and stale cologne. It smelled as though it had been passed from hand to hand, collecting the essence of each person's skin, the way a bee collects pollen from many flowers . . . only this with a far more deadly sting.

According to Corey, the town's rumour-mongers believed Samuel escaped conviction because his father was a friend of the judge. But what if the rumours were wrong? What if Samuel had walked free not because of an obliging judge but due to a bona fide lack of evidence? Evidence that I now held in my hands?

I checked the drawer and sure enough, right at the back, was a small cardboard box of twelve live brass rounds. They'd have to be surrendered to the police along with the revolver. I should take them now, while Bronwyn was at school. I placed the revolver and box of ammo on the floor beside me and went to shut the drawer . . . when something caught my eye.

A corner of yellowing paper was poking from beneath the floral drawer liner. Digging under the liner, I pulled the paper out. It was an envelope: large and mottled with age-spots, its flap secured with a strip of brittle tape.

Inside were two colour snapshots.

In the first, a dark-haired boy of about ten stood in the shadows at the base of an enormous bunya pine. The boy had Tony's eyes and Tony's cheeky grin and he was waving at the camera. Nearby on a sunny patch of grass sat a child's inflatable bathing pool, a pristine blue sky mirrored in the water. In the left corner of the photo a woman stood at a clothesline. She was tall and heavily built, her hair pulled severely off her face. She was in the process of pegging a man's shirt to the line, glancing over her shoulder as though taken by surprise. Next to the woman, obscured by her raised arm, stood a girl with long fair hair. A shaggy lawn grew up around them, freckled with daisies and darkened in the centre by the shadow of the unseen photographer.

I flipped the photo. On the back was written, 'Luella, Glenda, and Tony. Magpie Creek, 1980.'

The second photo was a blurred and grainy Polaroid, the paper creased and tattered along the edges as if it had spent its life in someone's pocket or wallet. It showed four children, two boys and two girls – all were laughing as if at a private joke, their eyes locked on one another. The boy on the far left was curly-haired and ever so faintly familiar. The other boy – who I recognised at once – was Tony, probably about eight years old. One of the girls had fuzzy ginger hair and a broad freckled face, her brilliant smile dimmed only by the gappy absence of a front tooth. Apart from the missing tooth, Corey Weingarten had hardly changed at all.

It was the girl in the centre of the group, though, who captured my attention. She was grinning widely, her face framed by white-blonde plaits. For a single disorienting moment I thought I was looking at my daughter's face. Of course it wasn't Bronwyn; the girl in the photo would have been a few years older than Tony when the snap was taken. By now she'd be in her mid-thirties, perhaps with children of her own.

I flipped back to the photo of Tony under the pine tree, and studied the girl near the clothesline. Then I re-examined the four kids, convinced it was the same girl in both photos. Who was she? And why was she the very image of my daughter?

The revolver would have to wait. Placing it back in the dresser drawer with the box of brass cartridges, I locked up and hid the key in the back of the wardrobe. Then, collecting the photos, I dashed along the hall to the kitchen and grabbed my car keys.

7

The airfield car park was deserted – there was just one other car, a sporty leaf-green Mercedes. I parked beside it and hurried along the gangway toward the office.

The door was open, but the cluttered space was empty. I went back along the narrow path and headed to the runway. Two small aircraft were parked on the strip, but there was no sign of Corey's Cessna. I scrutinised the sky, but it was a vast tranquil sheet of nothingness – no planes, no clouds, not even a stray bird.

'Hello there.'

I whipped around. Corey had emerged from the darkness of the maintenance hangar and was striding towards me, grinning happily. She wore grimy overalls and a baseball cap that did little to restrain her exuberant hair. As she drew nearer she must have sensed my mood. She gave my arm a friendly squeeze and peered into my face.

'What's up?'

'I've found a couple of old photos,' I told her without preamble. The photos were already in my hand and I held them out. 'Tony was easy to pick, and you're in one of them. I was hoping you might be able to tell me who the others are.'

As she examined the photos, her smile slipped. She tried to recover it, but it seemed to hang a little crooked. She motioned for me to follow her into the hangar.

The huge shed was dark and cool. In the centre sat the Cessna. Its doors were flung wide, making it look like a grotesque dragonfly. The smell of sawdust and diesel hung in the air, and as I breathed it in I grew calmer.

Corey wiped her hands on an oil-blackened tea towel, then took the photos from my fingers. A warm breeze lifted strands of her hair about her face, and the peak of her cap shadowed her eyes. She examined each image for a long time, saying nothing.

I grew impatient. 'Tony's grandfather had them tucked away in a drawer,' I told her. 'I can understand why he'd have a picture of Tony. But why would he want a photo of the other kids . . . and that's you, isn't it?'

'Yeah. And the curly-haired boy is my brother, Danny.'

'What about the blonde girl?'

Corey gave me an odd look. 'That's Glenda.'

'She looks like Bronwyn. Were she and Tony related?'

Corey studied me for an eternity. Her eyebrows were drawn as though she was trying to nut out a complicated maths problem. Then her shoulders slumped. 'He never told you.'

A twinge of irritation. 'Told me what?'

'Hell, I assumed he told you *something*, the basics at least – '

'What?' I nearly yelled, feeling the first nibble of panic.

'Come on. We can't talk here.' Grabbing my arm, she hauled me across the hangar, out into the glaring sunshine and along the narrow gangway in the direction of the office.

We entered the dusty space with its bulging file cabinets and desk of radio controls, cluttered bookshelf and map-covered wall boards. Corey went to her desk and selected an old gramophone record. Sliding it from the paper sleeve, she plonked it on the turntable. A noisy orchestral overture boomed into the room, quickly joined by a strident male baritone whose voice rattled the windows. Corey gestured to a pair of scruffy leather recliners. I sat on the edge of one while she flopped on the other.

'Bloody Tony,' she said over the music. She wrenched off her baseball cap and wrung it between her hands. 'How could he not have told you? Glenda was his sister.'

'*Sister*?' I wanted to correct her – Tony had no sister, I knew that as a fact because if he had, he'd have mentioned her ... Wouldn't he?

Of course not.

I realised that I'd constructed a mental picture of Tony's early life that was entirely built on assumptions. Since he never spoke about his parents, I'd assumed them dead. Because he made no mention of any siblings, I had surmised that he didn't have any. But now, in the space of a heartbeat, all that had changed.

'So what about Luella?' I asked Corey. 'Was she his ... ?'

'Mother.'

I looked back at the snapshot. The tall woman at the clothesline had been photographed by surprise and she didn't look happy about it. Yet despite her alarmed expression, she had a kind face – oval-shaped with small, almost slanted eyes and a generous mouth. She was nothing like Tony and even less like the blonde girl, Glenda. But as I studied her, a rare excitement began to rush through my veins.

'Bronwyn's grandmother,' I said wonderingly. 'Where is she now? Does she live locally? And what about Glenda? She's Bronwyn's aunt. I can hardly believe it. Bronwyn's going to be over the moon to learn she's got family up here.'

Corey tore her eyes off me and stared through the window at the sky. 'Glenda died twenty years ago.'

'Oh.'

'In a rockslide accident at the gully.'

'The gully?'

'You know that waterway running through your property? A few miles north, it deepens into a gorge. Locals call it the gully, but that's a rather humble name for such a spectacular piece of geography. It's a deadly place, too. There's been a few accidents there over the years.'

The music surged around us, an ocean of thunderous sound.

'And Luella . . . is she alive?'

Corey nodded. 'She lives here in Magpie Creek, quite close to the airfield. Out past the turnoff, on William Road. But she might as well be dead as far as any of us are concerned.'

'Why do you say that?'

Corey was hunched forward on the edge of the chair, her face tilted away from me. She seemed smaller, as though she'd shed her protective adult shell and now sat childishly vulnerable.

'Luella Jarman hasn't spoken to anyone since Glenda's death. She was . . . oh hell – Luella was the one who found Glenda's body.'

'God. How awful.'

'She refuses to see any of her old friends, won't even open the door to the pastor. I can't tell you the amount of times I've popped in to visit and been disappointed. I've heard she travels up to Brisbane every month to do her shopping, but apart from that she rarely leaves the house. And now that Tony . . . Well, now he's gone too, I can't help worrying that Luella has burrowed even deeper into her shell.'

'Surely she'd want to meet her granddaughter?'

Corey's face was bleak. 'Luella's been through so much – and she's been alone so long – that I can't even guess at her mental condition. She lost everyone, you see. Everyone who mattered. Even if you did take Bronwyn to meet her, there's no guarantee that Luella would even open the door.'

I nodded. Corey was right. I knew how loss could hollow a person, cause them to lose touch with the outside world. My rational mind said to concede defeat, turn back now . . . But my heart refused to listen. Suddenly it was racing hard, pumping a wild tempo of hope through my veins. All I could think of was how much it would mean to Bronwyn to meet her grandmother.

'I'd like to try.'

Corey's broad face was full of pity. 'Oh, Audrey, I understand why you'd want to, I really do. But you must forget about Luella. It's not worth the heartache – not for you, and certainly not for Bronwyn. Luella was always a timid sort of person at the best of times. She had a rough trot as a kid, from what I can gather, and I don't think she'd be in any state of mind to cope.'

At my questioning look, she added, 'Samuel was her father. She was just a little girl when all that business happened with her mother. It was terribly sad.'

'And you're worried that now, with Tony's death so recent, another shock might send her over the brink?'

'Exactly.'

I filed this information away for later, not wanting to lose the thread we were on. I knew Corey was right, and I knew Luella must still be grieving for Tony. But I couldn't find it in myself to give up. Not yet.

'I came across a news article,' I said. 'A man's remains were dredged from a dam near here. Am I wrong in thinking it was Tony's father?'

Corey sighed. 'I was wondering if you'd heard about that. It's a complicated story. Why don't I start at the beginning?'

I nodded.

She hugged herself, shrinking deeper into her chair. 'The day of Glenda's funeral, Tony ran away from home. Some people speculated that running away was his reaction to grief; others said that guilt drove him away . . . that he'd been there when his sister fell, that an argument got out of hand and Tony pushed her – '

'Why would they say that?'

'It was common knowledge that Glenda knew that gully like the back of her hand. She'd grown up nearby, spent a lot of time exploring the property and was aware of the danger zones – the gravel traps and unstable embankments. Everyone knew she was good in the bush, not prone to taking risks . . . to some, it seemed more likely that she'd been pushed.'

'You knew her well, then?'

'We were best friends. I was gutted when she died. I'll never forget the awful moment Mum sat me down and told me. October 1986, the day before my sixteenth birthday.'

Something in Corey's face, a rawness, made my heart go out to her. 'Tony would never have hurt her,' I said gently.

Corey slouched deeper into her chair. 'You and I both know that, Audrey . . . but people need explanations, clear-cut answers. When none are forthcoming, they simply make them up.'

The baritone continued to wail, and its ponderous libretto vibrated through me. I inched forward on my chair, suddenly reluctant to yell over the noise.

'It's all really sad – but lots of families experience tragedy, and most pull through. Why do you think Tony didn't cope?'

Corey tugged the tips of her hair, as if trying to tear the strands from their roots. 'Maybe he blamed himself . . . for not being there when Glenda most needed him.'

'How do you mean?'

'The night Glenda died, their parents had a terrible row. Luella told Cleve she wanted a divorce, and asked him to leave. Things got nasty and Cleve walked out. Glenda must have over-heard them and run off, intending to hide at her grandfather's until it all calmed down. She would have been devastated by the row, she adored her father – and in that state of mind, all it took was one careless step . . .'

'Why did Luella want a divorce?'

'There were rumours that Cleve was seeing another woman. After he disappeared, we all assumed the rumours were true.'

I remembered the *Courier-Mail* article. 'Until recently.'

Corey nodded. 'A group of agricultural scientists found a vehicle half-buried in the mud at Lake Brigalow Dam. Inside was a human skeleton. It turned out that the car was Cleve

Jarman's, and the skeleton matched his build. The police won't confirm anything until the forensic tests are finalised . . . which could take years, because the tests are expensive and the car was submerged for so long – but there's no doubt in my mind it was Cleve.'

'Was Tony close to his father?'

Corey's face brightened. 'Yes, very. They were a tight-knit family. Great people, all of them. Danny and I loved visiting; the Jarmans always made a fuss over us. Luella would bring out homemade scones and jam, or sandwiches, and the most marvellous cakes – she'd done a pastry chef's course in Brisbane and really knew how to bake up a storm.'

'What about Cleve?'

'He was lovely. A real comedian, too. He'd tell funny stories, he even knew magic tricks. He had a little dog he'd trained to howl along whenever the telephone rang, it was hilarious. Cleve had been scalded on the face as a kid, he had these white patches on his cheeks – I used to wonder if that's why he went out of his way to charm everyone, so people wouldn't focus on his scars. He needn't have bothered, we would have adored him whatever he looked like.'

I was growing more confused as Corey's story unfolded. 'If the Jarmans were so wonderful, why do you think Tony never spoke about them? Why would he have kept his past a secret . . . especially from his own daughter? And why did he . . . ?' I couldn't finish that particular sentence, but when Corey met my gaze I knew she'd been thinking the same thing. Why did Tony kill himself?

Collecting her baseball cap from the floor, Corey jammed it on her head. 'To tell the truth, Audrey, I'm as baffled about it all as you are.'

I sensed our conversation had burnt itself out. I certainly felt drained and empty. As I joined Corey at her desk, I saw the paleness of her face and guessed she felt the same. We had reached a sort of bottleneck – without real answers, there was only so much mileage to be had from guesswork and speculation.

Corey slipped the gramophone needle off the old record, cutting short the moaning baritone. 'Come on,' she said, nudging my arm and heading for the door. 'I don't know about you, but I'm parched. Fancy a quick beer?'

'Another time. School gets out soon, Bronwyn'll be anxious if I'm late.'

I followed her outside, waiting while she locked the office door. A gust of dry wind lifted her hair, brushing its tips against my bare arm. As we trod along the concrete gangway to the car park, I wondered if I'd ever smell diesel fumes again and not think of her.

'Oh well,' she said with a sigh, 'I've still got oil to change and a cracked cylinder to deal with. I guess I can wait 'til Saturday to see you again.'

The mention of our impending barbecue cheered me. 'It'll be fun – the girls can run wild in the garden while we put our feet up and enjoy a bottle or two of Crown. Have you ever seen the sunset from the verandah?'

'If memory serves me correctly, it's pretty spectacular. We could set ourselves up on a couple of deck chairs like Glenda and I used to do as kids. Bitch about Tony, make a night of it.'

'Sounds riveting.'

Corey beamed. 'You're on, kiddo. See you then.'

In the quarter-hour that it took me to drive back to town, the sun slipped behind the clouds and the sky turned overcast. The roadside trees were soon swarming with shadows and by the time I pulled up outside the school gate, lightning spikes were jabbing the horizon.

I hurried across the schoolyard, scanning the few remaining figures that milled in the quadrangle, seeking my daughter's blonde head. She was easy to spot: taller than most of the other kids, she was slouched against the admin block wall in a patch of dappled shadows. To my surprise, she wasn't alone.

A man was with her, a teacher I assumed. He was describing something with his hands while Bronwyn and another girl watched intently. As I drew nearer I recognised him. His hair was combed – sort of – and he wore a clean T-shirt and jeans; but there was still the same aura of wildness about him that I'd discerned that morning in Hobe Miller's front yard.

Two pairs of eyes swivelled towards me as I approached – Bronwyn's sapphire ones, and the dark, almost black gaze of her young companion. It took the deaf man a second longer to register my presence, and as he spun to face me I prepared myself for the irate scowl he'd presented that morning.

When he saw me, though, his face lit up and his smile left me dazzled. I couldn't even return the nicety; I felt my features settle into a look of dismay.

Bronwyn sprang forward. 'Mum, this is Jade and her dad, Danny. They're teaching me sign language. Cool, huh?'

'Er . . . yes.'

'Hi, Ms Kepler,' the dark-haired girl said, and flashed me a grin almost as glorious as her father's. She was Bronwyn's height, with a perfect oval face and almond-shaped eyes. She was lankier than Bronwyn, but equally as pretty. The two girls made an arresting pair.

Danny shook my hand in greeting, his palm cool and dry despite the heat, his calloused fingers gentle around mine. Then he looked at Jade and made a series of swift gestures.

I remembered Corey telling me about her brother and his daughter Jade. Danny was a vet, called out early that morning to attend an emergency.

Jade sighed. 'Dad's got something to tell you. I'll translate, is that okay?'

'Oh . . . sure.'

She watched her father's fast-moving hands. 'He says you caught him at a bad time this morning . . . Mr Miller's dog had just had puppies and had accidentally rolled on two of them and that everyone was upset. He says he doesn't usually take his clothes off in public – ' Here, Jade rolled her eyes sideways at Bronwyn, who giggled, then went on, 'But poor Alma – she's the Millers' dog – was terribly distressed, and Dad and the two Mr Millers got covered in blood trying to restrain her.'

'Gross,' Bronwyn said, with a wary look at me. She shifted her weight, moving fractionally closer to Jade. 'How many puppies?'

Danny signed swiftly, and Jade translated, 'Six, including the two that died. The remaining four are healthy.' Jade glanced back at me as her father's fingers continued to move. 'He says he's sorry if he alarmed you.'

I shifted my features into a mask of composure. Inwardly, I cringed. The explanation behind my uneasy visit to the Miller property had turned out to be benign. Corey's brother, the vet. Alma and her puppies. Hobe's abrupt behaviour due to worry about his dog.

'I wasn't alarmed at all,' I told Danny, recalling that he could read my lips. I knew I was speaking too loudly, but I felt self-conscious again. 'I guessed it was something like that – I mean, it's not as if I thought you were a serial killer or some kind of maniac on the loose just because you were covered in all that blood – ' I managed to stop babbling when Danny's expression grew confused.

He frowned at Jade, who signed swiftly back at him. He turned back to me and grinned wickedly, his fingers flying once more.

Jade snickered. 'He says you took him by surprise, too. He was probably more startled than you were.'

Thunder rumbled and the first drops of rain began to spit onto the pavement around us. Looking across the shadowy schoolyard, I saw that the sky had darkened further and now bulged with purple clouds. I looked back to find Danny observing my face, his expression unreadable.

'Well, it was nice to meet you,' I told him briskly, then found a genuine smile for his daughter. 'You too, Jade.'

Jade smiled, her almond eyes tilting at the corners. 'Aunty Corey told me that we're coming over on the weekend. I guess I'll see you then.'

'Can't wait. You and Corey will be the first visitors that Thornwood's had in a long time.'

Jade looked pleased. 'I don't suppose Aunty Corey remembered to tell you that we're vegetarians?'

'No, she didn't mention it, but I haven't shopped yet ... What can I get you?'

'Oh, don't go to any trouble, we'll bring tofu snags and lentil burgers, that's what we normally do. Besides, Aunty Corey says it's rude to turn up empty-handed.'

'It won't matter to me if you're empty-handed,' I told Jade, and this time my smile came easily. 'As long as you show up.'

I snuck a look at Danny. He was watching me hopefully.

'Why don't you join us?' I said as casually as I could.

Danny nodded, keeping his gaze on my lips. He didn't bother signing, Jade wasn't watching anyway. Her head was bent close to Bronwyn's – they were talking quietly, no doubt saying hurried goodbyes and making plans for the next school day.

I attempted a smile, squirming under Danny's close scrutiny. I took advantage of the uncomfortable lull to berate myself: why hadn't I thought to wear my good jeans instead of this old patched pair I'd thrown on ... and what had possessed me to wear such a daggy T-shirt?

Danny made a lazy sign, knowing full well I couldn't read it. His hands were large and lightly freckled, graceful. I looked up and met his gaze, and a jolt of awareness went through me. He was unsettlingly gorgeous, but it was more than that. Maybe his silence, his intensity of focus; or maybe the intimate way he searched my face as if trying to see under the skin. Whatever it was, it was making me edgy.

I tapped Bronwyn's arm, and started backing away.

'See you Saturday,' I called to no one in particular, and made a hasty beeline for the car.

'You like him.' Bronwyn's long fingers drummed the dashboard. 'And Jade thinks he likes you.'

I snorted, glad to be inside the familiar cocoon of my Celica and out of the rain. My brain was throbbing – not with pain, but with a tangled knot of thoughts that would take some serious unravelling to get in order.

'I barely spoke two words to the man.'

'Mum, you babbled.'

'And that's a crime, is it?'

'Not a crime . . . just a dead giveaway. You like him.'

'I was only trying to be polite because he's deaf.'

'Jade said he was looking at you a bit gooey-eyed.'

I snorted again, trying to sound incredulous. 'Which makes me think that Jade's imagination is as equally out of control as yours.'

Rain pounded the roof. The cloud-bellies came alive with threads of flickering light.

Bronwyn looked at me. 'Did you know Jade's mum died?'

'Yeah . . . Corey told me.'

'She was deaf, like Jade's dad. It was really sad, she got caught in a thunderstorm and a big heavy tree branch fell on her.'

I looked at Bronwyn, aghast. 'That's awful.'

'Jade said her dad never got over it. He and Jade's mum got married young. They met at a peace rally in Brisbane, love at first sight, that sort of thing.'

'Oh. I see.'

'Jade thinks it's time he met someone.' She looked pointedly at me. 'You know. Moved on.'

'Hmmm.'

'What about you, Mum? Jade thinks you'd be perfect, and her dad's obviously keen.'

I blinked at the glossy blacktop unrolling ahead of us, willing the rain to fall harder, willing the sky to crack open and flood the road – anything to create a diversion from the current conversation topic. When the sky failed to respond to my internal command, I sighed. 'And you had time to discuss all this, did you? In the few seconds before we said goodbye? I didn't realise that speed-gossip was now part of school curriculum.'

'It's not. I'm just getting good at reading the signs,' Bronwyn said mysteriously.

'Oh? After ten minutes of lessons?'

'Signs are not just about hand signals, Mum. Jade says that because her father's deaf he's good at reading a person's face and the way they move their body. He's sensitive to shadows and temperature, too, even the feel of movement in the air. Jade says that a deaf person's other senses grow keener to make up for the one that's missing.'

I changed gears and eased the Celica up to ninety.

I'd once shared student digs with a deaf girl – years ago, pre-Tony, at the start of my first year of art college – and her loud, garbled sentences had taken ages to decode. It occurred to me at the time to learn a few phrases of Auslan, but despite my efforts she was determined to speak rather than sign, even though it meant endlessly repeating herself. Danny Weingarten was the opposite; judging by the notes, and by his daughter's easy role as translator, it seemed he was equally determined to remain silent.

'You and Jade certainly covered a lot of ground in one day,' I told Bronwyn. 'I'm glad you've made a new friend.'

'Not in one day, Mum. One *afternoon*. We didn't even sit together at lunch . . . I was having a bit of a bad morning,' she added quietly.

I looked at her. 'Why?'

Bronwyn twisted her schoolbag strap. 'Oh, you know . . . first day at a new school and all that.'

She looked small, vulnerable. My heart tightened.

'I hated first days,' I confided. 'Every time Aunt Morag got itchy feet, I was thrown into a different school, and the kids weren't cool like they are now, and the teachers – well, let's just say they'd have been right at home in a Charles Dickens' novel . . . My life was a veritable nightmare,' I concluded mock-gloomily.

Bronwyn giggled. 'Mum, you're such a drama queen.'

I grinned. 'You were telling me about Jade.'

'Well, she found me in the library. She'd just come back from lunch with her Aunty Corey, who'd told her they were coming over to our place on Saturday. Jade and I hit it off straight away. Then later, in class, she put her hand up when the teacher asked if someone would like to volunteer as my buddy.'

'Buddy?'

'You know, because I'm new – a buddy is someone who shows the new kid where the toilets are, where to line up for assembly, that sort of thing.'

I'd reached the turn-off. If I hooked left, the road would veer west towards Thornwood. Driving straight through the intersection would take me north to the airfield and from there – if I continued past the landing fields – I'd reach William Road.

I flicked the indicator and slowed to turn toward home . . . but then kept going straight. The Celica rattled as the tarmac gave way to gravel, and the crack in the windscreen inched off on another tangent. The trees along the verge grew thicker, so tall they appeared to join with the low-hanging stormclouds, crowding out the last shreds of colourless daylight. Was it really only four o'clock? It looked more like midnight.

Bronwyn noticed we weren't on our way home. 'Where are we going?'

'I want to show you something.'

'What?'

'It's a secret. You'll see.'

'A secret?' She pondered this morsel, her brows pinched. 'You *do* like him, then? Jade's dad, I mean?'

I rolled my eyes. 'When have I ever liked anyone?'

'Never.'

'Well, I've no intention of starting now.'

'You said we came to Magpie Creek to make a new life.'

'We did, but that doesn't mean I'm going to lose my head over the first guy who comes along.'

'Did you really see him half-naked?'

'He was just washing the blood off his arms after whelping the old man's dog.'

'Did he have nice muscles?'

'Bron!' I actually growled.

'Well, did he?'

'I didn't notice,' I responded frostily. 'Anyway, that's beside the point. Your dad was the only man for me. I could never love anyone else.'

Bronwyn affected a theatrical eye-roll. 'So you keep saying.' Unzipping her bag, she retrieved her drink bottle, took a noisy swig, then palmed shut the sipper top. 'So what's this secret? If it's not your mad crush on Jade's dad, then what is it?'

There were only two dwellings on William Road: one was a small boarded-up shanty that was obviously abandoned. The other – which came into view now – was a beautiful highset Queenslander sitting in the midst of an overgrown garden. Slowing the car, I pulled onto the verge opposite and cut the motor.

'I found a couple of photos.'

'What – that's your big secret?'

'Have a look in the glove box.'

Bronwyn yanked open the compartment and withdrew the envelope. She examined each photo carefully, her head bent nearly to her knees.

For a long while we sat in the steamy silence – me listening to the patter of raindrops on the roof, and Bronwyn scrutinising the photos as though they held long-sought answers to her life's most puzzling questions. When she thought to flip the larger photo over, the sight of the handwritten inscription made her gasp.

'I knew it,' she said excitedly, 'it's Dad as a boy. Who are the other kids? That blonde-haired girl looks like me.'

'That's your father's sister, Glenda, who died. And the redheaded girl is Jade's Aunty Corey . . . The other little boy is Jade's dad. They all grew up together.'

'Jade told me her dad and my dad were friends when they were kids.' She considered the photo for a long time. 'I wish Dad was still here. I miss him.'

I let my gaze fall on the dark-haired boy in the photo, seeing in my mind's eye the man he would later become – attractive, intelligent, sexy and wickedly funny, a brilliant artist . . .

'I miss him, too.'

The Celica's cooling engine ticked noisily. Steam rose off the water-slicked hood. The rain was so light now that I could hear individual drops pattering on the roof. Bronwyn's attention drifted to the window, focused on the house across from where we'd parked.

It was much like other houses I'd seen in Magpie Creek – the weatherboards could have done with a coat of paint, and the guttering was flecked with rust – but its period features were intact: decorative iron lace, stained-glass windowpanes, a leafy verandah and wide stairs. Pink roses frothed along the front gate, shadowed by tall poincianas that partly obscured the house from the road. On either side of the boundary fence was bushland, thickening behind the house as it escaped uphill. A massive black bunya pine towered over the rooftop, its great arms jabbing the sky. The pine hadn't changed much since the photo of Tony and Glenda and their mother had been taken beneath it, and its curiously contorted trunk was unmistakable.

Bronwyn's gaze lingered on the tree, then darted back to the photo. When her mind made the connection, she shot a questioning look at me.

'It's the same tree,' she said. 'Is it Dad's old house?'

'Your dad grew up there, but it's your grandmother's house.'

'I have a grandmother?' Bronwyn's eyes went wide. 'A grandfather, too?'

'Honey, I'm sorry ... your grandfather Cleve died a long time ago.'

She latched her gaze back on the house. 'Oh, Mum, does my grandma know we're here? Have you spoken to her? What's she like? When can I meet her?'

'Well, this is the secret bit, Bronny. Your grandma – Luella – never leaves her house. Apparently she's a bit of a hermit. And now, after what happened to your dad, I'm worried she might be too upset to see anyone.'

Bronwyn looked thoughtful. 'She'll want to see us, though, won't she, Mum? I mean, we're family.'

'I don't know, Bronny. I hope so.'

'Can we go in? Do you think she's home?'

'It's a bit late in the day. Why don't we come back on the weekend, bring her something special?'

'Flowers, you mean?'

'Sure.'

'Maybe a box of chocolates.' Bronwyn studied the house, her eyes alight with curiosity and longing. 'I'll make her a card, too. Oh, Mum, I can't believe I've got a grandmother!'

Her excitement infected me. My heart rate picked up. My hands grew damp. Questions began to tumble through my mind. Then, one question in particular. And though I knew I had no right to ask it, and knew as well that the time when

I might broach the topic was a long way off – it niggled like a thorn in my psyche, sharp and all-consuming.

Luella, what really happened the night your mother died?

As I examined the lovely old house with its boisterous garden and daisy-sprinkled lawn, I sensed that even if did win Luella's trust enough to ask, the odds were that she would have no answers.

Her cosy nest of a house seemed to be hiding beneath the protective arms of the great bunya pine. I imagined her inside, pottering in her darkened rooms, trapped for the past twenty years in a self-imposed prison of sorrow and loneliness. Did she have other family? Or was she – like me and Bronwyn – adrift without relatives, a solitary unit forced by circumstance to stand alone?

As the old Celica rocketed back along William Road in the direction of town, Corey's words echoed in my ears.

It's not worth the heartache . . . Not for you, not for Bronwyn –

But Corey was wrong. Bronwyn and I had weathered heartache before and survived it. If it came to that, we would survive it again.

After a dinner of pizza and salad and shared jam lamington, we flopped on the couch in front of the TV and channel-surfed for a while before bedtime.

Bronwyn wandered off to her room, Harry Potter tucked under her arm. When I checked on her later, she was curled on her bed, hugging her book like a ragdoll, lost to the world.

In the watery moonlight, she might have been a princess from a fairytale – her hair fanned across the pillow, kinked by the heat, and her features were serene as an ice carving. Her eyes moved under their lids, as though following the antics of some astonishing dream-spectacle.

I marvelled over how much she'd changed in the last twelve months. She'd shed her baby-faced plumpness, grown taller and leaner. There was more of the teenager about her, less of the child. Yet so subtle was her transformation, that if I hadn't been observing her I'd have missed it.

It seemed I wasn't the only one taking notice. After what I'd learned today, Tony's withdrawal from his daughter's life made sense. For so long I'd feared that he was distancing himself from Bronwyn to punish me. Or worse, that he was pulling away from both of us, letting us fade into the past, just as he'd let his early life fade.

How wrong I'd been.

Tony hadn't been withdrawing from Bronwyn ... but from the memory of his dead sister. Bronwyn's resemblance to Glenda had been there all along, of course, but Tony must have noticed the likeness growing stronger with each passing year, until he'd been unable to bear it. Which made me wonder if there was any truth to what Corey had told me. Had Tony argued with his sister the day she died; *could* he have pushed her? Is that why he'd run away from home – to escape the guilt and horror of what he'd done? Was it also why, twenty years later, he'd found it necessary to withdraw from Bronwyn's life, unable to endure the sight of her face? It pained me that I'd never know.

Adjusting the sheet across Bron's narrow shoulders, I kissed the top of her head and then crept back to the kitchen.

This part of the house still smelled pleasantly of onions and tomato, and I found it comfortingly ordinary. As I washed and dried the dishes, stacked them in neat piles in the cupboard and folded our pizza boxes into the recycle bin, I tried to pretend that nothing existed beyond these familiar domestic tasks. For a while it worked. There was just the quiet run of the tap, the clink of dishes, the soft call of a boobook from the dark garden outside.

I had a quick shower to cool down, got into singlet and undies and brushed my teeth. Switching off the lights, I padded down the hallway to my room, climbed into bed. Then tossed and turned, cursing the infernal heat that glued the sheets to my legs and back. My eyes were gritty from lack of sleep, but whenever I tried to close them they kept snapping open to re-check the bedside clock.

Was it really only midnight?

For the first time since arriving at Thornwood I found myself missing the hum of city traffic, the blare of car horns and sirens, the rattle of trams, and the reassuring blaze of streetlamps. Noise, glare, distraction; was that why people flocked to the city? Not for jobs, not for lifestyle . . . not even for the anonymous crowds to lose themselves among – but for the constant never-ending distraction?

Wrestling the sheet off my legs, I flopped back on the mattress. A heat rash burned on my neck and I felt the urge to scratch until I drew blood. Instead, I tried to meditate . . . only to snap awake minutes later, more impossibly strung-out than before.

Finally the dam broke.

Images poured into my mind – a child's bathing pool full of sky; four small faces crumpled in laughter; a girl with white-blonde plaits and a skinny dark-haired boy with too-large eyes. A tall woman with a kindly face trapped inside the prison of her own house. Human bones dredged from a dam, and rocks sliding down a deadly precipice. People I'd never met began to murmur their secrets. The dead rose up – pleading, cajoling, calling me to listen to stories that I had no desire to hear.

Only one voice was absent.

'Samuel,' I whispered into the darkness. 'Where are you? Why won't you talk to me?'

The room was stuffy, the air like a furnace. Despite the cool shower, my blood felt on fire. Rolling out of bed, I groped for my slippers and tiptoed down the hall.

The instant I crossed the threshold to the back bedroom, I felt calmer. The voices in my head fell quiet, the dream-rush of images ebbed away. I told myself it had nothing to do with being near the photo of Samuel Riordan; nothing to do with the way his solid presence soothed me ... and nothing to do with the lonely ache in my ribcage that made me want to wrap myself around a large warm body and forget, just for a little while, that I was alone.

I fell heavily into the sheets. Sneezed a couple of times, curled in a ball and dragged the pillow over my head. When nothing happened, I threw the pillow on the floor and rolled onto my stomach, burying my face in the mattress. I'd wake up with wrinkles, but I didn't care. Sleep was what I wanted ... sleep, and the sweet silence of oblivion.

A splinter of awareness in the back of my brain told me I was dreaming, yet in my drowsy state I could have sworn that the man lying beside me in the bed was real.

At first I thought it was Tony; dreams often resurrect the dead. He was sobbing, which is what made me think of Tony. There had been so many nights broken by his nightmares ... so many nights pieced back together with calming words, cups of tea, back rubs.

But this wasn't Tony. Tony had been skinny, bony, disarmingly boyish. The man beside me was a solid weight, fleshy, big-boned. And somehow I understood that he wasn't anguished because he was waking out of a nightmare, but because he had just fallen into one.

'Samuel ... ?'

Wrapping my arms around him, I drew him tight, just as I'd once done with Tony, pressing my lips to the top of his head, murmuring comfort. His hair smelled of sunlight and sweat, his skin felt hot.

A coil of my hair fell across his face. The strand was very long, kinked by soft waves that gleamed in the moonlight. I brushed the lock away, letting my fingers linger on his cheek and trail down the side of his neck into the hollow at the base of his throat.

Samuel shivered. 'Aylish.'

'I'm here,' I whispered. The voice wasn't my own. Or rather it was, but it sounded raspy, as though much time had passed since I'd used it.

Samuel didn't appear to hear.

I tightened my stranglehold. The heat of him burned like fever against my breasts, scalding the inside of my arms, my belly, my thighs. Yet he shivered, as though a cold wind swept over him . . . as though my touch was made of ice.

The moon slid down the sky. Cicadas sent up their first tremulous chorus, then fell again to silence. Soon dawn would come and that knowledge filled me with dread.

He was slipping away.

Or perhaps it was me, retreating into the place my mother had called the Alcheringa, the Dreaming. I clung tighter, but my arms felt scrawny around his shoulders, slender vines encircling the trunk of a vast river gum. I held him with more force, sending tendrils of myself around him, drawing him near, binding his flesh to me, twining his heart and soul to mine.

'Aylish,' he whispered.

'I'm here, Samuel. I'm here.'

Yet even as I spoke I felt the substance of my body begin to dissolve, like a night mist melting in the sun. I felt my core respond to the pull of something greater and vastly more eternal than either of us; something I could not – dared not – resist.

I clutched him with sudden desperation, fearful of letting go. Fearful that this moment might be our last. A tremor flew across his big body and with a jerking motion he curled away from me, wrapping his arms around his chest as if to close me out. I pressed from behind, draping my arms over his shoulders, resting my cheek against his back, but it only seemed to make him shiver all the harder.

Night was escaping.

The moonlight faded and I could hear the scratch of leaves against the window. Birds began to chirp awake, serenading the approach of another piccaninny dawn. I drifted mournfully, no longer able to feel the bed beneath me, or the heat radiating from the body of the man beside me. Soon he would become invisible to me . . . as I already was to him.

I nestled closer, one last attempt to cradle him against the tremors, to ease his sorrow. I thought he must be asleep, but then his voice entered the stillness.

'What have I done?' he murmured, his voice coloured by an emotion I didn't understand. 'God forgive me, what have I done?'

8

Still dark. The night outside, silent. A delicate breeze wafted in the window, cool and delicious with the scent of lilac. I reached across the bed, my palm smoothing over the sheet, seeking but not finding.

The emptiness confused me.

A moment ago he'd been real. Solidly real. Now, the cool expanse of space jarred me, dislodging me from the dream world into the thin atmosphere of actuality. I remembered where I was: the old sleigh bed in the back room. My gaze flew to the wall. Samuel's photograph was a hazy rectangle trapped within its ghostly frame. I couldn't see him from where I lay, it was too dark. I could still feel him, though: the sleeping weight of his limbs, the warmth of his skin, the soft fuzz of chest hair, the quiet thump of his heart –

Rolling myself into the quilt, I burrowed deeper in the bed. Sneezed a couple of times, then groped in vain for a hanky. Ridiculous to feel so shaken by a dream. A foolish dream brought on by talk of accidents and murder, by my constant re-reading of Aylish's letter. Yet it had seemed so real, as though it wasn't a dream at all – but a memory.

I found my hanky and blew my nose, then flopped onto my back and lay staring at the ceiling.

I'd been sixteen when Aunt Morag died. She'd gone quietly in the night, stealing away without so much as a murmur. I'd found her the next morning, her body cold and rigid. So small. I'd always thought her a large woman, robust and tall as a man. The morning I found her I saw how mistaken I'd been. It was odd to see her lying there so still, her waxy eyelids resting shut. Her body deflated now that the largeness of her persona had gone elsewhere.

When I was little, her fleshy arms had sheltered me, her stories had chased my nightmares, her cackling laughter had filled the emptiness that always seemed to hang around after my father's death and my mother's desertion.

Now, as I lay in the quiet darkness of the back bedroom, the warm lilac-scented air drifting through the window reminded me so much of Aunt Morag that I longed to be a child again, snuggled in her arms, slipping easily, and so eagerly, from the chaos and disappointment of the waking world and into the tranquil haven of my dreams.

My eyelids fluttered half-mast.

A lilting voice entered my darkness. A man's voice. With it came the scent of wildflowers, of sun-warmed skin and salty sweat. The weight of a warm body nearby, and me unable to stop myself reaching for him, my lips forming the shape of his name . . .

Samuel.

I struggled upright, gasping. Rolling to the edge of the bed, I stood shakily. When had it become morning? Hazy dawn light trickled through the windows. An orange sun rode the distant hills, burnishing the sky with gold clouds.

I went to the dressing table and peered into the mirror. My face was chalky, except for my cheeks which flamed crimson. I'd bitten my lips so hard they were the deep blood-red of winter roses. My eyes shone in a way that made me uncomfortable. The sensible woman I'd worked so hard to become was gone. In her place, a wild-eyed stranger.

Why was I drawn to this room night after night, like an addict craving her next fix? Was I really that lonely? Had my life become so vacant that I was clutching at dreams for emotional fulfilment? Or had being in this old house dislodged something within me that was now struggling to get out?

Disjointed sounds drifted along the hallway from the kitchen. Cups clattered, a chair scraped the floorboards. Bronwyn was up and about, she must be wondering where I was. The radio's muffled chatter worked on my nerves, and I knew the fragile bubble of my dream would not survive long in the harsh light of day.

Already it was receding like an outgoing tide. I tried to draw it back, tried to hold tight to the sweetness, to the memory of the man I'd clung to in sleep, his lilting voice, the intoxicating scent of his skin and hair, his solidly reassuring nearness.

But dreams were no match for the waking world; in the end I had to let it go.

Hobe Miller didn't say much as we walked around the house. His silence didn't surprise me. After the edginess of our previous encounter, I'd half-expected him to show up in a crotchety mood. Instead he seemed thoughtful, reserved. As though something more weighty than my disorderly garden was pressing on his mind.

To compensate for his quietness, I found myself chattering nervously as I pointed out the broken verandah rails, the cracked bathroom window, the buckled steps, the mango branch that scraped the eaves.

'Will the old iron roof need replacing?' I wanted to know. 'Must the tank water be specially treated? The water tastes good, but how do I know it's safe to drink? And how often should I clear the guttering? Is bushfire a problem, will it improve matters if I pay an arborist to prune the trees? And if I cut back the old rose vines, will they reshoot?'

Hobe acknowledged my barrage of questions with a nod, recording everything in a tiny notebook, his minuscule writing so neat it looked typed. Every time he paused to jot another memo, I snuck glances at him. He reminded me of a TV person-ality from the seventies, vaguely debonair despite the scarecrow clothes and awkward black tape covering one lens of his glasses.

Finally he shut his notebook.

'Your water tank'll need a good clean,' he informed me. 'Ideally, a tank should be scrubbed out every two years, depend-ing on the condition of the roof and pipes, as well as ridding it of any tree detritus, or dead possums and frogs that might have fallen in . . . which'll mean drinking bottled water until the rain fills it up again. Taste's a fair indicator that all is well, but I'll test it to be sure. You'll need to remove leaves from the gutter-ing every month or so. Bushfire might be a problem, so have an early escape plan and keep the house area clear of debris . . . and why go to the expense of an arborist, when I can prune those overgrown trees m'self? As for the roses, I suspect they've carked it. Treat yourself to some new ones, lass. Better yet, plant something else that's more suited to the climate.'

The morning was ablaze. By the time we reached the edge of the garden, about halfway up the hill, my skin was damp and I wished I'd remembered to wear a hat. The air crackled and the trees clung tight to their thirsty leaves. Hobe seemed unboth-ered by the heat, but as we climbed the rocky embankment he drew out a handkerchief and mopped his face.

Below us, the homestead looked stately and serene with its iron lace eaves and glimpses of stained glass shimmering in the early light. The mossy brick pathways wove in and out of the trees, and a froth of red and orange nasturtiums spilled from overgrown beds. It seemed impossible that such tranquillity could harbour so many secrets; even more unbelievable that those secrets may have involved brutal murder.

Hobe seemed as absorbed by the outlook as I was. There was much I wanted to ask, but I knew I'd have to tread carefully.

'Lovely view, isn't it?' I said, hoping to break the ice.

Hobe frowned down at the homestead. 'Hmmm.'

I tried a different line of attack. 'Corey told me you've lived in Magpie Creek all your life. She said if I ever needed to know anything about local history or landmarks, then you're the man to ask. She called you a walking encyclopaedia.'

Hobe looked stunned, then his face wrinkled into a radiant smile. 'Young Corey said that, did she?'

I nodded. 'Actually, I was hoping you might know some interesting walking trails. My daughter's a real nature buff and since a lot of Thornwood is bushland, we're both keen to explore.'

Hobe's blue gaze darted down the hill to the house. 'Tony's daughter?'

'Yeah.'

'Corey told me, I hope you don't mind me mentioning it.'

'I don't mind, Hobe. It's no secret that Tony and I were never married. It didn't work out between us. He met someone else and married her. And yes, Bronwyn is his daughter.'

'Bronwyn? That's a pretty name.' His voice trembled and he kept his attention directed at the homestead. 'Poor kid, losing her dad like that. A horrible loss for you both.'

'It was hard,' I admitted. 'More for Bronwyn than for me. But she's a bright girl, she'll be okay.'

'Nature buff, eh?'

I couldn't resist a smile. 'She has her heart set on becoming an entomologist.'

Hobe blinked, then shook his head in wonder. 'A little bug lady, is that right? Well, she's come to the right place if she wants to study insects – this place is crawling with 'em!'

We laughed louder than the quip warranted, but it was as if an invisible barrier between us had dropped away. The glow in Hobe's face became luminous, his eye shone.

'How old is Bronwyn?' he wanted to know.

'Eleven.'

'A good age. Old enough to ask questions, but not quite old enough to know better than you do.'

'Bronwyn must be on the cusp, then. There are times when she seems to know a great deal more than me. Do you have kids, Hobe?'

He shuffled, averting his gaze back to the house. 'It's just me and my brother, two old bachelors rattling around up at the bungalow. I never married. I guess I was too busy taking care of things around the property, and keeping Gurney out of trouble. My brother's a bit slow in the head, born that way – but good company most of the time. I suspect a lot more goes on under the surface than he lets on.'

Hobe walked a short distance along the embankment, picking his way around clumps of brown tussock grass. When I joined him, he pointed along the ridge to where an outcrop of boulders jutted from a neighbouring hill.

'You see that protrusion of stones, halfway along? That's Bower's Gap, it's about half a mile from here. At a clip it'll take you twenty minutes, thirty at most. There's not much to see at present, everything's burnt brown by the heat. But come spring, the north face of the hill will be a carpet of wildflowers.' He looked back at me and smiled, his glasses flaring in the sun. 'Wait 'til young Bronwyn discovers the butterflies that congregate there, millions of 'em, glorious to see.'

'Sounds perfect.'

'There's plenty of wonders in these hills, Audrey. I don't mind saying it's a magical part of the world. As a young fella I used to walk for miles deep into the national parks. Sometimes Gurney and I would camp out for weeks at a time. I was obsessed with trying to picture what it was like millions of years ago when these hills were really alive.'

Hobe pulled in a deep breath, his nostrils flaring. 'Did you know that Magpie Creek was settled smack bang in the middle of a volcano remnant?'

'Yes.'

He seemed pleased. 'Wild days, they would have been, with the air boiling and all those monsters lumbering around the place. Of course,' his good eye glittered, 'by the time I arrived on the planet, the countryside around here was all dairy grazing. The first farmers cut down all the trees – the beautiful old rose-woods and red cedars and brigalow. Now it's just grass and wire fencing and dozy cattle. Poor old *Tyrannosaurus Rex* is long gone.'

His gravelly laugh was infectious. I found myself grinning back.

'It still has a presence here, though, doesn't it? The volcano, I mean.'

Hobe tore his eyes back to the hills. For a while we stared silently at the distant mountains, burnt-brown and barren, prim-ordially beautiful.

'This place gets to you,' he went on, almost to himself. 'It crawls under your skin, works its way into your bloodstream. I used to knock about with the old blackfellas who lived up at the Crossing. They believe the land is a kind of mother-spirit, that it gives birth to them, and when they die it swallows them back up. They consider themselves to be the keepers of the earth and trees and birds and wildlife ... that they're the earth's sacred custodians. That's why their sense of place is so strong. When you settle into land like this, you get a taste of what they were on about.'

The sun had climbed the sky. I could feel my skin begin-ning to redden. My restless night was catching up with me. I felt languid, my eyes wanting to droop in the harsh light. The stillness folded around me, soothed me. No longer so eager to extract Hobe's hidden secrets, I found myself wanting to reveal my own.

'I never felt as though I belonged anywhere until I came here,' I admitted. 'The moment I saw the place, I knew. The house and garden, the hills behind and the view over the valley from the front ... it felt right, somehow. Like reaching your destination after a long journey.'

'Yep,' Hobe said faintly. 'Exactly like that.'

There was no breeze. The birds had stopped prattling, there was only the hum of a lonely bee, and the whisper of wind in the dry grass. All else was still. The moment unravelled, hung suspended. Then a group of crows lifted from the branches of a nearby red gum, barking mournfully as they flapped into the sky ... and the spell was broken. A solitary cicada began to chirp in the nearby bushes, and was soon joined by a chorus of birdsong. Cattle bellowed in the distance, and the scent of eucalyptus drifted up from the valley.

'Better get on with it, then,' Hobe said. 'Never fear, Audrey, we'll have your garden in ship shape before you know it.'

'We?'

'Gurney helps me out sometimes. He's a good worker, loves to feel needed. I'll get him to trim your grass, no extra charge.'

'Oh Hobe, of course I'll pay him.'

'Well, just a few bob if you like. He does several other lawns in town, makes a good job of it too. Keeps to himself, not a chatterbox like his brother.'

I smiled at this, recalling the man I'd seen on my first visit to Hobe's bungalow, the day I'd stopped to ask directions. He'd been taller than Hobe, with sparse snowy hair and a face that seemed frozen in an aspect of perpetual bewilderment. I also recalled his alarm when he'd heard that I was looking for Thornwood.

'I hope he doesn't mind coming here?' I asked. 'To Thornwood, I mean.'

Hobe shook his head. 'It's just that we've always avoided this property in the past. Sounds silly now, us being close neighbours and all. We've barely set foot on the place these last twenty years. I suppose young Corey told you I was none too fond of Samuel Riordan?'

I nodded. 'She also told me about his murder trial. I must confess, I'm curious to know more.'

Hobe adjusted his glasses. 'Well, now. There was never any concrete proof that Samuel Riordan was guilty of murder ... but mark my words, lass, he was a scoundrel. I used to call him the black snake – if you were fool enough to cross him, he'd strike before you could blink.'

'You think he was guilty?'

Rubbing a knotty finger under his good eye, Hobe looked at me warily. 'Perhaps.'

'Why?'

'I suppose it was the war that changed him, turned him sour ... that's what people say, at any rate.'

'Did he see active service?'

Hobe looked uncomfortable. 'He was a prisoner of war, lass. Spent several years in a Jap camp. Now, those boys of ours did it tough over there. I don't mean any disrespect to them, none at all. They helped save this country, poor bastards – and the women too, trading their young lives so that those of us back home could carry on in freedom and peace. I suppose Samuel did his fair share of the saving, he might even have been a hero like they said. But when he came home he was damaged somehow, not right in the head. Some say he'd have been better off copping a Jap bullet. Better for all of us.'

'What do you mean, not right in the head?'

Hobe raked his sparse hair, thoughtful. 'An old fella I knew had been a war prisoner. He came home changed too, only not for the worst. He said that after the horror years of a Jap camp he developed a powerful awareness of the smallest kindnesses. He'd get all misty-eyed when his wife laid out his slippers or made him a cuppa. Poor old bloke, he reckoned that being deprived of compassion and gentleness all those years had turned him about, made him appreciate things more.' Hobe's attention slid away, darting from sky to hill to tree then back to sky, apparently unable to settle on any one thing. 'Not Samuel, though. He came back cranky as a cut snake. When he died, I wasn't the only person in Magpie Creek to breathe a sigh of relief.'

I conjured the face of the man in the photo, trying to picture him as a snake, a scoundrel. Impossible. To me there was only the gleam of desire in his dark eyes, the appealing curve of his perfect lips, the seductive half-smile that made me feel warm and somehow precious. If a rotten core lay beneath that fetching mask, then I was well and truly blind to it.

'Audrey – ?' Hobe was frowning at me. 'I've troubled you with all this talk, haven't I? You're pale as a grub. Come on, lass, we'd best be getting back. I've got sheets of glass to buy and a shed full of offcuts to sort through. That bathroom window isn't going to fix itself, now, is it?'

The walk down the hill provided a welcome distraction. Somewhere between the vine-choked back garden and the shady path that meandered beside the house, I regained myself. Soon, I silently vowed, I'd be soaking my weary bones under a cool shower. Swilling caffeine, munching a breakfast of reheated pizza. Immersing myself in normality, breaking free of the uneasy residue left by my dreams.

As we rounded the house, a glimmer of peacock-blue caught my eye; Hobe's pristine Valiant was like an oasis of colour in the sun-browned landscape. Even my beloved Celica, parked a few metres away, looked neglected by comparison.

We walked down the slope in silence. I was no longer edgy around Hobe. Odd, I felt nearly as comfortable with him as I did with Corey.

Hobe darted forward. At first I thought he was heading down to his car – that perhaps he'd said goodbye and I'd been too absorbed in my thoughts to hear him. But he waded through the grass towards the fig tree, and crouched in the shadows beneath the sprawling canopy. He was looking at something on the ground.

As I approached, I saw it was a straggly white pom-pom. It let out a shrill pip and began to flap its stubby wings.

'Poor little bloke.' Hobe studied the fig tree's dark underbelly of branches. 'He must have been turfed out of his nest in last night's windstorm . . . or by crows. There's no sign of any other chicks. Probably got themselves snatched by feral cats.'

'What is it?'

'A little boobook hatchling – cute little fella, isn't he?'

'Will it live?'

'Raptors – that is, birds of prey – are pretty tough. But it's always hard to tell. Doesn't look like he's got anything broken after his tumble from the nest, but I don't like to take any chances.' He got up and went down to the Valiant, retrieved a cardboard box from the boot, and hurried back.

'Why's its beak opening and closing like that?' I asked. 'Is it in pain?'

Hobe placed the box near the little bird. 'He's hungry. I reckon once he has a decent feed he'll be right as rain.'

I didn't like the bird's chances. It's soft feathers looked ruffled, the brown and white markings chaotic, its open beak a sign of distress rather than hunger.

Hobe didn't seem worried. He pulled a towel from the cardboard box, then placed it over the little owl. With infinite gentleness, he bundled the bird into the box, so all we could see was its round face and huge golden eyes.

'What'll you do with him?' I asked

'Normally I'd put him back in his nest. Seeing as that's been destroyed, I'll have to play mum for a few days, get him vet checked. I'll make him up a nest box at home and keep him warm, give him a feed on the hour. See if he'll take a bit of minced grasshopper, a few eyedroppers of water.'

'Sounds like you've done this before.'

'I might have. Once or twice.' His lips twitched. 'I'm a carer for WIRES, lass. You know . . . wildlife rescue?'

I grinned. 'Bronwyn'll be keen to know all about that.'

Hobe seemed chuffed. Picking up the box, he stepped from the fig tree's shade and headed down the slope towards his Valiant. The grass smelled warm as we moved through it.

When we reached Hobe's car, I huddled in the meagre shade of a nearby eucalypt while Hobe placed his box on the passenger seat and buckled it in.

'Me and Gurney'll be back in a few hours,' he told me. 'I'll grab those glass panels and some timber offcuts. Gurney can start on the garden this arvo. Providing all goes to plan, we should be done sometime tomorrow.'

He lingered, apparently reluctant to leave. A feeble chirring sound issued from the box, and he peered in, readjusting the towel. The baby owl let out a mournful hoot, then fell silent.

'I hope he survives,' I said helpfully.

Hobe beamed. 'I'll bring him back on the weekend. Bronwyn might like to watch me set him loose.'

'Sure.'

The hatchling gave another worried peep, which made us laugh.

'You'll have your hands full,' I told him, 'with four new puppies and now a baby owl.'

'Ah yes, never a dull moment at the Miller residence.' He regarded me thoughtfully. 'Listen, Audrey, why don't you bring young Bronwyn up to the bungalow sometime. She can choose a pup, if she'd like one. Alma's a great guard dog, and I'd be relieved if at least one of her litter went to a good home.'

My smile faltered. We'd never had a proper pet – unless you counted composting worms, or the hordes of beetles and butterflies and mantises that Bronwyn habitually brought home. She'd given up badgering me for a dog years ago, worn down by my unwavering refusals. But we'd come up here for a new beginning, I reminded myself; maybe it was time for a change of tack?

'She'd love that.'

Hobe's brilliant eye danced in the dappled sunlight. 'Would she, Audrey? Would she really?' He looked up towards the house again, shaking his head as though marvelling at the sight of it.

I was a little overcome myself. In less than an hour my opinion of Hobe Miller had altered dramatically. Corey was right, he was turning out to be a bit of a treasure. I wondered how far I could push our newly established familiarity.

'Hobe? Can I ask you something?'

He was still considering the homestead. 'What's that, lass?'

'Who was Aylish?'

He jerked his head around and stared at me. His brows were furrowed, and his good eye snapped with electric blue light. 'Young Aylish Lutz . . . Well, she was the one they said Samuel murdered.'

'Tony's grandmother?'

'That's right.'

A breeze whispered through the grass and curled around my ankles. Hearing Hobe validate my suspicions brought a heaviness to my chest, as though a stone was wedged in there. Aylish had loved Samuel, her letter had made that clear. So how had he come to betray her so brutally?

'He didn't, though,' I heard myself say, 'did he . . . ?'

Hobe's brow wrinkled. 'Who's to know for certain, Audrey lass?' he said kindly. 'The old boy *was* declared not guilty in a court of law, after all . . . maybe the accusations were nothing more than a bunch of old hogwash.'

'You don't sound very convinced.'

'Well, now – '

'What makes you think he was guilty, Hobe?'

Hobe looked down the hill. 'I was just a speck of a thing in forty-six when it happened – so I'm only going on hearsay, you understand. Y'see, young Aylish got herself in the family way, and there was no question in anyone's mind that the father was Samuel. They'd been thick as thieves for years. They planned to marry, but then Samuel was deployed to Malaya. Got himself captured in forty-two when Singapore fell, and by the time he returned to Magpie Creek he'd changed his mind about marrying her.'

'Why?'

A wedge of sunlight pierced the fig tree's canopy and carved Hobe's craggy face into sharp relief.

'Samuel was a doctor, a good one from what I've heard. He specialised in tropical diseases, and at the start of his service he made quite a name for himself as an RMO – that is, a regimental medical officer. After the war, doctors were in high demand. At least they were in little backwaters like Magpie Creek, and Samuel was keen to set himself up. But there were those who speculated that marrying Aylish would have wrecked his career.'

'Why would they think that?'

'Young Aylish was part-Aboriginal, lass. Her father Jacob was a Lutheran pastor who'd run an Aboriginal mission up north in the twenties. He'd fallen for one of the dark lasses there, wanted to marry her. Of course the church refused, but Jacob couldn't give her up. She bore him a little daughter – Aylish – and they spent the next decade in relative peace. Old Jacob once confided to me that those years at the mission were the happiest of his life. But then tragedy struck. Aylish's mother died of scarlet fever. Jacob left the mission and brought his little girl with him to Magpie Creek. Raised her good, too. All the old-timers only ever sing her praises, and Jacob, poor old bugger, he worshipped the ground she trod on, so he did. After she died he turned into a shell of a man. Never recovered.' Hobe shook his head, as if trying to dispel the sadness of what he'd just told me.

I felt it too, a dirty, oppressive sort of sorrow that lodged in the vicinity of my heart and made my lungs ache. But with the sorrow came a fierce curiosity.

'Where did they find her body?'

Hobe opened his mouth to answer . . . but then went rigid. His face was pale, and his eye grew wide behind the lens of his glasses.

I turned in time to see Bronwyn on her bike flying over the grass towards us. Earlier that morning, before Hobe arrived, she'd been immersed in a school project, head bowed over the kitchen table threading cicada shells into a sort of macabre daisy chain. I'd half-expected her to muscle in on my discussion with Hobe, curious about a new face, but obviously she'd been too absorbed . . . until now.

Her cheeks glowed from the sun despite her sunhat, and her long hair whipped her shoulders. She beamed at us, lifted her hand off one wobbling handlebar in a quick wave, then veered away from the fig tree and continued down the slope along the service road.

Hobe stared open-mouthed, as though at a ghost.

'That's Bronwyn,' I told him.

She coasted the bike until she reached the overhang of trees at the edge of the road, then looped back uphill and resumed her furious pedalling. It wasn't until she disappeared behind the house that Hobe finally spoke.

'She . . . the girl . . . she's the image of – '

'Tony?' I forced a smile. 'Everyone says that. They were very close. Not only in looks, but in temperament as well – '

Too late I realised what he'd been about to say.

Glenda. She's the image of Glenda.

Hobe's gaze was still fixed on the spot where Bronwyn had vanished, as though half-hoping she'd rematerialise. The baby owl was chirruping in its cardboard box, but Hobe didn't appear to notice. To my astonishment, his good eye filled and a single tear popped over the rim and vanished into the rugged terrain of his wrinkled cheek.

'Well, then,' he said, brushing self-consciously at his face and throwing a guarded glance at me. 'I suppose I'll be off. Best collect those window panes while the day's still young. We'll get started after lunch, if that suits you?'

'Oh . . . sure.' I tried to shrug off my disappointment. He seemed eager to get away. 'I've got a fill-in job later this morning, a wedding shoot. I should be back mid-afternoon.'

Hobe nodded, but I could tell his mind was elsewhere. There was a stretch of silence as he continued to stare up at the house, then he shook himself, as though out of a daze. He gave a jerky little wave and climbed into the Valiant. The engine growled to life, and a moment later the car was engulfed behind a billowing plume of dust.

For a long while I stood in the fig tree's sizzling shade, clutching my elbows, listening to the quiet natter of birds. The world seemed so tranquil, so at peace. And so at odds with the havoc raging inside me.

'Mum . . . ?'

Sneaking my fingers around my ribs, I stared bleakly out at the sun.

Aylish Lutz . . . The one they said Samuel murdered.

Closing my eyes, I summoned the image of Samuel in the rose arbour: his intense eyes, his reluctant smile, the rigidity in his broad shoulders that might have been repressed anger. Foul-tempered, Hobe had called him. Malicious. When he died, people had sighed with relief.

'Mum, it's quarter to nine. We're going to be late!'

I whipped around to find Bronwyn standing by the Celica. Her school uniform was rumpled, but her shoes had been polished and her hair brushed into a shiny tail.

She stared at me, horrified. 'You're not even dressed.'

I looked down. Ratty cut-offs. Threadbare T-shirt. Runners, no socks. It would have to do. I stalked through the grass and collected the keys from Bronwyn's outstretched hand. As I did, I saw my fingers. Crusts of blood clung to one thumbnail, and the cuticle was a black half-moon. I'd bitten it in the night, in my sleep. Night biting was a habit I'd shaken years ago. When had it crept back?

Diving into the Celica, I revved the engine as I waited for Bronwyn to buckle up. Then I tore off down the service road in an explosion of dust and gravel.

I didn't much like the picture of Samuel that was taking shape in my mind. I could understand that he'd endured much in the war, and that his suffering must have made it tough for him to re-enter civilian society; but so many ex-servicemen and women had readjusted, so many had thrived. Why had Samuel failed? Worse, to my mind, was the implication that he'd believed marrying Aylish would ruin his career as a doctor. It stung, as though his rejection had been, not of Aylish, but of me.

Clamping my fingers around the steering wheel, I helmed hard against the bumpy road. The Celica kept wanting to get away from me, to skid out of control on the loose rubble, to bounce off over the potholes and take me somewhere I didn't want to go.

Winding down the window, I dragged in a lungful of warm air. It tasted of pine sap and dust, of grass and flowers. It tasted alive. I drank it in, trying to flush away my thoughts of death, my thoughts of betrayal and murder.

I'd fallen head over heels for Thornwood. I didn't want to leave. I didn't want the past to uproot me, to chase me away from where I belonged. But Samuel's presence in the house was tangible. He had once walked the same floorboards that my daughter's soft feet now trod; he had breathed the same air that we now breathed, slept in the same darkness that now settled over us. His blood flowed in my daughter's veins . . . and his dreams flowed in mine.

If he'd been a murderer, then how could we stay?

The truth was, I couldn't let myself believe that Samuel Riordan had murdered anyone. Which meant that somehow, if I wanted to continue living here, I would have to find enough evidence to prove, at least to myself, that he was innocent.

The potholed dirt road ended and the tarmac began. The Celica stopped jolting and our ride became smooth. I looked at Bronwyn. She had her headphones on, staring out the window adrift on her thoughts.

I tried to swallow the lump in my throat, tried to shake free of the shadow that had settled around my heart. Yet it refused to budge. If anything, it was growing darker by degrees.

Aylish and Samuel were starting to feel very real to me. Like family members, or very close friends. I felt keyed up whenever I thought about them, kept having flashes that I'd known them intimately, loved them. It was as if a part of me had flown back into the past to join them, and was now unable to return. I felt lost . . . and utterly, wretchedly, alone.

Only twice before had I experienced such feelings. The first time was when Aunt Morag died. The second was that memorable day when Tony had sat me down and tried to explain why he must marry someone else.

The third time, insanely enough, was now.

My face hurt. My head throbbed and my rarely worn heels were killing me. I wished I could stop smiling.

In a leafy park beside the Brisbane River, a hundred wedding guests mingled under lofty Moreton Bay fig trees. It was midday. The sky was cobalt blue, the sun glowed white. Seagulls squawked overhead, their cries drilling through the muffled din of traffic, giving the atmosphere a holiday air.

The bride wore a classic frothy white strapless – she was a big girl, glorious and busty, with gardenia buds in her glossy dark hair and a luminous smile. The groom gathered her at intervals for a kiss, or swept her in a circle causing soft fragrant petals to rain onto the grass around them.

Poor fools, I thought. Love doesn't last. It was a bitter lesson to learn, but thanks to Tony I'd topped the class and earned a master's degree in disappointment many years ago. Call me cynical, but I'd never seen love make anyone truly happy. The most contented person I'd known was Aunt Morag, and she'd flown solo all her life. 'Free,' as she so often declared, 'of all the heartbreak and frustration you get from loving a man.'

I adjusted my tripod and swivelled away from the wedding party, pulling long focus on the twin flower-girls. They'd clambered into the lower branches of a nearby pine tree, their shrill laughter mingling with the cries of the seagulls. Their dresses, frothy white to match the bride's, were hitched into their undies so their skinny little legs were free to climb. They were giggling madly, flicking twigs at each other, their faces flushed, their eyes glittering bird-bright. Drunk from too much cake and cordial, too much joy.

My shutter began to whirr – perfect shots: a group of guests milling unaware in the foreground, the flower-girls perched like a pair of snow-white hens on their branch in the middle-distance, while all around them butterflies danced like wisps of bright paper among sprays of silvery sunlight.

Then the composition broke apart. The cluster of guests dissipated and the butterflies flew away. The little girls ran back to their mothers. I followed their progress through my lens, but the shutter remained still.

The sun skimmed behind a cloud – or so it seemed – plunging the world into night. The park vanished. I found myself in a dark landscape where tall ironbarks raked the starless sky, their branches bowing and swaying in the wind. I saw a dirt track lit by moonlight. Then, motion. A child was running along the track, her thin legs carrying her away from me. It wasn't Bronwyn – this little girl was no more than a toddler, only three or four, and wearing an old-fashioned dress – even so, I felt a mother's panic as she disappeared ahead of me into the shadows.

Danger in the trees. Stalking . . .

I jerked back to my senses. And back to the brightness of the riverside park with its lofty blue sky and quiet babble of voices, back to the sunlit trees and seagulls and wide-flowing river. Back to a world that wasn't skewed by dreams – a world to which I was fast becoming a stranger.

As soon as my hands stopped trembling, I packed up.

I'd taken over five hundred shots – half during the reception, and half at the park – and I was confident there'd be more than a few triumphs in the mix. Besides, I could see the bride was restless. A new chapter of her life began today; she must be eager to turn the page and get on with it.

As I made my way back to the Celica, my camera bag banging against my hip, the tripod gripped in white-knuckled fingers, my thoughts returned to Aylish.

Had she dreamed of her wedding day with Samuel? Had she planned her dress, fretted over guest lists, pondered their future together? Had she – like the bride I'd photographed today – come alive when the man she loved stood near? And what about Samuel, had he truly loved her . . . or had his intentions been darker, driven by the self-serving delusions of a damaged mind?

I stumbled on my heels and tripped. My tripod clattered to the ground. When I stooped to pick it up, my bag swung forward and knocked me off balance. By the time I reached the car park I was sweaty and flushed, my mood in the scrapheap.

The Celica roared as I gunned the motor. Peeling away from the kerb, I joined the glut of traffic heading to the highway. My vision in the park had rattled me, but I knew it was just the beginning. My curiosity was getting out of control; I could feel it starting to burn, starting to manifest the first red-hot symptoms of unruly obsession. I needed to know the facts – not just rumour and hearsay, but *real* facts.

I checked the dashboard clock. Hobe and his brother would be well into the garden at Thornwood by now. Magpie Creek was a good hour and a half away. Calculation told me that if I blew the limit I could do it in fifty minutes.

9

By the time I got back to Thornwood, the sun was witheringly hot. Grass drooped, leaves relinquished their grim hold on life and wafted earthward, twigs crackled as though on the verge of spontaneous combustion. Even the lorikeets seemed irritable, shrieking and calling to each other as they congregated at the birdbath and tried to cool off.

The Millers had made good headway on the garden. The lawn was mowed, the edges trimmed, and the intruding mango limbs humanely amputated.

I showered and slipped into something more me – cut-off jeans, tank top and bare feet – and then spied on the Millers from various windows, marvelling that they seemed untroubled by the excruciating heat.

Hobe declined my offer to help him carry the glass panes up from his battered utility. As his brother Gurney shied away from coming near the house, Hobe had to make two trips. First came his toolbox and an armload of timber offcuts. Then he donned rigger's gloves to bring the glass. By the time he'd set up camp in the bathroom his face was shiny pink, his snowy hair glued to his scalp.

He got to work chiselling putty from around the broken window panes. First he removed each section of damaged glass and wrapped it in newspaper, then re-measured the new inserts.

I interrupted under the pretence of offering him an iced coffee, and when he politely regretted that he'd already had his solitary cup of the day, I decided to get straight to the point.

'I've been thinking about what you told me this morning.'

He had his back to me, so I didn't see the expression on his face, just a glimpse of his profile as he half-turned.

'What's that, lass?'

'I'm curious, Hobe. Where did they find Aylish's body?'

Scraping his chisel along the base of the window frame, Hobe tapped out another chunk of putty, spraying debris over the floor.

'They found her up at the gully,' he said quietly.

'On Thornwood?'

He nodded. 'She'd been bashed and left there to die.'

An alarm rang quietly in the back of my mind, but I ignored it. Establish the details, I cautioned myself, before you go getting any crazy ideas.

'That's why you think Samuel was guilty, isn't it? Because Aylish was found on his land.'

Hobe pondered the window and scratched his stubbly chin. 'I'm going to have to remove the entire sill, it's rotten through. Good thing I brought along that extra timber.'

'Hobe . . . ?'

He sighed. 'What does it matter now, lass? Too much time has passed. Stop fretting about Samuel Riordan, what he did or didn't do. Thornwood's yours now, it's your home. Don't let the past drive you out of it.'

He was right, it shouldn't matter; it was useless trying to unearth facts that were simply too deeply buried. I kept trying to let it go. And I kept failing.

Aylish might be dead and Samuel long gone, but to me they'd become real. So real that if I closed my eyes I could smell the sweet fragrance of roses, hear a young woman's tinkling laughter drifting across the garden, and see – so clearly that it made my eyes water – the tall man slouched in the arbour, his angel's face lit by a devilish half-smile.

'Is it much of a walk . . . to the gully, I mean?'

'It's on the northern boundary, lass. Back in the direction of town. Borders the national park, might take you a thirty- or forty-minute hike from here. Why do you ask?'

'Well, I was planning to take Bronwyn up to see that flower place you were telling me about – Bower's Gap, wasn't it? But I'd be interested to see the gully now, perhaps I'll go there instead. The light's perfect at this time of year. I could get some really lovely sunset shots.'

Hobe placed his mallet on the windowsill. 'There won't be much at the gully right now. You'll have to wait 'til spring to see the flowers. If it's photos you want, you and Bronwyn'd be better off sticking with Bower's Gap. There's more of a view, and it's safer. Less of a hike, too, only twenty minutes.'

'Safer?'

A hornet hovered near the now-glassless window, darting to and fro, probably scouting for a nesting place. Hobe waved it away.

'There's been a few accidents at the gully over the years, the place is well known for being dangerous – rockslides, earth collapses, trees coming down after heavy rainfall.' He gave me a measuring look. 'You should warn Bronwyn, tell her not to go wandering off into the bush alone. You know what kids are like, they get side-tracked with all the exploring they like to do. Will you do that, Audrey? Will you tell her?'

Birds whistled outside and the hornet droned, but in the bathroom the stillness – though it lasted less than a heartbeat – was explosive.

'Don't you find it strange,' I said thoughtfully, 'that Aylish and her granddaughter Glenda Jarman both died at the gully?'

Hobe brushed a line of putty crumbs from the sill. His face seemed old, the lines deeply carved, his inner light dimmed.

'Like I said, lass, that place has seen more than its share of accidents over the years, what with earth collapses and tree falls and suchlike. It was sad about young Glenda . . . very sad. But she wasn't the first to take a wrong step up there.'

The bitter and desolate sorrow that coloured his voice shocked me.

'Did you know the Jarmans well, Hobe?'

The hornet whined in the stillness, darting at the empty window then dropping back as though undecided. Somewhere in the garden below, a lonely whip-bird cried.

'Well, now,' Hobe mumbled, 'I saw them 'round town on the odd occasion, but no, I can't say I had all that much to do with them.'

He turned away and began to peck at the remaining putty with his hammer and chisel. After a while his good eye peeked around and saw me still watching. With a sigh, he laid his tools on the sill.

'Don't you hate it? You hit sixty and your memory starts to dry up like a billabong in a drought.' He shook his head and shuffled past me, pausing beyond the bathroom door to look back. 'Left my fool spirit-level down in the car, means another trip. Perhaps I will have that cold drink after all,' he added, 'I expect I'll be parched by the time I get back.'

He went out to the verandah and vanished down the back stairs. I hurried to the lounge room window and watched him cut across the grass and down to the service road.

Gurney was fossicking in the back of the ute. He looked up as his brother approached. Hobe slumped against the car, his shoulders stooped. Dragging a large handkerchief from his back pocket, he mopped his face, blew his nose. Gurney must have asked him a question, because he shook his head and then stared away down into the valley. Gurney continued to hover, wringing his hands as he shambled about. Even from my vantage point at the lounge room window, his distress was palpable. He kept glancing up at the house, then back at Hobe, his face creased with worry.

'Oh, Hobe,' I whispered, 'what just happened?'

This morning, up on the embankment overlooking Thornwood's rambling garden, Hobe had confessed his love for the surrounding countryside. He'd painted a picture of hills carpeted in wildflowers and prowling prehistoric monsters, and told me of his boyhood fascination for the long-dead volcano. He'd spoken respectfully about the local Aboriginal people and had seemed to understand their connection to the land. I'd warmed to him after that, feeling compelled to spill my own private thoughts, wanting to trust him the way I'd wanted to trust Corey.

And yet, just now, he'd lied.

I remembered his shock at seeing Bronwyn this morning, obviously triggered by her resemblance to Glenda. He'd been so overcome by emotion that he'd shed a tear. And yet, when I'd asked him just now, he'd denied knowing the Jarmans and taken off like a startled lizard.

Hmmm.

As Alice said when she stumbled down the rabbit hole, things were getting curiouser and curiouser.

'Pizza *again*?'

'I thought you loved pizza?'

'I do, Mum. Don't get me wrong, I'm not complaining – just reading the signs.'

I settled myself on the couch, grabbed a plate and loaded up with ham and pineapple. 'What signs?'

'That time is of the essence. That one of us is too busy with other things to be bothered cooking. That there are secret activities going on. That one of us is hiding something. And it's not me.'

I paused, a slice raised halfway to my lips. I lowered it back to the plate and looked at her. She was nibbling a corner of cheese and tomato, blinking innocently at the television. Pretending interest in David Attenborough's segment on termites which she'd watched a million or more times already.

'Hiding what?'

She shrugged, eyes on the TV. 'You tell me.'

My stomach knotted as a vision bloomed in my mind: Bronwyn discovering the old revolver I'd locked into Samuel's dresser drawer. Handling it, rummaging in the box of live rounds . . . I felt suddenly ill. Why hadn't I disposed of it, surrendered it to the cops as I'd initially planned?

'What did you find?' I asked carefully.

Bronwyn took another dainty bite, chewed and swallowed. 'Come on, Mum, own up. A secret pastime, perhaps? A private little project? Something you're not quite ready to share?'

Not the gun, then. A parade of other guilty suspects shuffled past. The clean sheets I'd put on Samuel's bed, the carefully hand-washed quilt and my own favourite pillowcases. My books piled on his bedside; the frame displaying Samuel's photo de-tarnished and fitted with new glass; Aylish's letter tucked into the top drawer . . .

I shrugged. 'Sorry, you've lost me.'

Bronwyn contemplated her crust the way a torturer might eye their next victim. I could almost hear her brain ticking over: Will I draw it out slow and painful, or act fast with the advantage of surprise?

'Mum,' she said reasonably, still considering her crust, 'I think I'll become a vegetarian like Jade. It's more humane, plus it's way less taxing on the planet. Can I?'

So, it was to be slow and painful. Shoving my plate onto the coffee table, I drew my legs up under me and wriggled around to face her.

'What do you mean, a secret pastime?'

She smiled then, a luminous smile that lit up her face. 'That sounds like the voice of a guilty conscience.'

'Actually it's the voice of an annoyed mother who's too tired to play games.'

'Whatever.'

'Come on, Bron, what've you found?'

Setting down her plate with unnecessary slowness, she reached under the coffee table and drew out a small pile – several instruction books and a companion DVD.

My heart sank when I recognised the book covers, but at the same time I felt drunk with relief.

'Oh. That.'

'It seems I'm not the only one learning about signs,' Bronwyn said triumphantly, tossing the DVD onto the lounge between us, holding up the manuals to read.

'*A Time to Sign – The Easy Way to Learn Sign Language* . . . and this one, *Something to Sign About – Eleven Fun Children's Songs* . . .' She peered over at me, eyes agleam. 'Really, Mum, children's songs?'

'I thought it best to start with something simple,' I told her stiffly. 'Anyway, I don't see what the big deal is, it's only – '

Bronwyn twittered happily. 'Oh Mum, you *do* like Jade's dad, don't you?'

I glared at the TV. 'I'm only being polite because he's deaf. Besides, he's coming to the barbecue on Saturday and I'd hate him to feel left out just because he's hard of hearing. Someone's going to have to talk to him.'

'Someone? You mean aside from me, Jade, and Aunty Corey?'

'It's just the polite thing to do, Bron. Besides, if the four of you get caught up in a sign language conversation, how am I supposed to join in unless I know it too?'

'You're telling me you *don't* like him, then? That you're going to all the trouble of learning sign language just so you won't feel left out?'

I picked up my plate, bit the corner off a pizza wedge and feigned absorption in the program. David was leaning on a huge termite hill, instructing the camera to enter. Suddenly there were busy white bodies everywhere, gathering and swarming like . . . well, termites.

'Mum? Stop ignoring me. It only makes you look more guilty.'

I sighed. 'He's nice, okay? Just not my type.'

'Why not?'

'He just seems . . . I don't know, a little wild.'

Bronwyn snorted. 'Mum, you're hilarious, I can't wait to tell – '

'Don't you dare!'

She shook her head. 'Let me guess, Dad was the only man for you?'

'Something like that.'

'You know, Mum, one day I'm going to grow up and leave home, and you'll be alone. You'll get lonely. That is, unless you can forget Dad and move on.'

I looked at her, found myself trying to analyse her words, probing for a hint of pain or a shadow of unresolved anger. Trying to determine if her casual-sounding comment concealed a cry for help. Her face was calm, her eyes deep blue and still as lake water.

'Move on, maybe,' I told her. 'But we don't have to forget.'

'I'm not saying *I'll* forget him. Just that you should.' Tossing the sign books aside, she reached for the remote. Inching up the volume, she settled herself comfortably and resumed the slow demolition of her pizza.

She was right. I *was* hiding something.

Only it wasn't a romantic plot that hinged on learning sign language. The truth was, how could I think about any man when my head was so full of Samuel and Aylish?

After the dishes were done, I hurried out to my studio at the far wing of the house. The long narrow room had once been part of the verandah, which, with the addition of a timber wall and line of tall windows, had been converted into a sunroom. Soon after our arrival I'd spent several days scrubbing bird poo from the floorboards, polishing the windows, and freshening the walls with creamy white paint. The furnishings I'd kept simple: my print drawers, an aluminium tripod lamp, my cherished Eames chair and an antique desk. Under the windows at the opposite end of the room sat my huge drafting table – a pair of sturdy trestles topped by a recycled oak door. I'd even dragged out my old developing trays and enlarger. They were dinosaurs in a digital world, but I loved having them around – they reminded me of those giddy, intoxicating first days of my love affair with photography.

Sitting at my laptop, I plugged in the satellite USB and connected to the internet. Typing my request into the search engine, I waited while the State Library of Queensland website loaded. I used Bronwyn's public library card to set up a user account, then followed a link to the Historic Australian Newspapers site. There was only a handful of Queensland newspapers – the earliest of which was the *Moreton Bay Courier* from 1846. I clicked on the more recent *Courier-Mail*, dating between 1933 and 1954. The site took forever to load. When the page appeared, I saw it was useless: either the newspapers after 1939 were non-existent – which was unlikely – or they hadn't yet been digitised and uploaded to the site.

Retracing my steps to Historic Australian Newspapers, I typed in a series of connected keywords – 'Queensland', combined with '1946', 'Magpie Creek', 'murder trial'. My hopes began to flag as I trawled through nineteen pages of links to possible articles – Atrocities by Japanese, War Prisoners Starved and Beaten, Death of a Swagman – but failed to find anything even remotely related to what I wanted.

On the brink of giving up, I made a last-ditch attempt and typed in: 'Aylish Lutz'. Within seconds I was staring at a patchwork of blurred newsprint. At the centre, flanked by articles and advertising sketches, was a single block of highlighted text. At first I was mystified – it wasn't even from a Queensland paper. Then I enlarged the image and took a closer look.

The Argus (Melbourne, Vic.: 1848–1954)
Monday, 18 March 1946, page 1

MAN ARRESTED FOR MURDER
BRISBANE, Mon. – After 30 hours' investigation by police under direction of Sub-inspector B. McNally, a man was arrested on Friday night charged with the murder of Miss Aylish Lutz, 22, whose body was discovered early Thursday morning in a bush clearing fifteen miles west of Magpie Creek, Queensland.

The police discovered signs of a violent struggle, as well as several human teeth and patches of blood where the victim had tried to drag herself away from the scene. A post-mortem examination held on Friday showed that Miss Lutz died of injuries sustained when she was bashed across the head and body.

A further examination today confirmed that Miss Lutz had been battered by a wooden implement thought to be a wheel spoke or club.

I flew out of my chair and raced along the hall. Aylish's letter was already scored into my memory, but I had to be sure. Bursting into the back bedroom, I retrieved the letter from the bedside and unfolded it in the light.

Aylish had written the letter on Wednesday, 13 March 1946, asking Samuel to meet her at their secret place. The following morning – Thursday – her body had been found in a bush clearing near the gully.

Back at the desk, my fingers sped across the keyboard. I jabbed the Enter key and waited, convinced there'd be nothing. First time lucky, second time empty-handed, wasn't that how it worked?

Apparently not.

The Sydney Morning Herald (NSW: 1842–1954)
Wednesday, 20 March 1946, page 3

WAR HERO ARREST

BRISBANE, Wed. – Returned war hero Dr Samuel Riordan appeared in Magpie Creek police court, Queensland, accused with having murdered Miss Aylish Lutz, 22, a coloured woman, daughter of Lutheran minister Rev. Jacob Lutz on Wednesday.

Miss Lutz was found with her head battered half a mile from the doctor's homestead.

Several witnesses came forward and declared that Dr Riordan and Miss Lutz were seen arguing in the main street of Magpie Creek the morning of Wednesday last. Another witness affirmed that he and Dr Riordan had parted company late on Wednesday evening. Both men had been drinking. Dr Riordan pleaded not guilty in the preliminary hearing and will be remanded in custody to reappear at Brisbane Supreme Court in June.

I sat back, the jagged black and white words flashing in my mind. Arguing in the street. Drinking. This was damning behaviour, even without Aylish's letter asking Samuel to meet her the night she died. My hope of finding concrete proof of Samuel's innocence was fast shrivelling. In its place was a growing sense of dread.

Backtracking, I clicked on another link.

The Sydney Morning Herald (NSW: 1842–1954)
Friday, 14 June 1946, page 4

JUDGE RULES LACK OF EVIDENCE IN MURDER CASE
BRISBANE, Fri. – Accused war hero Dr Samuel Riordan, 30,
of Magpie Creek, Queensland, walked free from the Brisbane
Supreme Court yesterday after the judge ruled there was not
enough evidence against him.

Dr Riordan had been on trial, accused of murdering Miss
Aylish Lutz, 22, also of Magpie Creek, in March last. Justice E.
Redmond discharged the jury today after ruling that there was
not enough evidence against Dr Riordan for the case to continue.

None of the articles mentioned a child, which made me wonder.
Had Aylish suspected that her meeting with Samuel might end
badly, and so changed her mind about taking her daughter
to meet him? All I had to go on was her letter, but aside from
Aylish regretting that they'd argued, there'd been no undertone
of hesitation or worry.

I made another keyword search – 'murder' with 'Magpie
Creek'. The computer turned up fourteen pages of prospective
links. I eliminated each of them, until only one remained. It
was short, and there was an air of finality about it which told
me that the case had been abandoned.

The Mercury (Hobart, Tas.: 1860–1954)
Tuesday, 17 September 1946, page 13

MURDERER OF WOMAN NOT TRACED
BRISBANE, Mon. – No trace of the murderer of Miss Aylish Lutz,
22, who was battered and left for dead at Magpie Creek, Queensland, in March last, has been found by police up to tonight.

For a long while I stared at the screen, deflated.

I'd gone looking for proof of Samuel's innocence, but instead
found only more reason to doubt him.

Corey had said that Samuel's case was discharged because his father was a friend of the judge. Power and influence were valuable commodities. It would only take a whisper for vital evidence to be overlooked. Worse, I knew that way back in 1946 there would have been those who considered the death of a young half-caste Aboriginal woman to be of no great import. A few strategically placed lies, a casual tip-off to the press . . . and the whole inconvenient affair would have neatly vanished off-radar.

I pored over my printouts, trying to read between the lines.

I hated the idea that Aylish had been murdered by someone she loved. Not because I necessarily wanted Samuel to be innocent, not even because I wanted their story to have a happy ending. But because dying at the hands of your beloved was wrong. Seeing in his face the intent to hurt you, to destroy you. Not just love lost; not simply indifference or hatred, but a look that says, You are mine, and I can do to you whatever I want . . . and since you mean so little to me, your pain will bring me great pleasure –

A shiver in the darkness. An unspoken whisper.

Not Samuel. For her sake, don't let it have been him.

But if not Samuel, then who?

Sixty years had passed since Aylish's death. If the police had failed to trace her killer back then when the clues were still fresh, what chance did I have of discovering anything now? Aylish was gone, and whoever had cut short her young life was gone, too. There was no point searching, because I already knew what I'd find: Nothing.

And yet how could I abandon her?

There were moments – when I sat in the derelict old arbour, or lay on Samuel's bed, or caught the ghostly scent of roses drifting in the warm air – when I felt so close to Aylish that I had trouble discerning where she finished and I began. It didn't make sense, this obsessive fixation, but somehow the fragments I was learning about her had burrowed under my skin. Each new slice of her story scared me, disturbed me . . . and excited me beyond explanation. Sometimes I liked to imagine that her heart pulsed within me, flooding me with feelings I'd never thought possible. Not for me, anyway. Aylish had opened a window into what it might be like to deeply love, and to believe that love wholly and unconditionally returned.

Only now I had to ask, had it all been a lie?

I shut my eyes, then wished I hadn't. A new image of Aylish came to me: She was lying on the edge of a bush track, the ground around her striped with shadows, its leaf-littered surface splashed with blood.

Despite her injuries she hadn't died immediately. She had tried to crawl away from the scene of her attack, taking shelter in the darkness. She'd drifted through the endless night, teetering on the brink from which there was no return, hovering through the clammy dawn, tasting the dew, feeling the crawl of insect-legs on her cooling skin, watching the bush around her come to life as she prepared herself to greet death. And she had waited. Patiently, because time was no longer a burden to her. Waited for someone to come along and find her.

Waited for Samuel.

10

Aylish, March 1946

The scent of fresh-baked bread lured me to the bakery window. There were scones today, and even a small hard-crusted raisin cake, and I stood a moment mentally counting the coins in my purse.

The main street of Magpie Creek was busy for a Wednesday. Young mothers hoisted along their grocery bags, or dragged toddlers by the arm. Older women collected at the kerbside to chat. Most managed to look smart despite the lingering shortages, and I knew first-hand the effort this took. Like me, they taxed their precious rations to boil up their own sugar-and-water setting lotion, and rouged their cheeks with beetroot juice. The clever ones cut up old curtains to refashion using dress patterns from the *Women's Weekly*, while the rest of us were still patching and mending and darning the clothes we'd purchased before the war.

In contrast, the men seemed shabbier, somehow depleted; their trousers shiny with wear, their shirts grey from too many washdays, their shoes thin-heeled and scuffed. The happy glow of victory still burned bright in most hearts, but the papers and newsreels were full of bad news. Prisoners of war, concentration camps in Europe, war criminal trials, and the devastation caused by two atomic bombs dropped on Japan. Grief and fear and the pain of separation had changed all of us; not a single soul was left untouched.

There were a lot of servicemen about, some on crutches or bandaged, others thin and hollow-eyed, looking at everything, curious and engrossed as though seeing their hometown for the first time. I'd stopped searching their faces. Stopped hoping. Become accustomed to keeping my thoughts trained on simple, undemanding things.

Like bread and cake.

Which, despite their tempting aromas, lost the battle against my frugality. I wandered a little way further down the street, but stopped again in front of the pharmacist's display. What was wrong with me? Normally I'd grab supplies and rush home to be with Lulu and Poppa . . . but for some reason I was lingering today, as if I had nothing better to do with my life than shop.

A jumble of jars and bottles filled with coloured powders were appealingly displayed in the pharmacist's window. Blocks of finely milled soap, a set of brass weighing scales, a copper mortar and pestle. I thought of the soap I'd been making through the war, a rough old brew of goat fat and water filtered through wood ash, scented with wild jasmine picked from the gully, then cured for a couple of months on a drying rack in the laundry. It did the job, but left my hands red raw. I examined the pretty paper-wrapped blocks in the display, calculating whether I could stretch my budget to such an extravagance –

'Hello, Aylish.'

I tensed. That voice. Whirling around, I faced the man who'd spoken . . . then slumped. Not him, not the one I'd been half-hoping, by some impossible miracle, to find before me. A stranger, this gaunt man with hollow eyes and an untidy growth of stubble. His uniform was shabby, his lanky body wasted. Sharp bones jutted from beneath his yellowish skin as if trying to push through.

'Aylish, it's me.'

'I'm sorry, I don't – ' The words I'd been about to say died on my tongue. His voice. I knew his voice. Then, as I searched the haggard visage, the features shed their mask of unfamiliarity and reassembled into a face I'd once known almost as well as my own. My heart stopped beating; the air became unbreathable.

'Samuel . . . ?'

He watched me, not bothering to nod or acknowledge my recognition. Just watched, as though fascinated by the array of emotions that must be swarming across my face. Disbelief. Uncertainty. And then . . . hope.

I allowed myself the rare luxury of a smile. When he smiled in return – a ghost of the bewitching half-smile that had once captured my heart – the gauntness and scars and jutting bones receded, and I saw my beloved Samuel clearly for the first time.

'It *is* you.'

He nodded.

Unable to contain my joy, I rushed at him intending to throw my arms around his neck and, not caring who saw, give him the loving welcome home I'd been dreaming about for so long.

Samuel flinched, stepped away.

'You're well then, are you?' he asked stiffly.

I froze mid-flight. The chatter and wash of voices from the street eddied around us. A motorcar rumbled past, churning up a slipstream of dust.

'Yes,' I managed through my shock, 'well enough.'

All of a sudden my neck itched, my skirt needed adjusting, I became aware of the pebble I'd collected in my shoe. The urge took me to look anywhere but at him, to hide my stricken embarrassment. And yet I couldn't tear away my gaze.

Samuel observed me with hollow eyes. 'How's Jacob?' he said flatly. 'Still up to his old tricks?'

'He's been ill,' I said with equal flatness, 'but he's on the mend now.'

This was ridiculous. Better Samuel was dead, than this. Better I was dead, than endure this chilly reception. Better to have lost him, after all. At least then my memories of him would have been sweet. I recalled that long-ago night at the hut when he'd loved me so ardently, and been so determined to protect me. Our soft words, our passion; the moonlit bed, and the warm rose-scented darkness. Wasn't it better to remember the man I'd once loved and believed lost, than to face this cold-eyed stranger?

'You never came to see me,' he said gruffly.

I blinked, not understanding.

'At Greenslopes,' he clarified. 'I wrote and told you I was in the hospital, but you never replied to any of my letters. I even telephoned the post office in February, but you didn't respond. I thought . . .' He pinched his lips together, as though unwilling to say more.

'What are you talking about, Samuel? What letters?'

He swayed on his feet. 'You promised, Aylish. You promised to write, but you never did. How could you ignore me like that, after . . . after . . . ' He cleared his throat. 'We talked about marriage, about a future together. Then you ignored all my letters, never wrote back. It was as if all we had together suddenly meant nothing to you. As if *I* meant nothing.'

Passers-by were staring now, openly curious. An annoying tear wobbled on the edge of my eye, and as I paused to dash it away, the meaning of Samuel's words finally took root in my scrambled brain.

'You wrote?'

He nodded, leaning nearer. 'Whenever I could, sometimes every day. Sometimes not for weeks. Then in forty-two when Singapore fell – ' He rubbed his mouth and glanced along the street. 'There were no more letters after that. I guess you heard about the Jap camps? Frustrating, it was, to be stuck there while the rest of Australia was off winning the war. Made a man feel worse than bloody useless.'

'I never got any of your letters.'

He looked back at me with those flat, empty eyes and went on as if I hadn't spoken. 'I was repatriated in December. I wrote from Greenslopes to let you know I'd returned.' He lifted the walking stick I'd failed to notice. 'I would have come to see you earlier, but I was a bit laid up. I thought if I sent a letter, you might come to visit.'

'Samuel.'

He blinked. 'What?'

'I didn't get any of your letters. Not one. Nothing came from Malaya, and there were no Red Cross postcards from the camp. And nothing from the hospital.' A horrible thought pressed into my mind. 'I sent you a ton of letters. Did you get any of them?'

He shook his head.

'Any parcels, or cards?'

'No.'

'Then where . . . ?' My question died on my lips.

At the end of the war the Red Cross had discovered thousands of letters and parcels rotting away in storerooms in some of the Japanese camps – letters that might have offered comfort and hope to countless prisoners. The contents of any parcels had been ransacked, the food eaten by guards, the cigarettes smoked, the photos and notes of encouragement from loved ones discarded, with not so much as a postcard delivered to its intended recipient.

Did that explain why Samuel hadn't heard from me? Possibly. But what of the letters I'd written before he was taken prisoner? The endless missives about life at home and how I yearned for him? The photos of Lulu, the cakes, the dreadful hand-knitted socks, the little blocks of soap? And why had the letters he'd written – sometimes every day, he'd said – never reached me?

'You told me you telephoned the post office. Who did you talk to?'

'Klaus Jarman's young fella, Cleve. He said he'd ride over to Stump Hill Road and give you my message the minute he finished his shift.' Samuel gave me a searching look. 'You didn't get the message?'

'He must have forgotten. Samuel, if I'd known you were in the hospital, wild horses wouldn't have kept me away.'

Samuel swallowed. The ice in his eyes showed signs of melting. His voice, when he spoke, had lost its edge of anger. 'Just now, a moment ago. You didn't recognise me, did you?'

'No.'

'Am I so very different?'

A moment passed before I could speak. 'It's true,' I said at last, 'you have changed. These past few years have taken their toll on everyone. But Samuel, it's time to put the war behind us and get on with life.' I dared to reach out and grasp his hand, to give his fingers a quick squeeze, shocked to feel how icy they were. I drew back. 'I have a little girl now. Her name is Luella . . . Lulu, I call her. I've told her all about you.'

'About me?'

'Of course, Samuel. Every time I look into her sweet face, I see you. She has your eyes and smile, and she's very smart. Cheeky too, just the way you – ' *Were*, I almost said, as if he was past tense. But that was how I'd come to think of him: The man I'd lost in the war. The man who came to life in my dreams, but who only inhabited the grey shadowland of the past.

Samuel apparently didn't notice my blunder. A slow smile transformed his gaunt face. The remoteness in his eyes dropped away and something else dawned there: a flicker of almost startled pleasure. He cleared his throat.

'Luella . . . Lulu, I've always loved that name. May I, if it's all right with you . . . oh, hell, Aylish. I'd love to meet her. Do you think I could perhaps visit – would this afternoon be too soon?'

Hope, at last. A glimpse of my old Samuel, the one who'd held me all night at the settlers' hut and chased away my ghosts.

The sweet man I'd wept over and prayed for every moment since he'd climbed into that old red rattler four and a half years ago and been transported out of my life. A smile began to bloom in me, starting at my feet, a fireball of love that coursed upwards, setting my whole body ablaze.

'Of course you must visit – '

Right then a truck clattered past, its exhaust pipe firing off a loud explosive pop. Samuel lurched away from the sound, grabbing my arm and pulling me into the pharmacy doorway, looking around to find the source of the sudden noise. The truck rattled off, and Samuel turned back to me. His already grey face had turned paper-white and broken into a sheen of sweat.

'Samuel . . . ?'

'I'm all right,' he said quickly, letting go my arm, brushing at his chest with trembling fingers, nodding as though to reassure me. 'Just a bit . . .' He wiped his mouth. 'A bit jumpy.' He stared along the street. More and more people were sending us curious looks, some turning their heads as they passed, nodding in acknowledgement of Samuel's uniform. Once or twice a male hand shot out to pat him on the back, several voices called to him.

'Welcome home, mate.'

'Good on you, son.'

'Your father would've been proud, Samuel – '

I braved reaching again for his fingers. This time I grasped them and didn't let go.

'Of course you must visit us,' I resumed. 'I'll be taking Poppa to the doctor in Ipswich this afternoon, but tomorrow's his birthday, we've planned a little shindig, nothing flash, just the three of us. Would you like to come? Please say yes, Poppa would be so thrilled to see you, and Lulu . . . well, she'll be over the moon.'

Samuel's large fingers curled around mine. A tiny, almost insignificant show of warmth, but it caused my heart to drop open like the petals of a great soft flower. Everything was going to be all right. Samuel was alive, he was home. And he loved me still, I knew he did, it was there in that gentle squeeze of his fingers, and there in his dark eyes as they searched my face with evident longing. I didn't mean to race ahead, but the honey-sweet words were already forming on the back of my tongue. We'll be a family, I yearned to say. At last, we'll be a proper family. You and me and Lulu together, just as I dreamed. We'll be married and put this whole sorry wartime episode behind us –

Samuel's eyes narrowed. 'What about you, Aylish? Are *you* pleased to see me?'

I gazed up into his dear face. Pleased? Could he not guess how I'd missed him, how sick with longing I'd been while he was away? How worried, how desolate, how lonely I'd been? Of course not, how could he? The letters I'd written to him were probably still mouldering away in some forgotten camp storeroom.

I smiled. 'You have no idea how pleased I am.'

But this time Samuel didn't return my smile. A change had come upon him. My familiar Samuel was gone, the cold stranger had returned. His eyes were empty again, his mouth grim. Withdrawing his fingers from mine, he gripped my wrist hard.

'You didn't even know who I was.'

I tensed. 'Samuel, let go. You're hurting me.'

'Have you met someone else, Aylish? You have, haven't you?'

'No! Don't be ridiculous, Samuel.'

'That's the real reason, isn't it?' He jerked down on my wrist. 'That's why you never wrote, why you never came to see me at Greenslopes.'

'Stop it, Samuel, you're hurting me!' I tried to pull free, but he held firm.

'And the little girl, she's not mine, is she? She can't be, I've been away for years . . . what do you take me for, Aylish, a bloody fool?'

'You're wrong,' I cried, sensing curious looks around us, knowing that we were making a scene, but too upset to care. 'I *did* write. I don't know why you never got any of my letters! There's no one else, Samuel. How can you say that? There's only ever been you. And Lulu . . . of course she's yours, she's nearly four, why would I even tell you about her if she wasn't your daughter? Please, Samuel . . . you're not well – '

'Well enough to know a lie when I hear one.' He released my wrist as if touching me repulsed him. Then he added quietly, chillingly, 'You'll be sorry for this. By God, Aylish, you'll be sorry.'

His mouth worked as if he wanted to say more, but instead he made an animal sound in the back of his throat. A snarl, a sob, I couldn't be sure. Turning, he limped away along the street, his stick jabbing the pavement, his shoulders set; a tall emaciated bear of a man careless of the pedestrians dodging out of his path.

11

The Lutheran church was on the airfield road north-west of town. It was perched on a plateau of threadbare brown grass, a tiny whitewashed chapel with a tall roof and twin cypress trees guarding the entryway. Under one of the cypresses was propped a gleaming vintage motorbike.

Leaving my Celica on the verge, I hurried across the grass towards the little cemetery tucked away at the rear of the church. I passed a few modern plots – flat marble plaques implanted in the arid soil, invisible unless you were standing over them. The older gravesites occupied the furthest corner of the property, marked by a wire fence and shaded by red gums. On the other side was a paddock of dry lucerne inhabited by ghostly-white Brahman cattle. Behind them in the distance, a huddle of purple-blue volcanic hills.

I took my time weaving between the graves, pausing here and there to crouch and touch my fingers to weathered names, dates, endearments. I'd brought along my old Minolta but now that I was here it seemed too intrusive to start shooting; even the barely-there whirr of my shutter would have been out of place. The morning was too serene, the graves too peaceful. Deep quietude cocooned the graveyard, occasionally broken by

164

the slipstream of noise as a solitary car sped past. I might have drifted through a crack in time and into another world.

The graves in this section were largely pre-war; many of the inscriptions were written in German, evidence of the immigrants who'd settled the area in the 1870s.

One tiny marker begged a closer look. I knelt beside it and brushed at the flaking inscription until letters appeared: In Loving Memory of Mary Irene, Aged Eleven Years. Same age as Bronwyn. The blackened headstone struck me as too sombre a final home for the spirit of a vibrant eleven-year-old girl and I hastened away, only to stumble upon more children's graves. One of them, surrounded by a collapsed iron-lace border, lured me back. Its unadorned headstone bore a single date – 21 April, 1907 – but there were two names: Edith, seven years, and Wilma, two days. Beloved daughters of Napoleon and Isabella.

My breath caught. How had she fared, the mother of these two lost girls? Had she stood where I now stood, a bereft young woman hugging her ribs in an attempt to hold herself together, fighting a losing battle against the grief that would tear her apart? How could she have moved on, how could she have taken the first step back towards life, when life had betrayed her so cruelly?

A raucous cry interrupted my reverie, drawing my gaze skyward in time to see a pair of grey-green dollarbirds swoop from the branches of a gnarly old red gum at the furthest end of the cemetery. Tumbling and rolling around each other, their coin-like underwing markings flashed white as they hawked for butterflies. They swept off across the paddock, diving over the Brahmans before riding an updraft back to their tree. I found myself following them, curious for a closer look. The sunlight warmed my arms, I grew languid. It was peaceful here, I hadn't heard a car for more than five minutes. There was just the dollarbirds' barking cries, the murmur of cattle, and the ever-present whisper of windblown leaves.

I loitered beneath the dollarbirds' tree, gazing up. It was a pristine day, the sky a cobalt dome, the sun gloriously hot. Everything seemed so *alive*. It was an odd observation to make in a graveyard, but I could feel the energetic hum and thrill in the air around me, like swarms of invisible insects. I felt alert, in the grip of a sort of vertigo, as though I was standing on a precipice with one foot lifted in the act of striding out over the edge . . .

Reflex made me look down.

The grave at my feet was neglected. Weeds struggled through cracks in the masonry slab, and the headstone – a massive granite cross engraved with a Celtic knot – was pitted by what looked like bullet holes. As though someone had used it for target practice.

I brushed at the flaky stone, and when that failed to clarify the ravaged lettering, I sat back and pondered it. Regarding it through narrowed eyes, I could just make out the 'S' at the start of the inscription, and the 'R-I-O' that I presumed were the first three letters of the name Riordan. Everything else was chipped away – dates, epitaphs, loving memories – as though the elements had seen fit to wipe all trace of him from the face of existence.

I knelt closer. Not the elements; I'd been right first time. Someone *had* taken pot-shots, probably with a small calibre rifle, and from a fair distance. Not enough to shatter the headstone, but adequate to pit the granite surface and spoil it with rings of shallow chipping. I glanced around, puzzled. I hadn't noticed that any of the other graves were vandalised. Just this one.

Who would bother to deface a gravestone – bored kids, local louts with nothing better to shoot at? And why this grave? Was it coincidence, or had resentment and suspicion followed Samuel into death and beyond?

'That's the nature of tight-knit communities like Magpie Creek,' Corey had told me. 'People know each other's business, and they have long memories – '

Gravel bit into my knees. The sun had burned a heat rash on my shoulders and a headache had begun to gather behind my eyes. The liveliness of the morning seeped away. I was limp with exhaustion again, or maybe it was defeat. I entertained the idea of stretching out on the sun-warmed slab among the shards of powdery rubble and weeds, laying my head above the place where – six feet below – Samuel's bones nestled in the dark earth.

Foolish thoughts.

I stood, brushing grit off my jeans legs. The dollarbirds had flown away, leaving the Brahmans to snore in peace. Silence reigned supreme, there was only the creak of windblown eucalypt branches and the distant drone of a plane.

Whatever I'd hoped to find here – a sense of communion perhaps, or a touching of spirits that might validate my belief in Samuel – eluded me. My quest to prove Samuel's innocence had turned up little in the way of absolute truth. At least, not the truth I wanted. Hearsay, innuendo, prejudice, unfounded accusations; and now the senseless destruction of a gravestone. All fragments of a larger story whose ending I was beginning to dread.

Since I wasn't really looking, I found her easily. She'd been laid to rest at the edge of the old section that slumbered in closest proximity to the church – nearer to God, perhaps.

I stopped, my heart squeezing out a few extra beats in confused surprise. Aylish's final resting place would have been impossible to miss. It was a humble affair, elegant in its simplicity, uncluttered with sentiment. The grave itself was protected by a masonry slab, cracked and pitted by the passage of years, not so different from any of the other graves that surrounded it, apart from a glaring absence of weeds and rubble.

And a vase of fresh roses.

The headstone was traditional, a simple arch with a circle engraved at its heart. Inside the circle was a relief carving of a wildflower: a delicately stylised waratah. I bent to read the inscription.

Aylish Lutz
Beloved of Jacob
Taken to God, 13 March, 1946
Aged 22 years

Once again I had the giddy sense of falling forward. *Taken to God*. They were only words, but they spoke in a chill whisper of that distant night. I could see her so clearly in the eye of my mind. She was curled in the shadow of a tall boulder, her limbs skewed under her, black trails of blood leaking from her wounds, her face hidden from the moonlight. As she waited.

Waited for death. Or for Samuel. Whichever came first.

I was on my knees, though I didn't recall making the decision to move. Reaching for the roses, I bruised a petal between finger and thumb, disturbing its dark-red perfume. Not a dream, then. Real. The great blowsy roses were plump and unwithered, their stems erect, the water in the vase clear. They'd been placed here late last night or early this morning.

Minutes crawled by.

In the privacy of my secret mind, I was coming to feel that I knew Aylish intimately. Out here – in the dust and sunlight and baking heat of reality – I had no claim on her. She was a stranger to me, a faceless young woman who had died sixty years ago.

Yet someone remembered her. Someone cared enough to clear the detritus of time from her grave, remove the weeds. Bring roses. I touched the crimson-black petals again, drank in their scent. In this heat, they'd be dead by nightfall.

It could only be Luella Jarman, I reasoned. But after all I'd learnt about Luella – the elusive hermit who drove an hour and a half into Brisbane to avoid being seen at the local shops, and who refused to open her door even to old friends – the image of her tending her mother's grave seemed unlikely.

I looked over my shoulder at the church.

I couldn't see the entryway from here, just the tall siding with its leadlight windows. The door had been ajar when I arrived, and I hadn't heard anyone's car arrive, nor had I heard the old motorbike rumble to life and roar away. The place looked deserted, but there was a slim chance that the pastor or church attendant might be skulking about inside.

It was a long shot, a wild gamble; a wager thrown forward by a brain in the grip of unhealthy obsession. Of course, I could stake-out the cemetery for the next week in the uncertain event that Aylish's visitor would return, but that seemed insane. Wasn't it easier to ask?

Before I could talk myself out of it, I was weaving my way back through the gravestones towards the little church, my heart set on beating the odds.

The darkness was cool, a relief from the scorching sun. Muted light filtered through the stained-glass windows, drenching the gloomy interior in crimson and green, gold and subterranean blue. The dry air smelled of furniture polish, turpentine, candle wax, musty books . . . and curiously, of chocolate.

I could still hear the barking chant of the dollarbirds, but their calls were distant now, subdued and otherworldly. As my eyes adjusted to the dimness I began to make sense of the topsy-turvy shadows. Pews draped in white, a stone basin on a pedestal, a bookshelf crammed with hymnals.

Beneath my feet the floor was gritty. I noticed that the sheets covering the pews were splattered in paint, as though a renovation was in progress. I'd assumed correctly: further along I spied paint tins and a dusty old ladder, boxes of cleaning gear.

At the far end of the central aisle was a tall rose-glass window, its details obscured by a shadow that seemed out of place. I studied the shadow for several heartbeats before I realised what it was.

A man.

'Hello?' I called. 'The door was open, I hope you don't mind me coming in . . . ?'

No answer. He must be praying, I decided. I would wait.

My feet rasped on the dusty floor. Looking around, I wondered where I should sit. Close to the front, to facilitate an effortless introduction; or tucked in at the back to appear more respectful? In my indecisiveness I bumped into a pew corner, my knee banged sharply and I muttered a profanity.

The man shifted, half-turned as if listening. The light from the rose window struck his profile.

For one heart-stopping moment I thought I was seeing a ghost. The features silhouetted in the pink-lit window might have been chiselled from solid shadow. The swooping brow and straight nose, the strong jaw and sensual mouth . . . I found my thoughts flying to the photo of Samuel in the rose arbour, but then instantly dismissed it. While Samuel's hair was close-cropped and sleek, this man's shock of unruly curls appeared on the brink of mutiny.

He shifted again and came more fully into the window's ruby light. The illusion broke apart. He was no longer other-worldly, just a man of flesh and blood in faded Levi's and a brown T-shirt. He looked around and saw me. Not surprised, just curious. Silently poised, as though waiting for me to speak first.

Which of course, we both knew was inevitable. Danny Wein-garten customarily refused to utter a word.

'Oh,' I said. 'It's you.'

He walked towards me, slowly, as though this dusty capsule of a church with its kaleidoscopic light and eerie stillness was immune to the passing of time. He had the sort of build that was both brawny and fleshy, which could go either way: with neglect, it could turn to fat . . . or with concentration of effort, be converted to ironman muscle. The face, however, was a different story. No matter how his body fared, his features would remain about as close to perfect as those of any face – any living face, I amended – that I'd ever seen.

He moved his hands. I got as far as 'you thought', then had to guess the rest.

'I . . . uh, no. Well actually, yes – '

I slumped with the realisation that if I'd been talking to anyone else I might have gotten away with it. The tilt of Danny's head and his narrowed eyes told me that I'd failed the lip-reading test and already lost him.

'What are you doing here?'

His lips moved as he watched mine, then he made a gesture with his hands that I missed. When I stared in speechless confusion, he took out his notepad and pencil.

Enjoying the silence. You?

I shrugged. 'Being a tourist.'

It was disconcerting to have a man pay such close attention to my mouth, especially when I was talking.

He scribbled again and passed me the leaf.

Lutheran church big attraction?

'Not bad, though I prefer the Presbyterian. Don't you have enough silence?' I added, then cringed the moment the words were out. Wasn't that a tactless thing to say to a deaf man?

Danny lifted a brow and scribbled. *Not all silence is created equal.*

I blinked. 'I thought all silence was . . . well, silent?'

Depends on state of mind. Absence of sound is not necessarily silent.

I smiled. Twisted as his logic was, it made an skewed sort of sense. 'Do you always speak in poetry?

He scratched out another note. *Give me more time, a bigger page, I might write novel.*

'Don't you get tired of writing all these notes?'

He tucked the notebook under his arm and made a lazy motion with his hands.

'Signing is . . . easier,' I interpreted painstakingly, and that made him smile. Slowly, knowingly. Then into high beam. He wasn't watching my lips now; his gaze was direct, straight into my eyes.

It had been such a long time since anyone had flirted with me – openly or otherwise – that at first I missed the obvious: the prolonged eye contact, the big warm smile. Anyone would think I'd have been flattered, glad for the boost to my self-esteem. After all, Danny was a fine-looking man. And yet when the penny finally dropped, all I felt was panic.

I took a step back. Groped for something to say, a way to lighten the sudden intensity: an offhand comment, a witty remark, or perhaps a polite enquiry about Jade. A chain reaction had begun in my chest and was travelling downwards, getting warmer on the descent. The shock of it rendered me mute.

Danny's fingers wound out another sentence, but my gaze was stuck on his face and I missed what his hands were saying.

I cleared my throat. 'Didn't quite catch that one.'

Back came the notebook. *Sorry about before, didn't mean to startle you.*

I could see by the enjoyment radiating from his eyes that he wasn't sorry at all. I shrugged, glancing at the door, wondering how abruptly I could make a getaway without offending him – then decided that maybe he deserved offending. I was a friend of his sister's, after all; wasn't there an unspoken law against flirting with family friends?

Something touched my fingers. Another note.

You thought I was someone else. Who?

I tried to appear distracted by glancing at my naked wrist, but was betrayed by the warm glow I could feel creeping up my neck. 'Actually,' I told him offhandedly, 'I thought you were praying.'

A crooked smile, the merest glimmer of a laugh. He made a rapid sign in explanation, most of which I missed, apart from one word right at the end that might have been 'chocolate'. Seeing my confusion, he motioned for me to follow him and, without giving me the chance to decline, strode off along the narrow aisle towards the rear of the church.

I hesitated, then reminded myself that if Danny had been here for a while – enjoying the silence, as he claimed – then he may have seen the person who'd put flowers on Aylish's grave.

We entered a tiny office at the back of the church. Sunlight streamed through a large window, making the room pleasantly warm. Shoved against the far wall was a battered old desk. Next to that, a bookshelf of dusty Bibles and atlases, stray hymn-books. A rickety trestle table was laid out with tea things: electric urn, piles of cups and saucers, canisters of tea and coffee. In the corner, the smallest fridge I'd ever seen.

Danny jogged my elbow, delivered another note to my hand, then went over and opened the fridge. Bottles clinked and tinfoil crackled while I read:

Sat. morning there's a fete here to raise money for restoration. Mum's on the committee, come along if you like?

I looked across at him, the excuse ready on my tongue: Sorry, we can't make it, on Saturday we'll be visiting Bronwyn's grandmother –

But when I saw the huge plate he was holding, the words froze before they even reached my lips. With a flourish he removed the sheet of foil and held the plate aloft for me, signing clumsily with one hand: *I made them, have one?*

I stared. First at the plate, and then at his face. Then back to the plate. Arranged on a delicate paper doily was an assortment of truffles encased in tiny baking cups. They looked like something from the pages of a gourmand's recipe book, the sort of treat that appeared effortless to create but was in fact ridiculously tricky.

'You made them?'

He nodded, motioning again for me to try one.

'Oh, I couldn't . . . Aren't they for Saturday, for the fete – ?'

Another lopsided sign: *Please.*

'Well,' I regarded the chocolates, my brain already skating ahead, assessing my preference, 'since you insist . . .'

I had meant only to pop it in, chew and quickly swallow, just to be polite. But the moment the chocolate touched my tongue I felt my spine unravel, and if my mouth hadn't been full I'd have uttered a sigh of sheer joy. The chocolate was fine and creamy, vaguely bitter, smooth and yielding as honey. Then I bit down and nearly lost my head. Inside the chocolate shell was a sweet cherry preserved in liqueur, heady and intoxicating. It was the singular, most bracing pleasure I'd had in . . . well, far longer than I cared to admit.

The soft hint of a laugh, and I opened my eyes – when had I closed them?

Danny gave me the thumbs up sign: *Good?*

I nodded distractedly, then pretended sudden interest in the view through the window. I walked over and found myself gripping the sill, gratified by what I saw, no longer having to feign the diversion.

It was just as I'd hoped: a direct line of sight across the brown grass to the nearby graves. Although I couldn't see Aylish's stone from my vantage point inside the church, anyone wandering there would have been in clear view.

Behind me, the fridge door sucked open, whispered shut. I could still taste the cherry, and the smooth dark aroma of chocolate had apparently entered my bloodstream. I found myself hastily re-calculating Saturday morning, wondering if I could squeeze a detour to the Lutheran fete between our scheduled visit to Luella's and our necessary trip to the shops. Perhaps several of Danny's chocolates would provide a remedy for Bronwyn's inevitable disappointment when Luella failed to answer her door?

A slip of paper feathered along my wrist.

I turned from the window, grasping the note. Danny had sidled up beside me. It was a perfect opportunity to ask him about Aylish's grave, to find out whether – by some wild coincidence – he'd happened to see anyone lingering in the cemetery that morning. He was watching me hopefully, waiting, I realised, for me to read what he'd written.

Corey said you photograph. Were you shooting graves?

I had to re-read the note a couple of times. At first I thought he was referring to the imposing Celtic headstone pitted with bullet holes. The feeling of vertigo flashed back; suddenly I was out over that precipice again, falling into thin air –

Then I twigged. 'No. No photos today. Just looking.'

Danny tore off another leaf. *See anything you liked?*

A tickle of pleasure. That smile. Was he flirting again? I decided to ignore it and get down to business.

'There was one grave that caught my attention.' I paused. Despite my need for answers, I was strangely reluctant to drag Aylish's name into the bright light of actuality. To me she was a creature of dreams, fragile as a moonbeam, insubstantial as a wisp of cloud – yet so real that I felt as though I'd – not known her, exactly . . . but understood what it was like to *be* her. It was a seductive feeling, one I felt compelled to protect.

Danny jotted another note. *Tony's grandmother.*

I nodded, disconcerted that he'd second-guessed me. 'Someone's been tending it,' I told him. 'Weeding, clearing rubbish. They put fresh flowers on it.'

Danny pressed nearer the window and looked out.

In the light streaming in from outside, I saw that his features were not as impossibly perfect as I'd first thought. His eyes were more grey than green, and freckles scattered his nose and cheeks. Stubble on his jaw, and a tiny nick of pink skin the shape of a crescent moon near his top lip, like a fingernail print – a scar.

Who? he spelled slowly, keeping his eyes on the graveyard.

I had to touch his arm to draw his attention back to my lips. 'Luella?'

He looked baffled, so I repeated the name. Again, he gave an almost imperceptible shake of his head, then passed me his notebook and pencil. While I wrote, he leaned over my shoulder. Though there was no contact, I was aware of his heat against my arm.

No, he signed sharply when he read the name. *Not her.*

He must have seen the question in my face, because he took the pencil and scribbled beneath what I'd written: *Luella avoids town. If she came here regularly then Mum or Corey would've seen her.*

I wasn't convinced. 'Are you sure?'

A swift sign. *Yes*. Then another note. *Besides, she won't set foot in a graveyard. Tony once told me she thinks they're bad luck.*

That I understood. Luella had lost her mother, then her daughter and husband, and now her son. From her perspective, graveyards were very bad luck indeed.

'Then who?'

Danny shrugged and shook his head, his eyes on mine.

Maybe it was the chocolate, or the oppressive morning heat – perhaps a combination of both – but I was no longer panicked by his attention, by his nearness. I even found myself hoping he might attempt to flirt again.

Another scrawled note. This one took me by surprise.

I saw you at Tony's funeral.

I looked at him, doing a mental backtrack, trying to remember. 'You were there?'

Me and Corey, he wrote.

'Tony would've been pleased.'

Danny shrugged. He made a noncommittal sign whose meaning eluded me, then turned his attention back to the window.

I touched his arm again. 'You and Tony were friends . . . when you were kids, I mean?'

A nod.

'What was he like as a boy?'

A distracted thumbs up. *Good.*

I had the feeling he'd lost interest in the conversation – meanwhile my curiosity was ablaze, and I couldn't help wondering aloud.

'Why do you think he ran away from home all those years ago?'

Danny barely glanced at my lips, but looked hard into my eyes. Then sliced the air with his little finger.

Bad.

I didn't need a handwritten note to further explain what he meant. Something bad had happened, and though Danny Weingarten might – or might not – know what that something bad had been, it was clear he had no intention of saying any more about it.

Turning from the window, he strode across the room. He checked the fridge was shut, then jingled a set of keys from his pocket and stood in the open doorway looking back at me. He attempted a smile, but his eyes were guarded.

In the space of a morning I'd had a fair bit of practice at reading the signs. Hand gestures, body language, innuendo. This last one came through loud and clear. I was getting my marching orders.

12

rriving back at Thornwood, I parked on the service road and gazed up the rise toward the house. In two days, the Miller brothers had transformed the overgrown yard into something resembling a stately, although still somewhat feral, botanic garden.

Gone were the strangling vines and piles of deadwood and overreaching tree limbs. Clear pathways now wended through corridors of foliage. Emerald hydrangea leaves unfolded from the shadows, and new delights had emerged from the forest of weeds – a huge bird's nest fern with fiddleheads the size of my fist, and clusters of pink tropical orchids that swayed in the warm air.

My skin tingled as I drank in the scent of cut grass and frangipani. A few months ago I'd been living in a cramped, cold bluestone renovator in gloomy old Albert Park, struggling to pay my heating bills and squirrelling every spare cent into my nest egg. Hemmed in by timetables, appointments, to-do lists.

But here . . . Life seemed expansive. There was peace and quiet, the scent of wildflowers, and cool sweet rainwater to drink. Best of all was knowing that my daughter now had what I'd never had: a safe, permanent home.

There was a definite spring in my step as I went along the path and around the side of the house, heading uphill towards the rear of the garden, drawn by the lonely whine of a brush trimmer. Pushing through the tangle of trees, I stepped over burst pomegranates and fallen avocados that lay rotting on the path. Halfway up the hill I paused in a shady patch to mop the sweat streaming from my face. The trimmer's buzz died, and the garden fell to silence.

The sky was brilliant, but the shadows beneath the trees were damp and dark, humming with insect life. I continued on, my footfall muted by the carpet of leaves and pine needles. Soon the brick path petered out, became a dirt trail. A few minutes later I thrust aside a curtain of flat monsterio leaves and found myself on the edge of a trimmed grassy clearing.

In the centre of the clearing grew an immense beech tree, spreading its graceful arms skywards. Dainty blue-and-white flowers hovered above the leaf bracts, smudging the air with sweetness. The trunk was broad, its pale grey bark smooth except for a blackened cave-like opening at its base. The trunk must have been struck by lightning some time ago; the resulting fissure was hollow and large enough for someone to crawl into. From this damaged section of trunk sprouted several ladder-like branches, and I recognised it as the tree in which Bronwyn had found the old biscuit tin. The lowest branch was swaying, its leaves trembling as if in a gale. There wasn't even the merest puff of breeze. Going closer, I saw I wasn't alone.

A man had climbed onto the lower branch to lever himself up the side of the tree. He was reaching into the junction between two boughs, his arm plunged to the elbow in a deep knothole.

'Hobe – ?'

The air seemed to hang suspended, an instant of troubled calm before the storm. He snatched his hand from the hollow and leapt off the branch, clouting his head in the process, dislodging his glasses. Whirling to face me, he let out a surprised grunt. His sapphire-blue eye was wide and curiously naked.

'Lost something?' I enquired.

Hobe stepped away from the tree, dusting his palms together, straightening his glasses.

'Er . . . no, lass. Just checking for possum damage – luckily it's all under control, nothing to worry about. Lovely old white beech, rare to see one in cultivation like this, shame to think of it at the mercy of the elements. Well, now . . .'

He patted his pockets, located his notebook and made an exaggerated show of ticking something off a list. Collecting his trimmer, he saluted me with a cheerful grin, then made off along the path, down the incline in the direction of the house, vanishing behind the monsterio.

'Everything else is pretty much done,' he said, when I caught up. 'All the trees are pruned back from the eaves and the gutters cleared – a good thing too, could be a storm's about to blow in . . .'

He waffled on as we trod back down the hill, filling me in on the day's progress in fastidious detail: The pile of dead branch loppings he'd stacked beneath the house would make excellent kindling come winter. He'd send Gurney back in a few weeks to have another go at the lawn – after years of drought, he explained, if rain did eventuate I'd be able to stand at my window and watch the grass grow. And if it was all right with me, he'd mulch the vegie patch with clippings to encourage earthworms.

I was only half listening.

Possum damage? I frowned over my shoulder. As we descended along the overgrown path, the beech tree's upper- most branches were visible above the thicker, glossier foliage of mango and wild fig. Its branch tips raked the sky, its leaves shimmered grey-green beneath sprays of waxy blossoms. It had no doubt co-existed happily with possums for a hundred or more years.

I glared at Hobe. His leathery face glowed pink and his scalp shone with sweat. He was halfway through explaining the procedure for gutter clearing – the correct implement to use, the right way to prop the ladder, and how the leaf dross made marvellous compost tea.

In my mind's eye all I could see was the giant beech with its pale scaly bark and burnt-out trunk, and the odd ladder-like branch formation sprouting from its flank. I could still see Hobe reaching into the fork of it, his arm sunk to the elbow as he groped around in search of something.

And it wasn't possum damage.

Another image: Bronwyn sitting on the garden bench before school, her hair a curtain around her flushed face as she tried to prise open the battered biscuit tin.

Pretty, isn't it, Mum?

She'd found it in an old canvas haversack, she'd said. Aside from the tin, there'd also been clothes, makeup, a hairbrush. Rotten, all of it; she'd tossed them away, kept only the tin. The tin containing a girl's diary.

Hobe caught me staring, and grinned.

'Don't forget about that puppy,' he said affably. 'Tell young Bronwyn she can come over and pick one out any time she likes.'

'Will do,' I said fake-brightly, avoiding his eye.

Something was off, and I couldn't say what. Only that the easy camaraderie I'd shared with Hobe Miller yesterday was gone.

I dashed inside for my chequebook, cursing the dust that puffed off my jeans legs and sandals and sifted onto the floor. As I passed the back bedroom, I realised that I'd forgotten to ask Hobe about Aylish's grave and whether he knew of anyone, other than Luella, who might want to remember her with roses. It seemed irrelevant; all I wanted to do right now was get rid of Hobe as quickly as possible and pursue the thread of this latest mystery.

I raced down the stairs and into the front yard, catching up with Hobe at the service road. Gurney had finished loading the mower and rake and pruning saws into the ute's tray and had secured it all with rope. He now sat in the passenger seat, seatbelt fastened, sweat trickling from his sparse hair. He twisted around as Hobe and I approached, and grinned happily when I thanked him again for the work he'd done. Hobe fastened his trimmer into the tray with the other tools. It was rude of me, but I couldn't seem to raise the same enthusiasm when I thanked him.

Scribbling a cheque, I tore it off and handed it over. Said goodbye and watched him shamble around to the driver's side and get in. When he waved, I pretended to be distracted by something in a nearby tree. Then, even before the rusty utility had vanished in a miasma of dust, I was sprinting back across the fresh mowed lawn towards the house.

As with most high-set Queenslanders, the laundry was located downstairs. It was a rustic space, partitioned off from the rest of the under-house area by lattice walls. The stone floor had seen better days, and I was still waiting for the plumber to arrive and install my washing machine taps. The laundry was clean and cool, a shady haven when the heat of the day became too intense. Best of all, my hand-washed clothes were dried in record time by the breeze gusting up from the valley.

I crossed to the sink. There on the edge of the concrete tub was the ruined diary Bronwyn had found. It didn't look like much: a water-damaged wad, its clasp broken, its cover buckled and discoloured by rust and dirt and mould. I had set it on the sink the other day to wash my hands, intending to salvage it after I'd dropped Bronwyn at school. Then, after my unexpected reunion with Corey and consequent dash to the Millers', I'd forgotten it.

As I held the diary, I had another flash of Hobe with his hand sunk in the tree hollow, groping around as if in search of something. A haversack, perhaps. Full of female things – hair-brush, makeup, clothes . . . and an old tin box safeguarding a diary. Hobe hadn't seemed too bothered to find it gone; he'd seemed more shaken by the fact that I'd caught him looking.

Possum damage indeed.

It wasn't until much later that night, after the dinner dishes were done and Bronwyn had escaped to her room, that I worked out how best to peel apart the diary's fragile pages without destroying them. Filling a saucepan with water, I placed it on the stove and cranked the gas. When the water boiled, I took off the lid and let the steam billow out. Then I clamped the diary in the jaws of my barbecue tongs and positioned it over the steam.

The smell of mould invaded the kitchen. The wrinkled wad of paper began to respond. The cover softened. The inner pages grew damp and began to peel apart. When the clump looked pliable enough, I carried the book to the table and sat over it, separating the fragile top sheets with a butter knife.

The first few pages were furrowed, blotched with yellowish water-stains, brittle as bark. Tight lines of neat cursive filled every inch of space; some words were lost beneath mildew, or faded – but most were legible. I leaned closer, drawn by the gravitational force of my curiosity.

KEEP OUT! Private property of Glenda Jarman
Monday, 8 September 1986
Is the whole world mad, or what? I was hoping to start this new diary by celebrating my progress on the romance front. There was just this one annoying incident:

I took Corey down to the creek this afternoon to update her on the new developments with Ross. Or lack of development, which is in itself a topic worth discussing. Anyhow, Corey's been sulky lately, a real misery guts – I only wanted to cheer her up.

We sat on the embankment, chewing Redskins and drinking Coke. There's me getting high on the sugar rush, meanwhile Corey's looking all moony and sad. Setting aside my Coke bottle, I put my arm round her shoulders to ask her – for the gazillionth time – what was wrong, but I didn't get the chance.

She kissed me.

On the lips, with her tongue, the way I've told her I'd like to kiss Ross. Dammit, what was she thinking? Me and Corey have been besties forever, how could she do this to me? Worse, she knows I love Ross, why did she have to go and get all weird?

Sigh. I like Corey, love her I suppose . . . just not like that.

Not like she wants me to.

We haven't spoken since. I admit I was horrid to her, pushing her away, shouting at her. Shock talking, I guess. Normally when we fight she rings me, only now it's nearly 11 p.m. and I still haven't heard. I feel like shit.

Thursday, 11 September 1986
In answer to Monday's question: Yes, the whole world IS mad. And me? I'm the maddest of them all.

Bloody Tony.

Just found out he's the reason we're not going to school camp next week. He fessed up that he accidently (on purpose?) let slip to Mum that I was keen on someone at school – the dork! Him and Mum are thick as thieves, I should have bloody well known not to trust him. He was really sorry, panicking that I'd go ballistic and do something crazy – which I nearly did, but then he gave me a funny little drawing of a bird with Ross's face and love-heart wings, which was so daggy and annoying of him, but what can you do? He's a shit sometimes, but a loveable shit.

Sigh. I'm hunched in bed with the blanket over my head writing by torchlight, sweating like a porker. There's a pain in my chest, probably just my stupid heart breaking. I hate knowing that after next Friday I'll have to wait for next term to see Ross again, two scummy weeks! All the while knowing he's at the mercy of those pathetic Gorgon sisters at camp, they'll be laughing and flirting, the bitches, and Ross no doubt having a grand old time. Rats. It's going to be torture.

Friday, 19 September 1986

Good news on the romance front, though a sad day as it's the last before the hols and I'll have to wait forever to see Ross again. I painted my nails pink for the occasion, though it's against school rules. Just for luck, you understand.

Look, I know he's happily married, and I know he's got two little boys who he adores (which only makes me love him more), and his wife seems nice – but what can I do? Everyone knows you can't help who you fall in love with.

So the good bit was this: Ross says to me, 'Hey, Glenda, since you're not coming to camp I've got just the thing to keep you busy over the holidays.'

I rolled my eyes as if to say, Great, more homework – which made him laugh. He handed me a page torn out of the newspaper.

'I was reading the weekend *Courier-Mail* and found this. It's a short story competition, the prize money's pretty good. I reckon you should enter.'

I took the page. There was a picture of last year's winner, a dumpy woman in slacks, and a blurb about what sort of story they wanted. Family drama, totally humdrum. The entry form at the bottom caught my eye, though. In particular the dollar sign next to the winnings.

'Wow,' I gaped, 'that's more than I earn in a month of baby-sitting. But . . . family drama.' I wrinkled my nose. 'My family's boring. What would I write about?'

Ross shrugged. 'Remember what I said in English: no one's boring once you scratch the surface. For some people you might have to scratch a bit harder, but there's always a story lurking. So have a think. I'm sure you'll come up with something.'

He smiled one of his big heart-stoppers and looked right into my eyes. Of course, I melted. My hands shook just a bit as I walked away, folding the entry form and slipping it into my bra against my skin. I was pleased that Ross had been thinking about me on the weekend, pleased that he thought my writing was good enough to maybe win a competition. I would win, too. Never mind the pink nail polish. Take it from me. Winning a great big juicy story prize is a far better way to impress your teacher.

Thursday, 25 September 1986
The holidays are duller than dishwater but I've decided to pass the time working on my prize-winning story.

So there I was this arvo on the back verandah, trying to rustle up ideas. Basil was flopped in the shade beside me, snorting in his sleep, no doubt dreaming of hunting rabbits, as rabbits are the love of Basil's life. While I pondered, I shelled peas for Mum, popping a few in, they're yum. If Mum has one talent it's growing vegies. We've got a freezer full that she forced early in her hothouse, they're small but they out-flavour those soggy prepacked ones in the shop. Mum says to let them thaw before shelling, but I never do. Straight from the Kelvinator, frosty and sweet.

The days are heating up, soon it'll be stinking hot. Since Dad's a retard and won't let me and Tony have iceblocks like every other living person on the planet (on account that they'll rot our teeth), I have to make do with frozen peas.

While I shelled, I spied on Tony. Had a bird's eye view from my perch on the back steps. He was down in the bush paddock sitting on a big old stump, his head bent over his drawing book, sketching bark or seedpods or dragonfly wings, God where does he find this stuff? You'd never know it to look at him, but he's really clever. Mum's got his little paintings framed and hung up all round the house, and Dad's forever spouting on at the post office about his talented kids. I always roll my eyes when he says that, but of course I'm secretly pleased.

Anyway, there I was mulling over story ideas, when I saw Mum sneak along the side fence. Hello, I thought, what's she up to? She doesn't usually go into the paddock. Her face shone pink in the heat and she was wearing her good apron. Tony must have heard her coming because he looked around. They spoke for a moment, and then Mum slid something from her apron pocket – it looked like an envelope. Tony took it, and then Mum put something into his hand, a five dollar note? My sneaky brother squirrelled the money away and leapt to his feet, packing pencils and sketch block into his satchel. Then he trotted off along the track in the direction of Grandfather's.

Mum watched until Tony vanished, then came back to the house. A minute later she disappeared inside.

Tossing my peas aside, I raced down the stairs and through the gate, hurtling along the track after Tony –

Damn. Mum's calling, dinner's ready.

Gotta go.

Friday, 26 September 1986
So anyway, yesterday. Tony's nowhere. Gone. Vamoosed. Can you believe it? As if he'd racked off down the Bermuda Triangle. Nowhere.

So I just kept walking along the track. I'll go to the hollow tree, I decided. It's a monster white beechwood tree, blackened by a long-ago lightning strike, really old. It's on Grandfather's property, worth the forty-five minute hike it takes to get there.

By the time I got to the gully I was puffed. Only another thirty minutes to the tree, but the heat was out of control. Sweat drenched my T-shirt and I was parched. As soon as I went down the track and into the gully, I sighed with relief. It was shadowy and cool, all ferny and dark. Down there the air smells like creek water, muddy and delicious. Like another world. Millions of bell miners inhabit the trees. You can't see them but you can hear them. It's like being in a huge jar with these bright little

chirps echoing at you from all sides. On and on they go. Sometimes there's a gap in their song, and it's dead quiet. Eerie. Then
off they go again, dizzyingly beautiful. People say they sound
like bells, that's why they're commonly called bellbirds, but to
me they're more like thousands of girls' voices singing the same
ringing note over and over and over.

I reached the creek and paddled for a while. Sitting at the
edge, resting my feet on a big mossy rock, enjoying the cool tug
of the water. Lacy ferns grew along the bank, nodding in the
stillness. The place was like a fairy glade, green and spotted
with sunbeams, bright with birdsong.

I got to thinking about Grandfather – at first, how awesome it
was that he left this property to me and Tony when he died, and
how we can come here whenever we like. Over two thousand acres
of bushland, all ours. Then I remembered how much I miss him.
He was such a cool old guy. He and Mum never saw eye to eye,
but it wasn't on account of what happened back in the war days.
If Mum thought for a minute that the rumours about Grandfather
were true, she'd never have let us kids within cooee of him.

Murder. God, how awful.

I don't know how Mum coped, knowing her own mother was
killed. If it was me, I'd have cracked up. I couldn't imagine
growing up like she did, putting up with all the gossip and
shame. I guess that's why she and Grandfather didn't get on – he
stayed away from her when she was little, Mum says, because
he couldn't cope with seeing her after her mum died, that he was
just too sad. But I reckon it was something else . . . like maybe
Grandfather wanted to spare her more heartache by not reminding her of what she'd lost.

It happened yonks ago, back in the forties. Mum was a
toddler, three or four. Grandfather would've been a young man.
Me and Tony used to talk about it sometimes, but only in a
hush. We didn't know much, and never asked. Could tell it
was too painful for Mum to talk about. Dad stayed silent out of

respect, too. Even so, we heard things. Whispers, snatches of gossip.

Sometimes one of the oldies at church will cluck her tongue and mention Grandfather, but no one else much remembers. Once, I went into the post office to give Dad the lunch he'd forgotten, and overheard one old biddy whisper to another, 'She's the granddaughter of that girl the doctor murdered . . .'

Crows picking over dry bones, that's what Dad would've called them.

So there I was in the gully, sitting in the cool shadows and thinking about my poor old grandma, when all of a sudden I get this full-on rash of goosebumps. I looked around. My grandmother had died right here at the gully. Maybe on this very spot.

I started shivering, as if a wintry change had come over the gully. The creek water looked dark, the shadowy ferns no longer quite so friendly. High in the trees the bellbirds were chiming away, but now they sounded shrill, almost urgent, as though their song was a warning.

Crazy, I know, but I couldn't stop shivering.

Ross is right, I thought. All you have to do is scratch the surface . . .

And that's when I had my brilliant idea.

Saturday, 27 September 1986

'Mum, I've got an idea for that story competition I was telling you about,' I began, testing the water. 'But I'm going to need your help.'

'Oh?' She looked up from the ironing board, which she always insists on dragging into the kitchen so she has a view outside. She smiled encouragingly. 'What's that, love?'

'I'm going to write about my grandmother . . . only I don't have much info about her.'

Mum looked taken aback. 'But Glenny, you've got a whole album of photos of Grandma Ellen, and Dad's told you plenty of – '

'I don't mean Dad's mother.'

'Oh.'

'It's all right, isn't it? I mean, it was a long time ago. And we both know Grandfather didn't kill her, he couldn't have. So it's a mystery . . . and a kind of love story, all mixed into one.'

Mum set the iron aside and went over to the sink, turned the tap on full and washed her hands. She grabbed the soap and washed and washed, as if my question had somehow made her feel dirty.

'Mum – ?'

She splashed her face and gave it a good scrub with her palms, then groped in the drawer for a clean tea towel. 'I don't think you should, pet.'

'Why not?'

She looked over her shoulder at me. Her face was blotchy as if someone had squeezed lemon on it. Her eyes were big and brimming with worry.

'I just don't. I'm sorry.'

I sighed, realising my mistake. I could have argued with her, pointed out that I had every right to know about my grandmother – but I knew it would hurt her too much. Mum must have had a horrible time after her mother died, she'd only been a little kid. It wasn't her fault she couldn't talk about it.

'Never mind, Mum,' I said. 'I'll think of something else.'

And I tried. I really tried. In the end, the story of my grand-mother nagged. It was as if her ghost was restless now that I'd raised the topic of her with Mum. As if her story had sprouted wings and flown free of its box, impossible to tuck back out of sight. One way or another my grandmother would have her tale told . . . and I would be the one to tell it.

Sunday, 28 September 1986

Mum was at church, rostered on morning tea. Dad was out in the garden, planting spring onions. He'd made neat little rows in the soil with a broom handle, and was using a length of old wooden ruler to space the seeds.

'Dad,' I began, cautious after Mum's response, 'I have to ask you something, but I'm scared you'll be angry.'

It was a joke, of course. Dad's never angry. Taurus the bull: stubborn and reliable, slow to lose his cool. On the rare occasion that a Taurean does fly off the handle, say the astrologers, then watch out. It must be true, because I've never heard Dad raise his voice, not once. I like to think of him as 'mild-mannered' – a regular Clark Kent, except no Superman hiding beneath his crisp white shirt and boring brown workpants. Of course Dad wasn't wearing his good gear today, just old King Gees and a khaki shirt rolled at the sleeves, but you get the drift.

Dad looked up and grinned, his ears pink from the sun despite his hat. A bit of hair flopped into his eye and he blew the strand away.

'What's that, Glenny?'

'Well . . .' I looked at the sky, then checked my fingernails. The pink polish I'd put on for the last week of school to impress Ross was mostly chipped off. Just lots of little flakes bravely clinging, but I didn't have the heart to remove them. They'd been lucky, after all.

Dad gave a snort and went back to his onions. 'Out with it, then.'

I sighed. 'I'm writing a story, it's going to be really good, I might even enter a competition.'

'Hmmm,' Dad said, marking out the next row with his broom handle. 'What's it about?'

'My grandmother.'

My voice was kind of tight when I said it, maybe that's why Dad looked up. He gave me a curious look.

'Mum's mother,' I explained, then hurried on. 'It'd make a great story – you know, the mystery about how she died and all that. The problem is I hardly know anything about her.

Mum doesn't like talking about her, and all I've got to go on are rumours and an old newspaper clipping that doesn't give much away, and . . . well, not much else.'

Dad set aside his broom and stood up. Hands on the small of his back, he stretched his spine and looked at the sky. I heard a bone pop, and Dad sighed.

'You want to hear what I know about her.'

'Yes.'

'Not much, I'm afraid.'

'Did you ever meet her?'

Picking up his ruler, he went to the next row and shook some black seeds from a packet into his palm. He was silent for a time, as if he'd forgotten I was there. He walked the seed line, measuring, and making little indents in the soil with his thumb, then poking in the seeds.

I waited. Dad loves his privacy, a quality he shares with Mum. He rarely speaks about the past, and when he does you get the feeling he's making half of it up as he goes, embroidering the facts to be more amusing or maybe just to disguise the bits he doesn't want to give away. I suppose that's where my love of stories comes from.

Dad cleared his throat. 'I knew your grandmother in the war days. I was just a lad of eight or nine. She was . . .' He paused to smile up into the overhanging trees. 'She was beautiful. Long dark hair and brown eyes. Slim, and as graceful as a bird.'

'How did you know her?'

'She was all alone, so she came to stay with us.'

'She *stayed* with you? I never knew that.'

'Yes.'

'Why was she alone?'

Walking along the row, compacting the soil over his onion seeds, Dad trained his eyes on his feet. 'Her mother had died, and her father was interned on account of him being a German immigrant. That's what happened in the war, the government was worried about security – though you'd never meet a more patriotic fellow than Jacob Lutz, your great-grandfather. He loved Australia, always said this country saved him . . . Anyhow, Jacob had been Magpie Creek's Lutheran pastor for years, but on account of him being born in Germany, the Commonwealth Investigation Bureau made all these ridiculous accusations and sent him down to Tatura, an internment camp in Victoria. He was there for nearly three years.'

Dad fell silent. I waited. And waited some more. Then sighed. Dad was fifty-four, which was pretty old – but sometimes he acted *really* old, if you know what I mean. Staring into space, pondering. Forgetting things, getting his facts mixed up. He loved relating yarns about the old days, but they never quite seemed to match up from one telling to the next. This was one story I hoped he'd get right.

'Dad – ?'

He smiled distractedly. Picking up his broom, he began re-marking a seed line he'd scuffed.

'Your grandmother was happy living with us. She became one of the family – helping my mother with the chores, churning the butter, feeding the chooks, tending the little cornfield we had out the back, keeping the house nice. And your mum, she was just a tiny tot, a chirpy little thing with these big green eyes and a smile that made your heart melt like ice-cream in the sun. My mum – that is, your Grandma Ellen – adored her little Lulu, and spoilt her rotten. We all did.'

'I can't believe Mum never told me.'

'Well, Glenny, it wasn't all fun and games. There was a war on, and life was hard . . . but it was exciting, too. We had a couple of servicemen billeted with us. Most families in Magpie Creek had two or three boys staying with them. Army, or Air Force. A few Navy. Your grandmother used to cook up big shank stews with beef, and corn from the garden, and split peas. We had cream and buttermilk, and eggs from the chooks. Fresh vegies and fruit. Families in town – or worse, in the cities – did it hard, eking out their coupons for a measly pound of butter a fortnight, or two pounds of sugar. They were interesting times. Rewarding if you kept your wits about you.'

Collecting the hose, he twisted the nozzle and directed a fine spray onto the onions. The mist showered rainbows over the bare soil, sending up the rich chocolatey odours of old manure and compost and dynamic lifter.

'Dad?'

'What's that, Glenny?'

'Why did they blame Grandfather ... you know, for what happened to my grandmother?'

Dad stared at the rainbows for an age, as though mesmerised. Just when I'd given up on getting an answer, he said quietly, 'Your grandfather had a bad time of it in the war. Got himself taken prisoner, you know all that. He was very sick afterwards, and I suppose folks thought he might be capable of hurting someone.'

'But he wasn't, was he?'

A long pause. 'No, Glenny. No, he wasn't.'

The sound of a car roared into the stillness. Dad turned off the water, coiling the hose over the tap. 'There's Mum,' he said, ruffling my hair as he passed me on his way to the house. 'I'd better put the kettle on.'

Saturday, 4 October 1986

Been working like mad on my writing project all week. What started as a ploy to impress Ross has ballooned into something much bigger. Mania. Obsession. I simply HAVE to tell my grandmother's story. It's as though she's standing behind me saying: 'Glenda, everyone else just wants to sweep me under the mat, forget me. As if they wish I'd never existed. You're different. You understand. I want my voice heard, and you're going to help me.'

I did understand, too. My beautiful grandmother had been attacked and left to die at the gully, lying there all night in the damp leaves, her poor head aching and her blood seeping into the dirt. Someone had done that to her, and I just couldn't find it in my heart to believe that it was Grandfather.

Dad was always telling me to stand up for what I believed in. Trouble was, I'd never really believed in anything. Saving the whales was all very well, it was cruel how they speared them and cut them up to make perfume and stuff . . . but how was I supposed to get all fired up about whales when I'd never even seen one?

My grandmother, on the other hand, was a blood relative. There were no photos of her – none surviving, anyhow – and to be honest, I'd never really thought about her all that much until now. But blood was blood. And my grandmother deserved her voice to be heard.

So there I was, writing up a storm, trying to get the ending done before lunch. I'd decided that the person who killed my grandmother was a tramp, passing through Magpie Creek on his way north to the goldmines up at Ravenswood in search of work. I'd found a book in the school library about the post-war days. There'd been tons of men on the drift, travelling from town to town in search of work . . . I'd never know for sure, of course, but it fitted in well with my story.

I was just getting to the bit where they meet, it was coming along okay, too – when I heard shouting. A man's voice, it sounded like Dad. My heart somersaulted. Dad never shouts. At first I thought he must've amputated his foot or something with the hoe. I rushed out to see what the matter was, but stopped halfway along the hall. I could smell chops cooking, and fried potatoes.

Dad was clearly in pain, but he wasn't yelling for an ambulance. When the jumble of words started to make sense to me I slumped against the wall, sick to my heart.

'You promised, Lu,' Dad was saying. 'A long time ago, you promised . . .'

'Cleve, it's not what you think.'

'All these years, all these bloody years you – ' Dad choked on the next words, which I couldn't make out. I heard something rattle and crash to the floor, smash.

I ran to the kitchen. Mum was sweeping up a broken glass with the dustpan. Dad stood with his hands braced on the table, slumped over as though he'd lost the strength to hold himself upright.

Mum wrapped the bits of glass in newspaper and placed them in the bin.

'Please, Cleve . . . calm down. We need to talk it over quietly. And,' she added, with a glance at me, 'in private.'

Dad's head jerked around. He saw me and his lips trembled. His face was blotched red, his scars stark white. Turning back to Mum, he lifted his arm and shook the scrap of paper crumpled in his fist.

'How long?'

Mum seemed to shrink. 'Just the once.'

'I don't believe you.'

'Cleve, you're overreacting, it was just – '

Dad actually growled. He shot upright and crossed the kitchen to stand over Mum, his body trembling.

'Overreacting?' he said, his face close to hers. 'Oh, Lu . . . you have no bloody idea.' Pushing past her, he went out the door and down the back steps.

'Mum?' I said. 'What happened?'

Mum shut her eyes, took a long while to open them. 'Glenda, it might be best if you make yourself scarce for a while, love. Your father's very upset.'

I stared at her. 'What've you done?'

She just looked at me. She'd had us kids late in life; she'd been nearly thirty by the time she'd had me, but people always said she could pass for a woman half her age. Now, she appeared small and frail and old.

Shouting came from the yard. I ran out and saw Tony sitting under the pine tree. He'd been daubing away at a little watercolour – it was a yellow finch perched on a spray of peach leaves, crazy how I remember that. Dad's shadow fell on the page and Tony looked up.

'Did you deliver this for your mother?' Dad demanded, thrusting the piece of paper into Tony's face.

Tony kept his eyes on Dad. He didn't speak, just nodded. I groaned inwardly. He was going to give Dad the silent treatment, he'd learnt that from Danny Weingarten. I wished he wouldn't.

'How long's it been going on?' Dad yelled.

Tony shrugged.

Dad was trembling. I started to worry he was having a turn, maybe a heart attack or stroke or something. Whatever it was, it had converted him into a Dad I didn't recognise.

He put his face close to Tony's. 'I ought to teach you a lesson you won't forget in a hurry, my lad. You hear me, boy? How long?'

I didn't catch what Tony said.

'Maybe a while, eh?' Dad's voice broke. 'Maybe a bloody while! What's that supposed to mean, you idiot? Weeks? Months? Flaming years?'

When Tony didn't answer, Dad grabbed him and dragged him across the yard to the shed. I followed, more scared than I'd ever been in my life.

'Dad,' I pleaded, hanging off his arm so he'd let go of Tony, 'what's going on? What's Tony done?'

Dad shook me off and pulled Tony into the shed with him. He unhooked his hunting knife from the tackle bag hanging near the door then, jamming the knife into his belt, he hauled Tony through the shed and into the front yard towards the Holden.

The front flyscreen door slammed. Mum stood at the top of the stairs. 'For God's sake, Cleve! Let him go. Come inside and talk it through like an adult.'

Dad ignored her. He gave Tony a shove. 'Get in. And you stay here,' he said, looking around at me, but I hopped into the car beside Tony. Dad didn't even bother to remind us about seatbelts. He just jumped behind the wheel and gunned the motor, screeched into reverse and backed out onto the road. A moment later we were rocketing south in the direction of town.

My last view of life as I knew it came when I looked back through the rear window. Mum was standing on the grass verge staring after us, clutching the sides of her head like a crazy person.

The following pages were gummed together. I wanted to know more, wanted to carry on reading, but my eyes felt like cinders. I was seeing flickers of shadow at the edges of my vision; I needed to sleep.

Tucking the diary against my chest, I went through the lounge room and down the hall. When I reached Bronwyn's door I didn't stop to listen like I usually did, just continued past to my own room. Flopping onto the bed, I lay unmoving.

My brain sifted through what I'd read.

Aylish had lived with Cleve's parents during the war, after her father was interned. She'd been happy there, and everyone had adored little Luella – or Lulu, as they'd called her then. All of which was juicy enough to ponder in depth – but after reading about Cleve's emotional outburst, I was stymied. He'd obviously discovered the letter Tony had delivered, but why had it outraged him so?

My head felt huge and swollen, invaded by dead people, crowded by memories that weren't mine. I wanted to get up and steam open the rest of the diary, read what Cleve was planning. Teach Tony a lesson, he'd said. But a hunting knife ... Holy crap, what sort of a lesson was he planning?

My head spun.

I needed sleep. Craved it. Depended on it. Without it, tomorrow would be a disaster. I'd be flustered and frazzled and end up making a ham sandwich out of the day.

Trouble was, my curiosity was alight. Even now, at two-thirty in the morning, eyes agog with exhaustion – all I could think about was rushing back to the kitchen, re-boiling my pot of water, steaming open more pages. And finding out what Cleve planned to do with that hunting knife . . .

What the hell.

2 a.m. Sunday, 5 October 1986
Oh God, I can't bear to write it. But I have to. Ross says if I'm going to be a writer then I have to face things even if they're painful. That's what writers do. Confront fearful things, then write about them.

Dad sped towards town, past the airfield and through the roundabout, then headed south along Briarfield Road. We passed the turnoff to Grandfather's place and kept going. It took a while to realise where he was taking us, but then we saw the big gate and the steep drive that led up to the Miller property. I knew the place pretty well, because me and Tony used to come here years ago, when we were kids. Mum used to send us over on Sundays with jars of jam or pickle – that is, until Dad found out and put a stop to it. Lazy good for nothings, he called the Millers; I won't have them teaching my kids how to fail at life.

Even before we approached the house, Dad started honking the horn. The sound of it ripped through the afternoon, and Mr Miller and his brother appeared on the verandah.

Dad parked the Holden and hurtled out, just as Mr Miller was coming down the stairs. They met halfway across the yard, and Dad gave Mr Miller a shove. Then he started yelling.

'Stay away from my family! You hear me, Miller? Stay away or I swear I'll kill you.'

Me and Tony huddled in the car, cramped together, holding hands. Don't look, Glenny. Don't look. I think that's what Tony was saying, but I can't be sure. I knew he was right, I didn't want to look – but my eyes refused to obey. They kept staring, staring right at Dad and Mr Miller.

Dad was shouting, his words slurring together, not making sense. His arm shot out and he punched Mr Miller in the chest. Mr Miller staggered, but caught his balance. It took a second for him to act, but then he came at Dad like an angry bullock, fists first, throwing a good one right into Dad's face, then one to the stomach.

Dad bent double. He looked winded, hands on his knees, gasping. Mr Miller's younger than Dad, a good ten years, maybe more. I could see Dad's face was blotched and sweaty, his chest heaving for breath. He was having a heart attack, I was sure. Then he let out a bellow and threw himself at Mr Miller. I thought I saw sunlight flare off something in his hand.

There was a horrible screech. Then I saw the blood.

Mr Miller fell to his knees, his hands gripping his face, covering his eye, blood streaming between his fingers. He was making a horrible noise, a sort of screeching bellow, over and over as though he had lost his mind. He yelled something at Dad, but his words were muffled by his hands.

Dad stood back, trembling all over. 'Stay away, you scheming bastard,' he said in a weird voice, staring down at Mr Miller. 'Stay away – '

A rifle fired, the blast cracking off Dad's words. Dirt flew up near Dad's feet. Dad jerked around. He staggered a couple of steps towards the Millers' house, and I saw that Mr Miller's brother was standing on the verandah holding a rifle. Dad began to charge at the house, but Mr Miller's brother raised the gun again and took aim.

That's when I screamed.

The rifle went off again. Dad stumbled and dropped to his knees and for one terrifying moment I thought he'd been hit. But he got up and ran back to the car. As he got nearer I saw the blood speckling his shirt and face and arms. I was sick with fright. He wiped at himself and I realised he'd cut his hand. Climbing into the car, he sat staring through the windscreen, shaking so hard I thought he was going to pass out.

Dad didn't say a word on the ride home. When we turned onto William Road, I braved a look at him. He'd stopped trembling, but his face was blotched. He looked different. Empty, somehow. As if the dad I knew had gone and left this vacant shell of a man in his place.

4 a.m. Sunday, 5 October 1986

Can't sleep, keep hearing the floorboards creak and doors rattling, keep worrying that Dad's prowling around. I've never felt scared in my bed before, it's not a feeling I like.

Dad's fight with Mr Miller keeps replaying in my mind against my will. The more I try to blot it out, the bigger and brighter it seems to get.

God. It feels like my real Dad died and the man who drove us back from the Millers' is someone else. A stranger. Someone bad. Someone straight out of a splatter movie or nightmare. Maybe that's it. Maybe I'm having a nightmare, maybe this whole mess is nothing but a stupid dream.

I just wish I could wake up.

13

'Mum? Are you all right?'

I blinked awake. Sunlight poured through the kitchen window, showering light on the wooden floor. Outside, the sky was eggshell blue. Birds were going wild in the mango tree, as though the dawn of another day was something to celebrate.

Bronwyn stood nearby, peering down at me, a concerned frown crinkling her brow.

'Here, drink this.'

She slid a cup towards me. Coffee-scented steam rose up. I wanted to grab it and start gulping, drench my system with caffeine and haul myself to full consciousness, but I couldn't yet trust my trembling hands.

Bronwyn shuffled closer, her frown morphing into a worried scowl. 'Are you sure you're okay? You were talking in your sleep.'

I scrubbed my hands over my face. I felt groggy, still anchored in a drowse as though the greater part of me couldn't wait to sink back into oblivion. 'What . . . what was I saying?'

Bronwyn shrugged. 'I think you were calling someone's name.'

A barb of half-remembered fear. 'Whose name?'

'I couldn't make it out, but you seemed upset. You must have been dreaming.'

When I closed my eyes to remember, the darkness behind my lids shifted and I glimpsed a bush track. I'd been running along it, calling out. The trees on either side were gilded by moonlight, their branches raking the sky, their sinewy trunks bowing and groaning in the wind. Somewhere ahead of me, a child was fleeing into the night, a little girl . . . startled by something in the trees –

'You didn't want to wake up,' Bronwyn informed me, shuffling her feet and twining her fingers in knots. 'I was shaking you for ages. You looked comatose, I thought there was something wrong. Mum, you scared me.'

When I pulled her into a hug she stiffened and tried to wriggle away. After a moment, she gave in and stood meekly, no doubt waiting for my display of sentimental weakness to pass.

'I'm sorry,' I whispered. 'I'm sorry I scared you.'

She got free and stepped away, brushing at the creases on her dress, eying me with concern.

'That's okay, Mum. Feeling better?'

'Sure.' I pressed my lips to the rim of the cup and let the fragrant steam engulf me, breathing it deep until the last traces of dream residue were gone.

'Is the coffee okay?'

'Yeah, good.'

'You haven't tried it yet.'

I took a sip. It was piping hot with extra sugar and a splash of milk. 'Perfect,' I said, drumming up an appreciative smile.

Bronwyn was studying the misshapen diary spread open on the table in front of me.

'A good read?' she asked, frowning.

Odd how the brain works. In my dazed state I'd forgotten last night's reading marathon. It crashed back with sudden clarity: Glenda's story competition and her father's revelations about Aylish – and then, most startling of all, his brutal attack on Hobe Miller.

God, poor Hobe.

Whatever he'd done to provoke Cleve Jarman's attack, it seemed an extreme sort of punishment. And an extreme reaction from a man whose daughter had described him as 'mild-mannered'. Then I remembered. Cleve in the kitchen shouting at Luella, brandishing a scrap of paper. And standing over Tony in the garden, yelling, 'Did you deliver this for your mother?' A letter. Was that why Cleve attacked Hobe, because of a letter? Were Hobe and Luella – ?

Bronwyn tapped her foot. Pulling out of my uneasy thoughts, I looked at her. I could tell she was miffed about me reading the diary she'd found. But, after what I'd just learned, I said a silent thank you to the universe that she hadn't shown more interest in it . . . at least, not until now.

'Actually, it was quite boring,' I told her. 'Just a bunch of waffle.'

'Whose was it?'

I hesitated. If she knew it was Glenda's diary, she'd guess that it must contain snippets about her father and would insist on reading it. I weighed up the consequences, and decided that – for now, anyway – a lie was the best policy.

'No idea, some girl.'

'Can I read it?'

I gulped some coffee, tried to act indifferent. 'Well, sure. When I'm done. It's a real snore, though. A waste of time. Don't know why I bothered.'

'It kept you up all night.'

'Not all night. Apparently I was dead to the world when you found me.'

She considered me through narrowed eyes. 'Mum, you fell asleep on your arms at the kitchen table, with all the lights blazing. How can you say it was a boring read?'

I drained the rest of the coffee so I wouldn't have to answer. It scalded my throat on the way down, but it did the trick. My heart began to pump again and my brain cleared.

'It's Saturday,' I remembered, leaping to my feet and tossing the diary up on a shelf with a pile of recipe books. 'The barbecue's today. What time did I tell Corey? Four? What time is it now? We'd better get a wriggle on, I still have to buy sausages – '

'Relax, Mum. It's not even eight o'clock. In the morning,' she added, scowling.

I slumped back on the chair, relieved. There still remained the better part of the day to prepare. Shop, make salad, chill beer. Shower and freshen up. Pump my body with caffeine and create a façade of normality by the time everyone arrived –

Bronwyn was still hovering. 'Aren't you forgetting something?'

It was then I noticed what she was wearing. The new pink polka dot dress she'd bought with her Christmas money. Her good white sandals. She'd done her hair differently, too. Pigtails with white ribbons, very girly, she hadn't worn it like that for ages. Despite her height, she seemed younger than her eleven years.

'What's going on?' I asked.

She rolled her eyes. 'You promised we'd visit my grandmother today.'

A familiar emotion rolled over me. Guilt. I'd forgotten. But with Bronwyn's reminder, I felt a ripple of eagerness. Luella was a direct link to Samuel and Aylish. After what Corey had told me, I suspected Luella would be too fragile to cope with being questioned about them, but there might be other more subtle clues at her house – photographs, or mementoes; conversation threads that might unravel a little more of Samuel's story. I knew it was early days to be planning intimate heart-to-hearts with a woman I'd not yet met, but I couldn't stop myself hoping.

'There's no guarantee she'll open her door,' I warned, as much for my own sake as for Bronwyn's. 'Remember what I told you about her being a hermit.'

Bronwyn flipped a pigtail over her shoulder as though its presence irked her. 'There are worse things than hermits, Mum.'

'She might not like getting intruded upon.'

Bronwyn sighed. 'Nothing ventured, nothing gained, Mum. That's what Dad used to say and I agree with him.'

Before I could muster an argument, she'd escaped out the door. I listened to her thump along the verandah and down the stairs into the garden. When the twitter of birds and the rasp of windblown foliage were all I could hear, I went to the window and peered out.

The sky had turned from eggshell to aquamarine. Cabbage moths flounced in the air, weightless as paper scraps. I guessed that Bronwyn had escaped to her jacaranda bench, no doubt to tally the minutes until we made our trek to William Road.

Her carryall was propped near the kitchen door in readiness for our departure. I couldn't resist a peek. Inside was the box of Cadbury Roses we'd bought, albums of photos, mostly Bronwyn and her father, and a handmade glitter-encrusted card. 'For My Grandmother' she'd written in fancy letters. The card stirred an odd mix of feelings. Envy, because it had been a very long time since she'd bothered to make a card for me. Protectiveness, because there was a strong likelihood that her quest to meet Luella could end in disappointment. Jealousy, because I feared that my daughter might need someone other than me to fill the void her father's death had left behind. And a giddy, illogical sort of fear that I might lose her.

Crazy, I reasoned.

Still, it couldn't hurt to take an active stand against this newest threat. Grabbing a pair of secateurs from the utility drawer, I headed outside.

The flowerbeds were overflowing – the bobbing heads of roses and gladioli, sunflowers and daisies and gerberas created a brilliantly hued concerto in the harsh light. Bees hovered, and butterflies sailed from leaf to leaf looking for a tender spot to mark out their eggs.

I walked uphill towards the sea of nodding flower heads, planning which combination would have the most impact.

A big bunch, I decided, showy and brazen and bursting with colour and scent. Wobbling roses, perky gerberas, maybe a few sprigs of timeless lavender; a shrewd and ingenious combination of cottage garden with reliable old-world charm.

I might not be able to fill any voids, but I had a pretty good idea about how to impress a prospective grandmother. If you can't beat 'em, Aunt Morag had been fond of saying, then you might as well go down with all guns blazing.

We stood at the door for an eternity. Both of us wide-eyed, nervous. Bronwyn hugged the massive bunch of flowers to her chest, her carryall with its bulging cargo of chocolates and photo albums slung over her shoulder.

The verandah was cool and shady, dark beneath its canopy of white wisteria and climbing roses. The outlook was pleasant – bushland and distant hills, the pretty garden – but I had the jitters. Someone was watching us. I didn't know how I knew, only that I had the feeling of eyes peering through the shuttered windows, eyes that were as curious as our own.

'Come on,' I told Bronwyn. 'We've been here five minutes, I don't think she's going to answer. We might as well head home, come back another time.'

Bronwyn put on her most pleading face. 'What if she was out the back and didn't hear the first few times we rang? Please Mum, just a bit longer?'

Before I could answer, she reached out and pressed the doorbell. Muffled electronic chimes burbled deep inside the house. I waited to hear footsteps, waited to hear the creak of floorboards, the rattle of the door being opened.

There was only more silence.

'We can't stand here all day,' I insisted. 'We have to prepare for tonight – the salmon isn't going to marinate itself, you know.

Besides, there's a fete over at the Lutheran church. Why don't we pop in on the way home, Jade might be there?'

'No.'

'Come on, Bron, your grandmother'll still be here next week. We can come back then, have another try.'

Ignoring me, she shot out her hand and rapped on the flywire door.

'Gran! Gran, it's me, Bronwyn!' she cried shrilly. 'Gran, please come out, I've brought you something.'

'Bronny, I don't think it's a good idea to . . .'

Bronwyn kept knocking. The flywire door shuddered and clanged, making a horrible racket.

'Gran, please come out. It's Bronwyn, your granddaughter. I've come all the way from Melbourne to see you!'

I sighed. 'Bron, you're making a fuss. Even if Luella *is* inside, she won't want to open up now. What must she be thinking?'

Bronwyn's eyes filled. 'I don't care what she thinks. I just want to see her, talk to her. You don't know what it's like, Mum. I really want to meet her.'

'Then you're going about it the wrong way. Carrying on like this is only making things worse – '

There was a soft click.

We froze. A mouse-like scuffle came from behind the door, and then the snicking sound of a deadlock tumbling in its chamber. Behind the flywire screen, the front door rattled.

And swung open.

In the dim half-light of the entryway stood a woman. She was tall and stout; her pudgy face was blank with shock. She shuffled forward, peering through the flywire, blinking her small grey-green eyes. She wore a fifties-style floral dress, and her grey-streaked brown hair was teased into a bouffant bun, dressed with a velvet ribbon – white, like the ones in Bronwyn's hair. Her makeup was perfect, as deftly applied as a movie star's.

For what seemed like a full minute she didn't speak, just stared through the flywire at Bronwyn as if looking at a ghost. When she spoke, her voice was high and soft, husky.

'Glenda? Dear God, my Glenda . . . is it you?'

'Mrs Jarman?' I said quickly. 'Luella, forgive us for dropping in unannounced. I'm Audrey Kepler, and this is my daughter, Bronwyn. She's Tony's daughter – '

The woman looked at me, but only for a second. Her eyes turned back to Bronwyn, large with disbelief. Bronwyn beamed back, her eyes aglow.

'Gran? We've brought you flowers. I hope you like them.'

A puff of breath escaped the woman's lips.

'Bronwyn?' She wagged her head from side to side, as if unable to grasp what she was seeing.

Bronwyn held out the flowers. 'For you, Gran.'

The flywire door squealed open, and Luella Jarman blinked in the dappled light. As she gazed at Bronwyn her eyes welled. Twin tears spilled over the rims, splashing down her plump cheeks, painting lines in the powdery make up.

'My dear girl,' she whispered huskily. 'My dear, dear girl.'

Then she grasped Bronwyn's hand and drew her close, careless of the flowers as she enfolded Bronwyn in her vast fleshy arms.

We followed Luella into a dim hallway, deliciously cool after the heat outside. Through wide arched doorways I glimpsed a formal sitting room. The walls were high and white, punctuated by black-framed pictures. Heavy drapes muted the light filtering through tall windows. Polished floorboards gleamed like spilled ink, and there were bulky lounge chairs and cabinets displaying figurine collections and silver trophies. Bookshelves groaned under the weight of countless books.

I caught a whiff of Pine O Cleen from further along the hall, but that was soon eclipsed by other aromas: rose perfume wafting from the bunch of rumpled flowers Bronwyn carried, a faint musty animal smell. A dog, maybe. Furniture polish. Hairspray. Freshly baked cake.

We emerged into a sunny buttercup-yellow kitchen with double doors that opened onto a wide verandah. The benchtops were the same dark wood as the floor, brightened by a colourful retro cannister set. A groovy sixties sunray clock ticked on the wall above a breakfast nook; below it sat a pine table and four chairs.

Glenda's diary was still fresh in my mind, and I couldn't help picturing her and Tony breakfasting at that table. They would have measured their mornings and afternoons by that clock, eaten and laughed and bickered under this roof, perhaps eaten cereal from those gaily coloured canisters. They'd been a long time gone from this house, yet I imagined I could feel their lingering presence, as though the air had never quite managed to fold itself around their absence. It was a sad feeling, an emptiness within an emptiness, a dislocated sense of being where I had no right to be, knowing what I had no business knowing.

'Such a surprise,' Luella was saying, apparently mesmerised by Bronwyn. 'Such a wonderful, wonderful surprise. I can't believe I have a granddaughter, a beautiful little granddaughter . . . I must be the luckiest woman in the world.'

Pleasure shone from Bronwyn's eyes as she watched Luella bustle about the kitchen.

'I brought photos to show you, Gran. Most are of me and Dad, but there are some of Mum, too.'

'Truly? I can't wait to see them.' Luella still seemed dazed, but she managed a shy smile for Bronwyn. 'If your mother has time, I might even be persuaded to bring out my own snaps – your father as a little boy . . . and our dear Glenda. You resemble her, you know.'

Bronwyn nodded. 'I've seen her photo. We could be sisters, couldn't we?'

A brittle intake of breath, then almost inaudibly, 'You could indeed.'

While the kettle boiled, Luella selected three floral teacups from a glass-fronted cabinet and stacked them on a tray. Her chubby fingers worked swiftly, gathering the implements of morning tea: sugar spoons, delicate plates painted with cornflowers, crisp linen napkins, a jug of fresh milk, lovely old silver cake forks. She removed a jam sponge from the fridge, then filled the teapot with scalding water. The only thing out of place was the quavering in her hands. Nerves, I surmised, and who could blame her? Twenty years without company, shut up in her house with little outside contact; I was amazed that her one display of strain was a slight tremor.

'Dad was a famous painter,' Bronwyn chatted on, 'really clever – he won all these awards and travelled overseas, had lots of exhibitions to show off his work . . . Oh, but you probably already know that, don't you, Gran?'

Luella chuckled. It was a pretty laugh, throaty and warbling. 'Why yes,' she told Bronwyn with a hint of the conspirator, 'in fact I followed my son's career in the newspapers. He did well for himself, didn't he?'

'Everyone loved his pictures,' Bronwyn agreed, 'they bought heaps of his work and he became very rich. He painted landscapes; his early ones were small, the size of postcards . . . but Mum says as he got more confidence his paintings became bigger and bigger. Abstracts, he called them, but if you looked hard you could still see the trees and rivers, that sort of thing. Do you have any of Dad's paintings?'

She stopped talking long enough to peer around at the walls, which made Luella laugh again.

'Oh yes, darling. I've got some lovely watercolours of flowers and birds, even a view of this house from the top of the hill. They're in the lounge room, and there's a couple in the hall. Why don't you wander through and have a look? Then come out to the verandah and we'll cut the cake.'

Bronwyn scampered off.

'Can I help you with that?' I offered, as Luella hoisted the tray.

'No thanks, dear, it's lighter than it looks. Although you might bring the silverware? And grab that packet of Iced Vo-Vos, there's a love.'

In the twenty minutes I'd spent in Luella's company, I had been pleasantly surprised. I'd been expecting her to be mousey and drab, fearful of her own shadow, perhaps even somewhat deranged . . . but Luella Jarman was none of those things. She spoke in a formal manner, yet her voice radiated warmth. She was a large woman but she moved gracefully, as though each gesture, each step she took, had been rehearsed.

There was another reason her friendly nature boded well. If she was this easy to get along with on our first meeting, then she might be open to discussing her parents after all. Perhaps not today . . . but sometime soon.

Collecting the forks and biscuits, I followed her through the double doors – which, I noticed, were fitted with deadlocks – out to a wide shady verandah.

'It's a perfect morning, isn't it?' Luella piped, unloading her tray onto a large cedar table. 'So clear and tranquil, except for those kookaburras cackling fifty to the dozen. You'd think they'd just heard the joke of the century.'

'And look at that view,' I agreed, 'it's breathtaking.'

Beyond the yard stretched a vista of grey-blue bushland, dotted with Bangalow palms that swayed in the warm air. Purple volcanic hills languished on the horizon.

The yard itself hadn't changed much since the photo of Tony under the bunya pine. There was the wonky paling fence, the shaggy lawn overrun with daisies, the clothesline where Glenda and Luella had been taken by surprise. Everywhere were red and yellow nasturtiums – cascading under fruit trees, pushing up through garden seats, or spilling from a variety of planters including an old clawfoot bathtub. Framing the view was the magnificent bunya, stretching its arms as if to embrace the four corners of the sky. The soil around its base was carpeted with brown needles and clumpy pinecones; tucked behind the tree at the end of a meandering path was a tall glass-panelled hothouse –

A sharp bark made me whirl around.

At my heels stood a stocky bull terrier, its lips drawn to reveal rows of yellow teeth. I took a startled step backwards and the dog growled. It was white with a tan mark on its head like a handprint. Its eyes were dull with age and its coat mangy, but it seemed alert . . . and I didn't like the look of those teeth.

'Don't mind Gruffy,' Luella said, stooping to dance her fingers along the top of the dog's head. 'He's not used to having visitors . . . Now, take a seat, love, and make yourself at home. Do you like sugar in your tea?'

She busied herself slicing cake, arranging generous segments on plates, fiddling with dessert forks. Just as the silence was about to reach saturation point, Bronwyn burst onto the verandah. Plonking herself at the table, she took a hungry bite of cake and watched Luella pour her a glass of lemonade. When the cake was demolished and her glass emptied, she dragged her carryall onto her lap and took out the presents she'd brought for her grandmother.

Luella exclaimed over the chocolates and card, which she positioned next to her teacup, shaking her head all the while in amazed disbelief. She dabbed at her eyes with a large hanky, but the brightness of her smile said her tears were of the joyful variety.

An hour later Bronwyn and her grandmother were still poring through the last of the albums, examining Bronwyn's school photos. Luella wanted to know everything: what Bronwyn had loved best about school, what she was good at, what subjects – if any – she struggled with. She even asked the names of Bronwyn's classmates, and Bronwyn was eager to recite them for her.

I stifled my hundredth yawn.

It took all my available willpower to resist the urge to dig in my tote and check my watch. No amount of inconspicuous twisting and craning in my seat had yielded a glimpse through the open doorway to the kitchen clock. I was starting to get jittery. There was shopping to be done, a barbecue to prepare. And I was hoping to find a few moments to steam open the rest of Glenda's diary.

Meanwhile, time was ticking away.

My bladder came to the rescue and I excused myself. The bathroom was old but clean, tiled in white with fluffy towels and fresh cakes of Imperial Leather. The window overlooked the back garden, framing the huge pine tree and revealing a glimpse of distant mountains. Like the windows in the kitchen, this one was fitted with a security grille and deadbolts.

I washed up at the sink, grimacing at the pallid sleepy-eyed creature staring back at me from the mirror. I made a mental note to add a hot shower and mud-mask to the afternoon's to-do list, then went back into the hallway.

This wing of the house had a more lived-in feel than the formal lounge and dining room near the entry. Four closed doors lined the hallway, their brass knobs glinting in the muted sunlight. I paused outside the first room, curious to know what lurked within. Surely a quick peek wouldn't hurt?

Quiet sounds floated on the still air. The clink of Luella's teacup, the sing-song murmur of her voice. Bronwyn's chirping giggle. The roar of cicadas, and the scratch of Gruffy's claws on the decking as he chased rabbits in his sleep.

I reached for the doorknob, peered in. It was a lovely room, all pale pinks and florals and white walls, though disappointing in its ordinariness. A double bed sat centre stage, overlaid with a mint-green chenille bedspread. It was a cosy, pretty room, but unremarkable. Even more regrettable was the obvious lack of photographs. None of Tony or Glenda, nor any of Luella's late husband Cleve. Not even a single snapshot of Luella, and none of Samuel.

The next room was sparer. A single bed was pushed against the far wall, its blue eiderdown freshly laundered, its pillow propped against the headboard. There was a flimsy desk crammed at the foot of the bed, topped by a solitary atlas. The only extraordinary thing about the room were the drawings tacked to every wall: butterflies, blossoms, frogs and caterpillars – tiny pencil sketches, a few of them washed with fading watercolour.

Tony's room.

Despite the obvious care in its upkeep, a mood of sorrow and loneliness seeped from every corner. Feeling like the intruder I was, I retreated along the hall to the next room.

Like Tony's, it was preserved exactly as it had been when Glenda lived here. Wallpapered with yellow roses, it was light and airy as a dream. The bed was freshly made, the pillows plumped. On the window seat sat a scattering of well-loved teddy bears and a knitted ragdoll. There were signs of the sixteen-year-old, too: a David Bowie poster tacked opposite the door, a make-up box, a pile of dog-eared *Dolly* magazines and a school jumper draped over the back of a vanity chair.

The next room looked like an office, though judging by the dust it hadn't been cleaned for some time. There was no bed, just a desk and a large leather recliner with an antique lamp standing to attention beside it. Bookshelves groaned under the weight of hundreds of books – dusty old Penguin classics, cookbooks and gardening books, rows of well-thumbed paperbacks perched along the upper shelves like roosting pigeons.

The only evidence that this might have once been a bedroom was a wardrobe tucked like an afterthought behind the door. It looked to have once belonged to a child; painted blue, with a model ship perched on top.

The murmur of voices from the verandah reminded me that I'd been gone too long . . . but I couldn't resist.

Crossing to the wardrobe, I opened the door.

The smell of mothballs puffed out. On one side was a hanging space, empty but for a scattering of dry moth bodies. The other side held shallow drawers, the kind for keeping underwear. The top drawer contained a jumble of paperwork: house deeds, rate notices, defunct utility bills. In the next drawer was a skipping rope, a cigar box of dried roses converted to dust, and a collection of pastille tins crammed with rusty hairpins and pearl buttons. In the bottom drawer I found a large photo album, its spilling pages held intact between the covers with black ribbon. Untying the ribbon, I opened the book and turned the flyleaf.

According to the handwritten legend, the first photos had been taken in 1931, and those that followed were in chronological order. They were all of the Jarman clan. Mostly matchbox-sized, they portrayed groups of people whose faces had blurred over time. Children on horseback, men shouldering rifles with dogs at their feet, women holding babies. I searched for names I recognised, but it wasn't until I'd flipped through half a dozen pages that things got interesting.

Above the caption, 'Cleve, 1939, age seven', was an empty space; the photo had been removed. A page later were more gaps where other snapshots should have been: young Cleve and his father fishing in 1940; Cleve outside the post office in 1942. Several pages on, I came to another blank space; this one was labelled: 'Cleve and Luella, just married, 1968.' I flipped through the album, bypassing snaps of Tony and Glenda as kids, early ones of Luella looking trim and serious. But then the empty gaps became more frequent than images. It was plain to see that every photograph of Cleve had been removed – from childhood snaps to those taken later as an adult. Not even family pictures had been spared. If, according to the caption, Cleve had been present, the photo was missing.

I recalled what Corey had told me about the Jarmans, and how they'd been such a tight-knit fun-loving family. But then hadn't she also said that Luella had asked Cleve for a divorce? Hmmm, I thought. Just goes to show that what you see is not always what you get. Pondering this, I retied the ribbon and replaced the album in its drawer.

As I was shutting the wardrobe, a frenzy of barking erupted from the verandah.

I spun around, dashed into the hallway, then forced myself to linger a moment while my heartbeat stabilised.

That was when I saw the little painting.

Tony's of course – his confident lines and vibrant colours were unmistakable, even in this earlier rendering. It was one of his smaller offerings, not much bigger than a page taken from a paperback, restrained behind the glass of an oversized frame that exaggerated the painting's delicate beauty. It was a botanical study, a native sundew with golden tentacles and sticky crimson hairs. There was even a tiny fly trapped on one glistening pad. As I studied it – breath held, gaze trapped as surely as the little fly – a memory surfaced.

It had happened one summer, clear in my mind because I'd been pregnant with Bronwyn, hideously uncomfortable yet glowing with a joy I'd never before known. Tony and I had been strolling the garden of our new Albert Park house when he'd spied a tiny cabbage moth snared in a spiderweb. The moth was twitching feebly by the time we found it, its body gummed by sticky strands, a big golden orb spider rubbing its legs at the web's perimeter. Tony insisted on stopping and it took him the best part of ten minutes to free the sad little moth, which fell into the grass and was lost, no doubt to perish anyway.

Tony was depressed afterwards. I remembered wondering if all artists harboured such peculiarities. That was in the early days, of course, before I came to know that Tony was pretty much one of a kind.

A string of yelping barks shattered the memory. I hurried back to the verandah. I'd been gone too long, I could feel the guilty flush creeping into my throat. Luella would guess I'd been snooping. To cover myself, I came up with a lie and measured it against my tongue so that it'd sound natural: You see, I followed Bronwyn's example and took a peek at Tony's paintings, I do hope you don't mind, they're rather lovely aren't they . . .

I needn't have bothered.

Luella was teasing the dog with an iced biscuit. She was smiling, her cheeks aglow and her skin dewy with perspiration. Gone was the timid, hesitant woman who'd opened the door to us a couple of hours ago. In her place stood someone who had blossomed to life.

'There you are, dear,' Luella said when she saw me. 'Poor old Gruffy was just doing a little dance for Bronwyn. I think it might have been a bit much for him.'

Bronwyn giggled. 'Mum, you should have seen him, he got up on his hind legs and hopped around, just like a tubby little man.'

'Why's he panting like that?' I asked, thankful that Gruffy had stolen the limelight. 'Is he all right?'

Luella patted the dog's head. 'He's not as young as he used to be . . . but look at his little face! He's positively beaming – why, the dear old boy hasn't had this much fun in years.'

Bronwyn studied her grandmother, her face alight with open adulation. 'You look different to the photo,' she commented out of the blue.

For the first time since I'd met her, Luella's reserve slipped. Her bright smile sank away and her face fell. In that moment she looked old, and I glimpsed the frightened, lonely woman behind her meticulously made-up mask.

'What photo?'

'The one of you and Dad and Aunty Glenda, out on the back lawn. Mum found it at the house. Dad's about ten, he's standing near a little blow-up pool, and you and Aunty Glenda are hanging washing on the clothesline.'

'Just the three of us?'

'Yep.'

Luella reached forward and touched Bronwyn's face. 'I can't say I remember that snap, pet. Perhaps you could bring it over next time you visit, I'd so love to see it.'

Bronwyn looked at me for consent, and I nodded. 'We'll make copies of our other photos as well,' I told her. 'I'm sure your Gran would love to have those baby shots, and your first years at school. And what about the studio ones of you and Dad . . . we could put them all into a little album?'

Bronwyn beamed, and we both looked at Luella.

She was sitting back in her chair, her pudgy hands clasped on her lap, twisting the ring she wore on her pinky. Tears quivered like raindrops on her lashes.

'Bronny, I think your gran's a little overwhelmed. Why don't you go and explore the yard for a while, let her have a bit of a rest?'

Bronwyn looked concerned, but got up and turned to make her way to the verandah stairs. Before she reached them, she darted back to Luella's side and planted a kiss on the older woman's cheek. Then she raced down the steps and across the yard, into the shadows of the bunya pine. A yelp broke the silence as Gruffy dragged himself out from under Luella's chair and lumbered after her.

'Luella, we should leave. We've overstayed ourselves.'

'Oh no! No, dear . . . please. I'm just a bit teary from the excitement. I'll be all right in a tick.'

'We must have given you quite a shock, I am sorry.'

Luella smudged away her tears. 'No need to apologise, Audrey. Bronwyn's a delightful girl, I'm so pleased you brought her to see me. It's been an emotional day and I suppose it won't hit me until after you've gone. But you will come again, won't you? How long are you staying in town? I'm afraid I've been so absorbed in the moment that I forgot to ask.'

I hesitated, then said softly, 'Actually, Luella, we live here now. In Magpie Creek. We've been here since December. We're living at Thornwood.'

Luella blinked. For the briefest of moments she looked stunned, but then her face lit up. 'Oh, my dear. That's just wonderful. Wonderful! But how . . . ?'

'Tony left the property to me in his will. We were together for eight years, but we never got married. It didn't work out between us. We separated when Bronwyn was six, although they had frequent contact. He was always good to her, a brilliant father. The best. Giving us Thornwood, I suppose, was his way of making sure Bronwyn would always be secure.'

Luella nodded. I saw the curiosity in her eyes, sensed her need to hear more about Tony's adult life, to fill in the gaps between his leaving home at fourteen and his death a few months ago. But like me, she was too polite, or perhaps too wary, to ask.

Instead she said, 'It must have been hard for you, Audrey, raising a little daughter on your own. You've done an admirable job. She's a credit to you.'

'It was easy,' I admitted. 'Bronwyn's so bright. Mature for her age, she always has been. Sometimes I feel as though she's light years ahead of me, almost as if I'm the child and she's the adult.'

My comment was intended to perk up the mood, but Luella's face grew sorrowful. Her chair creaked as she shifted her weight.

'Tony was a bit like that,' she said. 'But he was also an odd lad. While the other boys were kicking a football around the oval, or dashing around the place on their bikes, Tony was off by himself in the bush, collecting seed pods and wildflowers to draw. He was a friendly boy, funny and intelligent . . . but there was a dark side to his nature. A side that made you oftentimes wonder what he was really capable of.'

Her words had been spoken kindly, but they left me feeling damaged somehow, as though I'd fallen against something sharp, lost a layer of skin, been wounded in a subtle part of myself that I couldn't quite locate.

I reached for words to defend Tony, to explain that he'd been a good father despite his often lengthy absences from our lives; that he'd been a kind-hearted man, a good man despite his many failings. But the words wouldn't come.

Instead, I had a flash of Tony in the yard as a boy. Standing where Bronwyn now stood in the shade of the bunya pine. His dark head bent over a drawing, absorbed ... then looking up in surprise as his father's shadow fell on the page. Angry words; then, the hunting knife, the hot dusty ride in the Holden; and finally the terrifying, devastating attack that he and Glenda were forced to witness.

At that moment, I felt the keen opening up somewhere inside me of a breach; a gap, a chasm – as though I had overlooked something vital, but no matter how I probed, it remained just beyond my grasp.

14

Bronwyn insisted we decorate the back verandah with paper lanterns and fairy lights, and I had to admit the touch of whimsy lifted my spirits.

Our visit to Luella had been a roaring success. Bronwyn raved about her grandmother all the way home, unable to contain her admiration. She'd already made plans with Luella to visit again tomorrow, Sunday. I was happy for her, I really was ... but underneath the gladness lurked a darker emotion. Despite my own esteem for Luella, I couldn't deny that her bond with my daughter had tweaked a green nerve of envy.

Reaching up, I adjusted a lantern that had fallen awry, then ducked into the kitchen to collect another tray of food. When I returned to the verandah, Bronwyn was hovering at one end of the picnic table, peeling foil off the potato salad. As I balanced the loaded tray on my hip and offloaded another couple of foil-covered dishes, she wrinkled her nose.

'Pooh, what's that smell?'

'I don't smell anything out of the ordinary. Onions ... beetroot maybe?'

She made a performance of sniffing the air. 'Mum, it's you! You're wearing perfume!'

I sighed. 'And that's a crime now, is it?'

She stopped peeling foil and stared at me incredulously. 'But why?'

'So I feel nice.'

Her eyes went wide as if I'd just replied in an alien tongue. 'You've never wanted to feel nice before. Why now?'

'I just do.'

Rolling her discarded tinfoil into a wad, she narrowed her eyes at me. 'It's for *him*, isn't it?'

At my blank non-reaction, she elaborated. 'Jade's dad. I knew it, I was right. You do like him, after all.'

Candles fluttered in hurricane jars, and one of my favourite tracks came on the stereo, a haunting song with an undertone of funk. Dusting my hands on my jeans, I tried to escape back into the kitchen but Bronwyn trailed me like a bloodhound.

'No point ignoring me, Mum. Perfume's one thing, but that blouse is a dead giveaway.'

I stalled at the sink and gazed at my top in dismay. Silk, tied at the waist, the neckline softened by a narrow ruffle. I'd thought it looked okay, which had inspired me to supplement the effect with a light mist of scent. Vanilla Musk, a fragrant oil I'd bought as a single-and-loving-it present to cheer my flagging spirits after Tony left. It hadn't worked, of course, so I'd stashed the perfume away as a reminder never to go there again.

'What's wrong with the blouse?' I queried, feeling foolish. 'You always complain that I never make an effort.'

Bronwyn's hand went to her hip as she considered this.

'Well, there's effort . . . and then there's *effort*. And Mum, I have to say that you look really good. For a change,' she added pointedly.

'So my appearance meets with your approval?'

'Sure.' She dunked her wadded foil ball into the bin and wafted out, gloating triumphantly to herself.

'Wow, thanks,' I muttered, regretting that sarcasm was wasted on an eleven-year-old. Whipping off the tea towel I'd tucked into my jeans waistband as an impromptu apron, I stalked through to the lounge room window and peered out.

No dust cloud. No sign of a car.

The kitchen clock said three forty-seven. I toyed with the idea of steaming open a couple of diary pages and catching up with Glenda. Her world had come vividly alive for me since visiting the house she'd grown up in: the sunny kitchen with its loud clock and lingering cake aromas, the leafy verandah, and the girly bedroom at the end of the hall wallpapered with yellow roses. I was coming to understand her far more intimately than I'd ever have been able to through second-hand accounts from Tony. Her thoughts, her private longings, her fears. Part of me felt like the worst kind of criminal for reading her diary, but it was too late now to give in to any flimsy sense of remorse – Glenda's story had become too compelling.

A car horn honked. An instant later Corey's leaf-green Mercedes roared through the eucalypts at the edge of the service road, dragging with it a blustery swirl of dust.

Bronwyn beat me to the front verandah and was already racing down the stairs. She shrieked when she saw Jade spill from the car, and tore down the slope to greet her. They hugged like long lost relatives, then ran off around the side of the house, laughing and talking and shouting all at once.

I helped Corey drag a cooler bag of what I suspected were lentil burgers and soy snags from the boot. She'd brought beer, too – twin six-packs of Crown Lager. Just as I suspected, Corey was a girl after my own heart.

'Danny's running late,' she informed me, hoisting the beer into her arms, her hair burnished like bronze wire by the afternoon light. Wrangling a crumpled note from her pocket, she thrust it into my hand.

'He said to give you this.'

I read the now-familiar handwriting: *Audrey, gone to see a sick lamb, will be there soon, cheers Dan.*

'He had an emergency callout,' Corey explained, 'and had to arrange for his nurse to go with him.'

Oh, hello. 'Nurse?'

'He suspects his little woolly patient might have a heart murmur, and part of the test for that is to listen to the heartbeat via a stethoscope. It's unavoidable, as it's the only way to know for certain in this case if something's wrong. Danny has an arsenal of whiz-bang gadgets designed to monitor pulse and breath and guage blood oxygen, but once in a while he needs to listen. Since for him listening is a dual impossibility – typical man that he is, as well as being stone deaf – he employs the assistance of a vet nurse. Danny hates to admit his limitations, but there are things he can't risk overlooking. Hence, Nancy.'

'Of course.'

'She's a real sweetie – just out of vet school, a local girl and a bit of a firecracker. You'd like her.'

I smiled stiffly. 'Yeah, well . . . I hope you're hungry?'

'Starving.'

'Great!' I slumped off along the path, feeling flat as an image of Nancy flashed through my mind: tall, blonde, supermodel gorgeous. God, a firecracker – what did that entail, exactly? Danny was probably smitten with her, and who could blame him? Working closely together, relying on each other for important information. Providing encouragement when things went wrong, celebrating small victories. Well, good luck to them –

'Hey, it's amazing!' Corey had stomped up the stairs behind me and now stood beaming about the lounge room. 'I'm impressed, Audrey – it's not what I was expecting at all.'

Her smile infected me, and I gladly abandoned my fixation with Nancy the Firecracker.

'I knew you'd love it,' I said, grinning back at her. 'Come on, let's dump this stuff out back and I'll show you around.'

'I can't get over the furniture.' Corey appraised the dining room in wonderment. 'You're right, Audrey, it's not creepy at all, it's stunning. Smart move, to mix your own pieces in with Samuel's old stuff.' She drifted over to a set of tribal masks hung near the doorway. 'What are they, African – ?'

'They're from the Sepik River. Aunt Morag acquired them when she lived in New Guinea in the nineteen-fifties.'

'Aunt Morag lived in New Guinea?'

'Born there. Her parents were missionaries.'

'Fascinating . . . I can see we're going to have to discuss the old dear in microscopic detail. I'm dying to hear all about her – oh.'

She'd stopped in front of a series of framed photographs: Bronwyn dressed as a fairy, her wings sparkling in firelight, her tutu decorated with tinsel stars. The photos had been snapped at a bonfire party we'd attended years ago. At three, Bronwyn had been delicate as a pixie with her mop of flaxen hair and sharp little features, delighting everyone with her tireless dancing. Further along was another snap of Bronwyn, age six, in the botanical garden at Daylesford being swarmed by ladybirds.

'Audrey . . . are these yours?'

'Yep, early ones on film, before I converted to digital. This one here,' I said indicating the ladybirds, 'was taken the year Tony walked out . . . I got a bit fanatical about trying to capture everything Bronwyn did. I guess I was still hoping that Tony would come back to us. Of course, that never happened – but I ended up with a lot of great images.'

Corey sighed. 'Tony always was a bit of a dork.'

I found myself smiling, remembering how Glenda had called him that too. 'I guess he was.'

'A loveable dork, though. I've got a ton of funny stories about him as a kid – him and Danny were joined at the hip, more like brothers than best friends, a right pair of scallywags, always up to trouble.' She looked more closely at the fairy photos, nudged me with her elbow. 'These are special, kiddo. Got any more?'

In my studio I dug out a folio of newer work that I thought Corey might like: informal portraits, many in stark black and white – a Sikh wedding; elderly twin sisters in their gothic Toorak mansion; a shy old Jewish man displaying his wrist for the camera.

'Poor old codger, look at that.' Corey bent closer to examine the numbers inked into the man's forearm. 'It's a beautiful shot, but so terribly sad. God, look at his dear old face, so trusting. How could anyone even think about feeling trust after what he must have been through?'

She marvelled a moment more, then continued rummaging in silence. The mood had sobered between us. It seemed the right time to tell her, but I was struggling with where to begin. I decided to dive right in.

'Corey?'

'Hmmm?'

'Bronwyn and I paid a visit to William Road this morning.' A pause. 'We met Luella Jarman.'

Corey straightened abruptly and looked at me, the photo pinched between her thumb and forefinger forgotten.

'Luella? You met her?'

'Yes.'

A pallor had risen, making her freckles dance across her face. 'How . . . how was she?'

'She was fragile,' I recalled. 'Nervous at first – although once we got chatting she seemed to relax. She and Bronwyn hit it off straightaway, they had a great old natter. Luella kept saying how pleased she was that we dropped in.'

Corey pondered my face as though she'd never noticed it before. 'How did she look . . . I mean, is she all right?'

From the concern in Corey's eyes, I knew what she was really asking: Had Luella neglected herself, had grief turned her into a shadow of the woman she'd once been? Had she, in her state of reclusiveness, let her house – and perhaps her sanity – fall to ruin around her?

'She seems well, as far as I can see. And she looked great. The house is immaculate, not a speck of dust anywhere . . . and she's got some lovely old paintings of Tony's dotted around the walls. We had morning tea on the verandah. She and Bronwyn spent most of the time poring over old photo albums. Luella must have enjoyed herself, because she invited Bronwyn back to see her again tomorrow.'

Corey blinked. 'I confess, I'm flabbergasted. Gosh, I'd so love to catch up with her, it's been years. Do you think she'd cope?'

Something in my expression must have betrayed my reservations, because she hurried on, 'Hey, I should wait a while . . . let her get used to seeing you and Bronwyn first, before having to deal with the swarming masses. Maybe in a few weeks, when she's feeling stronger?'

'I'll talk to her,' I offered, 'test the water. You could come along with us one day. I'm sure she'd be delighted to see you.'

Corey nodded, but she was obviously shaken. 'I must say I'm glad you ignored my warning . . . Poor old Luella, it's about time she had a bit of joy in her life. Heaven knows, it's been a long time coming . . .' She seemed about to say more, her lips parted and she took in a breath – but then faltered. To my surprise, her eyes filled. She blinked, not looking at me now, not even looking at the photo she still held in her fingertips, but somewhere in between.

I resisted the urge to slip my arm around her shoulders. I sensed she wasn't the type to accept physical comfort, and I wasn't the type to offer it. Besides, as Aunt Morag liked to say, the best remedy for anything was usually distraction.

'Come on,' I said, leaving the photos where they lay, patting Corey heartily on the back. 'Let's get that barbie fired up, I'm starving.'

By the time we reached the kitchen, Corey had regained her chirpy old self.

'I don't know where that brother of mine is,' she said, wrestling open her cooler bag, pulling out a pile of white-paper parcels, 'but he's holding up the show. Why don't we start without him? These tofu snags are starting to get restless.'

I glanced at the clock. It was nearly five. 'You're right, by the time everything's cooked, the girls'll be feral with hunger.' I grabbed the dish of marinated salmon steaks, and as we headed outside we passed the kitchen window.

The window looked onto the verandah and afforded us a clear view of Jade and Bronwyn, who were sitting side by side on the back steps. They had their backs to us, chattering quietly, heads together, taking turns to view each other through the wrong end of an old telephoto lens.

Corey nudged me. She put a finger to her lips, and we paused a moment to spy on them.

Jade adjusted the lens and passed it to Bronwyn.

'Eliza says it's worse when you reach fifteen, 'cos then they get all panicky about boys. Dad's already showing signs of queasiness if I so much as mention a guy in class.'

Bronwyn removed her eye from the lens and regarded Jade. 'Who's Eliza?'

'She's Aunty Corey's girlfriend. I call them Aunty Corey and Uncle Eliza.' Jade's dark eyes narrowed and she smiled mischievously. 'Aunty Corey's gay, didn't you know?'

Bronwyn shrugged. 'I do now.'

Corey groaned and shot me a woeful look. 'Serves me right for spying,' she whispered. 'Not the most dignified way to come out of the closet . . .'

I didn't reply. Jade had my full attention because she hadn't finished. By the look on Bronwyn's face, I wasn't the only one captivated by the unexpected revelation.

Jade was obviously enjoying herself. 'Have you ever seen two girls kissing?'

Bronwyn goggled. 'No.'

'It's a bit gross at first, especially when they start groping each other, but definitely worse when they – '

'Jade!'

Corey rapped on the glass, making both girls – and me – jump. Marching out onto the verandah, she tossed her parcel of snags on the bench beside the Weber.

'What?' Jade said, shrugging.

Corey gave her niece a narrow look. 'Haven't I told you about polite conversation? Audrey and Bronwyn don't want to hear the gory details of my private life . . . at least not before dinner.'

Jade shrugged again. 'Sure. Where's Dad?'

A resigned sigh. 'Running late.' Ripping open her paper parcel, Corey exposed a half-dozen limp grey sausages. She draped them onto the sizzling grill and prodded them with a spatula. Flopping into a nearby deckchair, she glowered at me, obviously awaiting my response.

I hovered over the grill, arranging capsicum kebabs in the gaps between Corey's sausages. That done, I wrenched the tops off two Crownies and passed one to Corey. She eyed me as she took it, but I only smiled and settled into the deckchair beside hers, losing myself for a moment in a long smooth swallow of beer.

It felt good to have company. It felt good to see Bronwyn enjoying herself with someone her own age. It felt good to sit on the shady verandah, listening to the hiss of the barbecue and the twitter of birds, free from any pressing agenda, and – for the moment – free from any nagging worries. I decided to give myself permission, just for one night, to forget about Samuel and Aylish and my quest to uncover their story. I felt the tentacles of obsession retreating, leaving me in peace for once as the knots of my relentless curiosity began to unwind.

My moment was short-lived. A distant rumble infiltrated the onion-and-herb-scented tranquillity. The sound was barely there at first, the faint hum of an errant bee, getting louder as the car approached.

I tracked its progress in my mind. It would be at the base of the service road, a black Toyota truck with chrome wheels and dog hair on the seats. Rattling along the potholed gravel, merging in and out of the shadows as it passed beneath the trees, along the rim of the valley with its bowl of emerald pastures, finally bursting through the eucalypt grove below the house as Corey's Merc had done an hour before.

'Dad's here!' Jade cried, and she and Bronwyn leapt up and ran out to greet him.

Corey took the opportunity, rounding on me the moment the girls were out of earshot.

'Audrey, are you so terribly shocked?'

A twinge of guilt. Glenda's diary entry about Corey trying to kiss her erupted in my mind, full technicolour. I should have confessed then. About the diary, about all of it. Glenda's story competition and Cleve's revelations about having known Aylish as a boy; his fight with Luella, and then his violent attack on Hobe Miller. About Bronwyn's discovery of the tin box in the tree, and how, several days later, I'd happened upon Hobe with his arm in the hollow trunk, searching –

But I'd waited too long. Corey was studying me, a tiny frown etched into her brow.

'Of course not,' I said. 'Anyway, I kind of . . . suspected.'

'Oh? You did? What gave me away? It was the boots, wasn't it, the Blundstones? Eliza always says my dress sense is too boyish – '

Corey's large earnest face with its smattering of pretty freckles and halo of red-gold hair was unnervingly close, and nearly my undoing. Her milk-chocolate eyes echoed the question, but I dared not open my mouth, even to put her mind at ease. I longed to confess the truth and be done with it, to lead her out to my room and pull open the bottom drawer of my bedside, reveal the water-buckled diary that had once belonged to her best friend.

But I couldn't tell. Not yet.

I lifted my shoulders in poor mimicry of Jade's easy indifference. 'Not the work boots. It was just a hunch.'

'Oh,' she said, and I was amazed to see her face relax with relief. It made me suspect that Glenda's outraged reaction all those years ago at the creek had scarred Corey, made her doubt herself on some critical level. Rejection at the best of times is a bitter pill to swallow, but how much more bitter must it have been for a teenage girl exposing her secret self for the first time?

Corey was still watching me, evidently as curious about my thoughts as I was about hers.

'So the boots are okay?' she asked doubtfully.

Despite my dark musings, I was suddenly laughing. 'The Blundstones are good. More than good – in fact, they're kinda cute.'

Her face rumpled into an uncharacteristically shy smile, which gained force until she was beaming at me with full voltage. 'Wait 'til I tell Eliza you said that. She'll be furious.'

We grinned and clinked bottles, swigged in unison. The beer was cool and sweet, quenching any guilt I still harboured over keeping Glenda's diary to myself.

Just then the thump of feet – two small pairs in sandals, one large pair in boots – thundered through the kitchen. The screen door clattered wide. Jade and Bronwyn burst onto the verandah, followed by Danny.

'What took you so long?' Corey demanded of her brother, not bothering to sign.

Danny's arms were full: a bunch of crimson gladioli wrapped in pink tissue, a bottle of red wine, an assortment of paper bags that bore the bakery logo, and a huge floral cake tin. Unable to sign, he shrugged at Corey, moving his lips in silent explanation.

I discovered that lip reading was not my forte; I had no idea what he was telling her. I kept my eyes on his mouth, intrigued. How did he communicate on the job when he had his arms full of injured animal? How did he manage to reassure frantic pet owners or worried farmers who didn't understand sign, didn't lip read? Did he resort to writing notes for everyone as he'd done for me in the church yesterday? Or did he dazzle them with his luminous thousand-megawatt smile and hope for the best?

He turned his attention to me. I'd been staring, and he seemed delighted to have caught me. With a flourish, he held out the flowers and trapped me in the headlight beam of the smile I'd just been contemplating.

I jerked out of my seat, slopping beer on my wrist as I launched across the verandah toward him.

'Let me help you with those,' I said, grabbing the flowers and the wine and making a beeline for the table. 'Gosh, these are beautiful, deep red too, my favourite, I just adore gladdies – ' I snapped my mouth shut, mortified. Not only had I just babbled, but I'd been facing away from him – he wouldn't have been able to see my lips in order to read them.

I heard a soft snort from Bronwyn's general direction and cursed under my breath. My cheeks felt hot. Aware that they must rival the flowers for colour, I stalled for time by shuffling dishes around to make room for the wine.

'What's burning?' Corey said, springing up to check the Weber. I heard a riotous hissing and crackling as she muttered over her sausages and repositioned the kebabs. 'You could toss on those steaks now,' she told me, 'everything else is done.'

'Righto.' I turned to Danny. *Thanks for the flowers*, I signed clumsily. *I'm happy you're here.*

He had unburdened himself of the bakery bags and cake tin, and was uncorking the wine. He paused to catch my eye and offer a speedy sign: pulling his hands away from his face, he hooked a finger back to his chest.

Thanks for inviting me.

He was wearing a pale green shirt and jeans that were flecked with dry grass. He looked a little rumpled, and his hair – curly, in need of a trim – stuck out in clumps as though he'd been dragging his fingers through it. I had a flash of him and Nancy the Firecracker in a hay barn: both of them pink-cheeked, aglow with sweat and beaming languidly as they dusted fragments of chaff from each other's clothing –

I realised I was staring again, and cleared my throat, making a hasty attempt at polite signage: *Your little sheep okay?*

A quizzical look, a half-smile. Then: Thumbs up. *All good.*

We inhabited a moment of awkwardness, Danny's smile gone now, just his curious gaze lingering on my face, as though waiting for me to speak further. I was grappling to think of something else to say, something to ask him that would alleviate the unease of our mutual silence. Instead, I found myself cataloguing his features, comparing them to Corey's. He had faint freckles like his sister, and a broad well-shaped face, but that's where the resemblance ended. His skin was paler than hers, his eyes verging to emerald rather than Corey's milk-chocolate. There was no hint of red in his hair, it was dark brown, lighter at the tips where the sun had touched it.

'Audrey, those steaks . . . ?'

I joined Corey at the grill and busied myself arranging the marinated salmon in the space she'd made for them. The steaks' raw underbellies met the hotplate with a splutter, sending up clouds of fragrant steam.

'Ready in five,' Corey proclaimed, wiping her forehead with the back of her hand then taking a thirsty swig of beer.

I fetched a wineglass for Danny, concentrating on pouring the wine so I wouldn't risk another babbled outburst, then helped Corey serve up. Tofu snags for her and Jade, salmon for me and Bronwyn and Danny, capsicum and feta kebabs all round.

Somehow we managed to eat heartily while debating a variety of topics – why vegetarian sausages were ideologically unsound; whether Jade would one day replace Nancy as her father's vet nurse; at what exact moment had Bronwyn first realised her passion for insects; and wasn't it exciting that Audrey had agreed to take Corey's portrait – all the while communicating with a jumbled amalgam of sign, finger spelling, lip reading, and way too many charade-like hand gesticulations.

Midway through our meal, I found myself wondering why Danny never spoke, why he rarely uttered a sound of any kind – except for the occasional raspy laugh.

I remembered my deaf friend from art school, Rhonda, the one who'd been so determined to communicate verbally despite never being understood. She always spoke at full volume, snorted and howled at jokes, yelled across the street to her hearing friends, and generally clattered about the place as if she was trying – by the sheer force of her loudness – to crash through the boundaries imposed by her deafness and connect more fully with the rest of the world.

Danny, on the other hand, seemed to be at home with his silence. Comfortable to converse via notes or lip reading or sign. Not bothered by the occasional misunderstanding. Corey had said he hated to admit his limitations. But perhaps it was more than that – perhaps he didn't feel the need to crash through any boundaries? Perhaps he was happy with who he was?

Mad thoughts. How did I know what Danny really thought or felt?

When the food was gone and the dishes cleared away, we sprawled on deckchairs and passed around the cake tin – which, to my eternal joy and gratitude contained a batch of Danny's mind-bogglingly delicious chocolate cherries. Corey seized control of the coffeepot and soon the dark bittersweet scent of coffee flavoured the onion-tinged air. The girls were lost some-where in the garden, probably in Bronwyn's secret bower under the jacaranda. I could hear their muffled prattling punctuated by occasional giggles.

'Oh, this is bliss,' Corey declared, stretching back in her chair, swirling the dregs of her coffee as she gazed across the garden. Shadows were shifting, the trees had grown gloomy and mysterious. Mosquitoes tried – without success – to infiltrate my stronghold of citronella candles and mozzie coils. Large floppy moths reeled drunkenly about us, and hordes of tiny black kamikaze beetles bombarded the chocolates, the beer, the table, and embedded themselves in Corey's hair.

Danny signed to Corey, his hands moving too quickly for me to catch more than the gist: something about shouting.

Corey glared at him, then looked over at me, her brow puckered. 'He always complains that I talk too loudly. Do I, Audrey? Do I shout all the time?'

She was doing it now, but I'd become so accustomed to her loudness that I barely noticed anymore. Even so, I had to bite my lips to stifle a laugh.

'I wouldn't say *all* the time,' I said, 'just most of it. But how can Danny tell?'

She slumped and let out a sigh. 'He says he can feel the vibrations of my voice from all the way over there, can you believe that guy? He has a hide, considering my volume is his fault.'

With a grimace at my questioning look, she explained. 'When we were kids, Danny could hear faint words if we shouted with our lips pressed against his head. Right here – ' She tapped behind her ear. 'I guess the habit never left me.'

Danny slapped his palms and made another rapid sign.

Corey rolled her eyes. 'I *need* to play my music loud,' she argued, 'it helps me think. Anyway, there's no cause for you to be rude, you're signing way too fast, Audrey's struggling to keep up. Slow down for goodness sake.'

Danny looked over at me and signed, *Sorry.*

Okay, I gestured smoothly. I'd been practising that one in the mirror. It seemed a good all-rounder, a handy one to fall back on in moments of linguistic uncertainty. It was one of the few signs that now felt second-nature to me.

Danny's smile lingered a moment too long. There was a spark in his eyes that made me want to start fidgeting. How could anyone be that gorgeous? One side of his face was shadowed, while the other was burnished by the gold light of a lantern. I went to look away, but then he was signing again, this time with slow precision.

Her shouting doesn't bother you?

I gave him a lopsided grin. 'My old Aunt Morag was a shouter, on account of her dodgy hearing aid. I guess I'm used to it.'

Danny looked baffled, but Corey updated him with a series of swift gestures. When understanding came he snorted, the only vocal sound – other than his raspy, wheezy laugh – that I'd ever heard him make. He was signing again, grinning. Dimples appeared, and his eyes glinted. I found myself captivated by the sight of his face, his gesturing hands forgotten.

Corey launched into another story, something about Danny and Tony finding a haunted cottage.

'It was a hut built by the original settlers,' she explained for my benefit, 'yonks ago, 1870s I think. A pretty rugged old outlook hidden away in the bush up there near the national park boundary. Anyway, the boys used to sneak up there sometimes and hide out, and one day Danny came home white-faced, sick with fright. He said that he and Tony had seen a woman's ghost – '

I was interested in hearing the tale, as it provided another glimpse into Tony's childhood. But the sight of Danny spellbound by his sister's story, his eyes intense and his mouth so serious, combined with the fluttering gold lantern light on his perfect features . . . and somehow my thoughts were straying again. Back to my college days, and my deaf roommate Rhonda. Near the end of first term she'd snared herself a boyfriend, I recalled. He seemed nice, a good-looking hippyish graduate. I was pleased for her . . . until the boyfriend started staying over. Unable to hear herself, unaware that her ecstatic cries must echo throughout the entire house, Rhonda hadn't been bothered by the thin walls. I, on the other hand, had cursed them. In the adjoining bedroom, I'd been forced to smother my head under the pillow, equally appalled and awestruck by the noise emanating from the room next door.

Danny was slumped forward watching his sister, his hands clasped between his knees. The semi-gloom seemed to exaggerate that rumpled, half-wild look he had about him. Maybe it was the windswept hair, or the brooding mouth that could at any moment flash a killer smile. Maybe it was the fact that he never spoke, that my conversations with him always left me feeling out of my depth. Or maybe it was just that in the five years since Tony left, I'd had so little to do with men – and certainly none as dangerously fascinating as Danny Weingarten.

My traitorous thoughts rushed back to the hay barn, but this time it was *me* there with him – me brushing straw off his arms, his broad back; me reaching up to smooth my fingers over that untameable hair –

Of course, Danny picked that exact moment to look at me.

I felt the heat rush to my cheeks and pretended interest in the label of my beer bottle, which I'd already half shredded off, meanwhile thinking how lucky it was that the verandah was so dark, and that the lanterns cast such patchy light . . .

When his attention drifted back to his sister, I looked away across the garden. The sun was plunging lower, deepening the eastern horizon to indigo, painting it pink in the west. The hills were turning from purple-grey to deep rose, a scene straight from one of Tony's watercolours.

Out of the blue, Corey remembered an urgent phone call she had to make, which I suspected was a ploy to leave me and Danny alone. As her voice drifted from the kitchen, Danny's green gaze remained on my face – as though observing someone without comment was the most natural thing in the world.

At first, it unnerved me. I shredded the label off my beer bottle while I ran through possible conversation starters: Had Thornwood changed much since he was here as a kid? Had he and Tony spent much time swimming in the creek? Did he ever get the urge to pursue a career as a city vet? It all sounded so trite, so far removed from what I truly wanted to ask: Are you and Nancy an item? Why won't you speak? Are you really the enigma you appear to be? I clamped my teeth together, then tried on a smile. When that didn't fit, I simply stared back at him.

He didn't seem embarrassed or bothered by our silence. I imagined he was used to it; for him, the world was always silent. I remembered what he'd said in the church yesterday, about not all silence being equal. I was beginning to understand. A lull hung between us now, devoid of talk, empty of conversation, punctuated by the chirp of cicadas and the pop of beetles against Bronwyn's paper lanterns, by Corey's muffled phone talk. And yet my awareness of him was acute, making it impossible for me to turn my attention elsewhere.

His hands began to move. *Can you hear the girls?*

I nodded, pointing in the direction of the jacaranda. I resorted to finger-spelling, stumbling on Bronwyn's name, forgetting the crosshatched fingers of the W, making a botch of it.

Bronwyn's . . . secret place.

Danny nodded. *Thornwood's full of them.*

My fingers tangled over themselves. *Easy to get lost.*

You like it here?

This brought a genuine smile. 'Love it,' I said, pulsing my fingers outwards from my heart. I drew my hand up from belly to chest, then made a diving motion with my fingers. 'It feels like home.'

His gaze left my lips and he smiled into my eyes.

Do you have a secret place?

Maybe it was the beer I'd consumed, or perhaps the afterglow of all those chocolates. Or the heat, or vague exhaustion after a long emotional day, or even the unaccustomed pleasure of having company. Whatever the reason, I found myself getting to my feet, beckoning Danny to follow. We went down the stairs, through the jungle of hydrangeas and along the path that led into the front garden. The Millers had done a beautiful job. In the dim light, the grass was a green carpet. The trees had been shorn of their wayward limbs and now stood in the shadows, their fallen leaves whispering under our feet as we passed.

When we reached the rose arbour, I turned to Danny.

'Not all that secret . . . but easily my favourite.'

He frowned as he looked around, no doubt taking in the tangled mess of leafless branches and gnarled trunks, the half-rotted flower brackets and desiccated rosehips. He ambled over to the bench inside the arbour and sat heavily. Reaching up, he snapped a hip from an overhanging bracket. Crumbling the dried pod in his fingers, he let it sift onto the ground, then looked across at me. I knew he was wondering – just as Hobe had wondered – why I didn't dig out all the old rose trees and plant something else here instead.

So I had my excuses ready: I'm waiting for winter before I replant; I'm still browsing bare-rooted stock catalogues; I've been distracted by other things, what with the move and everything . . .

But the question never came. Instead, Danny patted the bench beside him, motioning for me to sit down. Taking out his notebook, he scribbled a line, his words barely decipherable in the gloom.

I can see why you like it here.

'You can?'

Great view.

'Oh . . . sure.' I fumbled around a moment before perching on the furthest end of the bench, then followed his gaze across the valley.

The sun had swan-dived out of sight behind the faraway volcanic remnants. The sky was black, darkness had eaten up the garden. It was a glorious night, the air was restful and warm, tinged with the lingering after-scent of our feast. The girls were quieter now, but their disembodied voices floated in the stillness, a muffled counterpoint to the echo of Corey's erratic loudness somewhere in the house.

Fingers closed around my wrist. Danny playfully tugged until I gave in and inched closer to him. He opened my hand and began to trace his fingers across my palm. Goosebumps shot up my arm and into my scalp, I had tingles. Something radiated from him, not heat exactly, but a raw sort of energy that made me feel all weird and goosy, not quite myself.

He tapped his fingers on my wrist. I looked down.

Then understood what he was doing. He drew the letter 'Y', then an 'O'. I smiled. He'd abandoned his notebook in preference to my hand. I watched the words unfold.

You need new roses.

I laughed. Giggled, actually. Like a smitten fool. With every letter he drew, more tingles raced over my palm and up my forearm, shooting through my nervous system, turning my resistance to jelly. Butterfly wings fluttered up the back of my neck and into my hair. I tried to pull away, but Danny's strong fingers held me captive.

I'll plant them for you.

I shook my head. 'No.'

Yes, I'll even buy the roses. What's your favourite colour, pink?

With the drawn-out curl of his question mark, I had discovered a ridiculous thing about myself: I was ticklish.

'No,' I nearly yelled, yanking my hand out of his grasp. 'It's green.'

Danny sat back. He was looking into my face, his eyes shadowed by the darkness. Plucking another twig from the bracket near his head, he snapped it into bits, tossed the shreds onto the ground at his feet. He rubbed a circle on his chest and tapped his chin.

I like this secret place.

I smiled. I liked it too.

'Look at them,' Corey said later as we lingered on the front verandah, watching the girls dart about on the midnight grass below. 'Silly as a pair of wet hens.'

The potent cocktail of too much excitement, too many chocolates, and excessive giggling combined with the lateness of the hour had turned two mostly normal pre-teen girls into a couple of disorderly twits. Danny was trying to herd them towards his

Toyota to entrap Jade within and get home, but they kept shrieking and dashing off, garbling something about being chased by
a mob of ghosts.

'I should never have told them the story about Samuel's
haunted cottage,' Corey said regretfully. 'I seem to recall it had a
similar effect on me and Glenda.'

I watched the moonlit shapes rushing about on the lawn.
'Yeah, that old settlers' hut sounds pretty creepy.'

'I hope I haven't given Bronwyn nightmares.'

I looked at her. 'You said the same to me, the first time we met.'

She shrugged. 'I know, but Samuel's story was real. The cottage
isn't really haunted . . . although,' she added with a mischievous
lift of her eyebrows, 'it *does* exist . . . and if you ever find it, look
out . . .' She waggled her fingers and made a hooty ghost sound.

I gave her a playful shove with my shoulder, then turned my
focus back to the figures below. Danny had abandoned trying
to lure Jade into the car, no doubt deciding the only sensible
course of action was to wait until the girls ran out of steam. He
wandered a little way down the slope, standing with his back
to us, gazing into the gloomy trough of the valley, hands in
pockets, shoulders hunched as if against a chill.

Corey nudged me with her elbow. 'Thanks, kiddo.'

'What for?'

'We had fun. Even Danny enjoyed himself . . . for a change.'

I returned my attention to the man down at the edge of the
garden. 'How do you know?'

'Because he stayed. Usually he slumps off home in a mood
before the festivities have even begun.'

'Why?'

'Not everyone bothers with signing, Audrey. Not everyone
makes an effort. Many do, of course – but then Danny's not always
the easiest person to have around. He's hopeless with small talk,
says it's a waste of energy, then gets pissed off when people ignore
him. He's always been that way, even as a little boy.'

'I take it he wasn't born deaf?'

'No, he had meningitis when he was a baby – although I suspect he'd have been just as difficult with full hearing. The early days were the worst, of course, when he was learning to sign, and Mum and Dad were still trying to remodel their lives around how best to raise a deaf child. Things were slow to improve; he was always so frustrated when he couldn't make us understand. Trouble was, his tantrums weren't vocal, the way most kids' are. Things would start flying around the room . . . plates, spoons, shoes. Once – to Mum's eternal horror – he pitched the glass containing Grandad's false teeth at her.'

'He seems . . . I don't know, wary. Aloof. One minute we were laughing like loons, the next he'd gone all broody. I hope I didn't offend him in some way?'

'Hmmm.' Corey frowned at her brother's silhouette. 'There must be a storm coming.'

'Oh?'

'He can always tell, even when it's miles away. He can smell it or feel it, or – my personal theory – he senses the change in air pressure. Whatever it is, he's never wrong.'

'He doesn't cope with storms?'

Corey shook her head. 'Six years ago his wife Marci died in a storm. She ran out after her dog who'd taken fright, and a tree branch came down on her. It was one of those huge gnarly angophoras – in the days of logging, they were known as widow-makers. Corky wood, but heavy as all hell when it gets wet. Marci was deaf, too, so she didn't hear the branch crack loose. Danny found her pinned there, but by the time he'd rushed back to the house for the chainsaw and cut away the branch, she was gone. He blames himself, reckons he should have stopped her going after the dog, should have got the branch off her sooner. He's never forgiven himself.'

'It wasn't his fault.'

'No, it wasn't. But he's a stubborn son of a gun. We get a lot of storms this time of year, too. Poor old Danny's in for a rocky ride.'

'Why won't he speak?'

Corey stared down the dark slope at her brother. Her features softened. In the dusky glow of the verandah light, her eyes were no longer milk-chocolate. They'd lightened, turned warm and gold as honey.

'I suppose he does it to be contrary. And possibly to make a stand, in some warped way that only he can fathom. The one thing he hates more than being pigeonholed, is being considered weak. In a hearing world, being deaf is a disability, but Danny won't tolerate anyone implying he's disabled. If he can't speak as clearly as a fully-hearing person, then he'd rather not speak at all.'

'Wouldn't his life be easier if he tried?'

'Oh yes, but don't ever dream of telling him that. The last person who attempted to convince him to speak ended up with a broken nose.'

I considered the shadowy figure on the lawn with fresh eyes. 'I'll remember not to press him . . . Holy crap, it wasn't you, was it?'

'Lord, no! A teacher at school. The guy meant well, but Danny just lost his straw. He was about fifteen at the time – it was the year after Tony left and Danny wasn't coping. He insisted on attending the regular school, even though in those days Magpie Creek High wasn't suitably set up for deaf students. He'd been cautioned, told to return to the special school in Brisbane. They sent letters home, even threatened legal action – all to no avail. In the end one of Danny's teachers tried to reason with him, and offered to help him apply for a grant to get a hearing aid and learn speech . . . but Danny, in typical form, gave in to his primordial instincts and punched the poor guy in the face.'

'A bit extreme,' I observed.

Corey sighed. 'To him being deaf is nothing more than having green eyes when everyone else has blue. He refuses to acknowledge his limitations which, sadly, I must say, is not always to his advantage.'

'You have to admire him for standing on his convictions, though.'

'Hmmm . . .' she said doubtfully. 'But I expect when poor old Ross O'Malley was waiting at the surgery to have his nose re-set, he wasn't applauding my brother's commitment to his convictions. He probably wanted nothing more than to wring the little bastard's neck.'

I looked at Corey. 'Ross O'Malley? He teaches at the primary school now, doesn't he?'

'Yeah, I expect you've met him?'

'Not yet. He was away when Bronwyn started school. I've got an appointment for a catch-up on Monday.'

Corey snorted. 'Lucky you, something droll to look forward to. I must say, though, I've got fond memories of Ross. Twenty-odd years ago he taught me and Glenda at Magpie Creek High. Tony too.'

Glenda's Ross, I realised. 'What's he like?'

Corey jangled her car keys from her back pocket. 'Oh, a bit of an oddball, but nice enough. Somewhat haunted, I suppose.'

'Haunted?'

She studied her keys, weighed them in her hand, then looked at me. 'Not long after Glenda died, Ross left the school. We thought he'd had a transfer, but then a year later he was back. I couldn't help wondering if Glenda's death affected him more than he let on. She'd had a crush on him for ages. I was horribly jealous, I hated anyone who took Glenda's focus away from me. But after Ross came back the following year he was changed. Less confident, almost nervy. As though he'd aged into an old man. Later I heard that the night Glenda died, Ross's wife had a miscarriage and soon after that, his marriage ended. No wonder the poor guy had seemed so defeated.'

'You think something happened between him and Glenda?'

Corey let her gaze drift away, giving her attention to the dark valley. 'I don't know. Glenda and I had a sort of falling out, we didn't speak much in the months before her death. It's my greatest regret,' she added in an quiet voice. Then she shook herself and gave a husky laugh. 'I can't imagine that anything happened between them. Ross was her first real love – sadly, her only one. He used to be considered quite a dish, way back in the day, although to see him now you'd never believe – '

Whatever she'd been about to say was cut off mid-breath by the abrupt honking of a car horn. Down on the dark verge, the Toyota's headlights flashed. Then it rolled away along the service road, soon engulfed by the black trees. An instant later Bronwyn pounded up the stairs, her cheeks glowing crimson against the pallor of her face.

'Mum, Jade's going to the school camp next Friday, too. I can't wait!'

'Goodnight!' Corey bellowed from halfway along the path. 'See you midweek, if not sooner.'

Before I could reply to either of them, Bronwyn had escaped past me into the house, and Corey was clambering into her Merc, honking the horn as her brother had done, then roaring away along the access road.

I watched her headlights press through the morass of shadows, visible one moment, swallowed the next by the impenetrable black moat of bushland that enclosed Thornwood and safeguarded it from the outside world. I stood in the silence, letting the echoes of the evening float back: the conversations, the warmth, the outbreaks of hilarity. Even the sombre tone it had ended on.

After the chaos of my nomadic life with Aunt Morag, I'd come to crave stability. And yet I'd always been drawn to people who were edgy and unpredictable. Artists, musicians, poets. Outsiders who were shadowed by a darkness that was indefinable . . . yet strangely alluring.

Like Tony. Except that he'd been the best of both worlds – or so I'd first thought. Level-headed and practical. An inspiring companion, a considerate lover. Organised and ambitious, in control of his world. And yet the moment I scratched the surface a very different sort of man emerged: prickly and secretive, plagued by nightmares and long bouts of silence. In the end the chasm between us had proved too vast.

After he left, I consoled myself that inexperience had caused me to overlook the obvious: Tony was an artist, and by his very nature he was unpredictable. I'd made an error of judgement . . . next time I'd be more careful.

Only there hadn't been a next time. I'd been alone for five years, without so much as a glimmer of interest from the male species. In that time, I'd formulated and honed a vision of my ideal man: A quiet accountant-type without the merest hint of artistic ability. Trustworthy, reliable . . . perhaps even a tiny bit boring. For surely that was better than a man who promised to be there forever, and then ran off and married someone else?

I recalled the image of Danny Weingarten's face in the lantern light. His handsome features burnished gold, his gorgeous green eyes, his lingering smile. I remembered the spellbound way he'd watched his sister relate a tale from their childhood; and then the way he'd studied me as though trying to fathom what went on under my skin. I recalled the question mark that had given me tingles in the rose arbour, and the tug of desire that had woven its forbidden magic around my heart.

I sighed and turned away, eager to be back inside.

It had taken me a long time to find myself after Tony walked out.

However tempting it might be to stray from the path in search of chaos and excitement, I had no intention of ever getting lost again.

15

After they'd gone, I did a quick clean-up. Nick Cave crooned in the background, his beautiful *Nocturama* lulling me into a reflective mood. I did the dishes and then, still basking in the afterglow of the evening, filled a saucepan with water and set it on the stove to boil.

Soon, wafts of steam were dampening the air. The final leaves of Glenda's diary took longer to peel apart than the earlier ones. Starting at the back cover, I worked my way to the centre of the book. I was disappointed to find that most of the remaining pages were blank. Most . . . but not all. With luck, there'd be an entry that related the outcome of Cleve's violent attack on Hobe Miller.

As I crept along the hall past Bronwyn's room, I paused to listen. All was silent. I knew she wasn't sleeping, she'd still be too manic. I heard the rattle of a page and guessed she was immersed in a book.

On silent cat-feet I hurried down the hall to my bedroom, eager to catch up on a little reading of my own.

Saturday, 11 October 1986
One week since Dad's attack on Mr Miller. Dad's been charged with assault. His court hearing comes up in three weeks. He

keeps reassuring us he'll just get a fine . . . but I can't see how you can attack and hurt someone with a knife, and not go to jail. I'm scared. Scared for Dad . . . and, I'm ashamed to say, a bit scared OF him now. He's changed since that day. Become distant, somehow. I think maybe he's scared too.

Nearly five weeks since my fight with Corey. She's still not talking to me. What started as a stupid misunderstanding has now ballooned into an awkward mess, each of us too proud to admit we were both wrong. I suppose the kiss wasn't all that bad. If I'd known I was going to lose her over it I'd have bloody well kissed her back.

It's her birthday next Sunday. I've gotten her a book, one we both loved as little kids, *The Magic Pudding* by Norman Lindsay. Daggy, I know, and I probably won't get the chance to give it to her . . . but I so wanted to see her face light up and hear her laugh again, and I miss that silly snort she does that always cracks me up. I wrapped up the book and wrote a card, but I guess now it'll just languish away in my bottom drawer forever. Sigh.

Sunday, 12 October 1986

This morning I went to Grandfather's, dunno why, just moped along the trail in that direction, mulling things over, trying not to cry as I worried about Dad and what he'd done to Mr Miller.

The wildflowers are beginning to bloom. Tony'll be up there soon, sketching and painting — though he hasn't done much artwork since Dad took us to the Millers'. He escapes from the house more often than usual, but I know it isn't to draw or paint. He was friendly with the Millers, and I don't reckon he'll ever forgive Dad for what he did.

It was a scorcher of a day so I stopped at the gully for a drink of creek water. By the time I got to the hollow tree at the edge of Grandfather's garden, the sun was blazing and I started wishing I'd stayed at home. I had a headache from crying, and it depressed me to see Grandfather's garden so neglected and overgrown.

I was pondering whether or not to turn back, when I saw someone up ahead.

A man. He was carrying something in his hand. A fold of paper, it looked like. Too late I recognised him. My stomach dropped, there was no time to escape into the bushes and hide. I froze in my tracks. He'd seen me.

'Glenda – ?' Mr Miller's voice was ragged as a crow's. 'I'm sorry, lass . . . so terribly sorry. My brother told me you and Tony saw what happened – '

He was babbling like an insane person, but that wasn't what scared me. His head was bandaged, the strip of gauze twisted skew-whiff over his eye. The dressing was stained with dry blood, pink in patches, sunken over his socket. His face was pale and shiny with sweat, his whiskers stark white, his hands trembling. He looked wasted, barely human, more like a zombie than a man.

'Give this to your mother, will you – ?' He flapped his bit of paper, urging me to take it. 'Just a note to let her know I'm all right. Will you give it to her, lass?'

I cringed away. He didn't look all right. His voice trembled even worse than his hands, and he smelled of Dettol and fire-smoke, maybe a bit sweaty. He was acting all doddery and frail, no doubt on account of his injury.

The injury inflicted by my father.

I took a shuffling half-step back, and when I realised he wasn't going to follow me, I turned tail and ran. All the way home, gasping for air as though my lungs had shrunk to the size of peanuts. I couldn't breathe, couldn't let myself think. It was only when I reached the safety of the paddock next to our house that I allowed a couple of hot tears to splash over my lashes and down my cheeks.

I stumbled inside. Luckily no one was home – Dad gone fishing, Mum rostered at the hospital, Tony . . . God knows where.

I chucked my clothes in the hamper even though they weren't dirty, and got in my pyjamas, crawled into bed and pulled up the covers. The heat was wretched, but I didn't care. Better to sweat it out in bed, burn my tears into the pillow, pretend I'd come down with something contagious – anything was better than letting myself think.

I kept seeing him, though – his pasty white face, his shaky hands. His hair standing on end like the hair of a crazy person. One eye blue as a shard of sky, the other hidden behind a pink-stained bandage.

Burying my head under the pillow, I shut my eyes. Something was very wrong. Mr Miller had always been kind to me and Tony, back in the early days when we used to take the chutney. What had he done to make Dad hate him? Why had he been so upset about us seeing the attack . . . and why had he written a note to Mum to say he was all right?

The note.

I sat up. Looked around for a hanky, then wiped my nose on my sleeve. Thinking back to the day of the attack, I remembered how Dad had been yelling at Mum, waving around a sheet of paper. Then out in the yard he'd shown the paper to Tony: 'Did you deliver this for your mother?'

In all the fuss, I'd forgotten – but the memory crashed back to me now. Mum had given an envelope to Tony the day I'd been spying on him from the verandah. An envelope and – I'm pretty sure – she'd given him some money too. Inside the envelope was a letter . . . a letter which had somehow found its way to Dad.

A strong gut feeling came over me. If I could find that letter, the one that'd made Dad so upset, then I knew it'd explain why Dad had gone ape-shit and attacked Mr Miller.

Of course, Dad might have burnt the letter, or thrown it away – but I didn't think so. He's a hoarder, a real squirrel when it comes to mementoes or keepsakes, his little bits of evidence from the past. He's got boxes and jars and tins of things stashed all around the shed: rusty bolts, broken bits of machinery he was still getting around to fixing, old bike wheels, a collection of ancient Coke bottles. Mouldy stamp albums that had belonged to Grandpa Klaus, packets of seed, coins and paper notes from before the war.

If Dad had hidden that letter, then I had a pretty good idea where it might be.

'Mum – ?'

I jerked upright. The diary toppled from my lap and thumped onto the floorboards. Bronwyn was peering through the crack in my bedroom door, pyjama-clad and rumpled, sleepy-eyed. Her eyes sharpened, however, as they focused on what I'd dropped.

She gave me a questioning look, then said, 'It's late. I saw your light on, I wondered what you were doing.'

'Just revising my sign language lessons.' Retrieving Glenda's diary from the floor, I tossed it onto the bed among the jumble of Auslan manuals. 'Off to bed now, are you?'

She scowled, her gaze darting past me to the pile. 'I thought you said it was boring?'

'What? Oh, you mean this?' I laid my hand on the diary's buckled cover, ashamed when the first thought that came to mind was another lie. I shrugged it off, groping at least for a fragment of truth. 'I guess I got hooked, after all.'

'Did you manage to find out who it belonged to?'

Dragging in a breath, I looked my daughter in the eyes and said, 'Still working on that one.' Yawning, I tucked my legs back under the covers, settled the sheet around me, and relegated the pile of books to the bedside. 'Well, goodnight then,' I hinted. Reaching for the lamp, I flicked it off and plunged the room into darkness.

The moment the door clicked shut, I swung out of bed again and waited, my ears pricked. Faint footsteps padded down the hallway, and I heard Bronwyn's door rattle. I counted to twenty. Then, grabbing the diary from the bedside, I found my way across the dark room, slipped silently out the door, down the hall, and into the secluded privacy of my studio.

4 p.m. Friday, 17 October 1986
God, oh God, I wish I'd never looked.

At lunchtime, I told Mr Abbott I felt sick with period pain and he let me go home. I knew there'd be no one here. Dad's in Brisbane for work, and Mum's doing the late shift at the hospital, Tony's off somewhere. Perfect, I thought. Grabbing Dad's spare key from the windowsill, I let myself into the shed. It didn't take me long to find the letter. It was in a big old tin, all crumpled up and torn to bits . . . but I didn't even bother reading it.

Not after I'd seen the bundle.

It was a fat wad of envelopes with old-fashioned stamps, tied with ribbon. I took them back to my room and spent a couple of hours reading and re-reading them. And now I don't know what to do.

I have to talk to someone. Corey, maybe. We're supposed to be fighting, but I need her right now. This is bigger than a stupid fight between friends. Bigger than pride. All I need to do is say I'm sorry and that I love her and I want to be friends with her again. She'll understand, she's good like that. I'll ring her now . . . Just as soon as my heart stops crashing about and I can gather my wits to speak.

Then again, maybe I should tell someone higher up the chain, like a teacher. Maybe Ross? Yeah, Ross'll know what do to. Afterwards I'll go to Corey's and see if I can stay with her for a while. Even just the weekend. I can't face anyone here, not now.

At least, not Dad. And especially not Mum.

God. God. I wish I'd never looked.

6 p.m. Friday, 17 October 1986

I was shaking like a leaf when I rang Ross. I told him it was urgent, and he said he'd come and pick me up. There was thunder in the distance, and the first few sprinkles of rain on the roof. All I wanted to do was climb into Ross's big warm station wagon and try to feel safe again. But just before we said goodbye, I heard a car pull into the drive.

Since Mum was doing the late shift and wouldn't be home 'til after eleven, I knew it must be Dad. He'd freak if Ross showed up here, and I knew he'd never let me get into the car with him, regardless of Ross being my teacher. Besides, the last person I wanted to see right now was Dad. So I told Ross I'd meet him at Grandfather's house, where we could talk in private. Ross said he could be there in an hour and a half, which seemed like an eternity away, but then he insisted he'd drive me to Corey's afterwards, which made me feel better.

So I packed my bag, luckily remembering Corey's present at the last minute, and left a note on my pillow for Mum, saying I'd ring her once I got to the Weingartens'. Then I climbed out my bedroom window and raced up the hill towards Grandfather's.

Right now I'm huddled inside the hollow tree. The rain set in twenty minutes after I left home, dammit. A sprinkle at first, but by the time I got to the edge of Grandfather's garden it was bucketing down and I had to take shelter inside the burnt-out beech. I'm drenched, and the tree reeks – ancient charcoal and possum poo – but it's better than drowning in the deluge outside . . . or worse, sliding arse-over-turkey down the muddy slope.

Now I'm sitting here in the dark, just my little torch beam to write by. The bundle of letters is zipped inside my windcheater pocket. It doesn't weigh much but somehow it feels like a brick. My thoughts about those letters are a muddled mess, I can't even write about them. Every time I go there, my mind shuts down. Not true, it says. Just not true.

The wind is flying through the trees, making the leaves hiss and the branches groan. Half an hour's gone by but the rain isn't slowing. I've still got time to meet Ross. It took five minutes to pack, forty to get here – so I guess he won't show for another fifteen, providing he's on time. I should just brave the rain and run down the hill to Grandfather's house now, but there's no electricity and the place is creepy when the shadows come out. I'm freaked out enough after what I read in the letters.

It's silly, but I keep remembering something Corey once told me, about that old cabin up in the hills on the park border. It's a spoogly old place, I've only been there a handful of times 'cos it gives me the willies. Tony and Danny swear it's haunted. Doesn't seem to worry them, though – they're up there all the time when the weather's dry, doing whatever it is that boys do in the bush, pretending to be bushrangers or whatever.

Anyhow, one day Corey told me she dreamed about the old cabin. 'I was standing in the doorway,' she said in a whispery voice, 'looking inside. It was dark and someone was in there. I wanted to run away but was too scared to move. The cabin was dark, but over by the window stood a woman. The moonlight fell on her and I saw she was smeared all over in blood and could tell she was dead. But here's the worst part. She must've sensed I was there because she looked over her shoulder and stared right at me. I woke up screaming.'

'You baby,' I told her, rubbing my arms to chase the creeps.

'But Glenny,' she'd whispered. 'This woman . . . she had your face.'

Shit, what a drongo. It still scares the daylights outta me. I shouldn't have written it down. That's the one thing I worry about with writing stories – all those twists and turns in the tale, some of them scary, some sad – how does a writer avoid attracting that stuff into her own life? Ross says writers – artists and musicians too – are protected by their muse, but I'm not so sure. I once wrote a story about a girl whose mother died, and soon afterwards Mum went to bed for a week and refused to get up. I was so scared, I thought she was going to die. Worse, I convinced myself that because of my story, I'd killed her. And then one day she just got up, had a bath and washed her hair, then carried on as if nothing had happened. But it made me wonder – just how much power do words have?

I wish I had that power now, I'd make the rotten rain stop this instant. I just poked my head out. The landscape is lost behind a watery curtain, the trees are dark blurs, hazy as ghosts . . .

Damn. Ghosts again. I'd forgotten how spooky Grandfather's place can be at night. No one ever comes here except me and Tony . . . and just that once, Mr Miller. He looked a bit like a ghost that day with his crazy white hair, and eye bandaged and blotched with blood like something out of a horror movie –

Shit. I have to stop scaring myself. I need to wee again, and now I'm all nervy and jumping at shadows. Hey, the rain's stopped roaring on the leaves, it must be letting up. Just checked my watch, I've still got a couple of minutes to run down the hill and meet Ross –

God, who's that? Someone's calling my name.

It must be Ross, got here early and come looking for me.

Hang on, I'd better go and see.

That's where it ended. I flipped through the diary, causing a few careless rips in my eagerness to find just one more entry – a paragraph, a single sentence, anything. But the remaining pages were blank.

For a long while I huddled in my desk lamp's bubble of light, surrounded by darkness. My thoughts whirled like moths in a windstorm, battered this way and that by the fierce gale of my growing unease.

I realised I'd just read the diary entry Glenda had written the night she died. October 1986, directly before Corey's sixteenth birthday. I recalled something else Corey had told me, about Glenda leaving home because of her parents' row. Only there'd been no row. Glenda had come home early from school that day and found a bundle of letters in her father's shed. Letters with old stamps, tied with ribbon. Letters whose content had disturbed her.

Love letters, perhaps. From Hobe Miller to her mother?

By her diary entries, I'd surmised that Glenda had been closer to her father. I could understand how finding evidence of her mother's betrayal of him had driven Glenda to seek support from a trusted teacher. She'd telephoned Ross, left a note for her mother, and escaped out her bedroom window.

And then the storm. The rain.

The hollow tree.

God, who's that?

The following day, Luella had discovered her daughter's body in the gully, almost a mile from the tree. Glenda had died after an apparent rockslide sent her plunging down the steep gully wall to the rocks below. An accident. A tragedy. Case closed.

And yet . . .

Less than a week ago, Bronwyn had found Glenda's haver-sack hidden in the tree where Glenda had sheltered that night. Had Glenda's meeting with Ross resolved her fears about the letters she'd found? Had she changed her mind about going to Corey's, and headed home instead? If so, then why had she left her belongings hidden in the tree – her clothes and makeup, her hairbrush; the tin box that held her treasured diary?

I nibbled a ragged thumb nail. Again I had the feeling that a breach existed, a gap between the facts and my understanding of them. I knew I was overlooking something, missing a vital link . . . but whichever way I turned, the truth shifted, changed shape, morphed into something darker and more worrying.

A picture was forming. One I didn't much like.

An accident that might not have been accidental.

A death that wasn't what it seemed.

Then, another image broke into my mind's eye. A tall scare-crow of a man balanced on the ladder-like branches of the hollow beech tree in the clearing. His arm sunk to the elbow in a fissure at the tree's fork, searching for something that had lain hidden in the dark cavity for twenty years.

16

'Mum, did you realise there's a type of wasp that preys on cicadas?'

The morning air was cool and damp. It was eight o'clock and I'd just stepped out of the shower. Still in my robe, I made a beeline for the coffeepot. Bronwyn was already at the table, a plate of toast and jam within easy reach as she pored over a battered library book.

Scooping fresh grounds into the filter, I set the pot on the stove to boil. 'I expect I'm about to.'

Bronwyn bit into her toast, chewed and swallowed, her eyes never leaving the page. 'It's called a cicada-hunter, and it flies up into the treetops and stings the cicada to stun it. When the cicada falls to the ground, the wasp mounts it and rides along on it, sort of pushes it ahead with its hind legs, sometimes as far as a hundred metres!'

'Fascinating.'

'The best part is when the wasp drags the cicada down into its burrow and files it in a shelf with a whole bunch of other numb cicadas, then lays an egg right inside its paralysed body. Later, when the egg hatches, the baby wasp grub has a ready-made food source. Talk about gross,' she added raptly.

I blinked through the window, trying without much success to banish the vision of a helpless creature trapped in some ghastly hole, awaiting its fate as grub-food.

'Thanks for sharing that,' I muttered, 'it's really made my day.'

Bronwyn wasn't listening. Her head was bowed back over her book as she nibbled a toast corner, shaking her head in private marvelment. 'I can't wait to tell Jade.'

I hovered at the window while my coffee brewed. I'd had little sleep after reading Glenda's final entry, haunted by why she'd abandoned her belongings in the hollow tree. And by why, all these years later, Hobe Miller had gone in search of them.

There was one person who might know.

'So how are you liking your new teacher?' I asked Bronwyn. 'Mr O'Malley, isn't it?'

I'd been expecting her usual preoccupied monosyllable in response, so was surprised when her head jerked up.

'He's a creep,' she said darkly.

My brow twitched, but I knew better than to probe. The moment she detected the merest hint of curiosity she'd clam up and any useful snippets would be sucked into the black hole of info that was too good to be given out for free. So I poured coffee, feigned absorption in the newspaper, then said in a bored tone, 'That bad, is he?'

'Oh Mum, he's a total sicko. Jade hates him as well; she says he picks on me, and it's true. He's always asking me dumb questions, always staring. And he's coming to the school camp next week, worse luck.' Flipping the library book shut, she scrambled from her chair and delivered her plate to the sink. 'Why are you so interested, anyway?'

'I've got a meeting with him tomorrow afternoon.'

'Great,' she said bleakly, tucking her book under her arm and heading for the door. 'Might as well prepare yourself to be depressed.'

'He can't be that bad, Bron,' I reasoned. 'Corey mentioned him last night. He was her teacher when she was at school. He taught your father as well.'

Bronwyn looked back, surprised. 'He taught Dad?'

'And your Aunty Glenda. That's why he stares, because you look like her.' The noisy rumble of a car motor cut into our conversation. Bronwyn and I exchanged a look, then rushed into the lounge and peered through the venetians. A blur of white was parked behind a thick bottlebrush, but there was no other sign of our unannounced caller.

We both startled as footsteps thumped up our back stairs and along the verandah. The sound magnetised us to the kitchen window like a pair of iron filings, but our visitor had ducked out of sight into the alcove that sheltered the back door. There was a knock, and Bronwyn and I made a mad dash to see who it could be.

Hobe Miller beamed from the other side of the screen door. He was freshly shaved, his hair combed, and there was new electrical tape covering the lens of his glasses. While his shirt was still ragged, it was laundered and absurdly wrinkle-free, as though he'd spent the morning grappling with an iron. He was carrying a battered cardboard box.

'Young Bronwyn in?' he asked without preamble. 'I've got something to show her.'

Bronwyn elbowed me in the ribs and peered over my shoulder. 'Who is it?'

Hobe's face lit up. His eye glittered like a blue diamond. 'Hello there, young miss. Ever seen a boobook chick up close?'

The elbow dug into my ribs again, and this time Bronwyn managed to squeeze past. Shoving open the flywire door, she burst onto the verandah and stood looking up at Hobe, hands on her hips as she studied his clean but shabby attire, his taped-over lens, his wide grin, and the wispy skeins of hair that had escaped the smear of Brylcreem he'd applied and were now wafting greasily about his ears.

To my astonishment, she tipped her head to one side and offered her own hesitant smile. 'What's a boobook?'

Hobe made a sound – midway between a chuckle and a sigh of pleasure – and set the box on the decking. Like a magician unveiling a trick, he unfolded a cardboard flap for Bronwyn to peer in. Looking up at us from the centre of a loosely coiled towel was a disgruntled little powder-puff of a bird with huge gold eyes and brown and buff feathers.

'Cute little fella, isn't he?' Hobe said. 'He fell out of your fig tree a few days ago. I've been keeping an eye on him, got young Danny Weingarten to check him out for breakages. The little guy got a good report, so I thought it was about time I put him back in his nest. You interested in giving me a hand?'

Bronwyn tore her attention from the baby owl and twisted around to look up at me. 'Can I, Mum?'

I dug my hands deeper into the pockets of my robe. I hadn't yet made up my mind about Hobe. Outwardly he seemed kind, perhaps even someone I might have liked having around occasionally . . . but there was the question of his searching the tree hollow, and then his denial of having known the Jarmans when it was all too clear that he had.

Three sapphire-blue eyes were watching me – Hobe's wide with hopeful expectation, and my daughter's with a mix of curiosity and impatience.

Later, I would remember that exact moment. The sun blazed, but the air was still damp and delicate, touched by the sweet scent of blossoms and fresh-mown grass. A whip-bird was calling from the shadows of the garden, and a colony of bees hummed in the daisies. I was acutely alert, as though I'd consumed too much caffeine. Even so, I missed the one thing that should have been most obvious –

The moment passed. Hobe was still watching me. Bronwyn was already inching her way towards the stairs.

'Come on,' I told Hobe on a sigh, gesturing at the box, 'no point keeping a boobook from its nest.'

Was it relief I glimpsed on his face as he bent to retrieve the box, or had it been a trick of shadows cast by the leafy tapestry over our heads? Whatever it was, there was no mistaking the change in Hobe's attitude. He was suddenly chirpy; he stood taller and his face took on the aspect of a much younger man.

As I followed him along the verandah, I had a vision of him twenty years ago, face-to-face with Cleve Jarman. I could see him clearly – not the middle-aged man Glenda had known, but rather the older Hobe familiar to me now – pitiful in his shabby flannelette shirt and grubby workpants, the walking encyclopaedia who rescued fallen birds, the natural history expert who'd been pals with the local indigenous people. In my mind's eye he was kneeling in his front yard, hunched in shock and pain, blood spilling through his fingers as he clutched his face . . .

Pity pricked in my chest, a potent blend when combined with my current misgivings. I reminded myself of another Hobe – his arm sunk to the elbow in the old beech tree, seeking something that was no longer hidden there.

'That's why owls can fly silently,' Hobe was explaining to Bronwyn. 'Their wing feathers are very soft, almost furry because of the hairy little strands along the edges. Being silent gives them an advantage over their prey.' He placed the box with its precious cargo on the ground and retrieved a ladder from his ute.

Bronwyn stood nearby, hands on hips, as she gazed up at the fork between two boughs where Hobe had pointed out the nest hollow.

'What do they eat?'

Propping the ladder against the trunk, Hobe unfastened one of the callipers and lengthened the ladder's reach until the upper rungs rested on the tree's central fork.

'Well, the southern boobook owl – or mopoke, as they're sometimes called because of their distinctive call – fancy all manner of things to eat. Small mammals, like mice. Tiny birds, frogs and lizards, wee bats. And the usual bird-delicacies such as beetles and moths.'

Hobe made another trip to the ute and came back with a deep wicker picnic basket. The basket's interior was a hotchpotch of leaves and soft bark, feathery dross and twigs: a makeshift nest. He placed the basket on the ground beside the cardboard box.

'Are you ready?' he asked Bronwyn.

Bronwyn nodded and slid on the leather gloves Hobe had provided for her, then dropped to her knees beside the box. She opened up the top of the box and peered worriedly down at the little bird. 'He's huddling right in the corner, Mr Miller . . . he looks scared. Are you sure it's all right for me to touch him? Won't his mother reject him if he gets human scent on him?'

'Well, now.' Hobe tested the ladder's stability against the fig tree's fork, edged it nearer the trunk, then sidled over to join Bronwyn. Kneeling in the dirt beside her, he gave her an appraising smile. 'Birds are good mothers, she won't abandon him. She's probably been wondering where he got to. No doubt the old girl's hiding somewhere up in the leaf canopy watching us, keen as mustard to get her little fella back into the nest and give him a decent feed. Get ready now,' he added, giving Bronwyn a wink.

Bronwyn hesitated, but with an encouraging nod from Hobe, reached into the box. Her gloved fingers closed gently around the bird. She gasped. Her face was blotched pink, her eyes alight with awe.

'It tickles!' she said, glancing at Hobe. 'So soft, I can feel his little bones! What do I do now?'

Hobe held out the picnic basket with its improvised nest of leaves. 'Careful now, just lower him in. He'll scrabble around a bit at first, but then he'll settle.'

Despite her uncertainty, Bronwyn delivered the bird to the basket without mishap. Just as Hobe had said, the tiny owlet burrowed around for a moment, letting out a mournful chirr-chirr before tunnelling into the dross and settling to silence. Hobe beckoned me over, and the three of us peered down at the little owl.

Its fluffy feathers were buff-white with brown markings, its face described by a dark brown disc. Its golden eyes peered up at us, fierce for a creature so small.

'Good luck, little fella,' Bronwyn said, and we watched as Hobe climbed one-handed up the ladder, his free hand clutching the basket.

When he was close enough to the hollow fork, he propped the makeshift nest between his body and the trunk and extracted the tiny owl. I caught a glimpse of downy buff-white feathers as Hobe settled the bird into the hollow. He fussed a moment, transferring handfuls of leaves and twigs from the basket into the hollow, and then he was returning, his weathered old boots clunking down the rungs as he made his descent. When he reached the ground and found Bronwyn's eager face peering up at him, he beamed.

'Just as I thought . . . there were crow feathers in the nest. Rotten scavengers must have knocked our little friend out while his parents were off hunting. Anyhow, he's in good hands now. I saw his mother watching from a leafy bough. Once we depart, she'll fly down and give him a feed.'

Hobe peered up through the leaves, and Bronwyn followed suit.

Again I found myself studying the old handyman. I'd been right, he had made an effort today. Shaved, combed his hair, put on clean trousers, made a rudimentary attempt to shine his shoes. He was no male model, but it was the most presentable I'd ever seen him. Perhaps it was wash day, or he was on his way to town, but I couldn't help suspecting he'd made a special effort in anticipation of seeing Bronwyn.

'Come on, Bron,' I prompted, 'we'd better get a move on, you don't want to be late.'

Hobe's gaze captured Bronwyn's face, his eye sharp as a fragment of blue glass. He grinned. 'Off to church, are we?'

Bronwyn smoothed the crumbs of bark and leaf-litter from her jeans.

'I'm visiting my grandmother,' she told him proudly. 'My dad's mother, she's really nice. We met her yesterday, and had so much fun that she invited us back again today.'

While Bronwyn spoke, Hobe's face had frozen, then melted into a look that at first I couldn't read. Shadows flitted over him, disguising the true nature of his expression, but I'd have sworn that in the blue depths of his iris glowed something akin to hope.

Which made me wonder if he was still keen on Luella. Yes, I could see it in his sudden perkiness, in the warm flush that coloured his leathery cheeks. He must have loved her all this time ... but what had happened between them in the years since Cleve's disappearance? Why hadn't they reunited? Had Luella shunned Hobe, perhaps sensing that he might somehow be accountable for her daughter's fatal fall?

Hobe caught me studying him and had the grace to dip his head, reassemble his features, and attempt a watery smile. It failed dismally, more of a grimace really.

'Luella's well then, is she?' he asked.

'Very well,' Bronwyn chirped. 'Do you know her?'

'Ah ... I suppose you could say that we were once friends. Back in the old days,' he added with a sheepish look at me. 'She's a kind lady, your grandma. One in a million. Give her my regards when you see her ... will you do that, lass?'

'Sure will.'

I slid my arm around Bronwyn's shoulder and nudged her in the direction of the house.

'Goodbye then, Hobe,' I said. 'Thanks for bringing the little owl home. Good of you to let us watch.'

Hobe hesitated, his hand raised, his finger extended as though to put forth a query, but he'd left his question too late. Without another word I steered Bronwyn out of the fig tree's deep shade, across the grass and up the slope, into the safety of the verandah's gloomy shadows.

'Mum – ?'

Bronwyn might have been only eleven, but she was observant, sensitive to fluctuations in the unpredictable climate of adult moods. 'What's the matter? Did I say something wrong?'

'It's nearly time to go,' I said, looking pointedly at my bare wrist. 'You're not visiting your grandmother dressed like that, are you?'

My ploy worked. She glanced down and regarded her jeans with no small amount of apprehension, making a half-hearted attempt to brush off the remaining crumbs of bark.

'Of course not – you ironed my dress last night, remember? Besides, Grandy says it's important to look your best at all times.'

I lifted an eyebrow. 'Grandy?'

'She prefers it to Gran or Grandma . . . She says it's more friendly, and I agree.' She gave a prim little smile, then spun on her heel and vanished inside, letting the screen door slam behind her.

Down in the yard, Hobe's ute growled to life. The old vehicle made an unspeakable uproar as its assemblage of ancient parts coughed and gasped in unison. A jet of smoke burped from the tailpipe, then the car lurched forward and shot off with startling speed along the bumpy service road.

Between the three of us we managed to carry cheesecake and forks, a thermos of iced tea, cups and plates, a huge tartan rug and an armload of photo albums down Luella's back stairs and into the garden. We found a shady spot beneath the bunya pine, settled onto the soft carpet of pine needles, and Luella passed around serviettes.

The cake was divine, the tea refreshing, and the breeze smelled of roses and jasmine. Gruffy sprawled in a grassy patch of sunlight, his feet twitching in his sleep. Our peaceful morning tea had all the potential of becoming a memory that one day we'd all look back upon and smile . . . and yet, despite it being Sunday, despite the cloudless sky and warm perfumed breeze, my brain refused to relax.

All I could think about was what I'd read in Glenda's diary, about her final entry, how she'd climbed out her bedroom window to meet Ross, hoping he'd advise her about what she'd read in the letters she'd found.

Leaning back against the tree's rough trunk, I studied Luella's face, admiring her satiny skin and gentle smile and softly gathered hair – but also acknowledging that beneath the joy now shining from her eyes lurked a lifetime of sorrow. There was so much I wanted to ask her. What had been written in the letters Glenda found, why had they caused her such distress? Was it the shock of learning about Luella's affair with Hobe . . . or had the letters revealed secrets that were much darker? Perhaps if I knew those answers, then the other missing puzzle pieces regarding Glenda's fatal fall would slide into place too?

Bronwyn and her grandmother had their heads bent together, poring over more photographs.

'Here's that one I was telling you about, Grandy,' Bronwyn said, sliding a snapshot from the album balanced on her lap. 'The one of you at the clothesline with Aunty Glenda and Dad? See, you look different.'

Luella shifted her weight and took the photo, holding it aloft. 'Well, it was a long time ago . . . gosh, 1980, it says here on the back. I was younger then, dear. Thinner, too! Oh . . . look at them, Tony just a wee strap of a boy, he would have been eight when this was taken. And Glenda, a carefree girl of ten.'

Now might have been the time to steer the conversation in the direction I was most keen for it to go . . . but Luella's eyes were already brimming, and though she smiled to cover her emotion, there was a raw fragility about her that told me she was holding onto her sorrow by a thread. I remembered Corey's words: *Luella was always a timid sort of person, she had a rough trot as a kid, I don't think she'd be in any state of mind to cope.*

Luella tore her gaze off the photo and peered at Bronwyn.

'Your father loved to dash off by himself to sketch or paint,' she told her. 'He had such a flair for art. And Glenda, my dear Glenda – ' She looked back at the photo and her shoulders slumped. 'She wanted to be a writer, you know. Always making up stories, ever since she could talk . . . so clever. Pretty too, just like you, Bronwyn dear . . . but with a temper fierce enough to curl your hair – ' Luella let out a noise that was probably meant to be a chuckle, but it sounded more like a sob.

The sound of it galvanised me.

'Bron, honey, why don't you pack away the photos for a while. Have you told Grandy about your school camp?'

Bronwyn's face lit up and she abandoned her albums to launch into a monologue about how she and Jade and twenty other kids from her class were going camping for six days in Mount Barney National Park, and that she'd never been camping before but Jade had raved about how much fun it was, and now she couldn't wait . . .

Luella brushed at her cheek and then, as though sensing my attention, gave me a watery smile. It was barely more than a glance, a quick flicker of acknowledgement as if to say, *Isn't she adorable?*

Until that moment I'd been nursing a dull sort of envy at the firm bond Bronwyn had forged with her grandmother. The girl was happy – I could see it in her glowing eyes, hear it in the eager way she related school news to Luella with far more enthusiasm than she ever related anything to me.

But now, as I watched Luella beaming at my daughter with obvious pride and admiration, my resentment buckled. Aunt Morag used to say that people were so dazzled by the hardships they'd endured in life, that they forgot to consider their blessings. With a pang, I realised I'd become one of those people – looking for things gone wrong, forever brooding. All it took was a slight shift in perspective to see life through fresh, more appreciative eyes. I had my health, a job I loved, and now a permanent roof over my head. Most of all, I had my daughter . . . healthy, able-bodied. Alive.

And it was in that moment of disenchantment with myself that I determined to relax my stranglehold on things I couldn't control. I decided to practise going with the flow, to breathe deep and accept my daughter's relationship with her grandmother for the blessing it was. So I closed my eyes and sank back against the bunya pine's corrugated bark. The air was warm, the afternoon breeze sweetly fragrant. Pine needles, lemon tea, the faint apple tang of Bronwyn's just-washed hair. Cheesecake, sun-warmed grass. And roses.

I blinked, letting my gaze drift across the yard. There, a few feet away, climbing up the side of a trellis near the garden shed, was a rose bush. In the late January heat the few blooms were small and withered, but there was one rose lower down that caught my attention. Fleshy and so deeply blood-red it was almost black.

I got up and went over, crouched to breathe the flower's scent.

My heart flipped over.

I was no connoisseur of fragrance and I'd only ever smelled that particular perfume once before – but it was unmistakable. A sweet dark essence with a peppery hint of cinnamon.

'Lovely, aren't they?' Luella said. 'Are you fond of roses, dear?'

Turning, I saw that she sat alone on the tartan rug. Bronwyn had scampered off to inspect a statue half-hidden in a leafy corner, and I could hear her talking to Gruffy. I joined Luella, hoping I wasn't about to overstep the mark.

'I do like roses, though I'm not much of a gardener. Those are a distinctive variety, aren't they? Such a gorgeous perfume.'

'Yes.' A pause. 'The bush grew off a cutting taken from the arbour at Thornwood. Although the old tree has died now, such a shame,' she added. She looked away, seeking Bronwyn over by the hydrangeas, perhaps in a bid to remind herself that any discomfort she felt with me was worth enduring.

'I visited the Lutheran church the other day,' I said, testing the water, feeling my pulse kick up a notch. 'It's such a quaint old building, I thought I might take some photos . . .' I'd been about to spin a lie; I seemed to be getting rather good at doing that lately. But I caught myself in time. 'Actually, I was curious to see some of the old graves. There was one in particular that grabbed my attention, because it had been recently tended. And it had a vase of roses on it . . . in fact they were identical to yours.'

Luella must have heard something in my voice, because she looked at me and frowned. I sensed she was waiting for me to elaborate.

I sighed. 'It was your mother's grave, Luella. I'm sorry, but I was curious. Since I've been at Thornwood, I . . . well, I couldn't help wondering.'

She nodded, but seemed more puzzled than upset by my confession. Then, still frowning, she said, 'Who'd be tending her grave? Does the pastor employ someone now, a gardener? I wouldn't have thought they'd have the funds.'

'Oh, I thought . . .'

She looked at me, and understanding dawned in her eyes. 'You thought it was me?'

'Well, I . . . Yes.'

She slumped, her fleshy shoulders and arms caving in around her. 'Oh no, pet. I never go to the cemetery. Not to visit my mother, and I don't go to the Presbyterian to visit my daughter. They're sad places, graveyards, aren't they?'

Her simple comment tugged at me. Luella was a large woman, but at that moment she looked frail as a bird, sitting on the tartan rug, obviously uncomfortable with her legs tucked under her and her bulges straining against the floral fabric of her frock. I wanted to protect her, to soothe away her hurt and chase the pain of the past. Ridiculous, of course. How could anyone, let alone a virtual stranger, do that? Besides, I wasn't the type to go around doling out hugs.

'I'm afraid I've overwhelmed you again, Luella. I'm so sorry.'

She sighed. 'Don't mention it, Audrey love. It's not your fault. I expect you're feeling a bit overwhelmed yourself, getting tangled up in Tony's muddled family affairs.'

'Yeah,' I agreed, managing a feeble laugh. 'Just a bit.'

Luella smiled too. For the first time since we'd met, the warmth that she usually reserved for Bronwyn touched me. I dared to hope that this might be a sign that she was opening up, starting to trust me. Perhaps soon she might even be willing to talk more about her mother and Samuel.

'You know,' she began, and leaned a fraction closer, 'when I was Bronwyn's age – '

'Grandy!' Bronwyn sprang from the sunlight into the shade. 'Guess what?'

Luella looked around. She beamed up at Bronwyn and cooed, 'What's that, love?'

I breathed a private prayer that Bronwyn's interjection would be brief and that she'd dart off as quickly as she'd materialised, so Luella could then resume whatever it was she'd been about to disclose. But Bronwyn flopped onto the tartan rug and, grabbing a plate, scooped up a wedge of cheesecake no doubt to fortify herself, and then began.

'You'll never guess what I did this morning. I helped return a little boobook owl to its nest!'

'A boobook owl,' Luella marvelled. 'Goodness me! How did you manage that?'

My heart sank. This was going to be a train wreck. I tried to catch Bronwyn's attention, maybe distract her, but she was too intent on her grandmother, not even taking her eyes from Luella when she paused to gulp some lemonade. Then she was off.

'It had fallen out of the fig tree in our front yard last week, you see, and Mr Miller found it and took it over to Danny – that is, Jade's dad – to check no legs or anything were broken. Well, the little owl was fine, so this morning Mr Miller climbed our tree and set it back into its nest . . . and I helped him! The mother owl was watching from a nearby branch, and a few minutes after we pulled the ladder away she flew down to . . . to – ' She stopped.

Luella had gone pale. She was trying to act interested in what Bronwyn was telling her, but I could see the white strain around her eyes.

'Bron,' I said into the gap of silence, 'I think I've left my sunglasses in the car, honey, would you get them for me?'

She frowned. 'Mum, you had them in your hand when we arrived.'

I tossed her the keys. 'And check I left a window open, while you're there, otherwise we'll fry on the way home.'

She gave me a questioning look that said: Something's going on, you'll tell me later, right? I nodded at her silent request, not because I had any intention of filling her in, just to get rid of her. I waited until she'd vanished around the side of the house, before looking at Luella.

'Hobe's been to the house a few times,' I told her. 'He and his brother cleaned up the garden for me. He asked after you this morning, and said to give you his regards.'

'I see.'

Luella carved off a slice of cake. Her fingers didn't tremble, but there was a jerkiness to her movements, as though her gracefulness had come unstuck. She plopped the segment of cake onto my plate without asking, and cut another slice for herself. Spearing it with a fork, she lifted it to her lips. Chewed mechanically, swallowed.

'How is he?' she said stiffly.

'He's well.' This was ridiculous. 'Luella, are you all right?'

'Yes! Oh . . . not really.'

I sighed. 'We've done it again, haven't we?'

Luella toyed with her cake. 'It's to be expected, I suppose. It is overwhelming, I haven't had company in such a very long time. So many years have passed, and yet I find that the memories rush back faster and faster, and sometimes I can't control them. It's not your fault, Audrey. But you must forgive me. Seeing you and Bronwyn, as wonderful as it is . . . well, I suppose you've guessed that I'm not all that well equipped to deal with the excitement.'

'Under the circumstances,' I said quietly, 'I think you're doing a terrific job.'

She looked over at me, her eyes moist and wide. 'Did Tony tell you what happened between his father and Hobe Miller?'

'I know they had a falling out.'

She nodded. 'It happened a week or so before we lost Glenda. Cleve and I had a dreadful quarrel. He stormed off, took the kids somewhere in the car. It wasn't until much later that I learnt he'd gone to the Millers'.' She paused, staring at the crumbs on her plate as though hoping to find the right words among them. She sighed. 'There was a fight. Hobe was injured.'

'That's how he lost his eye?'

'Yes. Afterwards, Cleve confessed he'd had a turn of some sort, that he'd lost his head and wanted to punish me for our quarrel. The police were here, Cleve was charged, and the date for the court hearing set. Only Cleve never made it to the hearing, he disappeared the week before. He must have had another turn, because . . . well, I take it you know about his car being found in the dam?'

I nodded.

Luella's face was rumpled-looking, her cheeks pale. 'So now I can't help wondering if, after all these years, Hobe still bears a grudge against Cleve – and me – for what happened.'

Her mention of a grudge made me reflect again on Hobe's possible involvement in Glenda's accident. But I also remembered the glint of hopefulness Hobe had betrayed that morning. 'Luella, I'm sure he doesn't.'

She didn't appear to hear, captured as she was by some private thought. Bronwyn's voice drifted from the front yard as she called to Gruffy. In the stillness her voice was as eerie and disembodied as the call of a wood pigeon.

We left soon after.

As we stood in the front yard saying goodbye, Luella invited us back the following Saturday. Bronwyn regretfully reminded her that she'd be at school camp, but we could visit the weekend after, if that was all right?

Luella nodded, pleased . . . but I could still see the strain in her face and the tight way she held her shoulders. She gave Bronwyn a great big bear hug, then surprised me with a kiss on the cheek.

'Thank you,' she whispered, then before I could ask what she'd thanked me for, she had opened the gate and ushered us out onto verge where the Celica glimmered dark red in the sun.

As we drove away, Bronwyn was subdued.

'Mum,' she said as we turned the corner and left William Road behind us, 'Grandy's very lonely, isn't she?'

'I guess so, Bron.'

'It's a good thing she's got us then, isn't it?'

'It is good,' I agreed, keeping my smile bright.

But as we headed back towards Thornwood, a grim mood took hold.

There was a side to Luella that inspired in me a fierce sort of protectiveness, the sort I'd only ever felt for Bronwyn. And yet, she also represented the shadow-side of Tony's past, a past that Bronwyn and I had – until now – been excluded from. Perhaps my longing for a family and for a normal life for Bronwyn had clouded my judgement, made me leap in too hastily. Or perhaps I was a victim of my own curiosity. Whatever the reason, I felt way out of my depth.

Luella was the shadowy sun around which all the other mysterious planets revolved. Aylish and Samuel; Glenda, Tony, and Cleve. Even Hobe. She was at the heart of a family story that was becoming increasingly horrible . . . and which had started to feel more than I could bear. I'd wanted a safe haven, and believed I'd found it at Thornwood; but it was turning out to be a minefield of tragedy, deception and sorrow . . . and possibly even murder.

I looked at Bronwyn. Her face was glowing from the heat, a happy smile playing on her lips. Fear pricked along my spine. For the first time since we'd arrived, I wondered whether coming here had been such a great idea after all.

17

The following afternoon I arrived at the primary school for my two o'clock appointment with Ross O'Malley. The school was small, so the directions to his office were easy to follow: Through the quadrangle, up the stairs, then into a covered walkway. The receptionist told me I'd find Ross halfway along.

It was a pretty little school – picnic tables tucked under shady trees, areas of trimmed grass, colourful flower beds, quaint old weatherboard classrooms. When the walkway appeared, I ducked into its cool shadows and slowed my pace.

Glenda's final diary entry was still haunting me. Its conclusion felt all wrong, and no matter which way I looked at it, I couldn't get the facts to add up. The person who would know for sure, I reasoned, was Ross O'Malley. Had he resolved the issue of the letters, had Glenda felt better about them and decided to return home? Or had some other scenario unfolded that stormy night, a scenario that better explained why an experienced bushwalker like Glenda Jarman had fallen to her death?

'Hello there.'

A doorway had opened and a man stood there, eyeing me expectantly. He was big and pale, in his late forties with close-cropped hair and watery blue eyes.

'You must be Bronwyn Kepler's mum, Audrey isn't it? So glad you could make it, Ross O'Malley here, Bronwyn's teacher. Please come inside. You must be eager to know how Bronwyn's settling in – ?'

A fellow babbler, I realised, and smiled a little with relief as I followed him into his office. While I stood gazing about he continued to talk, explaining that Bronwyn's class was in the library right now, which appeared to be Bronwyn's favourite, and how well she was fitting in with the other students, and how pleased he was that I'd agreed to let her attend the school camp at the end of the week . . .

Glad to coast on the backdraught of his chatter, I took quick stock of the decor. A pair of mismatched chairs, a file cabinet and pot plant. A bare desk, just a computer and a jar of pencils, which made me wonder how on earth I managed to get anything done in my chaotic bomb-drop of a studio. I was about to take the chair Ross offered, when a flag of jewel-like colour snagged my eye.

I made a beeline for the far wall.

'Ah, yes,' Ross said, abandoning the thread of his monologue and joining me, 'this is the other reason I was so eager to meet with you. Wonderful, isn't it?'

It was a small watercolour, simply framed, depicting the delicate cup-like leaf of a pitcher plant. Its proud hood was a mass of translucent washes and crimson veins, convincingly lethal despite its light-handed rendering. It was eerily beautiful, as though the plant's subtle life-force had been trapped in the multi-hued pigment.

'It's Tony's,' I said, not bothering to read the scrawled signature at the base of the drawing. 'I've seen similar ones recently. Other pitcher plants, sundews, a couple of Venus flytraps. I never knew he was so keen on carnivorous plants – ' I bit my tongue, aware that I'd betrayed the extent of my ignorance about Tony, and in doing so, had perhaps also revealed my failings as a mother.

Ross shuffled nearer the painting and peered at it short-sightedly.

'I've always loved it,' he said. 'There was a time when Tony drew these plants obsessively – I found them scrawled in the margins of his textbooks, doodled on his class notes, even on essays he handed in – pencil, ink, watercolour . . . as though they were a mystery he was trying to solve. He knew all about them, too, where they originated from, why they'd adapted to eat insects, as well as how to propagate and care for them. He was a fount of knowledge, a highly intelligent boy – and in many ways a bit of an enigma.'

I looked at him. 'What do you mean, an enigma?'

Ross shrugged. 'Unpredictable, I suppose. One day he arrived at school and upended his desk, went through his books. The finches and gumnuts stayed, but every page with so much as a sundew tentacle or pitcher plant hood went into the bin in shreds. It was as though, overnight, his obsession for carnivorous plants had turned sour and he could no longer bear to look at them. This one here,' Ross gestured at the little watercolour, 'was one of the last ones he painted. He presented it to me after I'd taken him hunting the previous summer and taught him to shoot.'

'Hunting?' I stared at Ross, thinking I'd misheard him. Or that perhaps he'd confused Tony with another boy.

'I'm sorry,' Ross said quickly, 'I've rambled on, it's a loathsome habit of mine I'm afraid. You came here to find out about Bronwyn's progress, and I've bored you by wandering off along memory lane, I do apologise.'

He looked so sheepish, his brow knitted into an expression of worried concern, his beefy shoulders hunched to his ears, that I bit my lips – partly to restrain the new flood of questions that were clamouring to be asked, and partly to prevent a triumphant smile. Ross O'Malley seemed as eager to spill forth the past as I was to hear it. Perhaps, on his part, it was the result of too many years' silence – or the novelty of having a fresh audience. Either way, I felt a sudden rush of warmth for this awkward man. Ross was something of an enigma himself, a figment of Glenda's diary come to life. He was an unusual choice of paramour for a schoolgirl, yet I was beginning to see something of that deeply buried charm. He was also a potential wellspring of Jarman family history that I was powerfully keen to tap into.

'I'm interested in hearing about Tony,' I admitted. 'It just surprised me when you said you took him hunting. The Tony I knew hated firearms.'

'He was always a gentle boy,' Ross agreed. 'It must have been a horrible shock for you when he died, I am sorry.'

I nodded, curious about what he'd said before. 'Why do you think he tore up his pictures?'

'It was a mystery . . . though I suspect, as I do when a student displays sudden uncharacteristic behaviour, that there were upsets at home.' He looked at me. 'Tony had been a favourite of mine, I took him under my wing. I guess I saw something of myself in his studious nature. He was a troubled boy. I suppose he grew into a troubled man.'

'Troubled?'

'Oh, you know . . . artistic types always seem to have restless souls. That's what makes them so fascinating to the rest of us.'

'Ross, I hate to ask, but could there be any substance to the rumour that he was responsible for his sister's accident?'

Ross frowned. 'No, I'd wager my life on it. I do hope no one's been gossiping?'

I shook my head. 'I can't see him hurting anyone, least of all his own sister. But – and this'll sound awful – if he was driven to end his life because of guilt, because of remorse over something he did as a boy . . . well, somehow that would be easier for me to bear. If it wasn't remorse, then I have to wonder if his death was the result of faulty wiring in his brain.'

'And you're worried Bronwyn might have inherited similar tendencies?'

I nodded, grateful for his understanding.

Ross sighed. 'Audrey, we can't know what other factors were at work in Tony's life before he died. Depression, drug addiction. Or he may have been terminally ill and not wanted anyone to know. I think genetics are overrated – even if Tony was mentally ill, it doesn't mean that the illness will pass on to Bronwyn. Your daughter is an exceptionally well-balanced girl, Audrey. And don't forget, Tony was only one of her parents . . . I'm sure she's inherited many sound traits from you.'

A dubious assumption, I thought privately. But in truth I felt reassured, glad to have my mind eased of its fears about Bronwyn. Ross O'Malley's kindness, and his admission that Tony had once been a favourite, inspired a twinge of trust.

I found myself asking, 'You were fond of Glenda too, weren't you?'

Ross looked startled. 'Did Tony tell you that? Of course he did . . .' He blinked rapidly and wrung his hands together. 'Well now, Glenda was . . . she was one of my students, but we – I mean to say, there was never . . .'

He was a blusher, too; the telltale red dashes that crept across his cheeks marked him as a poor liar. He took out a large hand-kerchief, which I expected him to use to blow his nose. His face looked drawn, his eyes rimmed pink as though the effort of his attempted falsehood had diminished him. Instead, he used the hanky to dust along the top of Tony's picture frame and over the glass, giving it a shake before returning it to his pocket. Then, as though losing the inner battle with his conscience, he sighed.

'I *was* fond of Glenda Jarman. Nothing ever happened between us, you understand. She was just a kid of sixteen, more than a decade younger than I was at the time, but wiser than most people twice her age. My wife was a good, kind woman and I'd never have dreamt of betraying her . . . but Glenda fascinated me. We had so much in common, you see – we loved the same authors, were moved by the same ideas, shared a passion for stories and films and – '

He cut off, turning his gaze back to Tony's painting. 'That sounds awful, doesn't it? But I suppose I was one of those people who drifted along seeing everything in monochrome. A million grey shades of life, my life. Uniform and predictable. The only true point of departure from the tedium came from movies, or theatre . . . or things I read about in books. Adventures, family dramas. Thrillers, crime, romance. Opening the pages of a novel and vanishing into another world, or marvelling over other people's expression – Tony's wonderful paintings, for instance, or Glenda's short stories – that was when I felt most alive.'

He fell silent. While he studied the luminous little pitcher plant, I studied him – discomfited by his honesty yet recognising myself in his observation. There was a time when I'd existed through my fascination for Tony; lured by his charisma and dragged along at breakneck speed, my own fragile sense of purpose lost in the hectic exuberance of Tony's ambition. With him I'd felt vital, inspired. Apart from him, I was only half a person . . . or so it seemed to me then. Looking back, I saw I'd lacked the confidence to accept that my version of life – though quieter and far less dramatic than Tony's – was equally as valid.

Ross shrugged. 'Glenda was one of those people you occasionally have the good fortune to meet, who brings colour into the greyness of your life. When she died, the light went out of my world.'

'You spoke to her that night, didn't you?'

Ross tried not to react, but shock darkened his eyes. 'You've done your homework, haven't you?'

He must have thought I'd been snooping into police files or newspaper archives or old testimonials – which made me wonder how much of his involvement he'd confessed. Probably all of it, judging by his inability to lie. Rather than alarm him further and lose any trust we might have established, I decided to make a confession of my own.

'Did you know Glenda kept a diary?'

His face softened as realisation trickled in. His shoulders relaxed and he shut his eyes. 'Ah. God, I'd forgotten. Did Tony have it? Did he – '

I shook my head. 'It was hidden on the property. Bronwyn unearthed it a while back.'

There was such longing in Ross's eyes that I felt a pang of pity for him. After what he'd told me, he must be dying to delve into Glenda's private thoughts, especially any that might concern him.

'Her last entry caught my attention,' I admitted. 'She wrote it while waiting at her grandfather's place. She said she was worried about some letters she'd found, and that she'd spoken to you and you'd agreed to meet her, talk it over.'

Ross nodded. 'I recall that she did find some letters. They'd upset her and she wanted to talk.'

'What was in the letters?'

'She never said. I remember thinking it was all a bit mysterious . . . but she sounded so young on the phone, so vulnerable and afraid. My heart went out to her, I'd have done anything to help her. So I agreed to meet, but . . .' He looked at Tony's painting, and his face appeared to slacken into that of a much older man. When he spoke again, his voice was a whisper. 'But it wasn't to be.'

'You didn't see her at Thornwood?'

He shook his head. 'After I spoke to Glenda on the phone, my wife started complaining about stomach pains. She was a few months pregnant, so I rushed her up to Brisbane. Sadly, she miscarried that night. It was awful, and I forgot all about Glenda until later.'

'Did you ever doubt that Glenda's death was accidental?'

'What do you mean?'

'She knew the gully well, didn't she? Knew which areas were safe and which parts were treacherous, which parts to avoid. It strikes me as odd that she'd have made such a fatal mistake.'

'That's why you asked about Tony, isn't it?'

'Yes.'

Ross's gaze slid away, then came back. 'If anyone was to blame, Audrey, then it was me. Glenda was distressed on the phone. Then when I failed to show, she must've been even more angry and hurt. I imagine she rushed off home, in a mood, not taking notice where she walked.' Pulling out his hanky again, he blew his nose. 'No, Audrey, all the evidence points to an accident. The heavy rain, the cave-in on the edge of the gully, the gaping chunk of earth where she went over. The mess of rubble where they found her. There was never any speculation that her death was anything other than accidental.'

He sighed, then pulled up his wrist and grimaced at his watch. 'I'm sorry, Audrey, I've got to rush off, I'm going to be late for class.'

We said goodbye, and I lingered in the coolness watching him hurry along the walkway and vanish around the corner. Then I made my slow way back to the Celica, my thoughts weighing heavy on the diary stashed in the bottom drawer of my bedside table. Buried in darkness, just as it had been for the past twenty years. None of Glenda's entries was conclusive; none would stand up in a court of law as evidence to support my belief that she'd been the victim of something other than a fatal fall.

But it didn't matter what she'd written, did it?

The facts told a different story. Along with her haversack and hairbrush and a change of clothes, her diary had lain hidden in the hollow tree at the top of my garden for two decades, a good forty-minute walk from where – that rain-swept night – her falling body had supposedly caused a rockslide.

At the end of the week, I pulled up outside the school gates and cut the motor. We were an hour earlier than usual. Beside me in the passenger seat Bronwyn was jiggling in obvious excitement. She was wearing jeans, her new hiking boots, and her old terry sunhat jammed on her head. Her face glowed with zinc cream.

I reached over to straighten her collar. 'Remember what I told you?'

'Stay near the teachers at all times,' she recited, pulling free of me and searching the mob of kids swarming at the gates. 'Don't wander off alone, watch for snakes, and always wear sunscreen.'

'I'll miss you, you know,' I said. 'We haven't been apart before.'

'Yeah, Mum.' She was distracted, fiddling with her bag, itching to get going.

I sighed, trying to calm the butterflies dancing whirligigs in my stomach. 'Are you sure you've got everything?'

'Mum, don't worry! Me and Jade'll look after each other . . . Oh, there she is! See you in a week!'

With a kiss to my flushed cheek, she grabbed her backpack and sprang out of the car, then hailed Jade, who was bearing down through the hordes towards us.

They greeted each other with their customary exuberance, then shouldered their packs and trundled off towards the waiting coach. The teachers, Ross O'Malley among them, began to drove the kids into ragged lines. I kept waiting for Bronwyn to turn and wave, but she was too immersed in excited conversation with Jade and a skinny fair-haired boy. Five minutes later she was climbing into the coach, vanishing from view as the ragtag procession of kids swarmed in after her.

A dull ache pulsed in my chest. She was slipping away. Only eleven, but already drifting out of my protective orbit, into a wider and – for her, at least – more interesting world.

Sitting there in the sun-warmed car, searching the crowded coach for a glimpse of her, I couldn't help remembering how I'd been at her age. Plaits and long socks, hand-me-down school tunics that Aunt Morag had happened across in op shops. Geeky and quiet, a bookworm, painfully shy. For a long time I worried that Bronwyn would be equally afflicted with shyness, but she couldn't have been more different. Despite the absence of a dependable father figure and the presence of a reclusive work-aholic mother, Bronwyn had turned out, as Ross O'Malley said, to be an exceptionally well-balanced girl.

A motor rumbled to life, pulling me back to the present. The coach doors hissed shut and the huge vehicle left the kerb and heaved out onto the road. Scanning the windows, I saw only a blur of unfamiliar faces.

Then, as the coach navigated the corner, I glimpsed her at the rear window, she and Jade together, their faces pushed near the glass. Both of them looking at me, trying to get my atten-tion, waving furiously.

A moment later, the coach rumbled off around the corner, leaving behind nothing but a puff of thin black exhaust.

The house was empty without her. The rooms were full of echoes, the shadows restless. I caught myself hovering at the window, watching the dark trees along the service road. Or going into her room, folding and refolding the clothes she'd left scattered in her rush to pack for camp. Or trying to calculate what she was doing, right now, this red hot minute.

Whatever it was, I knew it didn't involve worrying about me.

I went out to my studio at the back of the house and browsed through some recent photos, then decided that moping around was getting me nowhere.

So instead, I went in search of Glenda.

I climbed the hill, picking my way along the path that wound up through the pomegranates and monsterio, up to the clearing where the hollow beechwood tree grew. Moonlight washed the old beech in silver, illuminating its bark, making the branches glow white against the black velvet sky. Around it, the bush was an inky scrim of shadows.

Despite the moon's far-reaching radiance and my focused cone of torchlight, it took me an hour to find what I'd come looking for. Beneath the overhanging boughs of a collapsed tea-tree, I found the remains of an old haversack. It was sodden and disintegrated, empty of anything except a couple of worms and a wolf spider.

For a while I fossicked in the bushes, training my torch under ferns and grassy clumps, wandering uphill then backtracking to lower ground, all the while keeping the gnarly old beech central to my search. After twenty minutes, my flashlight beam struck a soft glimmer of colour.

The hairbrush was plastic, its translucent pink body cracked and whitened by age. Most of its bristles had fallen away – a few remained, though, and I trained my light up close and searched for a strand of ash-blonde hair. Of course there were none, so I stowed the brush in the grocery bag I'd brought and continued looking. Soon I'd collected scraps of clothing, various articles of makeup, toiletries, a wallet, and the remains of a book riddled with slaters.

On my way back, I paused at the tree. Its white bark seemed to breathe in the darkness. The burnt-out trunk looked sinister. Shadows scattered in the probing cone of my flashlight beam, then re-formed into the outline of a man's skinny frame, assembling and fleshing out until I could see him with full clarity: Hobe Miller balanced there on a trembling bough, reaching into the fork between two branches, his arm sunk to the elbow as he groped around for what was no longer hidden there. Letters or a diary, it didn't matter which. What bothered me most was that he'd known exactly where to look.

I hugged my grocery bag and stared into the darkness.

The gully was thirty minutes from here. On the northern boundary of the property, back in the direction of town.

Well known for being dangerous – rockslides, earth collapses, cave-ins.

And murder.

Fear ran light fingers across my skin. Fear . . . and the overwhelming urge to see this gully, to wander among its shadows and lofty trees and sprays of sunlight, to absorb its particular atmosphere for myself. Not with the intention of finding anything, but to get a sense of the place where Glenda – and her grandmother forty years before her – had lived out the final moments of their young lives.

18

The following morning I set out early.

By the time I reached the top of the first hill I was puffing, my skin flushed with sweat, my hair damp beneath Bronwyn's old sunhat. The battered Minolta I kept for field trips and photographic note-taking was slung over my shoulder along with my satchel and waterflask, bumping me as I walked.

Pausing to look back the way I'd come, I could just make out the homestead's roof gleaming through the ironbarks, and the deeper green of its garden surrounds. It was a glorious day, the sky faded denim, the air tangy with the scent of leaf litter and wildflowers. Lorikeets flashed green and crimson as they swooped from tree to tree, their squeaky chatter disrupting the stillness. As I passed beneath a giant ghost gum, a flock of sulphur-crested cockatoos lifted and flew into the sky, shrieking like devils.

It felt good to be surrounded by nothing but thickets of tea-tree and black-trunked wattles and lofty red gums. There was no one else for miles, I could have been the lone survivor of an apocalypse, the last soul on earth adrift in the golden morning. I had to keep reminding myself that Tony and Glenda had walked this way countless times as kids, a shortcut from William Road to their grandfather's house; this lonely track had probably once rung with their calls and shouts and laughter.

Glenda had also come this way the night she died, upset after discovering the letters in her father's shed, impatient to see Ross. Only Ross hadn't showed, and Glenda had rushed from her hiding place to meet – not Ross, as she'd been expecting – but someone else.

I shivered and picked up my pace.

Ten minutes later, the trail veered downhill. Once or twice it vanished into an erosion gully, and I was forced to crab-walk down the steep embankments on my hands and bottom until I reconnected at the other side. I passed several cone-shaped anthills erupting from the earth like red boils. Further down, the landscape grew lush and wild. I was certain I could hear the faraway tinkling of bells. I stopped to listen, then decided it must be the sound of flowing water. Taking out the aerial shot given to me by Tony's lawyer, I studied it, iden-tifying what landmarks I could, and surmised I was close to the gully.

Following the watery babble, I pushed through a dense understorey of ferns and wonga vines. The treetops now formed a canopy, their dense mosaic of leaves cutting the sunlight to ribbons. The shadows underfoot were black, and rank with new smells: decaying vegetation and wet wood. Here and there wild orchids and bluebells thrust their jewel-coloured heads above the grey-green foliage, tiny embers of exquisite purple, pink, crimson, indigo.

Then, more chiming bells. I gazed up into the trees, but there was no sign of any birds. As I wandered deeper, the calls became more frequent. Soon I was surrounded by a melodic chiming. Bellbirds, I realised. Their fluty chirps and trills seemed to echo from all directions, as if the sky itself was singing.

Walking on, I came to a small clearing. At its very centre stood a lofty boulder. The boulder was taller than me and shaped like a shark's fin. Its grey elephant-hide surface was decorated with frills of lichen and moss. One flat face was turned to the sun, the other thrown into gloom, and the shadow it cast on the leaf-littered ground was damp and tombstone-like.

As I went nearer, I had the bewildering sensation that I'd been here before, a long time ago. Impossible. And yet I could see it as though in memory. The clearing had been darker then, more overgrown, the trees so thick they formed an unbroken canopy overhead. It had been night-time, and the wind had sobbed as it threaded through the leaves. *No, stop*, it cried, *Please stop –*

I shook my head to clear it.

Streamers of light fluttered through the leaf canopy, chasing the deep gloom from between the rigid, black-trunked iron-barks. Sunbeams picked along the spines of lacy ferns, turning them brilliant lime-green beneath the ghostly white trunks of imposing river gums. A cathedral, I thought. A sacred place which must have been of great significance to the land's indigenous custodians.

Standing in this enchanted, timeless clearing, I felt cradled by the soft light, swaddled in the cool green glow, embraced by the giddy chiming-song of the bellbirds. I was a shadow among a million other shadows, existing in perfect alignment, tapping into the greater flow.

So why did being here make me uneasy?

Crossing the clearing, I went to the edge of the gully and peered over. The embankment walls were steep, eroded by cave-ins. Trees grew at right angles up the sidings, their new shoots seeking the light. Boulders thrust from the soil like half-buried skulls. Here and there were fallen trees, their roots jutting skywards, their trunks making gangways over the gaping nothingness.

One wrong step . . .

Walking back to the fin-shaped stone, I sat in its cool shadow and took out my flask. The water was sweet and delicious on my parched throat, but it sat heavily in my belly. The air was humid, the heat made me languid. Leaning back, I shut my eyes and breathed out the tension. Felt myself slip into the past.

It was dark, so dark.

No longer morning. Something was wrong. My limbs were skewed beneath me. My skin burned, but my bones were made of ice. If I cracked open my lids I could just make out, through a haze of red, the tracery of moonlight in the treetops. Bats chirped and insects droned, the wind murmured in the branches. From below me in the gully came the pounding of the creek, a liquid heartbeat that drew the other sounds into itself and slowed them down until nothing remained but the sound of someone sobbing –

I snapped to my senses. My pulse raced as I got to my feet. These recurring half-dreams were becoming more intense, feeling more real. I knew the dreams were related to Aylish – I could feel her presence rubbing against my mind like a hungry cat, pressing me to take notice – and yet I was unable to pinpoint any order or meaning. Just that the tone of the visions was fearful, maybe cautionary, as though Aylish was – from whatever realm she now inhabited – trying to warn me.

Stowing my flask back in my bag, I moved away from the stone. The darkness of a moment before was gone; the clearing had returned to daylight. The eerie throbbing of the creek had subsided – yet still, all was not right.

The gully was almost otherworldly in its beauty ... and yet I couldn't wait to be away from it. Two young women had died here, forty years apart; one brutally bashed, the other with similar injuries attributed to a fatal fall. That the two women were related to one another by family ties – grandmother and granddaughter – hadn't escaped me. Was it an unfortunate co-incidence, or had more sinister forces been at work?

The bellbirds had fallen silent. The clearing seemed to be holding its breath. Even the sunlight dappling the leaves appeared frozen. I was no longer a part of the whole. Rather, I was aware of my isolation. Shut in by trees, miles from home. No one knew I was here. No one. Worry started to twist and churn in me. What if something happened to me here? What if I died? Bronwyn would be alone, an orphan; abandoned the way my own mother had abandoned me.

I'd been wrong to come here. The gully offered no answers, no revelations about the past, just shadows and dampness and mystery, and the mesmerising babble of a creek, trickling from its underground source, lapping into shallows that had once run red with blood.

Retracing my steps, I hurried back the way I'd come, leaving the clearing and reconnecting with the meandering dirt trail that led uphill and back to Thornwood . . . or so I thought. A few minutes passed before I realised my mistake. The gully had sunk from view behind me, hidden by an awning of tall eucalypt crowns draped in parasitic vines. Through a gap in the trees further down, I glimpsed the rounded peak of the fin-shaped stone. The lichen freckling its smooth surface glowed green and black and lavender-grey in the blotchy sunlight. It was a breath-taking sight, but I couldn't recall seeing it on my way in.

Which meant that I'd entered the clearing via a different track.

I looked down the slope in dismay. There was no way I was going to retrace my steps, go back through the gully clearing. I flashed on the creepy feeling I'd experienced near the stone, the dark dreamlike glimpses that had so unnerved me.

Better to keep going, I decided. Sooner or later I'd stumble upon the right trail; for now, all that mattered was putting distance between myself and the haunted shadows of the gully.

I continued uphill.

The stillness grew until it was dizzying – at one point I imagined I heard the muffled barking of a dog – but other-wise there was just the soft crack of leaf debris beneath my trail boots, the raspy tempo of my breath, and the eerie ever-present chiming of the bellbirds.

Twenty minutes later I stood at the edge of another, larger clearing surrounded by groves of lanky ironbark trees. Sunlight cascaded across the open expanse, turning the carpet of native grasses to silver.

At the far side of the clearing, sheltered beneath a stand of red gums, sat a little shack. It looked very old, its weathered walls and shingled roof all cut from the black ironbark that grew nearby. Along the front of the rickety verandah grew pink hippeastrums, gnarled lavender bushes, even a rambling rose bush with huge crimson blooms – a forgotten cottage garden in the midst of wild and lonely bushland. I guessed it was the hut Corey had told me about, the one built by the original settlers in the 1870s.

Despite its age and remoteness, the hut looked to be in sound condition. The narrow verandah appeared to teeter, but the palings were intact and the steps leading up to it looked sound. There was even a battered old cane chair propped at one end. The roof shingles were age-blackened, though some looked lighter in colour, more roughly hewn – as though they'd been recently replaced.

Approaching, I saw the door was ajar.

Standing at the foot of the steps, I was able to look up through the door and into the hut's interior. It was cool and dark and inviting, crammed with furniture and belongings.

As if someone was living there.

'Hello . . . ?' I called. My voice echoed in the stillness, and I felt silly. Of course no one lived here. The place was too remote, too isolated. There was no road, no electricity, no running water, nothing that even resembled a telephone line. Why would anyone bother? Besides, I reminded myself, it was on Thornwood land. If anyone was living here, I'd have known about it . . . wouldn't I?

The door creaked as I pushed it open. 'Anyone home?'

I half-expected to see Corey's ghostly woman standing at the window, but there was no one there. The place was small and shabbily furnished, darker than a tomb. A single bed jutted from the opposite wall, its ragged army blanket moth-eaten but clean, its stained pillow plumped just so. At the bedside was an upended wood crate, topped with a thick candle in a jar and a new-looking box of matches. I went to the bedside, pinched the candlewick. Brittle, freshly burnt.

The other furniture was dilapidated and old, but tidily arrayed. A deep shelf was stacked with ammunition tins – each one labelled in small white block lettering: powdered milk, matches, pencils, tea, flour, candles, rope. A camp table and chair were crowded under a small glassless window. Next to the table was an ancient meat safe with mesh sidings. I peered inside. Enamel dishes and cups, a jar of jam that looked older than I was, and a lump of mouldy bread.

Crossing to the window, I peered through and saw a corrugated iron water tank tucked against the house. Nearby sat a forty-four-gallon drum with an iron grate fitted over the top as a makeshift cooker. Next to it, another drum full of kindling. Someone's idea of a bush kitchen, I supposed.

A noise behind me.

I turned, but it was just a leaf scraping through the door. The breeze that carried it in smelled of sunlight and wildflowers – a fresh contrast to the musty, unwashed atmosphere of the hut.

As my pulse recalibrated, I took stock. The matches, the tins of provisions, the neatly made bed; the repairs to the roof and water tank, the fusty odour that was – the more I breathed it – clearly not the smell of nesting possums.

The hut was inhabited.

I tried to remember if Tony's lawyer had said anything about the settlers' hut being tenanted, but felt certain she hadn't. Which meant I had a squatter. I had no way of knowing how long they'd been here, but it looked like a long time. I turned to leave, my mind already mapping out the procedure for having them served with an eviction notice. First step, notify the cops. Then write to local council to apply for an unlawful tenant eviction form. When I'd lived my nomadic life with Aunt Morag, we'd had our fair share of eviction notices served us; it felt weird to have the shoe on the other foot for a change. But there was no other option; Bronwyn and I were living less than a mile away . . . it was too creepy to have an unknown element in our backyard.

I was halfway to the door when I saw, in a shadowy corner, the antique tallboy. Its carved detailing was chipped and flaking away, one of its fretwork panels hung loose. I turned the key, rattled open the door.

On the top shelf was what appeared to be a crude shrine. A collection of tiny porcelain doll heads was arranged in a semi-circle; they were old, their prim Victorian faces chipped and discoloured as if they'd been dug from the ground. In the centre of the circle was a carved wooden box, and on the box sat a tarnished picture frame displaying a black and white photograph.

I picked up the frame and tilted it into the light. It was an informal portrait of a young woman leaning against a tree. Sunlight cascaded around her, and she was smiling, the joy clear in her lovely features. The photo was dim and patchy with silver marks where the developer had succumbed to age – but the uncommon beauty of its subject was clear. Her windswept hair was long and thick, her face a perfect oval, her eyes dark almonds. A 1940s-style dress hugged her willowy figure.

I wondered who she was, and why her image had been trapped here, in this gloomy cupboard in the middle of nowhere. I wanted to rescue her. To slip her picture in my satchel and take her back out into the sun. The hut was on my land, I reasoned. The squatter had no right to be here without my consent. Which surely meant the dwelling and all its contents rightly belonged to me.

I ran a possessive finger along the side of the picture frame. What was it about these old portraits, why was I so drawn to them? Not *all* of them, I amended. Just this one. And the one of Samuel at home . . .

And then I knew. Not by deduction or any process of elim-
ination; but in my heart I knew. I took the photo over to the
window.

Please agree to meet me, she'd written. *Tonight at our secret place
. . . I'll be the one wearing a big happy smile for you.*

'Aylish,' I said, disquieted by the realisation. 'What on earth
are you doing here?'

I came very close to taking her. But in the end I listened to
my conscience. Lies were all very well when you saw good reason
for telling them . . . but stealing was just not my thing. The
squatter might be residing unlawfully on my land, but I didn't
need Sherlock Holmes to tell me I was trespassing, invading a
personal space . . . and that whoever lived here might not be all
that pleased to arrive home and find a stranger making off with
a treasured keepsake.

I replaced the photo and was about to shut the tallboy, when
my attention was drawn to the hanging compartment. Propped
against the back panel was a shaft of wood that might have been
the handle from an old tool, possibly an axe. One blunt end was
stained black, while its weatherworn grip was split and splintered.
I wondered why someone would bother to keep an axe handle
indoors – especially one that looked ready for the scrapheap.
I reached in and ran my fingers along its blackened length –

Smooth as skin. Almost warm.

I pulled away, repulsed.

But as I was closing the tallboy door, I paused again. The
wooden box under the photo had grabbed my attention. I'd
dismissed it at first as a plinth for the little picture frame, but I
saw now that it was carved with leaves and cherry blossoms and
obviously had once been valuable. It was so feminine, so pretty
and so out of place, that I found myself moving the frame and
pulling the box into the light.

Taking it over to the bed, I sat and balanced it on my knees as
I lifted the lid. It was full of letters. A bundle of letters, tied with

threadbare ribbon. I thought of Glenda Jarman, and wondered if these were the same letters she'd discovered that unlucky afternoon in her father's shed – the letters I had assumed revealed Luella's affair with Hobe Miller. But as I picked an envelope off the top of the pile, all thoughts of Glenda went from my mind. The stamps were old. *Really* old, threepenny stamps mostly, I guessed from the 1940s.

And the handwriting . . . I recognised it immediately.

There might have been thirty or forty envelopes, the majority made of diaphanous airmail paper, brittle with age and wear. I rifled through them and saw that most were from Aylish, addressed to Samuel via the Second A.I.F. Headquarters.

The remaining envelopes bore Aylish's name and her street, Stump Hill Road. The stamps were Malayan, obliterated beneath heavy black cancellation marks. Other envelopes bore no stamps, just the caption: *On Active Service*. Each envelope was well-thumbed, the paper soft and crumbly as though they'd been handled frequently and often read.

I ached to start reading, but I knew it was too risky; the squatter might return at any time, and I didn't want to be caught red-handed – especially since I intended to have him evicted.

A quick peek, then?

Outside, a windy gust blew something across the roof, startling me: a scrape of leaves, twigs? I held my breath, listening . . . but there was just the warbling of currawongs, the drone of cicadas, and the soft hush-hush of a breeze in the dry grass.

Heart thumping, I slid one of Samuel's envelopes randomly from the pile.

30 November, 1941

Hope you're well, Dream Girl?

No letters have arrived yet. I've spent a ridiculous measure of hours chasing the possibility of lost mail. The handling officer assures me that we are at war (really, mate?) and therefore missing mail is of least concern in the larger picture. But then after I let loose a few choice suggestions as to what he could do with his larger picture, he rushed on to say that such occurrences were rare.

Letters, like fate, eventually find their way to the recipient, no matter how circuitous the route. So I will wait, and I will try to have faith – in the mail system, in the larger picture, and mostly in you, my Aylish – for without faith I fear this sweaty, mosquito-ridden, noisy and erratic existence might very well get the better of me.

10 January, 1942
Love, last night I was terrified to close my eyes in case my memory of your face left me forever. Regrets taunted me, things unspoken rolled around and around in my head until I thought I'd go mad. Why haven't you written? Have you forgotten me so soon? My heart aches to think you've met someone else.

Crazily, I keep thinking about that first day we spent up at the old hut, and how I'd been ranting about the ironbark shingles and boring you with the history of the underground water tank dug by the original settlers. You were more interested in trying to get me to kiss you, remember?

I admit now I was an insufferable egghead, resisting you out of propriety, but – and I beg you'll forgive my plain-speaking, love – all the while thinking, 'Lord but this woman is beautiful, it scares me how much I love her,' and a bit later I privately added: 'My word, I can't wait 'til we're married.' All unspoken, of course, concealed by my pathetic veneer of gruffness. Now I long for those days when I used to rush up that track to the little hut, knowing you were waiting for me. Sometimes my longing for those happy times is like a physical agony.

Oh my Aylish, this is a letter of confessions, isn't it? How easy now to jot it all down on paper, even knowing the censor's eyes will read it first. But love, if one good thing can come from war, it's that the veils of conceit drop away and you clearly see the one thing that gives your life meaning. For me, that one thing is you.

Sleep well, my wild little sparrow, hold my poor old heart next to yours for safekeeping. Always and forever yours, Samuel.

I stopped reading.

The Samuel emerging from these letters was very different from the man I'd constructed in my mind. He wasn't – at least not at this stage of the war – a snake or a scoundrel, and he wasn't damaged and bitter. Judging by the bare emotion of his words, he had loved Aylish. Which told me that what happened between them after the war was less to do with Samuel's career, and more to do with his fear – brought on by her apparent failure to write – that she might have forgotten him.

I looked through the doorway to the clearing beyond. I'd already been here too long. The sun had climbed a few degrees higher into the sky, and the growling in my stomach told me that breakfast had been and gone and that it was time to head home.

But I couldn't. Not yet.

I had to read one more . . .

I located another of Samuel's. It was headed: A.I.F. Abroad, and dated 1 February 1942 – two weeks to the day, I noted grimly, before the fall of Singapore. It must have been Samuel's last letter before his capture.

My Pretty Sparrow,

No news is good news, they say – although whoever 'they' are have never waited four months to hear from their Dream Girl. I've still heard no word from you, is everything ship-shape, love? I worry constantly, which I know will make you laugh. At least I hope it does – make you laugh kindly, I mean. I only pray there's no news you feel reluctant to tell me. Aylish, please understand that it'd be far easier for me to receive a note of rejection than no note at all.

Do you regret our promises, have you reconsidered my proposal? If so, I will try my best to understand, as your happiness is my first priority. Please, sweetheart, put a poor fool out of his misery, a few words will do.

How's Jacob? Well and spirited, the last I heard from old Mrs Beetleman – and she added that you sang beautifully in church at Christmas. God, how I wish I'd been there to cheer you on – and I would have too, loud and long . . . though I know Pastor Lutz does not encourage heckling from the pews.

If you can be bothered, my Sparrow, send me a full and detailed report of life at home, for which I pine with every fibre of my being. Chin up, Dream Girl, I love you so very much.

A whimper.

I stopped reading. Held my breath to listen. For a moment there was only the noise of the bush – the chatter of lorikeets, bush flies droning, and the wind rustling the leaves. But then it came again. A whine sounding every bit like a wordless, drawn-out question.

I shoved the letter I'd been reading back into the envelope, and tried to tell myself it was nothing. A bird or a creaking branch, a false alarm. But then the sound of a dog barking shattered the peaceful quiet, followed by the gruff command of a male voice.

I shot to my feet, upending the box of letters onto the floor. On my knees now, scrabbling them back into the box, crumpling them out of order in my haste. One envelope had skated just out of reach, I lunged for it –

And froze.

A shadow flashed across the doorway, eclipsing the sunlight. I risked a look, but it must have been a bird or wind-bent tree, because there was no sign of anyone. At least, not yet.

Grabbing the errant letter, I shoved it into its box and stowed the whole dusty mess in my satchel, then scanned the room for signs of disturbance. Brushing the wrinkles from the bed edge I'd perched on, I checked the floor for overlooked letters, then went to the door and blinked into the brightness. For a moment, my crashing pulse was all I could hear. Then, from somewhere on the other side of the stillness, came the crunch of footfall. I heard a man's voice. And a low, cautionary growl that made the hairs stand up on the back of my neck.

Racing down the steps and across the clearing, I threw myself into a thicket of tea-tree and shoved my way through. As I ran, my Minolta bumped against my back and the satchel containing the box of letters seemed to catch on every branch. My feet thudded over the uneven ground, and I'd broken out in a sweat of nerves.

Soon I was far enough away to hope that I'd escaped without being detected. I slowed. Risked a look over my shoulder.

Something white flashed across the open expanse of sunlit grass, but that was all I saw. Lurching into a run again, I darted downhill, skidding on loose stones as I fought to put distance between myself and the pale shape coming at me through the trees.

Then I heard a warning growl, and a torpedo rammed into the back of my leg. The pain was instant, shocking in its intensity. I stumbled, lurched forward and fell against a tree, gasping as I twisted back to look at my attacker.

The dog was thickset and dirty-white, its sturdy body rippling with muscle, its square jaw pulled wide. Its lips were bared back and I had a flash of strong white teeth clamping into my denim-clad calf. I kicked out, but the dog bit down harder. Wheezing in shock, I lost my footing and crashed against the tree, smashing my face into the trunk when my leg gave out beneath me.

The dog whined and drove its teeth deeper. The world skewed. The tree dipped away, the stony ground loomed. Somehow my fingers found a knob of branch, curled around it, got a grip. I used the leverage to try and twist away, but the dog grunted and this time I felt the skin above my ankle pop and tear. There was a horrid grating sensation as if my bone was being wrenched from its casing of flesh –

Blind with pain and shaking so hard I could no longer trust my reflexes, I fumbled for my camera strap, tore it off my shoulder and swung the Minolta hard at the dog. I missed, managing to slam my camera into the side of the tree and send myself jarring off balance. I nearly fell, greying out as pain swooped up from my damaged calf, bright as a shard of lightning, reverberating in the nerve response sector of my brain. It was then, in that instant of dizzy confusion, that I sensed rather than saw motion twenty feet away in a patch of sunlight streaming between the trees.

A man stood there. So still, he might have been an apparition from a dream. Tall and big-boned, hunched about the shoulders, watching from a face that was pale as the moon, the skin gleaming –

Then he was gone. Just like that. I blinked, came back to the shadows, the man forgotten as my attention returned to the growling mongrel clamped to my leg.

My second swing was better aimed. The dog yelped as the camera connected with its head. The pressure on my leg eased. I wrenched free, and the dog snarled and lunged, but then shied away as the Minolta made another sweep towards it. I lost my grip on the strap and the camera bumped off over the ground. The dog growled, baring its lips to reveal pink-stained teeth, but it didn't rush at me again, and I didn't wait around to see if it was planning to. Clutching my satchel to my chest, I turned and ran.

19

Six stitches and a tetanus shot later, I was feeling duly sorry for myself. I paid my bill at the hospital then limped down the hill to my car. Folding the prescription for painkillers into quarters, then eighths, I delivered it to the abyss at the bottom of my tote and decided to instead apply my own failsafe remedy for dealing with pain: A trip to the baker's.

It was mid-afternoon. I stood in front of the bakery window, balanced on one foot like an egret, favouring the throbbing lump of agony that had once been my leg. I felt drained and sore after the morning's misadventure; tormented by questions and eager to get home and huddle in a sunlit window seat and mull over what I'd found.

Who was the man squatting up at the old hut, and why had he made a weird little memorial to Aylish? Because in hindsight, that was what it was. The arrangement of doll heads, the damaged old photo in its tarnished frame, the box of letters . . . they held some sort of meaning for him, but what? Had he known her? Or had he merely discovered the letters and photograph somewhere by chance and taken a fancy to them?

I remembered seeing roses rambling along the rickety verandah at the hut, big red roses. I tried to picture them more clearly in my mind, but they were hazy. At the time I'd been too curious to see inside the hut's interior. But I'd seen those same roses three times before. Surrounding Samuel in his sultry rose arbour portrait; climbing along the fence in Luella's back garden; and in a vase of fresh water on Aylish's grave –

Someone touched my arm. I spun around.

Danny Weingarten handed me a note. *What's wrong with your leg?*

I blinked in surprise. 'What . . . How did you – ?'

His hair stood on end and he wore a tattered flannelette shirt that made me wonder if he'd ransacked Hobe Miller's wardrobe. In the shade of the baker's shop canopy, his eyes were deep ocean-green. He frowned at the foot I still had hooked egret-like behind my knee, then scribbled, *I can smell antiseptic. What happened?*

'A dog bit me,' I blurted, still spinning from his sudden appearance.

Reaching out a hand, he touched the side of my face.

Black eye, he spelled with his fingers. *Dog do that too?*

'I fell while trying to get away.'

His frown softened. *Looks sore. You okay?*

I nodded, unable to speak. I wasn't used to anyone worrying about me, wasn't used to anyone slipping in past my guard. But the look on Danny's face – the concern in his eyes, the downward turn of his mouth, the way he was leaning protectively near . . . Suddenly I was limp as a kitten and wanting nothing more than to fall into his arms and weep.

Instead I cleared my throat, shrugged. 'It's nothing. I'm okay.'

How did you get bitten?

A moment's hesitation. Then I grabbed his arm and pulled him into the bakery doorway, checked that the storefront was empty, and shifted so that my face was visible to him alone.

'There's a man squatting on my property. Did you know there's a dwelling on the hillside overlooking the gully?'

Danny narrowed his eyes, an indicator he hadn't understood.

He passed me his notebook, and I jotted a brief outline of my morning – the walk to the gully, the trek uphill where I'd found the old place, then how I'd ventured inside only to find someone living there . . . though I omitted the part about stealing Aylish and Samuel's letters.

I know the place, Danny signed, then reclaimed his notebook. *A little hut in a clearing, me and Tony used to go there as kids. Happy memories. I went back after he ran away, but it wasn't the same. I haven't been there for years. You think someone's living there now?*

I nodded. 'When the dog attacked, I saw him. It was only a flash . . . he was a tall man, I got the feeling he was maybe in his sixties. Do you know who he might be?'

Danny shook his head and wrote: *He let his dog attack you?*

I shrugged. 'I guess he got a shock, finding someone in his space . . . but yeah, he didn't seem in a hurry to call it off.'

Danny's eyes darkened. He rumpled the top leaf off his notepad and shoved it in his pocket, then started jotting on the blank sheet. He got as far as, *Bloody* . . . then stopped, tucked the jotter in his waistband, and began to sketch out a series of signs that were too complex for me to follow. I expected him to slow down, or at least to acknowledge that I'd lost him and realise that maybe it was time to resume his note, but he only seemed to get more caught up in his now-private monologue.

I watched him, awestruck.

His thick hair stuck up as if electrified, and his expressive face made me think of a thundercloud. But it was his eyes that caught me and held me captive – not just green now but emerald fire, brilliant as sunlight on seawater, dark and dangerous and wildly beautiful.

He stopped as abruptly as he'd begun. Signed, *Sorry.*

I shook my head to let him know his outburst had lost me.

He scribbled out the word *Bloody,* and wrote instead, *I'm angry. I was swearing. I'm going to see this bastard, get him off your land.*

'But . . .'

To my surprise, Danny reached out and gripped my arm, did this rubbing thing with his thumb that was reassuring. Then he scratched off another note.

I'll go this afternoon, that okay with you?

'No,' I said, 'You don't have to . . .' Unable to finish, I looked up into Danny's face. I wasn't used to having someone offer to act on my behalf. I wasn't used to anyone standing up for me. It was a heady feeling, which at first I resisted . . . but at the same time I was drawn into it, like a moth lured by the glow of a bright flame.

'It's kind of you Danny, but – '

I cut off as a young woman approached us. She smiled at me as she took her place by Danny, touching him on the arm to get his attention.

She made a series of swift signs, all of which I missed. Then she looked at me, still smiling, and thrust out a slender hand. 'Hi, I'm Nancy, Danny's vet nurse.'

She was everything I'd feared. Tall, blonde, supermodel gorgeous. She had a lip piercing, and wore her hair plaited into kooky bunches that were pinned behind her ears. She wore a red embroidered shirt-dress, stylishly belted around her trim waist, offset by the coolest pair of cowboy boots I'd ever seen.

'Audrey,' I near-whispered as I shook her hand, 'good to meet you.' I was wearing my own rather embarrassing fashion statement: a Harley Davidson T-shirt that had once belonged to Tony, and a pair of Bronwyn's cast-off track pants.

'You live at Thornwood?' Nancy asked.

I nodded.

'Cool,' she said, bobbing her head, 'it's gorgeous country out there. How are you settling in?'

I deflated. Not only gorgeous, but nice as well. How could I ever compete with that, I wondered. Not that there even *was* a competition, but . . .

'Yeah, good,' I told her, but as the words left my mouth I realised with a jolt that they weren't quite true. It *had* been good to be at Thornwood, dreamily good, almost perfect . . . until recently. At first I'd been intrigued by the notion of proving Samuel innocent, and then by the mystery presented by Glenda's diary. But as time wore on, and especially now after the horror of this morning's dog attack – my dream home was beginning to feel a touch like a nightmare.

Nancy warmed me with a smile, then transferred her gaze to Danny, elbowing his attention back to her.

We should go, she signed, then gave me a dimpled grin. 'Nice meeting you, Audrey. See you around again sometime.'

Then she was gone.

Danny wrote in his book, then passed me the note.

I'm free later this arvo. I'll head up to the hut and sort out your squatter.

I'm coming with you, I signed.

No. You'll pop your stitches.

'My leg's fine!' I stood tall, placing my leg square on the ground, wincing as I forced a breezy smile. 'It's just a bit of a graze, really, the dog's teeth barely broke the skin. Nothing to fuss over, see?' I took a couple of tiptoe steps in place to prove my point. 'Besides,' I lied for good measure, 'I'm an experienced bushwalker.'

Danny studied my face for so long that I worried he was planning to lift my pants leg and inspect the injury for himself. Then he wrote in his book.

How about Friday? Give you a few days to recover.

'Friday's good.'

Friday *was* good. I was curious about the man who – until this morning, anyway – had been in possession of Aylish and Samuel's war letters. Curious too about why he'd created a memorial shelf for Aylish . . . and whether he'd been the one to take roses to her grave. It would have been foolhardy to confront him myself, but having Danny along for the ride meant safety in numbers.

Danny was scowling now, apparently in no hurry to go.

I shrugged. 'What?'

Stay out of trouble.

'Sure.'

He shook his head as he scribbled another note. *You're like a kelpie I had once. Always chasing cars. You know what happened to her?*

A kelpie? Grimacing, I took his next note.

She got hit.

Without another word, he turned on his heel and stalked off. I watched him cross the road, catch up with Nancy on the far kerb. He made a series of swift signs, and Nancy shook her head to all of them. Then they strode along the pavement, bumping shoulders like a pair of comfortable old friends. Just before they slipped into the hardware I thought I saw him smile.

I wanted to run after him, tell him he'd got it all wrong. I wasn't a car-chaser, not usually – back in Melbourne I'd tried so hard to be level-headed and dependable, normal and nice, quite boring really, a person he could've set his watch by. It was only now, after leaving all that behind and taking possession of Thornwood, that I'd changed. After spending the majority of my days surrounded by wilderness, accumulating a store of unguarded moments in which I'd shed my need to please anyone other than myself – change had been inevitable. But snooping in huts, stealing letters, getting bitten by dogs? I wasn't generally that sort of a person . . .

Maybe I *was* chasing a car that would stop suddenly and finish me off . . . yet wasn't it better to be chasing something – anything – rather than standing helplessly in the middle of the road waiting to get hit?

The urge to run after Danny was strong, but I decided to let him go. Danny was out of reach. Not just in physical distance, but emotionally, spiritually. We were worlds apart. He was gorgeous and volatile, a dark horse; a silent enigma driven by the need to prove himself, to make his mark on the world.

I was a mouse.

Drab. Uninteresting. Colourless.

Worse, my leg was throbbing up a bitch and I needed that cake.

After a toasted sandwich followed by a slab of sticky date pudding and several Panadol, I took the box of letters out to Samuel's room and sat on the bed.

Emptying them across the quilt, I set aside the ones I'd already seen and then began arranging the others in order of date, sliding out the fragile old notepaper and clipping each page to its envelope. A few were bent and grubbified after their excursion across the hut's dusty floor, and I came across several that had dark fingerprint-like stains . . . dried blood?

I noticed there was a break in Samuel's letters that spanned from February 1942 until December 1945. This gap came as no surprise. His last letter must had been posted just weeks before his capture.

On February 15, 1942 the Japanese had achieved what the Allies had, until then, considered impossible. Marching down the Malayan peninsula, the Japanese army had stormed the supposedly impregnable port of Singapore. Over a hundred thousand Allies, including 17,000 Australians, were taken prisoner.

This crippling blow – coupled with the bombing of Darwin four days later – had marked the end of Australia's perceived remoteness from the conflict sweeping the rest of the world. Suddenly everyone was building backyard bomb shelters, digging trenches in the schoolyards, stockpiling food and clothing and medical supplies in anticipation of shortages. Wardens patrolled the night-time streets, enforcing strict brownout laws. The entire country began preparing for the now very real possibility of invasion.

Sliding one of Aylish's envelopes from the pile, I unfolded the letter and smoothed it on the bed before me.

6 February, 1942
Darling Samuel, I went into the post office again this morning to pester Klaus Jarman about missing letters, but his answer is always the same: 'There's a war on, my dear, delays must be expected.'

Yet I can see in his eyes he's as puzzled as me.

He claims that some days there is more mail than the postal service can manage. Add to that the difficulty some of the hospital ships have had evading air attacks, and you've got a sure-fire recipe for late mail.

I was spoilt while you were at university in Sydney, I got several letters from you a week. Now, when I'm so desperate to know that you're alive and well and in good spirits, your silence terrifies me.

Yet I refuse to lose hope. I'm certain you're alive, don't ask me how. I know you'd never abandon me, not even by dying, so whatever your reasons for not responding to my letters, I understand it's not neglect that keeps you silent. I pray that you're safe and that my letters and parcels are by some miracle getting through to you, bringing at least a small degree of comfort.

14 July, 1942
Take heart, my darling Samuel, for you are the father of a healthy little girl. She entered the world on Tuesday 23 June, a 9lb bundle of perfection. I named her after your mother, Luella Jean – but I call her Lulu because she's such a bright-eyed little button. She has my thick hair, but otherwise her resemblance to you is striking – the wide intelligent eyes, the determined chin, the milky Irish skin. She's a real beauty in the making, and though only three weeks old, I can already tell she's going to be a brain just like her clever father.

A flush of warmth at this one, and a strange sort of sorrow too. It gave me a curious chill to see Luella's name written in Aylish's orderly copperplate, a reminder that the world of the past was real . . . at least, it once had been. Aylish might be long gone, but there'd been a time when she was flesh and blood, a young mother with the same fears and hopes for her little girl as I had for mine. Did that explain my connection to her? Or was there another cause for the feeling that an essential part of her lived on in me?

17 September, 1942

Samuel Dearest, as you can see by the return address I'm no longer at Stump Hill Road. After Poppa's arrest in August, some inspectors from the Commonwealth Bureau started showing up at peculiar hours – right on teatime, and once very late at night, no doubt hoping to catch me unawares – checking, so they claimed, on the welfare of my child. They affected concern for my marital status (or lack of it) and cross-examined me about the child's father and whether or not he was also a 'coloured' man. I tell you, my cheeks burned the whole time and I longed to let loose at them, but I bit my tongue. I'd seen other little light-skinned children taken from their Aboriginal mothers, and families so damaged by their loss that they never recovered. The thought of anyone taking Lulu from me was beyond my ability to comprehend – I only knew I had to prevent it at all costs.

One morning when the inspectors called, Ellen Jarman happened to be here delivering a bundle of khaki wool for the Red Cross's latest knitting campaign. Now Ellen has a sharpish tongue at the best of times, but that morning she was in fiery form and gave them an earful that still makes me blush to remember it. Samuel, those men couldn't get out the gate fast enough! Clutching their clipboards to their chests, they dived into their motorcar and drove off in a whirlwind of dust.

Afterwards, Ellen regarded me for a long while. Then she said, 'Don't be offended, Aylish dear ... but would you consider working for Klaus and me for a while – just until Jacob returns?'

I declined, but Ellen rushed on to tell me that with her sister taken ill and her home overrun by billeted servicemen, and her housekeeper recruited by the manpower commission to cook for the mess at Amberley, she was run off her feet. Which, she pointed out in her determined way, meant that her volunteer work for the Red Cross was suffering, and that I should consider my position in their household a vital contribution to the war effort. Besides, she added, seeing the reluctance that must have shown in my face, she could help watch over Lulu, and with the advantage of having been a trained midwife, she could help me give my little girl the very best of care.

While she spoke, I stared down Stump Hill Road watching the dust still swirling in the wake of the Bureau inspectors' motorcar. Knowing that the next time they came – or the next, or the next – I might not be so lucky.

I thanked Ellen and told her I'd consider her kind offer. But Samuel, my mind was already made up. As Poppa used to say, When the wolf is knocking at the door, you don't hang about waiting for him to come down the chimney.

31 October, 1942

Darling, you'll never guess where I am, notepaper balanced on my knees as I lean against a great shady stone? Yes, our secret ferny glade near the gully!

It's just as it was when we last came here – full of sunbeams and ringing with the songs of a million bellbirds, the air deliciously cool, and the shadows green with all the ferns shooting up between the trees ... and most wonderful at the moment are the lichens, so vibrant after the rain – gold, pink, purple-grey, and brilliant vermillion. I've picked a few frills to press into this letter, as you used to admire them so. I've also collected some young eucalypt leaves, a tiny piece of home for you.

Lulu is lying here beside me in a shady patch, kicking her little legs on the blanket I laid out for her, gurgling up into the sunny trees. I've been telling her the names of all the birds: whip-birds, butcher-birds, flycatchers, and whistlers. Though she's only four months old, she peers up at me with her big wise eyes and I'm convinced she understands every word.

All is well at the Jarmans', though I confess they are part of the reason I like escaping up here. It's an hour's walk pushing Lulu's pram (then another twenty minutes to carry her up the gully track), but worth the trouble. Don't get me wrong, the Jarmans are kind. While I sweep or do laundry or churn butter or scrub potatoes or run errands, Ellen hovers around Lulu, watching and fussing over her. She and Klaus adore our little girl, which is a good thing, isn't it?

And yet there are times when I get a touch of the green-eyed monster about me. In particular, those times when Lulu's smile seems brighter, her eyes more alight, her giggles chirpier because Ellen is near. And then Klaus comes home and tickles her under the chin and makes her twitter with glee, and young Cleve puts his two cents in, brushing her hair, or telling her stories, or tickling her ears until she's cooing like a baby dove. Meanwhile I'm stuck with the mop and broom or milking pail, watching from the wings, imagining I could happily strangle the lot of them (but not my Lulu, of course!).

So I bring Lulu up here to our magical glade, and tell her stories about the birds and lizards, and the flowers that emerge from the warming earth. I tell her about the Bunyip who dances in the shallows of the creek far below, and about the wise spirits watching over us from inside the trees ... and I spin stories about her brave daddy who's gone to war and how happy we'll be when he returns.

And you will return, dear Samuel, I know you will; there's no doubt in my mind or my heart about that.

24 April, 1943

Darling, don't be alarmed but I had a bit of a spill yesterday.

I'm all right, it was a stupid thing, I was overtired and not paying attention – anyhow, last night after tea I was scrubbing the back steps when my worn-out old shoes slipped on a soapy tread and I went tumbling, landing in an ungainly heap on the path below.

I wasn't hurt, just a few scrapes along the shin – and, of course, a severe dent in my dignity – but as I sat a moment to catch my breath, a cry came from indoors, followed by a mad scuffling. Before I could get to my feet, young Cleve burst out clutching a bottle of mercurochrome and oversized roll of sticking plaster. I protested, but he's a stubborn little fellow. While he dabbed my barked shin with a cotton wad, he took great pains to tell me he was learning First Aid in the Cadets.

'Aren't you rather young to be a Cadet?' I teased, knowing the entry age was sixteen.

'I'm tall for my age,' he said loftily, then had to confess: 'Dad lets me tag along to the weekend camps at Amberley. I'm not enlisted yet, but I do everything the older chaps do. We're learning Morse code and tons of other terrific stuff – identifying aircraft, that's my favourite. As soon as I'm old enough, I'm going to enlist as a pilot.'

I swear, Samuel, the boy is ten going on forty, such a little old professor, interested in everything and quite the know-it-all – in fact he reminds me of a certain handsome young doctor I used to know! Cleve's also a diligent collector of glass bottles and bald tyres and tin cans, and does the rounds once a week cadging old newspapers – all to be re-used in a variety of ways for the war effort. A couple of years back he started helping his father at the post office, sorting mail before and after school, and on top of that he still finds time to help me around the house, picking up after Lulu, drying the dinner dishes, chopping wood, and feeding the hens – making himself quite indispensable.

Honestly, Samuel, if I only had half that boy's industriousness ... and a quarter of his energy! It's just a shame Ellen seems to think so lowly of him – going cranky on him for the slightest slipups, nagging and criticising his appearance. I've even seen her humiliate the poor child in front of her Red Cross cronies. I do feel sorry for him at times. He doesn't appear to have any friends of his own, which might explain his dedication to filling his every waking hour with chores.

Anyway, his enthusiasm is touching, and it was so very kind of him to help me after my soapsud calamity – but his comment about the RAAF made me sad. I only hope that by the time Cleve is old enough to enlist, this wretched war is long behind us.

21 May, 1943
Hello Darling, did you get my Easter parcel? I know you'll love the photos of Lulu, and you'll be able to use or barter the cigarettes and soap and box of Anzac biscuits. My baking skills are wretchedly inadequate and young Cleve declared the biscuits akin to gnawing on shoe leather but I posted them anyway. Perhaps where you are, you'll be glad of them? This time I'm sending socks, hand-knitted, only marginally better than the biscuits, I'm afraid.

On top of my duties in the Jarman household, I've begun working at the telephone exchange, night shifts while Lulu (soon a year old!) sleeps under Ellen's watchful care. My shift finishes at ten o'clock and I wobble off home on my bicycle, dodging those blasted sandbags they've piled everywhere, ringing my bell so I don't run anyone over, navigating through the streets by pure luck it sometimes seems. The town is pitch black at that hour, not a streetlamp lit, no glimmer from a single window. Motorcars are forbidden after dark unless the headlights are blinkered by a restrictive blackout device, and though occasionally I hear one in the distance, I never see more than a faint wash of light on the road. Who'd have thought that all the way out here in Magpie Creek we'd be worried about getting bombed? It's true though, Samuel, ever since Darwin none of us feel safe anymore.

On the way back from town on Wednesday we heard that a Red Cross hospital ship, the *Centaur*, was torpedoed off the coast near Stradbroke Island. They say more than 250 soldiers and nurses were killed or drowned. We can scarcely believe it, all those lives lost, all those families stricken by the cruellest of blows. I swear the entire country has gone into shock.

Meanwhile, here at the Jarmans' we are drifting along, mostly content. Although the other night Ellen let it slip that, in the unfortunate event of something happening to me – not that it will of course, she hastened to add – then she and Klaus would like to adopt Lulu. She seemed nervous when she said this, and I had the feeling that she wasn't telling me everything.

I hid my distress by bringing out your mother's beautiful ring and explaining that the moment you were back from service, we were going to be married. At this news, Ellen shed a tear and congratulated me . . . but again I sensed that her reaction was only the tip of the iceberg. It's hard to explain, but I started remembering other little comments she's made. 'How young you are, Aylish,' she says, affecting a frown of concern. 'Only nineteen, and all alone. Why, it seems you're barely more than a child yourself.' Most recently she confessed that 'Our dear little Lulu is a ray of sunshine in my otherwise overcast life.'

I do try to remember how kind she's been, and how she saved me that day from the Bureau inspectors and their endless questions and forms. And I try to remember that, without my employment at the Jarmans', I would be a defenceless target for the men who come with their pale sorry faces and Bible talk and official reasoning, and then drag away your children.

7 December, 1943
Dearest, I've been restless of late, driven by a strange feeling that time is running out. Ellen keeps telling me to slow down, to pace myself before exhaustion sets in – but I can't.

I spring out of bed at piccaninny light, bathe and dress Lulu and get her fed – I'm lucky, she loves her food and never refuses a scrap of what I offer. It seems I'm always rushing around like a headless chook until it's time to flop – cleaning up or polishing or sweeping or picking vegies, or mopping up spills or kissing skinned knees, or cooking huge pots of food or baking bread for the growing ranks of people staying with the Jarmans.

I never sit still. Even if I could, by some miracle, find a moment to put my feet up, I wouldn't bother. There's a time-bomb inside me ticking down the hours, counting off the seconds – to what end, I have no idea. I keep thinking back to that night at the settlers' cabin, to our last night together. Samuel, do you remember how upset I was when I saw that pale face in the window? A ghost, I kept insisting. But I knew in my heart even then what I'd seen.

I'd seen death, Samuel. And death had seen me.

Ellen says it's the war. Death and loss are always close. We laugh and sing and natter to each other, chirpy as wattlebirds, but beneath the veneer of cheerfulness flows an undercurrent of dread. Sometimes at night I lie awake and fancy I can hear the world groaning on its axis and quietly weeping. Whenever I shut my eyes, all I see is newsprint: page after page of names – the dead and missing, all those boys and so many women, never to return. Ellen's right – the war has changed us all, and not always for the better.

This afternoon I left Lulu with Ellen and, hoping to dispel my dark mood, I rode my bike out to Stump Hill Road and climbed the hill to the gully. The day was warm and I found my feet taking me along the track to the homestead. The poor old house was overgrown with lantana and blackberry. It feels neglected since your father went to stay with his relatives in Warwick.

I'd planned to sneak up to the window and peer through, perhaps even take the spare key from the washhouse and let myself in. Remember, Samuel, how you always stalled whenever I asked to see inside the house? You said I belonged in the sun and shadows of the garden, a dark butterfly too delicate and wild to be trapped within the stifling confines of a great dusty old house . . .

A lot of old rot, now that I think back. What were you hiding from me, I wonder now? Or, perhaps it was me you were wanting to hide – in case your father arrived unannounced, or some society lady paid a surprise visit – ?

Forgive me, dearest, that was harsh. But I'm racked by loneliness, made bitter by your continuing silence. Horrid scenarios
play over and over in my mind 'til I'm quite sure I've gone mad.
Meanwhile, you're far away and unable to defend yourself. If you
were here . . . oh, Samuel, if only you were here!

Of course, I never made it into the house. The old arbour
called to me, and I ran along the path to answer. I could have
wept (I did weep, in fact) to see the state of it. The lovely old rose
canes were infested with water shoots and choked by weeds,
the bushes scabby with dead flowers, the precious hips (which
we once brewed by the handful into sweet pink tea, do you
remember?) now withered and turned black in the sun.

I lay in the arbour's heart, sunk into the grass among the
brittle deadfall of petals and thorny twigs. I shut my eyes against
the brilliant sun, and you came to me then, behind my closed
lids, and I swear you were standing right there before me, in
the archway, every bit as real as you were the day I took your
portrait.

Remember, it was soon after war broke out in '39? Your
father had hosted a Red Cross picnic in Thornwood's rambling
garden one sunny afternoon. I lugged Poppa's Argus Rangefinder
up the hill, taking portraits for a shilling donation to the War
Fund. You slipped me a crisp pound note and beckoned me to
the arbour, insisting that you be my first customer.

You looked so alive, smiling that crooked way you have,
eyes only for me. And me feeling the first giddy threads of love
beginning to tighten around my heart. How I loved you that day,
Samuel . . . how I love you still.

Do you ever think of me, darling? Are there roses where you
are – or is it all mud and darkness, blood and dread? Perhaps I'll
sing them to you anyway – fragrant buds and big heavy blooms,
sweet-tasting hips, all bursting with tenderness and desire – and
I'll pray that if nothing else, at least they (and I) will be there in
your dreams.

4 May, 1944

Darling Samuel,

This morning I woke late to find Lulu's crib empty. I suffered a split second of giddy terror – as if that time-bomb had stopped ticking, with me poised in the silent lull before detonation – but then I heard her sweet giggling drifting from the kitchen.

I went out to find Ellen at the breakfast table with Lulu on her lap, and Cleve sitting beside them sharing a huge dish of scrambled eggs and fingers of buttery toast.

Ellen's face was glowing, and Lulu's too ... but the most extraordinary thing of all was the transformation which had come over young Cleve. While I stood unseen in the doorway, Ellen extended her thin hand and stroked Cleve's cheek. The boy visibly melted, his eyes went huge as a puppy's, gazing at his mother with a sort of astonished gratitude. Of course, Ellen's attention went back to Lulu, who was cramming great fistfuls of egg into her mouth, spilling most of it on her pretty frock – but Cleve ... well, Cleve's gaze remained transfixed on his mother.

I swear, Samuel, I've never seen such a look of pure, wild, hopeful love. I felt embarrassed to be witnessing such a thing. It seemed private, and Cleve's response to his mother's brief kindness was heart-rending. It was one of those tiny, deceptively trifling moments that a much older Cleve might look back on and remember as being a turning point in his life.

I should have been glad for him, but a feeling of desolation washed over me. My position in life had shifted. What I'd thought was real and solid became, in an eye-blink, as flimsy as spiderweb. Ellen and Cleve and my own precious Lulu were the picture of a happy, tight-knit little family sharing their moment of cosy togetherness; while I was the solitary outsider.

2 March, 1945

Samuel love, at last I have some good news to relate. Poppa is coming home! I had a letter from him yesterday, he says he'll arrive in Magpie Creek at the end of June. Of course, I wanted to rush back to Stump Hill Road and start preparing the house for him, but June is still a way off and so I must be patient.

Last night I showed Poppa's letter to Ellen and told her my plan to return home. At first she acted pleased, but I could tell she was put out. She kept stalking about the room, throwing worried glances at me, asking Klaus over and over if Poppa's letter sounded strange to him, and if the poor old soul (Poppa would be outraged to hear himself called that!) might in fact be too ill to return to Stump Hill Road after his ordeal in the internment camp, and too frail to tolerate the carryings on in the house of a rowdy three-year-old.

Lulu is lively, but she'd be no burden on Poppa – quite the opposite, I expect. Poppa always rambles happily about her in his letters, excited at the prospect of playing the doting Opa and spoiling her rotten. I'm sure her sparkle will cheer him rather than send him to an early grave as Ellen seems to think.

Later that night, when Ellen had retired to her room and the lights were out and the house creaking, I thought I heard her crying. My own heart sank, my joy over Poppa's letter dried up. Why is joy always so short-lived? Why is it always overshadowed by guilt or fearfulness? For a long time after Ellen's weeping got lost in the noises of the night and was replaced by Klaus's soft snores, I lay awake.

I understood why Ellen was sad. It had nothing to do with worrying about Poppa's welfare – it was that she'd miss Lulu.

At midnight I wandered downstairs to fetch myself a cup of Horlick's. Who should I find slumped at the table in the dark, but young Cleve. He startled when I pulled the cord and flooded the kitchen with light, and swiped at his face, but not before I saw that it was shiny with tears.

'What's the matter?' I asked.

'Nothing,' he muttered, and sprang out of his chair, filling the kettle with water and setting it to boil on the hob. He reclaimed his chair, slumped again and avoided my eyes.

'Cleve, are you sick?'

He shook his head.

'Why were you sitting here alone in the dark? You have school tomorrow, it's very late.'

Still he said nothing, and I grew worried. He's turned into a large, lumpish boy, thirteen this year and somehow cumbersome in his own skin. Compared to other children I know, he seems already an old man, his bristly fair hair cropped close to his large head, a crease between his pale brows, and wide blue eyes where anxiety and worry swim continuously around and around like goldfish in a bowl.

'Cleve?'

Again he swiped at his face. 'I don't want you to go.'

Only then did I twig. A dozen memories poured in – Cleve and his mother at the breakfast table, the way they were always cosseting Lulu, the three of them the very picture of a happy family; countless cosy evenings around the wireless, Cleve playing with Lulu at his mother's feet; Cleve and his mother taking turns to read in funny voices from one of Lulu's story books before bedtime.

Cleve and his mother.

'We can't stay here forever, you know,' I told him.

Cleve nodded, but then he lifted his eyes and looked at me. A chill took hold. Stupid, I must have been very tired – but I thought I saw something else in those blue fishbowl eyes, something that troubled me. Resentment, maybe. Even hatred. Samuel, I know it sounds strange, but what I felt at that moment was very much akin to fear.

The moment passed. Cleve hung his head, and I doubted what I'd seen. Brushing off my misgivings, I hauled the spluttering kettle from the stovetop and made two cups of Horlick's. Any other time I might have sat by the boy, patted his podgy shoulder, offered words of comfort. Not last night. As soon as I'd set his cup before him, I muttered a hasty 'Goodnight' and made a beeline for my room.

16 March, 1945

Oh Samuel, I've fallen into such a dark mood.

An hour after tea tonight, as we were settling around the wireless for the seven o'clock broadcast, Lulu, who I'd just kissed goodnight and tucked into bed, started shrieking. I flew out to our room and snatched her up, sickened to discover that blood was streaming from her poor tiny arm. Ellen discovered a piece of brown glass in the cot. She glared at me as if I was the worst mother in the world, which I now fear to be true.

The wound wasn't deep, but nevertheless we flapped around in a panic, spilling iodine and Solyptol ointment all over ourselves and scattering bandages and cottonwool and rolls of gauze until the room resembled a camp hospital – but Lulu soon settled, quite the brave little trouper.

I swear, Samuel, I've no idea how glass could have found its way into my baby's crib – I've got hawk-eyes when it comes to her safety. Cleve was lurking in the doorway, watching the goings-on with a sullen smirk on his face. I remember thinking unkindly, Where's your blasted bottle of mercurochrome now?

24 March, 1945

Samuel, I'm about to burden you again with my woes, forgive me darling, I have no one else to turn to and I know you'll understand.

Late last night I overheard Ellen talking on the telephone . . . she didn't mention any names, but several times I heard her say 'the child', and 'the little girl', and then, 'the whole situation is most unsatisfactory'.

I lay awake after that, listening to the house creak and groan, my tears turning cold on my cheeks. This morning I waited until breakfast was out of the way before approaching Ellen. I told her that I was taking Lulu back to Stump Hill Road earlier than planned, so we could get the house ready for Poppa.

Of course we argued. I hadn't been expecting her to be quite so upset. She left the room crying, and I felt wrenched apart. With every fibre of my soul I wished I hadn't said anything to her. But Samuel, after overhearing her telephone call last night, how could I not?

I slumped at the table. Cleve hovered in the doorway, watching me.

'What?' I said, more harshly than I'd intended. 'What are you staring at?'

He didn't reply at first. Again I had the sense that he was older – far older – than his thirteen years. In the past twelve months Cleve has grown quite tall, nearly as tall as his father and certainly as thickly built. I hadn't noticed until now . . . I suppose I've picked up his mother's habitual tendency to ignore him.

'*You* can go,' he said heatedly. 'No one will miss *you*. But Lulu belongs with us now.'

'How can you say that, Cleve? She's my daughter. The only person she belongs with is me.'

'Mum says you're not fit to be a mother.'

I stared, speechless. It took a few moments to find my voice, and when I did it was barely more than a whisper.

'Then she's wrong.'

But Cleve had gone, I could hear him clomping down the hall to his room, whistling in that tuneless way he did, a sign that he was well pleased.

I sat at the table for a long time. Shaking. Holding onto my tears. Lulu started to cry and Ellen went to her, but I couldn't move. I just sat there thinking about the men in the grey suits with their clipboards full of forms and their black motorcar with its windows wound up . . . and for the first time since the war began, I felt afraid. Not for myself, but for our little girl. She's my life, Samuel – her sweet smile, her chirpy little voice, her sunny presence – she is more vital to me than food or water or air. If she was taken, how would I go on?

25 May, 1945

My Dearest, as you can see by the address, I'm still at the Jarmans'. Ellen made me promise to stay on until she finds another housekeeper – as if that's all I was to them, hired help!

Anyway, a while ago I mentioned how busy we've been bottling fruit and chutney for the upcoming Red Cross stall, another benefit for the Comforts Fund. Ellen still hasn't found a housekeeper to replace me, so I had resigned myself to staying longer, trapped in this awkward sort of purgatory, biding my time until some other poor victim arrived to take my place.

Oh but Samuel, that's all changed. After this afternoon's debacle, I can't stay.

Ellen had taken Lulu to her Red Cross meeting (where, no doubt, the lot of them would make a right old fuss over the little imp) and so I'd taken the opportunity to bottle up the last of the tomatoes.

Cleve came into the kitchen and began skulking around, fiddling with the chopping knife, accidentally (on purpose) knocking tomato skins onto the floor, dithering back and forth between the sink and the table.

A huge pot of tomato lava was bubbling away on the stove, and as I started ladling the brew into sterilised bottles, Cleve shuffled past and jogged my elbow.

Scalding sauce splashed my arm. I jerked back in shock and pain, and my foot came down on the trodden-in tomato skins that Cleve had neglected, despite my nagging, to pick off the floor. I skidded, almost losing my balance but somehow catching myself on the table edge. The ladle flew from my grasp and crashed onto the floor.

Cleve screamed.

I spun around. The first thing I saw was a blood-red splatter on his school shirt. In my jostled state I thought he must have cut himself with the chopping knife. He was buckled over clutching his face, bellowing like a wounded bullock. Then

I understood. The blistering hot contents of my ladle had splashed him.

I tried to drag him over to the sink to douse him in water and see how bad his scalds were, but he fought me off and ran.

The matron at the hospital said he'll be all right, though the burns are quite nasty and his poor face may be scarred.

Samuel, I can't quite describe how low I feel about this. It must seem to you a trivial injury in light of the horrors you are no doubt treating in Malaya – or wherever it is you are. But Cleve is a child, and because of me he will now be marked for life.

I thought it best to return to Stump Hill Road. Despite my promise to Ellen, I can't bear to stay here a minute longer. I'm a terrible coward to run away, but what else can I do? Events here seem to be conspiring to prove me a wretch of a mother. I'm scared to be alone and at the mercy of the inspectors . . . but I'm more scared of staying here.

3 September, 1945

Samuel, our repatriated troops from Singapore have been trickling home for some weeks now, and I'm getting worried. Where are you, love?

No one has heard from you, no one remembers seeing you after Singapore's capture in '42. I've written to the Red Cross, but as yet have had no replies. I've even gone to Brisbane on the train and walked out to the wharf and watched the wounded pouring off the hospital ships. I've cadged lifts to Toowoomba, and back to Brisbane, even Enoggera – to haunt the wards of the repatriation hospitals there – all to no avail.

Darling, what am I to believe?

I will address this letter to the Records Office at the Showgrounds in Sydney, and hope, by some miracle, that if you are alive it will somehow reach you.

Samuel, please be alive. Please come home to me. Whatever you have suffered we will face together. We'll build a happy life just as we planned, you and me and Lulu. We'll forget the war, and let the greater world carry on without us for a while ... What do you say, love?

The next letter from Samuel was barely legible. The handwriting wobbly and uneven as a child's scrawl, veering all over the page, the paper freckled with ink spots and torn in places where the pen had broken through. At the top was written 'Greenslopes, Brisbane' – which I understood to be the repatriation hospital built early in the war for returning soldiers.

3 December, 1945
Aylish Sweetheart,

I got home a fortnight ago, relieved beyond belief to be back on familiar soil. My first thought was to see you, my dear – but I'm confined to a bed at least 'til Christmas. Please don't worry about me, I'm well enough – just somewhat underfed and malarial, though the staff at Greenslopes fuss over me like a newborn.

It's palatial, this hospital. Freshly painted walls and beds (the colour of buttermilk), crisp sheets so clean they crackle, ceilings the very same hue as that curly moss that used to grow at the gully, a delicate green I could happily stare at all day (and oftentimes do). There are wide verandahs where a bloke can sit and watch the world drift by ... or daydream about his beautiful girl, and how much he longs to see her (hint hint).

I've heard there are even machines to wash the dishes, as well as electric-heated food trolleys. Sometimes it feels as though I've stepped through time into a very different world to the one I waved farewell four years ago. The food is top-notch – though the nursing staff are somewhat stingy with my portions, half-cupfuls at a time due to my dodgy digestion. But oh, Aylish, it's good ... so very good. Stew with real meat, bread rolls and butter, sago pudding and poached rhubarb. Surely I've died and gone to heaven? Only there's an angel missing, an angel with a sweet smile and eyes that twinkle like black diamonds – how soon can you visit me, sweet Aylish?

Being home feels unreal – as though I'm not home at all, but in some halfway place, a limbo of sorts, a pleasant dream ... a dream I'm terrified of waking from.

I crave to be back at Magpie Creek. I crave company and laughter and lightness. Yet I fear it, too. What if I return only to find that I've forgotten how to banter, how to relate? How to fit in? I have to keep reminding myself that with my marvellous Aylish by my side I can do anything ... and I do still have you, don't I, love?

I don't know what you've heard about my escapades – probably bugger-all ... there are so many rumours whizzing around, so many contradictions, no one's sure of anything.

After being separated from my battalion in '42, I was taken off to Borneo and had no way of sending word home. I expect all the lads thought me a goner, and there'll be those in town surprised to learn I'm still around. In October last year when I reached Singapore – months behind the rest of the boys – I ran into a familiar face, do you remember Davo Legget from the timber mill? He broke the sad news about my father. It was a shock to think Dad's been gone all this time and me not knowing. You can imagine my grief – Dad was a hard sort of a bloke, we were never close ... and yet there was great respect between us, and I suppose you could say we loved each other in our way. I miss him terribly.

Which only makes me all the more impatient to see you, Aylish. I think of you constantly. Since we kissed for the last time and said goodbye on the platform at Roma Street, an image has remained imprinted on my soul: My beautiful girl standing there in the dusty September heat, tears swimming in her eyes and a smile trembling on her luscious lips – don't laugh, Aylish, that picture of you in my head was more vivid than any photograph – even though the snap you pressed into my hand that day has travelled with me, become as necessary to my survival as food or drink or oxygen. It grew tattered, but your memory never did. Heck, you're thinking, the damn fool's turned into a sentimental sap . . . and I guess I have. How could I not? My love for you is every bit as strong, if not a thousandfold stronger, than it was the last time I saw you that day at the station.

Aylish, please visit. Or at least drop me a line?

I sat back, rubbing the cramp out of my neck. Spread around me were dozens of letters, but not one of them had reached its intended recipient. It made sense that the wartime postal service had been unreliable, but surely *some* of their letters would have made it through? Shuffling through the pile, I noticed that although Aylish's envelopes all bore postage stamps, none had been franked. Mystified, I picked up the next letter. It was from Samuel, again from Greenslopes, barely half a page.

6 January, 1946
Aylish, did you get my letter?

As yet I've had no reply. I telephoned the post office and Klaus's boy answered, he agreed to pass on my message. That was over two weeks ago. Am I to understand by your silence that you don't wish to see me?

If you've met someone else, if your love for me has cooled, then please, my dear, write and kindly end our association. If my correspondence is inappropriate, then ask Jacob to write to me if you can't bear to write yourself.

5 March, 1946
Dear Aylish,

Just a note to advise that I'm returning to Magpie Creek next week. No doubt you'll want to avoid embarrassment. Never

fear, I'll try to be civil, but if you are engaged or are otherwise spoken for, please consider my feelings if we do happen
to meet.

Sincerely, Samuel Riordan.

P.S. I'm returning the photo you gave me at Roma Street,
I can no longer bear to look at it.

The afternoon was fading. Pink clouds streaked the sky and the
trees were gathering their shadows. I sat on Samuel's bed with
my aching leg propped on a pillow, staring at the letters he and
Aylish had written to each other.

In the 1940s the small post office at Magpie Creek would
have been hectic because of the war – letters and cards pouring
in from all over the globe, parcels going out. I could imagine a
young Cleve Jarman arriving early before school, then returning again in the afternoon, always making sure he was first at
the sorting table. In the midst of all that chaos it would have
been easy for him to palm a letter into his pocket. In the beginning, he might have been curious, pocketing the letters to read
in private, with every intention of later returning them. But
instead, in the end, he'd kept them.

Why? To punish Aylish? To hurt her for the perceived hurt
she'd inflicted on him? Or to spy on the private love she shared
with Samuel, a love that Cleve, as an awkward and lonely
teenager, felt denied?

A dark mood of my own was uncurling. How different would
Aylish's life have been if Cleve had not stolen the letters? Fate
might have led her and Samuel along a happier path. She might
have lived, married Samuel, had the joyful life she'd dreamed
about. And what about Luella? Given the advantage of a loving
mother and father, would she have grown into a woman with
the strength and foresight to somehow prevent the tragic
destiny of her own family?

I slumped.

Fate. Destiny. All very well in retrospect. But as I collected the strewn letters and began to file them back into their envelopes, I had to admit that there was no way ever to know. Any tiny, seemingly random or insignificant decision you made had the potential to change your life for the better ... or for the worse. The problem was, how did you know which decisions would lead to havoc, and which would prove benign?

I was about to close the lid of the box when I spied a letter I hadn't yet read. It had been tucked into the lining at the back, nearly out of sight. There was no envelope, but I saw from the slanting copperplate that it was from Aylish. Penned in early 1946, and written so hastily that splashes of ink dotted the paper like small blue freckles.

27 January, 1946
Dear Samuel,
I write in haste while my courage lasts. I have returned the revolver you gave me in 1941. I used the washhouse key and let myself into the homestead, I do hope you won't be cross. The weapon is now locked somewhere you're certain to find it. Forgive me, darling, but I didn't dare keep it any longer.

I will try to explain, but I suppose my dilemma will seem trifling to you. In my defence, remember I was raised a Lutheran and despite my sins I have always tried to tread carefully in the world and bring harm to no one. But I'm no longer the carefree soul you left behind, Samuel. No longer the girl who skipped beside you at the gully's edge, or giggled at the butterflies you captured. I feel hard and small, hemmed in by disappointment and a growing sense of dread that I can't explain. I still have the same body and face, the same legs you once said you admired ... but in the mirror lately I've noticed a darkness in my eyes that was never there before.

Last night, sometime before midnight, I heard the hens squawking in the chook yard. Recently we lost four of our best layers, and Poppa swore he saw a fox on Sunday, flitting through the fence palings with a fowl in its jaws. Poor Poppa was so distressed at the time, all red in the face and his eyes large and wet with worry. I thought he might be about to throw a turn, and became quite terrified for him. I only managed to calm him by promising that I'd find a way to trap and kill the fox.

Yes, dearest, you did hear right.

The Poppa who returned from two and a half years in Tatura is also a changed person. Do you remember how he used to say that killing tore at the human soul, and that it made us no better than animals? Well, Samuel, years of war have hardened his poor old heart. Especially when our meagre livelihood is under threat.

Since leaving my employment with the Jarmans in May last year, I've been able to bring in a small income by growing and selling vegies, as well as eggs and fresh-churned butter. There's also the ironing and mending I've taken on for some of the church ladies – but our eggs are in steady demand, and we couldn't afford to lose the small income they bring.

So Samuel, I dug out your revolver and loaded it the way you showed me. Outside, the yard was dark. There was no moon, but the starlight was glary enough to see by. I waited for my eyes to adjust, then trod barefoot along the path to the hen enclosure. I could hear the girls scratching their straw and nattering. The fox must be near. My blood galloped in my ears. I'd never killed a butterfly before, let alone a warm-blooded creature like a fox, but my heart was set. If I couldn't kill it, I'd scare it off for good.

I held the revolver in both hands and cocked the hammer. Then I stood my ground and waited.

And waited.

The revolver grew heavy, my arms ached. The girls were still restive, clucking and scratching. I sensed the night rolling by, the stars shifting on their axis overhead. There was still no sign of the fox. After a while, I decided to find a more comfortable perch, to wait out the night if I had to. Lowering the gun, I went along the path. I was approaching the enclosure when I heard a scuffle from the woodshed.

Turning, I listened.

The woodshed was behind me, between where I stood near the chook enclosure and the house. It was little more than a corrugated iron manger with three walls and a roof, stacked with firewood and kindling. I heard a soft crunch, like small clawed feet on woodchips.

I made my way back along the path, gripping the revolver tight in both hands. Careful not to make a sound, I approached the woodshed. Pausing in the open entryway, I waited for my eyes to adjust. Then, there at the back, I saw it. A shadowy hump of darkness outlined against the blacker pitch of the shed. I raised the revolver and trained my sights on the hump, held my breath as I slid my finger onto the trigger and braced myself in readiness to fire . . .

The shadow unfolded. Grew in height. It turned around to face me, and I found myself staring at – not a fox, as I'd thought – but the vague outline of a man. For an agonising moment nothing happened. Shock, I expect, Samuel. The moment must only have lasted for an eye blink, but it seemed to me as if I was standing on the brink of a hellish eternity.

'Oh dear God, Poppa!' I nearly dropped the revolver as shock left me and understanding came. I lowered the weapon and pointed it at the ground, shaking all over now and feeling the sweat begin to pour out of me. 'You might have been killed!'

The figure said nothing, and as it came towards me I realised it wasn't Poppa. I backed out of the woodshed door-way and retreated several steps along the path. The man followed and, as the dim starlight gathered about him, I saw I'd again been mistaken.

It wasn't a man, after all.

But a boy.

More than six months had passed since I'd seen him. He'd grown taller and filled out. I made a swift calculation. He'd be fourteen now, still a child, but nearly as tall and stocky as his father. With a stab of guilt, I noticed a whitish gleam to his face, as though it was streaked by skeins of moonlight. The last time I'd seen him his cheeks and brow had been puffy and weeping, blistered and pinkly inflamed.

'Cleve?' I said, my voice sharp with fright and horror at how close I'd just come to wounding – perhaps even killing – him. 'What are you doing here, creeping about in the dark? Does Ellen know you're here?'

He shuffled, but didn't reply. I wondered if I'd caught him in the act of stealing, but then had to admit there was nothing in the woodshed worth a ha'penny.

'Well?' I said, my concern turning to annoyance. 'What's up with you? Why won't you answer me . . . ? Has the cat got your tongue?'

Still he said nothing.

'You'd better go home,' I told him. My body was trembling. I was feeling sicker by the minute. The near-catastrophe played out in my mind's eye – the pistol blast shattering the night, and then me on my knees on the woodshed floor, trying in vain to revive Cleve's bleeding body . . .

The weapon seemed to writhe in my palm, greasy and warm, like an animal vexed by the loss of an easy kill. I understood then that the revolver was an evil thing and I wanted nothing more to do with it.

Cleve stepped from the semi-darkness and moved along the path, brushing past me, still without a word, and vanishing along the side of the house. A while later I heard the creak of his bicycle, and then the swish of his tyres on the road.

I stood for a long time, Samuel. There on the path in the star-light, waiting for the trembling to leave me. When it did, I said

a prayer of thanks, then turned to go back inside. I'd taken a few
steps when I remembered Cleve brushing past me, and how I'd
noticed an unpleasant odour.

He'd reeked of sweat, sour nervous sweat . . . which made
me wonder if perhaps he had been stealing after all? But
what? There was nothing of value in the shed. Wood, kindling;
but that was plentiful, scattered around for anyone to collect
for free.

Curious, I wandered into the shed and lit the kerosene lantern
that hung near the entryway. I looked around, but saw nothing
unusual. Neat piles of kindling, logs. A box of pinecones. Big
timber rounds stacked ready for splitting.

And Poppa's old axe head, forgotten on the floor.

I sighed and bent to retrieve it. The sharp edge gleamed
silver in the lantern light, the steel surface flecked with rust
spots. It had worked its way off the handle, and Poppa had been
promising for weeks to mend it. I'd given up nagging him about
it. It was only January, but Samuel, you know how fast winter
sneaks up on us here, it can catch you unawares.

I cast about for the handle, intending to prop it beside the
axe head as a reminder for Poppa. I searched among the stacked
logs and even in the box of kindling, but couldn't find it. In
the end I had to conclude that it had been stolen . . . or at least
secreted away in some improbable hiding place. Then an odd
feeling came over me. I looked back at the open entryway,
suddenly and inexplicably chilled.

What would Cleve want with an old axe handle?

Strange boy. Whatever he was up to, it had almost got him
killed.

Placing the letter on the bed beside me, I let myself slide down
the wall I'd been leaning on. Then somehow I was curled on my
side, staring along the bumpy terrain of the quilt at the piece
of notepaper with its blue-freckle splashes and dog-eared edges.

I couldn't know for certain. Too much time had passed. Logic said there wasn't any concrete evidence. Yet my bones ached with the terrible truth; my certainty was so strong that it seemed I'd always known it.

I recalled the news article I'd unearthed online.

A post-mortem examination confirmed that Miss Lutz had been battered by a wooden implement thought to be a wheel spoke or club –

I had another flash: the antique tallboy hiding in a shadowed corner of the settlers' hut. Inside its dusty compartment I'd found the greasy tool handle with its wooden shaft blackened by years of usage. Which had struck me as odd at the time because an axe handle belonged in the woodshed or under the house – not in a wardrobe that was clearly a storehouse of mementoes . . .

Unless the axe handle was a memento too?

As I lay there I was only half-aware of the day slipping away. Shadows flitted beyond the frame of the window – birds winging past, or trees swaying, or the passage of a cloud across the face of the sun.

After much deliberation, I decided not to tell anyone what I'd found.

Cleve was dead. And Luella had lived for sixty years without knowing the identity of her mother's killer. How would it serve her now, mere months after losing her son and when she was obviously still so fragile, to learn that she'd married and borne children to the man who had murdered her mother?

20

By Friday my leg was feeling better . . . though the same could not be said for my heart; it felt bruised and fragile after reading Aylish's letters, unable to beat quite as it had done before.

Although I knew the letters weren't conclusive evidence, there was no doubt in my mind that fourteen-year-old Cleve Jarman had killed Aylish. I longed to share the burden of that knowledge with someone, and to clear Samuel's name – but how could I, knowing that my disclosure would inevitably find its way back to Luella? The last thing I wanted was to add to her already vast store of sorrows.

So it was with a dull ache in my chest that I found myself back on the trail that led to the gully. Danny and I had set out from Thornwood at eight a.m. and had been walking for about forty minutes. My injured leg had flared up, especially after the steep climb, and was just starting to throb when Danny signalled to stop for a breather.

We found a rocky plateau overlooked by tall boulders that cast welcoming shade. Below stretched a spectacular vista of forested hills rolling to a pale blue horizon. There were distant glimpses of civilisation emerging through the trees like remnants of a lost world – brown paddocks, and a narrow dirt road that meandered to the east. There was no sign of the highway, and no other houses. Below us to the north-east, I could just make out the darkly treed depression of the gully.

Danny settled on a boulder and took two mandarins from his pocket, offered me one. I perched nearby on the flattest surface I could find, relieved to be off my leg. Content in the silence as I sailed my peelings into the shade of a stunted little bullock bush that looked as if it could use the nourishment. The mandarin was intensely sweet, seedy, gone in a flash. I wiped my fingers on my jeans, gazing at the distant hills as my thoughts escaped back into Aylish's letters.

I imagined Samuel hurrying along the track from Thornwood to meet Aylish at the settlers' hut, his skin moist from the climb and his pulse racing in anticipation of seeing her. At first I'd assumed they had met at the hut to avoid being discovered. After all, Samuel was the son of a wealthy doctor, while Aylish was the half-Aboriginal daughter of a poor Lutheran minister – which meant nothing these days, but back in the 1940s it would have created a scandal.

Now, sitting in the vast breathing stillness, basking in the warmth of a yellow day embroidered by birdsong – I came to understand what had really drawn them. Out here, there was space to breathe. No other soul for miles, no one to judge, no one to lay down rules and then insist that you abide by them. No one to criticise and find you lacking. No one to hem you in, tie you down, stifle you –

Something struck me on the side of the head. I flinched, envisioning a redback or flying snake or worse – then saw it was only a coin-sized fragment of mandarin peel.

I scowled at Danny. He was watching me, his eyes aglow, his hair on end, his lips on the verge of a smile. He took out his notebook, then came and sat nearby.

Leg okay? he wanted to know.

'Yeah, good.'

He patted his pocket, drew out a box of Panadol. *I brought these just in case.*

A flush of warmth. 'Thanks, that was thoughtful. I'm all right for now.'

He pondered me, as if deciding something. Then he wrote, *What happened with Tony, why did you split?*

Yikes, I thought. A million answers to that one. Tony grew bored with my constant probing, my questions, my need for reassurance. He became restless with our simple existence and went in search of greener pastures, wealth and fame and adventure. He needed far more out of life than I was able to offer . . .

I sighed. 'He met someone else.'

Bummer, Danny finger spelled, but his expressive face was anything but sorrowful. He dashed off another note to add: *He was an idiot.*

I had to smile. 'He found the right path, that's all. Carol, his wife, is lovely. She doted on Tony, looked after him. She helped him with his career, smoothed the way for him. But it was more than that, too. They just clicked.'

Danny looked thoughtful. He wrote: *You meet anyone else?*

I shook my head.

Why not? he signed, feigning astonishment.

'Too busy with my career. With raising a daughter.'

Back came the notebook. *And the real reason?*

I couldn't meet his eyes, so I stared at the parched little bullock bush. Stretched my leg. Pondered popping a couple of Panadol to take the edge off the pain that was just starting to flare. Then I had to confess.

'I never met anyone . . . anyone I clicked with, I mean.'

Danny nodded, studying my face as though my disclosure held utmost fascination for him. His obvious interest made me want to keep talking. There was so much I was curious about, and his unexpected inquisition about Tony had opened a doorway which would have made it easy for me to throw some questions of a more intimate nature back at him. Why did you offer to come up here with me today? Why do I get the feeling you're flirting? And how do you manage the loneliness you must feel being deaf in a tiny backwoods community like Magpie Creek?

Instead I found myself saying, 'Corey told me about your wife. I'm sorry.'

Me too, he signed, then finger-spelled, *Bad for Jade.*

'She's a great kid. She and Bronwyn are peas in a pod.'

Danny frowned. I reached for his notebook and wrote my comment. Danny smiled when he read it and signed, *Yeah, they're like sisters, aren't they?*

Crazy, how an innocent remark could make the heat fly to my cheeks. Mortified, I pretended interest in a magpie which had alighted nearby. It chortled, gaining volume until a full-throated song burst from its throat, sending shivers up my spine.

The corkscrew branches of the old angophora were black against the lake-blue sky, the delicate grey-green foliage motionless as a held breath. I liked being here, I found I felt comfortable with Danny. And yet my heart was at war. I was a leaf caught in raging floodwaters, being swept towards something I longed for . . . yet deeply feared. The speed and forward motion were exhilarating – but I was out of my depth, craving the familiar safety of solid ground.

From the corner of my eye I saw Danny lean back, scratching his fingers lazily through his chaotic hair, making the muscles in his arm bunch up. I tried not to look, but his fingers began moving in the air, and I had to turn my head to read them.

This place makes me think of Tony.

'Why?'

Danny took out his notebook. *We used to sit here when we were kids. On our way up to the hut, like we are now.*

Maybe it was the beauty of the landscape surrounding us, or the sun's scorching heat, or the vaguely edgy feeling I always had when Danny was near. Then again, maybe it was the secret I now carried in my heart, eroding it from the inside like rot in an apple core, making me throw all caution to the wind.

I found myself asking, 'Why do you think Tony never stayed in contact with anyone here? Not you . . . not even his mother? I can understand that he was grieving for his sister, but it strikes me as odd that he cut himself off from his past so completely.'

Danny shrugged. He looked at his hands for a long time, then began to write in his book.

The night he ran away, he came to say goodbye. It was late, Tony climbed through my bedroom window. He looked sick, pale and sweaty. He said he had to leave, that he'd done something bad.

That got me. 'Bad . . . like what?'

He began to write again, filling the small page with his looping scrawl. Tilting my head, I tried to read the top line but then he finished, tore off the leaf and passed it to me with a flourish.

I asked what had happened, but he wouldn't tell me. He seemed scared, kept looking around, jumping at noises.

Danny began another note, but halfway through he stopped. Tucking his notebook and pen into the waistband of his jeans, he began to sign rapidly, almost frantically, his gestures precise and fast and urgent. I wondered if he was swearing again, and watched, fascinated.

He must have known I was lost, but he didn't seem able to stop or slow down. His hands were graceful as they marked out a stream of silent words: forefinger skating the length of his arm, his fist slapping his open palm, the side of his hand slicing the air. Swift, almost violent gestures that – despite my inability to read them – were shockingly vocal.

I had come to believe that the language of the deaf was a precarious, abstract thing. Signing required physical effort; lip reading was dodgy at the best of times; writing everything down was time-consuming and tedious. Subtleties of tone, the warmth or chill in a person's voice, the harshness or tender-ness of pitch – all coloured a language, gave it a multilayered subtext that was vital to full communication. If those nuances were unavailable, flattened into a series of hand signals and voiceless gestures, how could you know for sure you were being understood?

And yet, without me catching a word, Danny's meaning came across loud and clear. His animated face, his tense shoulders, his fast-moving hands – the feeling of frustration and sorrow that radiated out of him – all spoke volumes.

Something bad had happened, and Tony felt responsible. Whatever it was, Tony's fear had infected Danny as well.

Danny stopped signing and took up his notebook. One page, two. Three. He tore the sheets off together, pressed them into my hand.

Tony convinced me to take him to the bus depot, he had a pocketful of change he took from his father's jar. After long arguing, I agreed. I gave him more dollars, then dinked him on my bike to the depot.

I flipped to the next page, ripped it a little in my haste.

We were too early for a bus so we waited 'til morning. When the first bus opened its doors, we hugged goodbye and Tony got on. I never saw him again.

And the next:

Later, I learnt gossip – that Tony had argued with Glenda the night she died, pushed her. I told Corey what he'd told me about doing something bad. She said: Take no notice, Tony would never do that. She said: Never tell anyone. So I never did. Until now.

My fingers shook as I folded the notes, tucking them out of sight with the others in my pocket. My leg was complaining now, bright threads of pain leaping and writhing along the edges of my awareness.

'Before, you said that Tony seemed scared . . . What might he have been scared of?'

Danny gathered the mandarin peelings he'd scattered around his feet and tossed them under the bullock bush on top of mine. He looked back at me, squinting against the sunlight.

Don't know.

The patchy shade seemed to grow hotter. I pressed my palms over my cheeks. They were burning.

'What about the bad thing he said he did? What could that have been?'

Danny shrugged, shifting his attention off me and into the treetops. I sensed him withdrawing. Leaning over, I grasped his wrist, forcing him to turn back and look at my lips. 'You think he had something to do with Glenda's accident?'

No.

'What then?'

Wish I knew.

I scrambled to my feet, hiding my irritation by turning away, glaring down into the valley. The pressure in my head was almost intolerable. The sense of space and freedom I'd been enjoying a while ago was gone. In its place was a bright red ball of anger.

Why had Tony left us Thornwood? He must have known I'd fall in love with the place, want to live here. The high-ceilinged rooms and his grandfather's gorgeous old collectables, the garden with its magical views . . . all elements Tony knew I'd go crazy for.

Hadn't he also known that I would, by my very nature, be curious about the past? His past? Hadn't he known that I'd pick away at the threads until it finally unravelled? And hadn't it occurred to him that my discoveries would not only trouble me, but cast their monumental shadow over Bronwyn as well?

Fingers touched the side of my face.

You okay? Danny wanted to know.

I nodded, but I wasn't. Not really. My mind was darting from memory to memory like a dragonfly skating over a muddy pond: Tony beaming at his newborn daughter. Tony teaching Bronwyn to use her first butterfly net. Excursions to the beach, fish and chips on the foreshore, the beaming smiling pair of them climbing the Elwood beach lookout, the salt wind putting roses in their cheeks . . .

Had it all been a lie?

Danny shifted into my line of sight. He tucked a strand of hair behind my ear.

You're burning. Forgot hat?

Before I had a chance to step away, he brushed his thumb beneath my eye, collecting the tear I hadn't realised I'd shed. Then he grabbed my hand. His palm was warm and dry, his fingers closing around mine with more familiarity than I had faculty to cope with. He tugged me out of the glaring sun and into the shadows of a nearby red gum. He seemed too near, the warmth of his body far greater than the heat radiating off the outcrop of stones. I tried to get my fingers back, but he wouldn't let them go. He lifted them to his chest, pressed my palm flat over his heart.

Something raced under my touch . . .

Now would have been the perfect time to utter some amusing quip and turn my attention outwards, across the sundrenched hills; to pull away, slam down the shutters, cocoon myself in frosty indifference – as my better judgement was urging me to do.

Instead I allowed Danny's gravitational force to draw me nearer. I felt the stillness of him quieten my ragged nerves, felt his calm aura radiate out and envelop me. Like him, I became motionless. And then, as he tugged me suddenly and surely against him, as his arms closed around me and held my body snug against his, all I felt was relief. Melting, warm-bath, half-sleepy relief . . .

For a moment I lost myself. My body sank against him and I remembered what it was like to feel safe and complete. Remembered, too, the comfort that the right man's arms could bring. I exhaled, feeling my doubts about Tony dissolve, feeling my fears evaporate. Feeling my faith trickle back as I basked in the simple pleasure of human contact.

Then I breathed in.

Fresh sweat and sunlight, a hint of soap. Dog hair, motor oil, the tang of citrus. I melted then, forgetting the danger. Letting myself notice the sturdy feel of his chest against my softness, allowing myself to steal a moment's pleasure as his arms tightened around me. Half-aware that I was entering risky territory, ignoring the warning bells as his nearness turned me half-drunk with desire.

Lifting my face ever so slightly, I felt the rasp of his whiskers against my cheek. I took another hit of his intoxicating scent, unable to remember ever breathing in anything quite so good. I heard his soft intake of air, felt him breathe me in too; and then his lips made contact beneath my ear, moved soft and warm over my skin. I only had to tilt my face a little, lift my mouth to his, satisfy my longing to taste him –

I sprang back, tearing from his embrace. Stumbled as my injured leg tugged its stitches and began to hurt in earnest. Loose rubble skated beneath my ill-placed boots.

One wrong step . . .

Danny grabbed my arm. I regained my balance and yanked from his grasp. The shock on his face turned to confusion, then understanding.

It's okay.

I looked at him. Couldn't speak, so signed, *No. Not okay.*

Danny's eyes were dark, reflecting my own bewildered longing, my confusion . . . but I couldn't have ventured back to him had my life depended on it. My brain was slamming down on what had just happened, pinching off sensation and warmth in a bid to recover what remained of my protective shell. I wanted to curse myself. I should have seen the signs: the Auslan books and DVDs, the smitten giggling in the rose arbour, the interest with which I'd listened to Corey relate stories about him. Worse, the silk blouse . . . and heaven help me, the perfume.

I had to turn away, and it seemed the only direction to go from here was down. But I took the uphill track, cutting across the stony plateau and pushing through tea-trees and straggly brigalow, heading blindly and inevitably into the scorching sun.

By the time we entered the settlers' hut clearing, my fear had dissipated, leaving in its wake a burning sense of embarrassment. I could hear Danny's footfall crunching through the dry grass behind me, and I wanted to turn around and explain that I was scared of losing myself again, falling into a love trap that would most certainly – for me, at least – end in more heartache. But I'd made such a botch of things already that I decided it was best just to move on.

As we neared the old hut, I noticed how empty it seemed.

The battered cane chair was still propped at one end of the verandah, and the door hung ajar as it had the day I'd come here alone, but the place no longer had the feel of being inhabited. I stopped at the foot of the steps and let Danny go ahead of me, already knowing what we'd find inside.

The derelict furniture remained, but the squatter had removed all other evidence that anyone had been living here. The mattress was bare of its army blanket, and the meat safe was no longer home to mouldy bread and jam. The candles, books, enamel cups and plates were all gone. Only the fusty smell of earth and stale body odour lingered. Leaves and twigs and bush detritus littered the floor and there was a dustiness to the place, as if the hut door had hung ajar for years inviting in the calling cards of windstorms, gales, cyclones; as if no one but possums and birds and the occasional lizard had set foot here for decades.

I stood in the doorway, watching Danny look around. He rattled open the tallboy, empty now of its shrine, the hanging compartment cleared of its gruesome memento. The squatter had surely noticed the box of letters missing, and I wondered how he was feeling about that. Annoyed, that someone had taken them . . . or just glad to have escaped his unlawful occupation of my property without confrontation?

I wondered if he'd known that Samuel and Aylish had used the hut as a secret trysting place – then amended that thought; of course he had, he would have gleaned that from their letters. I looked around with fresh eyes. Would Aylish recognise the hut now? How would she have felt to know that sixty years after her death, someone lived here . . . worse, that he'd been in possession of her private letters and the photograph she'd once given to Samuel?

I could only speculate about how the letters had come to be at the hut. A young Cleve might have stashed them here after Aylish died, fearing they'd be found in his possession . . . and probably guessing that Samuel would shun the place for the memories it held for him. For years the letters had lain here, gathering dust in some hidden nook, only seeing the light of day when the unsuspecting squatter had discovered them.

Yet something niggled. What about the roses? Was my gut feeling totally haywire, or was I right in thinking that the luscious red blooms twining up the verandah rails at the front of the hut were the same as the ones on Aylish's grave?

I went outside and down the steps. The roses had withered in the harsh sun, but I bent to sniff one anyway. The scent was dusty and faded, and yet unmistakable. A dark red perfume with a hint of cinnamon.

Danny thudded down the stairs and stood beside me, writing in his notebook.

Your friend has flown the coop. Covered his tracks. Wants us to think he was never here.

'Why?'

Maybe on the run from law. Or maybe an old bushie who likes to leave no trace.

He wasn't meeting my eyes. He seemed wary of me now. No longer flirty, but serious, almost businesslike. Not that I blamed him. I'd been giving him the signs – learning his language, digging out my prettiest blouse for the barbecue. Perhaps even, in my clumsy manner, attempting to flirt back. But the moment things got interesting, I'd run for the hills.

He touched my arm to get my attention, and crooked his finger for me to follow. I trailed him around to the back of the hut, past the water tank. The forty-four-gallon drum was upended, the woodpile cleared. The ground around it looked swept.

He was here a while, Danny signed.

'How can you tell?'

He indicated where the old guttering had been patched with a piece of tin, and then gestured at the roof where I could just make out the lighter shingles.

'He's done repairs,' I realised.

Danny nodded, then busied himself with further investigations, examining the water tank tap and then going over to look at a mound of tangled vines. I wondered if he was thinking about Tony, and their childhood exploits together. Tony had been a loner, happy to escape into his artwork, but I was patching together a picture of his friendship with Danny. They'd been like brothers, Corey had said. Joined at the hip, always in trouble. I could see them clearly, Tony with his saucer eyes, and Danny with his unruly mop of hair. Warmth crept in. My heartbreak over Tony had been severe, almost crippling at times . . . but I'd survived it. And my survival proved that I was now stronger – didn't it? I recalled how easy it'd been to melt into Danny's arms up at the rocky plateau, and how his embrace had felt so deliciously right, so tempting . . .

I turned away, retreating to the perimeter of the clearing, heading off in search of my Minolta. The old camera was no doubt damaged beyond help, but it had been a faithful old friend and I wanted it back.

Ducking into the tea-tree thicket I'd stumbled through before, I picked my way across the rocky ground until I located the smooth-skinned red gum I'd clung to during the attack. Walking in ever-widening circles, I searched outwards, lifting clumps of lomandra and toeing root hollows, scanning the leaf-litter and wandering downhill a way, all to no avail.

Back at the hut, I found Danny still poking around out back. He'd pulled aside the mound of vines to reveal a low circular structure that looked like the top few feet of a buried water tank. Rather than corrugated iron, the tank's walls were made of timber, thick planks set vertically in a deep round hole. It was topped by a huge flat lid constructed from thick boards bolted to a circular frame.

Danny was writing in his notebook.

It's the original water catchment, very old. The early settlers dug straight down into the soil, lined it with timber like a well. Me and Tony used to drag the cover off, climb down inside. Heaps of fun, but if rain came, it filled fast. Our parents would've had a fit if they'd known.

I smiled at this. Feeling brave, I touched Danny's arm to draw his attention. 'I'm sorry about before.'

He looked at me for a long time. I started to think he hadn't understood what I'd said, and that perhaps I should take his notepad and write it down for him, though of course that would lack the apologetic warmth I'd tried to convey in my smile . . .

Danny cupped the side of my face with his fingers, pressing his thumb ever so lightly against my lips. He didn't quite smile, but dimples appeared and he winked – which made the blood flutter through my veins and my knees go to jelly. Then, without another word, he headed off across the clearing.

I stared after him. Wondering, all over again, why he always left me feeling so dangerously, so excitingly, out of my depth.

21

The following afternoon, dosed up on Panadol to calm my throbbing leg, I pulled up outside the school gates to wait for Bronwyn. I spied Danny's black Toyota truck parked further up the hill beneath a poinciana tree, adorned with fallen crimson flowers ... but I slid lower in my seat, content to hide out. Our botched kiss at the rocky plateau had stirred feelings that I was still trying to untangle, and I wasn't yet ready to face him again.

Bronwyn appeared through the crowd of students and teachers. She hugged Jade and said goodbye to a group of other kids, then hurried towards the car. She waved happily when she saw me, and I had to swallow a lump of sudden emotion. Flinging open the car door, she deposited her rucksack on the back seat, and gave me a quick peck. She was tired and dusty and her clothes were muddy and grass-stained ... but her face glowed and she was brimming with stories.

Rather than our usual dinner in front of the telly, we sat at the table and, in between hungry mouthfuls of tacos and salad, she related a blow-by-blow description of her week. The great swimming holes they'd explored, the bush tucker lessons, the night excursions armed with torches to spot possums and wallabies and quolls. She rolled her eyes over the squashed tent she'd shared with Jade and two other girls, and raved about the prize-winning damper they'd made in a traditional bush oven.

'Mr O'Malley knows all about the bush,' she'd gushed. 'Jade and I reckon he's like that guy on telly who goes off into the wild eating grubs and stuff.'

'I thought you couldn't stand him?'

'Oh, but he's turned out to be really cool! He showed us how to make a flying fox and get across the river. And one night he told us these funny stories about Dad and Aunty Glenda, and Jade's dad and Aunty Corey, all the crazy things they got up to when they were kids. Mum, he's so funny, you wouldn't believe half the things he says.' She sighed happily. 'What did you get up to while I was gone?'

I recalled my trek into the hills; my discovery of the old settlers' hut and consequent encounter with the squatter's dog; I remembered Aylish's letters and their shocking disclosure about Cleve and the stolen axe handle; I thought about my return to the hut a few days later with Danny Weingarten, and our botched almost-kiss at the rocky plateau . . . And decided that some stories were best left untold.

So I just shrugged. 'Not much.'

'What happened to your leg?'

'A dog bit me.'

'Mum! How on earth did you manage that?'

I cut us both another slice of mudcake. 'Just careless, I suppose.'

The Sunday after Bronwyn returned from camp, I drove her over to William Road to spend the day with Luella.

'I won't come in,' I told her as I dropped her off at the gate. 'Say hello to Grandy for me, won't you? Be good, and I'll pick you up at four.'

'Okay.' She pecked me on the cheek, grabbed her carryall – today crammed with photos of the school camp – then hurried along the path and up the front stairs to where Luella waited in the doorway. I gave them both a wave, then threw a U-turn and headed back in the direction of town.

It was cowardly, but I just couldn't face Luella.

I needed time to absorb what I'd learnt about Cleve; time to prepare myself to look into Luella's gentle green eyes and hide what I knew. And I needed time to steel myself against the awfulness of it, against the taint that was now seeping through the cracks of Thornwood. I couldn't even enjoy knowing that I'd been right about Samuel, and right about his true feelings for Aylish.

All I could think about were the empty packing cartons stored under the house, and how much easier it would be just to uproot again and find somewhere else to live.

Somewhere with a little less history.

At four on the dot that afternoon I pulled onto the grassy verge outside Luella's house.

To my surprise Bronwyn was at the top of the stairs, waving to me. I started to wave back, wondering what she was up to, when I realised she wasn't waving at all . . . she was beckoning.

My heart sank. I got out of the car and went along the path. Bronwyn met me at the foot of the steps and grabbed my arm.

'Grandy's got something amazing to show you,' she announced, steering me up the stairs and into the cool shadows of Luella's hallway. 'A surprise. You'll love it, Mum,' she added, noticing my reluctance.

Luella greeted me in the kitchen, untying her apron and wilting my qualms with the magnetism of her smile. 'I've brewed fresh tea, that Earl Grey you're so fond of, love. And we've just pulled a batch of chocolate tarts from the oven.'

When I drew breath to politely decline, my lungs filled with air that was chocolatey-sweet, intoxicating. Something in me unravelled and I heard a little voice say, 'That sounds lovely.'

Bronwyn led me through the kitchen and out onto the verandah, where a feast awaited – Luella's delicate Noritake teacups sat in place beside a platter of fresh scones and hand-cut chocolate pastries that made me goggle in anticipation ... but Bronwyn tugged me past the table, down the back steps and across the garden towards the bunya pine.

'Close your eyes, Mum.'

Reluctantly, I obliged. Sunlight warmed my arms. Bright shards danced across my closed lids, turning the inside of my eyes blood-red. Blades of grass poked through my sandals, and I caught a whiff of jasmine, sweet in the sundrenched air.

We stopped. There was a grating sound, a latch sliding in its casing – then the smell of moist heat, of soil and fertiliser and clammy concrete.

'Watch your step ... Okay, now open your eyes.'

We were standing inside Luella's glasshouse. It looked ancient, pieced together with salvaged leadlight windows. It was shaded by the giant bunya, but along the western side it was a suntrap – ribbons of yellow and crimson and emerald light poured through the muted glass panels, creating rainbows in the humid air.

Workbenches had been built along both sides of the greenhouse and down the centre, leaving narrow walkways between. Crowded along the benches were hundreds of shallow plant pots sitting on trays of water. In the pots, the most curious collection of plants I'd ever seen. Some I recognised as the pitcher plants and sundews of Tony's early botanical studies. Others were strange carnival freaks, balloon-like heads suspended on slender stalks; massive tubes with purple veins and frilled lids, brackets of waxy florets.

'Wonderful, isn't it, Mum?'

'Oh ... yeah.'

Sounds filtered in from outside. Magpies and cicadas, the swish of wind in the bunya pine, the squeaky clothesline.

There was another sound, a muffled buzzing close by. I went over to the nearest bench and examined a shallow dish in which grew a flat rosette of leaves, each leaf tipped with glossy pink hairs.

'A native sundew,' Luella said. 'Each of those hairs is coated in sticky sweet-smelling glue. Insects flock to it, but then get stuck there and can't escape. The leaf curls up around the hapless fly or moth and digests it.'

She went along the workbench and pointed to another plant. Pairs of double-leaves nodded from thin stems; they looked like gaping mouths, deep crimson on the inside, fringed by teeth-like spines.

'It's a Venus flytrap,' Luella informed us. 'When an insect ventures between these leaf lobes, it bends the delicate trigger-hairs, then . . . snap! The trap fills with digestive fluid and begins to feast.' She gestured to Bronwyn, 'Untie your hair ribbon, pet – give it to me.'

Bronwyn obliged, then watched in fascination as her grand-mother smoothed the ribbon between her plump fingers and threaded it into the Venus flytrap's jaws. She gave it a jerky twist, and the spiny leaf lobes snapped shut. Bronwyn hooked her neck in surprise, and I had to stifle an inane snort. The ribbon hung limply from the closed lips of the flytrap, looking every bit like a long pale tongue.

Luella moved along, indicating another plant. This one floated in a small fish tank of water. A cluster of slender stems rose above the waterline, topped by yellow pea-like flowers. Submerged below was a hairy tangle of roots, studded with strange nodules that looked like white seedpods.

'It's bladderwort,' Luella said, bending to peer through the side of the tank, beckoning Bronwyn. 'Such a pretty flower, but don't be deceived – it's named for the bladders attached to the anchoring stems that grow beneath the water. Each bladder has a small opening sealed by a hinged door. Look closely, you might be able to see a pair of long hairs – yes, that's it, come closer . . . You see there?'

Bronwyn looked baffled, but nodded.

'When the hairs are triggered,' Luella continued, 'they lever open the bladder door, which creates a vacuum. The prey – in this case probably an aquatic invertebrate such as *Daphnia* – is sucked inside the hollow bladder and digested. Marvellous, isn't it?'

'Why do they do it?' Bronwyn blurted.

'Because they're hungry, of course.'

'But why do they eat insects? Why can't they just get their food from the soil, like other plants?'

Looking pleased, Luella mopped her hanky over her face. 'Why, these little beauties have adapted to grow in areas where the soil is thin or lacking in nutrients – particularly acidic bogs, or wastelands where nitrogen content in the soil is poor or non-existent.' She tucked the hanky back in her bra. 'Generally these plants lack an enzyme called nitrate reductase, which allows other plants to assimilate soil-borne nitrogen into food . . . that's why carnivorous plants rely on nutrients they get from insects.'

Bronwyn looked solemnly at the bladderwort, but my interest had shifted.

Over by a sheltered section of wall was a large earthenware pot containing a cluster of giant tubular pitcher leaves that towered over everything else. The tall leaves were twisted, with a puffed-up hood and a pair of petals extended like fangs.

'What about this, Luella?'

'Ah yes, that splendid specimen is one of my favourites.' She approached the plant, her face aglow with sweat and pleasure. 'It's a *Darlingtonia*, commonly referred to as the Cobra Lily – magnificent, isn't it? It belongs to the family of pitfall traps, otherwise known as pitcher plants.'

Bronwyn elbowed in beside me. 'What do *they* eat?'

'Pretty much anything that's foolish enough to crawl in – the usual flies and mosquitoes, wasps. Ants, slaters, silverfish. You see, like most pitcher plants, they have a brightly coloured visual lure at the lip of the trap – in this case, those fang-like protrusions – as well as the tempting sweet nectar that seeps from the hood. Look closer, my dear . . . do you see those little white splashes on the sides of the tubes? They're transparent aeriolae, or false windows – they trick the insects into thinking there's an escape hole. The insect struggles, but is further trapped by downward-pointing hairs, which direct them into the liquid below. The insect drowns, and eventually its corpse is dissolved . . . depending on the species of pitcher, the prey is broken down either by resident bacteria, or by enzymes secreted by the plant itself. The digested insect is converted into a solution of peptides, phosphates, amino acids, ammonium, nitrates, and urea – a veritable smorgasbord of essential nutrients!'

Stroking the largest lily trumpet, Luella gave an appreciative sigh. 'There are even pitchers that harbour insect larvae in their reservoirs. These larvae feed on trapped prey, and then provide castings which the plant absorbs. Instant fertiliser! Have you ever heard of anything so ingenious?' she added, almost to herself.

Bronwyn shook her head, obviously awestruck.

I felt somewhat awestruck myself. Luella seemed so proud of her plants, I wanted to say something complimentary – but while she'd been speaking, my imagination had run rampant. I'd imagined a beetle-sized version of myself climbing past the Cobra Lily's crimson fangs and into its mouth cavity. I'd followed the delicious trail of nectar, been confused by the transparent windows glimmering with muted sunlight. My tiny self continued its doomed journey, guided downward by the silky hairs until I was slipping and sliding, unable to stop myself splashing into the deep pool of liquid and bobbing helplessly among fly carcasses and mosquito husks.

'What happens – ' I cleared my throat. 'What happens if they don't catch any insects? Do they starve?'

Luella gave me a curious look. 'Goodness, no! They are, above all else, great adaptors. For instance, in winter when the insect population decreases, some pitcher plants produce special non-carnivorous leaves which assist in the absorption of soil nutrients ... temporarily, anyway. That's the beauty of these plants – they can adapt to virtually any environment, any circumstance, even lying dormant for years if they have to.'

Her face glowed with evident pleasure. A change had come over her. She appeared more youthful, more alive, her skin brightened by the intensity of her expression.

'You know so much about them,' Bronwyn marvelled.

Luella smiled. 'I suppose I do, dear. I find them fascinating, there's always something new to learn.'

I let my gaze roam. I'd just realised what was making the muffled buzzing noise I had noticed earlier. Sunlight had fallen on a nearby row of pitcher plants, illuminating the tall tubular leaves from behind and allowing me to see the tiny swarming shadows within. Flies, perhaps hundreds, trapped at the base of each pitcher plant reservoir, buzzing in a ghastly unmusical symphony – most of them droning like broken violins, while others were barely able to raise a frail hum.

The glasshouse was suddenly too hot, the air too humid to breathe. I inched towards the door, feeling two sets of curious eyes alight on me. I resisted the urge to look back. Shoving through the door, I stepped into the yard and made a beeline for the cool shade of the bunya pine.

Breathing the fresher air, I tried to clear the greenhouse scent from my lungs but the earthy, vaguely mouldy odour of peatmoss and damp soil made me think of the settlers' hut, of the closed confinement of the crowded little room, and the secrets it protected.

Again my imagination ran riot.

Now I was inside the musty tallboy, surrounded by chipped, grubby porcelain faces whose eyes fixed on me in the gloom. My one consolation, my letters, were gone. And nearby, very near in the dark hanging compartment, the greasy, blackened axe handle propped in the shadows . . .

'Mum?'

I wrenched around, blinking to clear my eyes. Bronwyn stood at the threshold of Luella's greenhouse, worry etched on her face.

'Are you okay?'

'Sure. But I could really use a cup of tea.'

Luella bustled us across the grass, back up the steps and onto the verandah, settling us into chairs around the old cedar table. Yet even after tea was poured, even as I praised Luella's chocolate tarts, even as my daughter prattled excitedly about the wondrous garden of carnivores we'd just seen . . . my thoughts kept returning to the settlers' hut.

Had the squatter discovered the photo of Aylish tucked in among the letters and taken a liking to it? Or had he known Aylish, had she meant something to him? All the people Aylish had mentioned in her letters – Samuel, her Poppa Jacob, Klaus and Ellen Jarman, and Cleve – they were all gone. Only one person was still alive, Luella; and either she'd lied about not leaving the flowers on her mother's grave . . . or someone else had left them there.

And that someone else, I felt certain, was the man I'd seen at the settlers' hut.

22

Aylish, March 1946

We hurried along in the darkness, me stumbling in my good shoes, Lulu skipping ahead. She was singing happily to herself, a half made-up version of a scripture song Poppa had taught her. Though it was late for her to be out – judging by the height of the moon, it must be nearly nine o'clock – she was chirpy as a bird, excited by our mysterious night-time expedition.

'Don't stray off the track,' I called.

'I won't, Mumma.'

She was a pretty child, good-natured and gentle, but with an occasional shrill temper that rivalled my own. Like me, she had inherited my mother's thick brown hair and my father's tendency to freckle – but she wasn't delicate-boned, the way we were. She had the skinny legs of my mother's people, but her frame was tall and robust, her features broad, her eyes wide-spaced and green like those of her own father.

My pace picked up.

Samuel, you'll see . . . All will be well between us again.

Tall trees loomed around us, their shadows carving the moonlight. Black ironbarks, red gums swallowed by strangling vines; lillypilly and wild jasmine drenching the night in scent, banksias shivering in the wind, and blackthorn boughs reaching their spines to snare us as we passed.

I cursed my shoes, wishing I was less vain, more prone to being sensible. I'd pulled my old patents out of the box they'd languished in most of the war. They were scuffed and thin-soled, so I'd buffed them to a molasses-shine, but now their glassy surface was dimmed by layers of dust. The heels wobbled over stones, threatening to overturn me with every step. To make matters worse I was running late. I'd got it into my head that if I kept him waiting a few moments then he'd be all the keener to see me, all the happier when I finally arrived. After all, we had already waited nearly five years – what were an additional five minutes?

Stupid, stupid.

Five minutes had somehow turned to twenty.

Slipping off my shoes, I started running barefoot, eager to close the gap between me and the small figure that trundled ahead. Eager to reach the gully where Samuel would be waiting. Lulu heard me and whipped around, startled. Then she grinned.

'Mumma? Are we playing a game?'

'Sort of,' I told her. 'Do you think you can keep up?'

She beamed and dashed ahead. I trotted behind, my feet bruised by the stones, my ankles wobbling nearly as much as they'd done in shoes. I'd grown up barefoot. At the mission, dirt tracks were all I'd known. When I was ten and my mum died and we came to live at Magpie Creek, Poppa insisted I start dressing properly. Frocks with petticoats, gloves. A hat, too. Always a hat. Not that I minded. It was the shoes I hated. No matter how hard I complained, Poppa persevered and by the time I was fifteen my barefoot days were long gone.

Looking over my shoulder, I conjured a picture of the little house we shared with my father on Stump Hill Road. Poppa had been sleeping when we left, snoring with the wireless turned up loud, one of his serial plays rattling the roof beams.

I hated deceiving him, but he'd said things about Samuel I didn't like . . . things that weren't true. He said Samuel might not be pleased to see his proud Irish features mirrored in the face of a little half-caste girl, but Poppa was wrong. Samuel would love his daughter the instant he saw her. His eyes would glint and he'd let out his booming laugh. Gathering her up, he'd press his whiskery cheek to her plump face and growl with pleasure . . .

I stopped running, resting my hands on my knees to catch my breath.

Lulu scooted ahead.

'Wait,' I called.

She pretended not to hear, but I sang out again and she paused at the edge of the track, gazing up at the sky until she heard me puffing behind her. She looked at my bare feet and frowned.

'Are we nearly there?'

'A few minutes more, that's all.'

'We're going to that bird place, aren't we?'

'Perhaps.'

'We normally go in the daytime.'

'But this is a special visit. You'll see.'

We started off again along the track, following it uphill. The trees grew thicker and the upper boughs joined over our heads. The way narrowed, flanked by boulders and stony outcrops. The gully yawned to our left, its banks becoming steeper as we climbed.

Lulu tugged my hand. 'Who are we meeting, Mumma?'

I laughed, excited and pleased and nervous all at once. 'Someone very special.'

'Is it another little girl for me to play with?'

'Much better than that.'

She wrinkled her nose. 'Will I like them?'

'You will indeed.'

'Why won't you tell me?'

'It's a surprise.'

'I don't like surprises.'

'You'll like this one. I promise.'

She grew bored with my teasing and bounded off again, singing her scripture song. Ahead, she found a branch of gum-nuts and skipped along with it, brandishing it over her head like a sword.

When I was little, my mum had told me stories about spirits who inhabited the night-time bush – Biami the protector, Bunyip the evil-doer, and wise Mirrabooka who watched from the sky. Mum taught me to respect the bush and its dark time, and I'd taught that respect to my own little girl. I'd sung her the spirit-songs and retold my mother's legends until they'd become a part of Lulu's being, and – I believed – would somehow keep her safe.

A twig snapped behind me.

I looked back, searching the trees. There were no swaying grass or branches, no glint of nocturnal eyes. No wallaby shadows or possums. And yet the hairs stood along my arms. We weren't alone.

I made a birdcall and Lulu trotted obediently back along the trail towards me, the question clear on her round face.

'Mumma, what . . . ?'

Her gaze strayed past me into the darkness. She frowned, and then her eyes went wide. Her lips parted, she gasped. I rushed to her, intending to swoop her into my protective arms, but she was too quick. She slipped through my hands like a lizard and fled along the shadowy track. I went to spring after her, but stopped dead as a hiss of sound came from the bushes.

A name.

My name. I whirled around.

'Who's there?'

No answer.

'Poppa, is that you?'

Of course not. He'd never creep through the trees. If he'd woken up to discover me and Lulu gone from the house, we'd have heard his irate yelling from here.

'Samuel?'

Wind rattled the leaves. Branches creaked. My fingers clenched around the ankle straps of my shoes, my nails buried in my palm. It was foolishness. No one had whispered my name. The bush was full of empty noises. Shivering treetops, brush turkeys scratching in the undergrowth, snakes on the prowl for food. Nothing to get weak-legged over.

I turned back to the track. It was deserted.

'Lulu?'

When she didn't reply, I began to run. Whip-birds chirruped and whistled in their nests, distressed by the thump of my passing feet, startling up from between the trees, flapping into the moonlight like feathery ghosts. While I ran, I called my daughter's name, my throat tight with panic. Where was she?

The track widened. The clearing was lit by patchy moonlight. In the centre, the tall stone curved its back against the night. A few hundred yards away, the ground plunged straight down into the gorge. The gully walls were steep, nearly vertical; the fall over the edge would be sudden and unexpected. Lulu knew the clearing well, we'd been coming here since she was small. Only, it was dark now, nothing looked familiar, and she'd been so frightened . . .

Crouching at the lip of the gully, I peered over the edge. Nothing to see, just moonlight on the treetops far below, the faint glimmer of water through the leaves. The sky seemed darker than it had a moment ago. And the night creatures, the whispering leaves, the cool night breeze – all of it suddenly still.

A murmur.

I lurched around, searching the trees. A grey cloud of dread folded around me, sharpening my senses but dulling my mind. Where was Samuel? It was well past the time I'd asked him to meet me. Had he stalked back to the homestead in a temper, angry that I'd made him wait? But he must have known by the contents of my letter how urgently I wanted to see him . . .

I went cold.

My letter. What if he hadn't received it?

Impossible. I'd delivered it to his door with my own hands. Had he decided to ignore it? I shivered, recalling the emptiness in his eyes as we'd stood outside the pharmacy this morning; the way he'd accused me of lying, of deceiving him. The way he'd looked at me, as if sickened by what he saw.

By God, Aylish, you'll be sorry . . .

Something moved at the edge of the clearing.

'Lulu – ?'

The darkness twitched, broke apart. A shadow-shape broke from between the trees, shuffling to the edge of the glade, dark in the blotchy moonlight. A figure. Not a child, not my little girl. Larger. It drifted closer, entering the clearing. Moonbeams danced over pale features. Features I recognised easily – how could I not? I'd come to know them almost as well as my own.

His voice cut into the gloom. 'Hello, Aylish.'

As if he had all the time in the world, he trod nearer and stood calmly. Watching me, perhaps waiting for me to return his greeting.

But my gaze had dropped to the object he clutched in his hand, a stick, I thought. Then, understanding dawned. The face of death, that pale grotesque ghost of a face I'd seen in the hut window on my last night with Samuel, had found me.

'What's the matter, Aylish,' he said, taking another slow step towards me, 'cat got your tongue?'

He came into the moonlight and I saw that the thing in his hand was not a stick after all, but the blackened, headless shaft of an axe.

23

Muffled thumping woke me. I sat up, blinking. Daylight glowed through my window, and magpies chortled in the trees outside. I thought I could smell toast.

The thumping came again. Someone was at the back door.

I looked at the bedside clock, groaned when I saw the time: eight-forty. Bronwyn was going to be late for school. Flying out of bed, I ran along the hall to her room. She wasn't there. In the kitchen I found a note on the coffeepot.

'Tried to wake you, sleepyhead, got the bus xx'

My relief – and the twinge of annoyance at myself that accompanied it – was short-lived. Whoever was at the door hammered again. I growled under my breath as I went to answer it, reasoning that if they were fool enough to continue making such a racket then they deserved to encounter me with unbrushed hair and ratty pyjamas.

'Oh. Hi, Hobe.'

He looked hopefully over my shoulder. 'G'day, Audrey. Young Bronwyn in?'

'It's Monday, Hobe. She's at school.'

'Of course she is, silly old me. I've got a little present for her.' He held up a box gift-wrapped in yellow paper with a card

364

attached. 'It's nothing much, just a neighbourly token. All right if I leave it with you?'

He'd ironed his flannelette shirt again and, absurdly, tucked a flowering gumnut in his buttonhole. My heart sank. Despite our rocky start, Hobe had been perfectly kind since our talk that day looking across the valley. I liked him. And he was a potential source of info about the events I so craved to understand. Yet I couldn't forget how I'd caught him searching the hollow tree . . . nor could I overlook the tear he'd shed the first time he'd seen Bronwyn.

'Hobe, I have to ask you something.'

'What's that, lass?'

'A few weeks ago when you cleaned up the garden, I found you up the hill searching the old beechwood tree . . . You weren't looking for possum damage, were you?'

Hobe's cheer withered before my eyes. His face grew slack and his eye clouded over. 'Well, now . . .'

'And then you got all weird when I asked if you knew the Jarmans and you said you didn't, when it's clear you did.'

He shuffled, his eye riveted unhappily on my face. Then suddenly he was looking everywhere else – his shoes, the decking, a leafy watershoot springing from the overhead grapevine.

'And Hobe, you've shown such an interest in Bronwyn, which is really nice . . . but I can't help wondering if there's something you're not telling me.'

He was staring down at the gift-wrapped box he held, as if willing it to spring open and reveal the answers.

'Oh Audrey,' he muttered in a strained voice, 'it's nothing at all, I assure you, lass, nothing at all . . . that is, I mean to say it's nothing to trouble yourself over. Stupid of me, I didn't mean to distress you, or young Bronwyn. I only wanted to . . . Oh, heck, I am dreadfully sorry . . .' He mumbled something I didn't catch – it sounded like further apology – then turned and fled.

I brewed coffee and drank it at the kitchen window, staring along the path where Hobe had vanished into the trees. I poured the dregs into the compost, then went onto the verandah and squinted up at the hillside. I could just make out the bald crest of the hill and, like a frayed yellow ribbon winding through the trees, the hilltop track that connected our two properties.

Hobe hadn't given me much of an answer; not with his words, at any rate. But his obvious distress spoke volumes. He was up to something . . . something that he clearly felt as uncomfortable about as I did.

Turning to go back inside, I saw Hobe's parcel propped near the stairs. The yellow wrapping paper looked vaguely grubby, the garden twine seemed tacky . . . but he'd gone to some effort – pretty pink butterfly stickers dotted the paper, and the card was hand-cut into the shape of a ladybeetle.

Kneeling, I read what he'd written inside.

'Every entomologist-to-be should have their own ladybird aquarium. Hope you like it, Bronwyn lass! Kindest regards from Hobart Miller.'

I tore off the yellow wrapping paper. At first I thought it was a doll's house. Closer examination revealed it to be a small fish tank with a wooden base and fretworked side panels – the wood had been whitewashed and carved with painstaking detail to resemble the iron lace on Thornwood's wraparound verandahs. Inside the tank was a tiny table and chair setting, complete with miniature teacup and saucer. The aquarium floor was strewn with flowers – rosebuds and gumnuts, nasturtiums, many of them blighted with tasty aphids. Swarming in attendance at this lavish feast were scores of scarlet and black-dotted ladybeetles. Hobe had gone to a lot of trouble. The effect was wonderful, Bronwyn would adore it.

I took the little aquarium into the kitchen, sat it on the counter, then dragged over a chair and peered inside.

The tea party was in full swing. The ladybirds flitted content-edly, stalking aphids or communing on the rim of their teacup. They seemed so at home, so happily busy and on purpose, that my misgivings about Hobe began to ebb. Had I misjudged him? Perhaps his interest in Bronwyn was easily explained. It was clear he still had feelings for Luella, so being curious about her granddaughter was perfectly reasonable.

There was still the issue of him searching the beech tree, and his denial about having known her family. I recalled her diary entry recording her terror the day she'd encountered Hobe on the track with his eye bandaged. Wasn't it possible that she'd also encountered him that rainy night at the hollow tree, while she'd been waiting for Ross? And wasn't it also possible that Hobe had spooked her again, which would explain her careless-ness at the gully?

I rested my forehead against the aquarium. The quiet flit-flit of the ladybirds soothed me and, crazily, made me envy them. They were so carefree and untroubled. All they had to worry about was where to find the next batch of aphids, and Hobe had pretty much taken care of that. Meanwhile I was caught in the sticky strands of a complex and powerful web. Tony's family web. Twisting this way and that in an attempt to break free, but only becoming increasingly tangled.

And yet, my entrapment wasn't entirely unwilling.

My family had no web. There was just me and Bronwyn. The two of us, winging through life together . . . but essentially alone. And there were times when it seemed better to become entangled with a family who had problems and conundrums and way too much history – than to have no family at all.

I followed the path up the hill, through the grove of pome-granates, past the hollowed out beechwood tree, and along a trail that led to the hill's bald crest. There were no trees at the crest, just boulders and grassland dotted with fiery red and gold wildflowers.

I stopped walking, lingering in the shade of an ironbark tree to mop my streaming face. The Miller track lay on the other side of the crest. As I approached, I saw a familiar lanky figure half hidden in the shadows of a rocky outcrop. His attention was fixed on the valley.

I followed his gaze. Below us to the north, thick bushland stretched nearly to the horizon, broken only by occasional patches of emerald pasture. A gravel road curved eastwards to join the broader black line of the highway. Nearby was the bare expanse of the airfield.

Hobe was looking west, which could only mean that the object of his attention was the solitary house perched along a lonely strip of unsealed road. It was a white house, surrounded by cleared land and adjoining a paddock of regimented fruit trees. I couldn't see the roses from where I stood, but the large bunya pine casting its shadow over the house was unmistakable.

I hadn't realised Luella's house was visible from here.

I started walking towards the boulder outcrop where Hobe stood. He must have heard my approach because he startled and his head snapped around. His leathery cheeks were wet with tears. Tugging a hanky from his pocket, he gave his face a wipe and blew his nose, then turned and slipped behind a crop of tall boulders. Seconds later he reappeared further down the slope, making haste along the narrow track in the direction of his home.

I called out, but when he made no reply I hurried after him.

The way was steep, overgrown with vines and brambles and littered with stones, some dangerously loose, others emerging half-buried from the soil. It wasn't until the track evened out and we were midway along the spine of a second, smaller hill, that I finally caught up.

'Hobe . . . ?'

He paused, pulling out his hanky again to polish his glasses and mop his eye, then prodding the limp rag back into the pocket of his workpants.

'Hobe, are you all right?'

He hung his head, but nodded, struggling his glasses back on. Only when they were in place did he look at me. He attempted a smile, but it was waterlogged and half-hearted.

'I've made an arse of myself, lass, and I'm very sorry. I'll just get along home now, be right as rain directly.'

I sighed. 'No, you haven't, Hobe. But I get the feeling that something's going on, something that involves my daughter. And I want to know what it is.'

Hobe considered me for a long while before speaking. 'You'd best come down to the house, then. You've every right to know the truth. I should've told you before, but . . . well, come on, lass – best get it done with.' Without further explanation, he loped off along the trail, the single lens of his glasses flaring in the sun, and his shoulders hunched as if the day's brilliance was suddenly too heavy to bear.

Hobe's old bungalow was just as ramshackle as I remembered. Paint peeled from the weatherboards, the corrugated roof was buckled and patched with oddments of iron, and the garden looked like a neatly arrayed junkyard. The vegie patch was a haven for weeds, but in among them I glimpsed neat rows of carrots and parsnips, with huge yellow pumpkins bulging out the sides.

As we went along the narrow back verandah, a clutch of tan kelpie pups spilled through the back door, nipping at Hobe's heels and trying to scramble up my legs.

Hobe hooked up one of the little wrigglers and tucked it under his arm, ushering me into the house ahead of him.

The kitchen was stiflingly hot, and obsessively clean despite the decrepitude of the decor. The plank floors were swept, the copper taps over the sink shone like burnished gold, the rustic timber bench tops were scoured and crumb-free. Hobe's brother Gurney crouched before an old wood-fired stove, stoking the flames. A frypan sizzled on the hob – bread and bacon and a tasty-looking scramble of eggs. Gurney took one look at Hobe's tear-stained face and started fussing.

'G'day Audrey . . . Hobe, can I get you something, old mate? A nice cuppa tea? The bacon's good'n fresh, are you hungry?'

Hobe waved his brother away. After a moment of pained indecision, Gurney seemed relieved to slink through the back door with his breakfast and disappear into the shed.

Hobe dragged a chair out from the table and gestured for me to sit. Slumping opposite, he tried to untangle the wriggling puppy from his shirt. I expected him to speak, but the silence stretched. There was just the sputter of the empty frypan, the puppy's eager snuffling, and a kookaburra's insane laughter somewhere outside.

Hobe tugged the puppy's ears, which made it squirm dementedly and try to clamp its pin-like teeth onto his fingers.

'I'll need to find homes for the little beggars soon,' he commented, still not looking at me. 'Alma's a fine mother, it seems a shame to take her pups away – but there're laws against keeping too many dogs about the place these days.' He sighed, placed the pup on the floor and sent it on its way with a gentle nudge. 'Seems there's a law for most things, and not many make all that much sense.'

Impatient with Hobe's nervous waffling, I jumped in. 'That day at the hollow tree, you weren't looking for possum damage, were you, Hobe?'

'No, lass.'

'And you did know the Jarmans.'

He sighed. 'Yeah. I knew 'em.'

Pushing to his feet, he opened the screen door and toed the puppy outside, where it scampered off with its littermates in a chorus of yips and yelps. Hobe came back to the table and sat heavily.

'Tony and Glenda used to come here when they were kids. Most Sundays they'd show up with something their mother had sent over. Fruitcake, or a jar of corn relish – the worst damn relish this side of the black stump, but the gesture meant everything to me. You see, Luella and I . . . I mean to say . . . Oh heck.'

He stood, went to the stove and rattled the frypan, peered into its greasy depths. Grabbing a leaf of newspaper from under the sink, he scrunched it around the inside of the pan.

'You loved her,' I said.

'That I did, Audrey. From the very first moment I saw her, I said to myself, "That girl is one in a million . . . and I'm going to marry her." I loved her madly. And after a while I learnt that she loved me, too. We were the same age, fifteen . . . just kids, I s'pose. But there was something good between us, a kind of belonging. Little did we know it then, but our young romance was doomed from the start.'

'What happened?'

Hobe tossed the newspaper in the bin and hung the frypan on a hook. 'We wanted to get married, but decided to do the decent thing and wait 'til after Luella turned twenty-one. Y'see, during the war Aylish and Luella had stayed with the Jarmans for a spell, and Ellen Jarman, Cleve's mum, had taken a real shine to little Luella. When Aylish died, Luella came to see Ellen as a sort of second mum, and so wanted her blessing to marry.'

Hobe wrestled the lid off a biscuit tin, and brooded over its contents. 'Anyway, when Luella was sixteen, Jacob died. She was all alone. Of course Ellen was keen for Luella to return to the Jarman household, but Luella refused. The house at Stump Hill Road held too many memories for her. It was her home, and she hated the idea of leaving it.

'But her being all alone in that remote little house set the stage for Samuel's entrance into her life. He was her only remaining blood-family, but he'd had nothing much to do with her until then. Luella always said he blamed her for her mother's death, that he never loved her – which was poppycock in my view, because how could anyone not love her?

'Anyway, Samuel sent her off to a fancy ladies' college in Brisbane, bought her posh clothes and lavished her with presents. She flourished, eager to please Samuel. He was her link to her mother, and she wanted him to love her. By the time she turned twenty-one, she was quite the young Miss . . . and Samuel considered her a significant cut above the likes of me.'

'He stopped you getting married?'

'No, lass. Oh no. I bungled that one all by myself.'

With a pair of oversized tongs, he tweezered half a dozen homemade Anzac biscuits from the cake tin onto a plate, then chose a pair of floral teacups.

'But you still loved her,' I said.

'Too right, I did. But the year Luella turned twenty-one was the same year the Yanks cracked down on Vietnam. Damn fool conflict, I was dead against that war from the start. Australia got dragged into it, and next thing I know Samuel had cornered me down at the Swan one night. He shouted me beer after beer, then explained how he'd be happy for me and Luella to get married . . . on one condition. He said to me, "Son, if you can prove yourself to be a brave and worthy man, then I'll not only give you my blessing, but sign over twenty acres of good land and a house so that you and Luella can kick start your life together." That's all he said, and like a trout snapping at a tasty fly, I went for it.'

'You joined up?'

Hobe's expression darkened. 'For Luella's sake, I wanted Samuel's approval. I knew how much it meant to Luella to have him on-side. So I rushed headlong into that god-awful war without a second thought, despite my pacifist leanings. Marched

off to be a hero, just like old Samuel had done in the forties . . .
damn near got my fool head blown off into the bargain, and
I did some things I've never – ' He cut off. For a time he stood
silently, pondering the kettle. When he resumed, his voice was
low, almost a whisper.

'The minute I arrived home I got stuck into the bottle. Made
a real arse of myself. My plans for proving my worth to Samuel
couldn't have gone more wrong. I knew I'd blown it, so I went
even further off the rails. Grog and pills, I didn't sleep for two
years, didn't dare – just stalked around in the bush yelling at
the top of my lungs and carrying on like a bloody lunatic. If it
hadn't been for poor old Gurney, I'd probably have starved to
death . . . or died of horror and shame, if such a thing exists.'
Hobe smoothed a palm over his lips. 'Worst of all, I pushed
Luella away. She wanted to help, but I couldn't bear for her to
see me so weak, so untogether. I told her the wedding was off.
Broke her poor heart, so I did.'

'And she married Cleve.'

Hobe's gaze went to the window. 'He was like a brother to
her. I suppose she felt safe with him. He was a real charmer.
Funny, had a knack for winning people over. Got himself a
university degree, too. Geology or history, I forget which. When
Klaus died in 1960, Cleve took over at the post office, so he had
everything to offer Luella – money, security, a stable future.
Samuel couldn't sign over his twenty acres fast enough.'

'But she never loved him, did she?'

Hobe looked defeated. 'In her way, I think she did. She was
very kind-hearted. Once, she told me that Cleve's mother had
wanted a daughter and so had never taken much of a liking
to her son. Cleve had a need to be loved, she said . . . a need
the size of a black hole. She thought that by being kind, she
could help fill that hole. Poppycock, if you ask me – staying
with someone because of what *they* need. In my view, Luella
deserved better.'

'You never married, did you, Hobe?'

He shook his head. 'How could I even look at another woman, after knowing Luella? She was one in a million. Still is, I expect. She was so beautiful. Inside and out. Never bothered with makeup, wore her hair unfashionably long. Dressed plain. But to see her smile, to stand near her and bask in the warmth that just seemed to radiate off her ... you'd feel good inside, a better man somehow, a more improved version of yourself.'

'That's why you kept seeing her ... after she married Cleve, I mean.'

Hobe's face was raw. 'How could I not, lass? She was my life. It took me three years to straighten myself out. I went to Luella and apologised for what'd happened. She admitted things weren't great with Cleve. He was a good husband, she said ... but she still loved me.'

Hobe took down a jar labelled 'TEA', unscrewed the lid, and scrutinised the grassy chaff inside. 'So we hatched a plan,' he went on. 'Luella said she could weather her marriage to Cleve for another year – just until we saved enough money to escape to the city. Adelaide, Melbourne, maybe even Perth. I hated the idea of losing her to Cleve, couldn't stand the thought of him touching her, claiming from her what she wanted to give freely to me. I hated seeing the pain in her eyes ... I can't count the number of times I loaded up the Winchester, started out along the track to William Road.'

He glanced over at me and frowned. 'Don't look at me like that, lass – I'd never have acted on those darker impulses. I was a man possessed by jealousy, hatred. By fear. In the war I killed, but it pained me something shocking to do it. I'm no cold-blooded killer. Even if I was, I'd never have subjected Luella to more heartache. I'd already hurt her enough.'

As each part of the Hobe puzzle fell into place, Luella's story began to flesh out too. Yet rather than satisfy me, Hobe's revelations only made me more curious. As the complexities unspooled, I could feel myself becoming more entangled . . . and it was a feeling I liked. 'What happened to your plan?'

Hobe rubbed his scalp. 'I had a nice little nest egg saved. We were going to make it large in the city, set up an enterprise selling home-made chutneys and the like.' He shook his head, smiled. 'Luella never was much of a one for cooking in the early days, she could burn water. But what she lacked in skill she made up for in gumption.

'That year, she did a fancy cooking course in Brisbane. She used to dream about one day having her own little bakehouse, you should've seen the light in her eyes when she talked about it . . . but it wasn't to be. The kids came along, and we decided to wait until they were older. Cleve started getting suspicious, and with him being the way he was – I suppose in the end Luella thought it safer for the three of them to stay.'

'Safer?'

Hobe dragged the kettle off the stove and flooded the teapot. 'According to Luella, Cleve was normally a placid man. But he couldn't cope with stress of any kind. If he felt threatened or humiliated, or even left out . . . he'd lose it. Big time. Lash out, then regret it later.'

As Hobe had found out the hard way – although I doubted that Cleve had been regretful after what he'd done to Hobe. I recalled Aylish's letters to Samuel. Over time she'd grown to dislike the young Cleve, maybe even fear him a little as events unravelled. The glass in Lulu's cot, the sulking and getting under her feet. The spiteful things he'd said when he learned she was leaving. And then the theft in the woodshed. It struck me that these were the actions of someone who, rather than lashing out in uncontrolled anger, had thought long and hard about what it was they planned to do.

Hobe seemed preoccupied with arranging the Anzac biscuits. He peered under the lid of the teapot then filled our cups with strong greenish liquid. 'Lemongrass tea all right, lass?'

I nodded, distracted. 'After Cleve disappeared, why didn't you and Luella reconnect?'

Hobe slumped. 'I tried, lord knows. After Cleve got suspicious, me and Luella had to stop our trysts. So we started writing letters. We used the big white beech tree at Thornwood as a letter exchange, midways between our two properties. It was kind of romantic, a secret place. It was also what started the whole mess. Cleve must have been snooping, because he discovered one of our notes.

'Later, after he went missing, there was no more need for secrecy. I went to see Luella but she wouldn't open the door. I hand-delivered dozens of letters, but she never responded. I figured her heart was all broke up after losing Glenda. I was mad with grief myself – but I had to respect Luella's wishes. It was clear she didn't want to see me. In the end I gave up trying.'

He attempted a smile. 'So when you and young Bronwyn showed up, I thought it might be good for Luella. I started checking the tree every few days, convinced it was only a matter of time before I'd reach in and find her letter.'

The realisation hit me hard. I saw how wrong I'd been about Hobe, how I'd twisted the facts out of proportion and let myself think the worst. 'That day you were searching the hollow tree . . . you were looking for a letter from Luella?'

He nodded. 'Nothing there, of course. I suppose now I've got to accept that she doesn't want to know about me.'

I warmed my palms on the brittle old teacup, recalling Luella's fears that Hobe still held a grudge for Cleve's attack on him.

'Don't give up, Hobe,' I told him. 'I'll have a whisper in Bronwyn's ear and get her to put in a good word for you. She and Luella idolise each other.'

Hobe brightened. 'You'd do that, lass? Would you really?'

'Consider it done.'

'Well, now . . .' He grinned into his cup, the steam rising from the tea fogging his glasses.

We sat in the quiet of our thoughts, listening to currawongs warbling outside. I stole a peek through my lashes at Hobe and saw that his smile had turned sorrowful. All those lost years, and the guilt and grief of a life that had somehow rattled off in the wrong direction. It was as though Aylish's death was a stone cast into some dark pond, and the ripples were still creeping outwards.

'Tony never spoke about his family,' I found myself thinking aloud. 'I'm only just beginning to understand why.'

Hobe's smile faded. He looked at me and nodded. 'His sister's death shook him badly, poor kid. He was only fourteen, hardly surprising that it unhinged him the way it did.'

'Unhinged?'

'Yep . . . poor little bloke went clean off his head.' Hobe dug under his glasses, massaged the empty socket. 'Y'see, the night before they found Glenda's body, Tony turned up here, must've been around ten o'clock. Poor little fella was covered in blood. Wild-eyed, as if he'd seen a ghost. He kept saying that his sister was at the edge of their grandfather's garden, lying under the old beech tree – the same damned tree Luella and I had been using as a post-box. Tony didn't know what had happened, only that Glenda was bleeding and hurt, barely conscious.

'Of course, Gurney and I rushed over to Thornwood. The leaves under the tree had been kicked around, but there was no sign of Glenda. Tony was beside himself, sick with fright. We brought him back to the house, and I managed to get some brandy down his throat. Poor Tony, he was jumpier than a cane toad, wouldn't sit still. And the blood – I thought he'd hurt himself, but he wouldn't let me near him to find out. He insisted on heading home to William Road. I offered to drive him but he got all teary again, kept babbling that Glenda might have recovered enough to take herself home via the gully. I convinced him to stay the night. Calmed him down and got him settled in the back room . . . but he must have taken off soon after. In the morning he was gone.'

Hobe drained his teacup. 'In those days, the Magpie Creek police station was unmanned at night. I rang Ipswich, but they said without an actual victim there was no point sending out a patrol. Then when they found Glenda the next day, the cops were all over us like ants on a honey-spill.'

I searched Hobe's face. Tony's version of events explained why Glenda had abandoned her belongings in the tree. But how had her body ended up at the gully, over a mile away?

'Didn't they question why Tony saw his sister at Thornwood, yet her body was found in the gully?'

'They said Tony's brain was addled with shock, that he got his locations confused.'

'Didn't you think it was strange?'

'My word I did, lass. But we were all so sick with shock and grief. You can't function when you're in that state. Later, I went to the cops and hassled them, but nothing came of it.'

He sat for a time, looking at his hands. I wondered what he was thinking; the lines on his cheeks looked deeper, the crevices around his mouth dark with shadow. An air of defeat sat heavily over him.

'About a month after Glenda died,' he went on, 'Gurney noticed his old Winchester missing from the shed. Now old Gurn was scrupulous with his firearms, always kept them racked up high, out of harm's way. Of course, these days you've got to have 'em under lock and key, which makes sense with all the ratbags around ... but back then the law was slacker. We puzzled over that missing Winchester for weeks, until it occurred to me that Tony must have taken it. And then last year when Tony died, the cops got interested again. Y'see, they'd finally found Gurney's old Winchester.'

'Tony used your brother's rifle?'

Hobe looked ill. He palmed his face and ran his fingers up into his sparse hair.

'That he did, lass.'

'God.' My voice was barely a whisper. My heart shrank into itself, took on the smallness of a pebble. It fell into a well of still, cold water and sank without a trace. 'Poor Tony.'

Hobe sighed and shoved away from the table. I acknowledged that our conversation was over, but after this last revelation I'd lost the will to move. The tea had grown cold, the biscuits lay untouched on their floral plate. An echo of sorrow seemed to linger in the kitchen. Then Hobe beckoned me to follow him through a doorway and deeper into the old bungalow's warren of rooms.

It was like stepping into a natural history museum.

Every inch of wall space was covered with picture frames – big 1950s landscapes, box-displays containing beetle or butterfly specimens, several faded old family portraits ... and water-colours, dozens of them, all fine examples of Tony's exquisite eye for detail: finches, frogs, gumnut blossoms, dragonflies.

Bottle collections stood to attention along windowsills and shelves, and rustic cabinets displayed antique gauges and clocks and dials; cages dangled from the ceiling, inhabited by taxidermied canaries and sparrows. Birds' nests hung in sunny windows, and the doors were furnished with cured animal hides – rabbits, dingoes, a kangaroo, even that of a moth-eaten red kelpie. Lined along the wide picture rails above us was an astonishing hoard of mummified creatures – dogs, cats, rabbits, snakes, and several specimens I couldn't identify. Assemblages of rusty machine parts served as candelabras, bookends, door-stops; a wind-chime of antique silver spoons clinked as we passed beneath it.

A narrow hall led to the back of the bungalow. We entered a small bedroom. Twin beds were crammed knee to knee in the tight space, divided by an antique bedside. The walls were crowded with more of Tony's watercolours. Spiky kurrajong leaves, blue lomandra flowers, fishbone ferns, a turtle ... and pencil studies of the various mummified creatures I'd seen earlier.

Hobe waved a hand at a wall of drawings. 'Young Tony was a talented kid . . . but I suppose you already know that.'

I marvelled, unable to resist doing a quick calculation. There must have been a hundred exquisite little paintings. I knew several art dealers who'd have given their eye teeth – and substantial quantities of cash – for any one of them.

'You have quite a collection.'

Hobe nodded, shuffling past. 'I expect they're worth a bit, but I'd never dream of selling them . . .' He shot me a sheepish look. 'You must think I'm a sentimental old fool.'

I shook my head. 'I confess, I've got my own stash of Tony's paintings under my bed. I put them away after he walked out, unable to look at them – but I can't bring myself to part with them either.'

Hobe averted his attention to an ink study of a black butterfly on a fig leaf. 'Tell me, Audrey – what was he like? I only knew him as a boy. He was a good kid . . . but I never got to know him as a man.'

I shifted uneasily. I'd avoided seeing Tony since we split five years ago, reluctant to stir up the quagmire of resentment and self-doubt that he'd inspired in me by marrying Carol. Those times when we met at Bronwyn's school carnivals or dance concerts or netball tournaments, he'd been politely distant, as if he believed that keeping me at arm's length was somehow kinder. Even so, those post-breakup memories of him had never been able to eclipse what we'd shared when we were together. Tony's smile had once been like a radiant sun to me, warming many a dark moment and distracting me from my various fears. He'd been funny and attentive, and I'd spend countless wintry nights enveloped in his arms. Most of all, he'd given me a daughter who meant the world to me.

'He was a wonderful man,' I told Hobe, and meant it. 'The best.'

Hobe looked grateful, and just before he turned away I saw his eye well.

I studied his profile. Beneath the leathery skin, he had a boniness that was unmistakably familiar. His sapphire eye, his snowy hair and willowy height . . . if I squinted, I could almost see in him a faint reflection of my daughter.

'Hobe?' I asked. 'Tony and Glenda were your kids, weren't they?'

Hobe froze, then pulled in a ragged breath. 'That they were, lass.'

'Did they know?'

He shook his head. 'It was for their own good, y'see. We thought it best to wait until they were older, after they left home. If Cleve'd found out, he wouldn't have coped. He doted on them, they were everything to him.'

'But they were your kids.'

Hobe smiled the saddest smile I'd ever seen. 'Good kids, too, so they were. I'd have done anything for 'em. Anything at all to make them happy, keep them safe. Even if it meant giving them up.'

'That's why you made the aquarium for Bronwyn, isn't it?'

Hobe seemed to shrink into his frayed shirt. 'When you and Bronwyn arrived, I saw it as a second chance. I'm sorry if I overwhelmed you both. I'm a foolish old man, I see now it was wrong of me to impose. I guess I was so eager to make a good impression that I botched it instead.'

It took a moment to swallow the lump in my throat.

'Don't apologise, Hobe. You were only being kind, and Bronwyn raved for days about her aquarium. I guess I'm a bit overprotective of her at times, which is crazy because Bronwyn's made of sterner stuff than I give her credit for.' An idea came to me, a way to make it up to him. 'You know, Hobe, I've been thinking it might do her good to have something to look after. Perhaps you could bring over a couple of Alma's puppies for her to meet?'

'I'll do that, Audrey, indeed I will.' Hobe attempted a smile, but he seemed distracted. Going over to one of the beds, he knelt on the floor and dragged out from under it a small dusty suitcase. He hoisted the suitcase onto the mattress, flipped the latches and yanked up the lid.

'Tony left this here one time. I got the feeling he'd been knocking heads with Cleve a bit, having a few rows. Glenda and Cleve were close, but Tony . . . he always seemed closer to his mother.' Hobe sighed. 'Anyhow, Tony would've been about twelve when he arrived on our doorstep claiming he'd come to say goodbye. He was running away from home, so he said. Of course, I lured him inside, talked him out of it. Eventually he went home, but he left his old valise here.'

Hobe sat on the bed, his face creased with a depth of sorrow I was only just coming to understand. 'Looking back now, I wish I'd let him go. Maybe then he'd have been spared the nightmare of his sister's death. Maybe he'd still be alive today.'

I sat on the bed next to the suitcase. 'You can't know that, Hobe.'

He didn't answer, so I drew the old case onto my lap and began to poke through Tony's belongings. Checked shirts, a pair of grubby jeans, rolled socks. A sketchpad of ink studies, a paint-brush rolled in a hanky, a tin of watercolour tubes: familiar lilacs and greens, cerulean and ochre, all dry and crumbled. At the bottom of the suitcase I found a large cigar box. The rubber band that had once held its lid in place had perished and fallen away. The contents of the box had tumbled out. I studied them, not daring to breathe.

A man's watch. A set of keys, a wallet embossed with the initials S.R.

'They were his grandfather's,' Hobe said. 'Old Samuel had them on him when he died. The police gave them to Luella, but she didn't want them. She gave them to Tony, and – apart from his paints and papers – those old relics were his pride and joy.'

Thumbing the rusty clasp on the wallet, I let it fall open. My heart nearly stopped when I saw the photo. It was a faded black and white snapshot of a young woman. She would have been about sixteen, achingly pretty, her oval face framed by long dark hair, her almond eyes alight with mischief.

I knew her. I'd seen another portrait of her just over a week ago, locked inside the dark cavity of the tallboy in the old settlers' hut.

'Aylish,' I breathed.

Hobe peered over my shoulder. 'No, lass,' he said. 'That's Luella.'

Understanding dawned. 'Samuel carried her photo in his wallet. To the day he died.'

'So he did.'

'He must have loved her, after all.'

Hobe had picked up Tony's sketchbook and was examining a tiny blue kingfisher vibrantly rendered in pen and ink wash.

'How could he not love her, lass?' he said softly. 'How could anyone not love her? She's one in a million.'

24

Luella was in her garden, a massive sunhat shading her face, her hands swamped in canvas gloves. She waved when she saw my car, met me at the gate, ushered me through, absurdly pleased.

'Why, Audrey! What a lovely surprise, I was just thinking about you and Bronwyn, wondering when I'd see you again – ' She frowned. 'What is it, love? You look peaky.'

'I've just come from the Millers' place,' I began, then floundered. On the drive over I'd planned my inquisition; there was so much I needed to know, so many questions aching to be asked. But seeing her concerned smile, catching the glimmer of worry in her eyes, knowing that just beneath the surface lurked the constant threat of more bad news . . . I found myself groping around for an easier, gentler way to confront her.

My voice was tight. 'Hobe has quite a collection of Tony's artwork, doesn't he?'

Luella's smile faltered. 'Oh, indeed . . . ?'

Insane, I felt the prick of tears behind my eyes. Then a sudden rush of anger – at myself, at Luella . . . and bafflingly, at Tony.

'Why didn't you tell me Tony was Hobe's son?' My voice came out all wrong, a twisted sharp thing that I didn't recognise as my own. 'Didn't you think Bronwyn ought to know her own grandfather? I've treated Hobe appallingly, thinking his interest in my daughter was inappropriate, maybe even perverse . . . I've just found out that it was because he knew all along that she was his granddaughter, and now I've made a terrible mess of the whole thing. How could you, Luella? How could you keep it from us?'

My outburst stunned me, but Luella didn't seem all that perturbed. With studied care she placed her secateurs on the rim of a birdbath and took off her gloves. Her hands were small and pink, damp. She gave my arm a firm squeeze.

'I'm sorry, pet. I really am. Every time I've seen you and Bronwyn I've tried to drum up the courage to tell you both about Hobe. And every time I've failed.'

I slumped, the anger gone as quickly as it had come.

'I was so mean to him, Luella. You should have seen his poor old face.'

'He'll get over it.'

'He told me everything. About how you met when you were young, and he went off to Vietnam then came back half-insane, and how Samuel influenced you to marry Cleve. Then the letters in the tree, and your plan to run away and sell chutney in spite of you being a terrible cook, which I can't believe because your cakes are just so . . . so – ' My outburst stalled. Tears pricked my eyes and I had to rub them away.

Luella dug in her sleeve and withdrew a pressed hanky, handed it to me. 'You and Hobe had quite a morning.'

'Yeah. I guess we did.'

She sighed, then turned and went along the path towards the house. When she reached the steps, she looked back.

'Come on,' she said huskily. 'I think we need a good strong drink. And I'm not talking about lime cordial.'

Luella poured sherry into tiny frosted glasses. I drained the sickly brew in one gulp, then dipped into my tote and removed the letter. Passing it across to Luella, I said a silent prayer that she'd understand.

She eyed the crumpled note with suspicion.

'What's this?'

'It's from your mother. She wrote it to Samuel after he returned from the war.'

Luella took the letter, but didn't unfold it right away. She turned it this way and that, obviously mystified.

'I found it at the homestead,' I explained, fumbling to find the right words. 'Samuel had hidden it behind an old picture frame. I guess he didn't . . . It was – oh hell, Luella. Please, just read it.'

She studied my face for ages, then got to her feet. I followed her down the stairs and into the shade of a rangy old plum tree, where we sat on a garden seat. The peppery scent of crushed nasturtiums rose around us. Somewhere high in the branches overhead an insect screamed, a prolonged cry that made me shiver.

Luella's face was pale. She smoothed the note on her knees and began to read.

Silence edged around us, punctuated only by the rollicking melody of a butcher-bird high in the bunya, and the soft creak of the clothesline. The day was balmy, and the sherry had thinned my blood. If my heart hadn't been skating around so erratically, if my mind hadn't been whirling, I might have curled up in the warm grass and drifted into a weary daze.

Luella folded the letter and sat back. 'It's dated the day of her death.'

'Yes.'

'She said she was taking someone to meet him – someone special. Do you think she meant . . .' She gave a dry cough. 'She meant me, didn't she.'

'I believe so.'

Tipping back her head, she peered at the sky. Her plump throat was satiny smooth and her face composed. I could tell – by the tremor of her lips, and the pink in her cheeks – that she was hovering in the eye of an inner storm.

'I don't remember her,' she said. 'Not well, at any rate. After she died, I used to pretend that little Lulu had gone to heaven with her, and that I was a different child. I even insisted that Poppa start calling me Luella, rather than . . . oh – '

The storm broke. Luella's face crumpled and tears began to rain. I hesitated . . . but only for an instant. Gathering her against me, I held her while she sobbed. She was a large woman, tall as well as fleshy – but there in the shade beneath the plum tree she felt frail and insubstantial, a small girl weeping inconsolable tears for her lost mother. I held her close, patting her back, soothing her as best I could with wordless sounds, the way I used to soothe my own child.

She pulled away, gave me a watery smile.

'You know, when I said before that I don't remember her, it wasn't quite true. I suppose it's safer to store my memories away, lock them where they can't hurt me. But Audrey, there are glimpses. Flashes here and there, like bits of a dream. I remember being in this leafy clearing, a fairytale place where the trees were full of birds. And Mumma reciting all their names – whistlers and butcher-birds, scrub wrens, flycatchers. And I remember that she always seemed sad. I don't mean depressed, but there was often a shadow behind her smile. Except for this one time when she glowed with happiness.' Luella looked into my eyes and tried to smile, but a tear rolled over her lash. 'It was the night she died.'

Something uncoiled in me, a dark sort of hope. 'You remember that night?'

She nodded. 'It's hazy, but it's always haunted me. We'd gone out late, walking along a dark track. I was scared at first, but then Mumma started singing and her voice reassured me. I just remember that she was beaming all the while, as if she was keeping a secret from me. We walked a long way. I never knew where we were going. I realise now that she was taking me to meet . . . to meet Samuel.' She peered at me through damp lashes. 'One part of the memory is even hazier, but it's the part that haunts me most. You see, I saw a face in the trees that night. A big pale face, like a ghost. It scared me . . . and I ran away.'

In the stillness, the insect in the branches above us shrieked again. I found myself remembering Bronwyn's story about the cicada hunter. Right then I felt like an ill-fated cicada at the mercy of a hunter-wasp; ridden along by the force of my curiosity, unable to help myself yet dreading where it must lead.

'Luella, did you recognise the face? Was it someone you knew, a friend of your mother's?'

She gave a strangled laugh. 'Lord, no. It was horrible, a nightmarish thing like a goblin or a ghost. Mumma used to sing songs about ghosts and bush spirits and tall white devils that came out at night with their firesticks. She was part-Aboriginal, you see. Poppa had established a little mission up near Townsville, after the first war. It had started out as a school but grew from there. My grandmother was his oldest student, very bright, she used to help with the younger kids. She and Poppa fell in love. They wanted to get married but the church said no. So they lived together in secret until my grandmother's death from scarlet fever in 1933. Much later, after we lost Mumma, there were those in the town who were cruel enough to suggest that her death was God's way of punishing Poppa for his sins . . . although how anyone could consider love a sin is beyond me.'

I nodded distractedly. The face Luella had described was haunting me. The face of a goblin or a ghost, she'd said. A childhood memory that had sprung into being decades before I was born . . . So why did I feel as though *I'd* been the little girl in the bush that night? As though I'd been the one startled by the monster? And why could I conjure so clearly the image of a big pale face haunting *my* dreams?

Ridiculous.

And yet I *had* seen that nightmarish face. Not buried in the distant past where it belonged, but recently. Just over a week ago. Peering through the trees, dappled by morning sunlight, pale and moonlike, almost gleaming . . . And it hadn't been a ghost; the man at the settlers' hut had been very much flesh-and-blood.

The breach, the chasm I'd been feeling, the sense that I'd overlooked something – shuddered and began to close. I thought about the stolen letters I'd found inside the tallboy at the hut, with its shrine of doll heads and the photograph of Aylish. I called to mind the splintered old axe handle propped inside the hanging compartment, a memento once burgled from a woodshed. I thought of the dark red roses scrambling along the hut's verandah rails . . . and how they so perfectly matched the ones on Aylish's grave.

Someone *did* remember her.

And as the gap in my understanding closed further, I realised who that someone must be. But if Cleve Jarman was alive, wouldn't he have contacted Luella, let her know he was all right?

Unless, of course, he'd been unable to.

Or unwilling.

Spider fingers crawled up my spine. 'Luella, do you have any photos of Cleve?'

'I burnt them. Why?'

'A couple of weeks ago I went up to the old settlers' hut. Someone was living there. A man. I didn't get a good look at him, just a glimpse. He was unkempt, as if he'd been living rough for years.'

Luella brushed at her skirt. 'I don't quite follow, pet.'

'I'm wondering if it was Cleve.'

'It can't have been Cleve. He died twenty years ago.'

I'd been prepared for her denial, I'd even been prepared to weather another spate of tears. After all, the subject of her husband was surely a sensitive one. I wasn't prepared, however, for the quiet steel in her voice . . . or for the determined mask that now shuttered her face. Her eyes gave her away. Below their watery depths I saw a shadow move, a dark shape that might have been panic pushing upwards trying to tear loose.

'The body they found in the dam could have been anyone's. Just because police forensics said it'd been submerged from around the time Cleve disappeared, it doesn't prove it was him.'

Luella blinked. I prayed she wasn't on the verge of losing it. I was in no frame of mind to give reassurance right now; it was taking every grain of self-control to maintain my own equilibrium.

'Seeing someone up at Dad's hut must have been a shock,' she said gently, as if talking to a child. 'But this man, this squatter . . . he's gone now, didn't you say? Oh Audrey, people come and go around here all the time. Seasonal workers, campers, conservationists – he might have just been a poor old bushie taking shelter for a few months.'

'There was something about his face,' I blurted. 'Parts of his skin seemed to gleam unnaturally in the sunlight.'

A pause. 'Gleam?'

My heart was sliding about, my palms were moist. I was labouring the point, but I couldn't stop, not now. 'Cleve's face was scarred, wasn't it?'

'Cleve did have scarring, but it was barely noticeable, even if you'd been standing up close. Trust me, Audrey – it wasn't Cleve you saw up at the hut.' She smiled kindly and patted my arm, then got to her feet. 'I've spooked you with my little ghost story, haven't I? Oh Audrey, it was a long time ago, nothing more than a childish imagining. Now, come along inside. I've got some cheesecake for you to take home for Bronwyn, I know how she loves her after-school treats.'

I caught up with her at the foot of the back steps. 'That's why Tony came home, isn't it? He suspected his father might still be alive.'

'I'm sorry, pet. You couldn't be more wrong.'

I felt her annoyance; I'd overstepped the mark and was heading into territory where I was unwelcome. But I couldn't pull back now.

'Tony and Cleve weren't close, were they? Which makes me wonder why, after twenty years away, Tony would rush back here in a state of near shock, with hardly a word to his wife . . . unless he suspected something?'

Luella's already pinched face turned grey. She looked at me for an age, but I sensed she'd forgotten I was there. Finally she turned and climbed the back stairs and vanished into the house.

I went after her. She wasn't in the kitchen, but I could hear her in the front of the house. Banging doors. Slamming windows. Doing a lot of thumping and clicking that – as I went along the hall – I recognised as deadbolts being engaged.

'Luella . . . ?'

I found her in the sitting room, hauling a heavy curtain along its track. The drape eclipsed the last column of light and the room fell into semi-dark.

'What are you doing?' I asked, though I could see perfectly well.

She ignored me. Another window wrenched along its casing then walloped shut. Another lock rammed into place.

My heart started to hammer. 'You believe me, don't you? That explains the deadbolts, the bars on your windows . . . you've always suspected.'

'I've done nothing of the sort. For heaven's sake, Audrey, I'm a woman living alone. Aren't I entitled to feel secure?'

'Security's one thing, Luella – but you've got more padlocks than Fort Knox.'

'The house was burgled once,' she said dismissively. 'Nothing was stolen, at least nothing of value. They ransacked the shed, took a few tools and bits and pieces. You know what it's like these days, every time you hear the news there're kids breaking into people's homes, running amok – '

One of Glenda's diary entries came to mind: *Dad's a hoarder, he's got boxes and jars and tins of things stashed all around the shed.* I recalled the letters I'd discovered up at the settlers' hut, and of the carved box they'd been kept in. I remembered the blackened axe handle with its greasy, skin-like patina. The dolls' heads, the photograph. And the ammo tins labelled with a hotchpotch of contents. Matches. Pencils, tea, candles, rope.

The man at the settlers' hut was a hoarder too.

'Perhaps it was Cleve who broke in?'

Luella spun to face me. 'No.'

'But the forensic tests aren't yet conclusive. Those remains they dredged from the dam might belong to anyone.'

She shut her eyes. 'I don't need any tests to tell me what I already know. It was him.'

'How can you be so sure?'

She went out to the kitchen, pulled shut the back door and rattled the key in the deadlock. Slamming the window, she hovered in the leafy sunlight.

'I *know* he's dead, Audrey.'

'But – '

'I saw him die.'

This took a moment to process. 'But if you saw him . . . if you knew, then why was he reported missing? Why didn't you tell anyone?'

She squeezed the deadbolt keys out of sight between her hands. 'I had my reasons.'

I stared at her. Why would she want everyone to think Cleve was still alive, if she knew he was dead? A chilling thought came to me. After reading Glenda's diary I'd come to suspect that her death was no accident. And when I'd heard Tony's story about finding her half unconscious beneath the beech tree, I'd understood why she'd never returned for her belongings. One question gnawed uneasily. If Glenda had been badly hurt, she'd never have managed to drag herself a mile to the gully. Which could only mean that someone else had taken her there.

I looked at Luella. She had found her daughter's body. Had she somehow arrived at the same conclusion? Is that why she'd allowed the police to construe that her daughter's death was nothing more than a tragic accident? Had she suspected the truth, and taken matters into her own hands?

'You knew,' I said flatly. 'You knew Cleve murdered her.'

Luella nodded.

'How?'

'Tony told me. Earlier that night, he'd found his sister up at Dad's. She was barely conscious, and kept mumbling something over and over, but Tony couldn't make out the word. He ran for help, but when he got back to Dad's, Glenda was gone. It wasn't until hours later that he realised what she'd been trying to tell him.'

'That it was Cleve.'

'Yes.' A pair of palm-sized roses bloomed on her face, as if she'd been slapped hard on both cheeks. Turning, she vanished into the dark hallway.

I found her in the floral bedroom. Pulling shut the window, she engaged the lock and closed the drapes, plunging the room into twilight.

'That's why you burnt his pictures.'

Again she nodded.

'Why?' I had to ask. 'Why did he do it?'

'I don't know.'

My world was shifting on its axis, changing gears, forever altering the course of its rotation. Slowly, inevitably, I was drawn by the gravity of a new understanding.

'Oh, Luella . . . you killed him?'

While she'd been standing there, she had dug her fingernails into the back of her hand. Half-moons of blood sat along her knuckles.

'I wish to God I had,' she said quietly. 'But no, it wasn't me.'

'Then who?'

She went across the room and stood in the doorway. 'The night she died, Glenda had been on her way to Corey's. She left a note, but there was a storm and I was worried. She always rang to let me know she'd arrived safely. Cleve's car was in the drive and the shed light was on, and I wanted to ask if he'd received a call from her, but when I knocked he wouldn't answer. Strange, I thought, then dismissed it. When Glenda still hadn't called by eight-thirty, I rang the Weingartens but no one was there. Thinking she'd taken the shortcut through Dad's and got caught in the rain, I grabbed my umbrella and rushed after her.'

Luella turned and went along the hall. In the bathroom she checked the window, then continued down to Tony's room and shut the venetians. 'When I reached the gully I saw something lying on the ground in the centre of the clearing. It was a shoe. My daughter's shoe.'

She was shaking her head now, tears wobbling in her eyes. 'It took me an hour to find her, but I was too late. My precious Glenda, on the gully floor. Her body half in the water. She was covered in leaves and dirt and bits of gravel sticking to the blood. And her . . . her head, it was . . .' She pulled out a hanky and mopped her face, then hurried back into the hall.

'I lay down beside her on the gully floor. Held her in my arms the way I'd done when she was a baby, rocked her. I can't remember how long I was there, it seemed forever. I heard something in the clearing above, the thump of feet and crying. I came to my senses . . . or rather, shook myself out of helpless shock and into something else, something raw and dark and full of hate. Anger, I suppose. I knew her death hadn't been an accident.'

'How?'

'It was her shoe. The one I found in the clearing. If Glenda had fallen accidentally, her shoe would have been lying at the edge of the gully, not at the centre. And I had a feeling,' she added softly. 'A mother's feeling.'

She entered Glenda's room and I trailed in behind. It was just as I remembered. Wallpapered with yellow roses, the bed made, the collection of furry toys propped on the window seat. A school jumper draped over the back of the vanity chair.

Luella picked up the jumper and brought it to her lips.

'I ran home. Stumbling, falling, getting up. Not knowing what I'd do when I got there.' She shook the jumper loose and refolded it, laid it back on the chair. 'I found Tony in the shed. The fluoro light was flickering and there was an unpleasant smell. Smoky, acrid. Tony was standing near the door. He had a rifle, an old Winchester, cradled in his arms. Ghostly white, he was . . . I shouted at him. Went over and shook him, but he didn't respond. He kept staring at the back of the shed. I turned to see what had transfixed him, and saw . . .'

I stumbled over to the bed and sat heavily. The roses on the yellow wallpaper seemed to fly around the room, dazzling me.

'Cleve,' I whispered.

Luella crossed to the window. Sunlight danced across her face. Her skin was damp; with sweat or tears I couldn't tell.

'My husband was a big man. He'd gone to fat in middle age and was nearly impossible to lift. Somehow, between the two of us we got him into the Holden and drove him out to the dam. I buckled him into the driver's seat, and jammed the old Winchester in the footwell hoping that when his body was found, the rifle would explain the gunshot wound. It wasn't a flawless plan, but I knew there'd be an inquiry. I disengaged the handbrake, and Tony helped me push the car down the slope into the water.

'Later, when it was over and we came back to the house, we couldn't look each other in the eye. I told Tony, Not a word to anyone. I needn't have bothered making him promise. Tony was all eyes, sick with shock. I wished I'd tried to console him,

but all I could think about was getting rid of all traces of Cleve
. . . especially evidence of Tony's involvement. I knew there'd
be questions, probably an investigation. It seemed easier to drag
out my bucket and mop, get busy with my soapy water, than to
deal with the horror of what we'd done.'

Luella drew the venetians. The light broke into ribbons and
the room dimmed.

'By the time I finished cleaning up it was eleven o'clock in
the morning. I had a shower, scrubbed the blood from under
my fingernails, did my hair and makeup, even ironed a clean
frock. Somehow I kept my voice calm while I telephoned the
police. Then I went back to the gully to say goodbye to my
daughter.'

We stood in the jagged shadows. Luella didn't cry. The tears
that had been wobbling in her eyes were gone, leaving her pupils
large and wet. She kept blinking, shaking her head as though
trying to disentangle herself from what she'd just revealed.

I felt somewhat twitchy myself.

Twitchy, yet calm to the point of numbness. Cleve Jarman
had been a bad man. He'd hurt his family beyond repair. He was
a murderer . . . but did that excuse what Tony had done? Did it
justify Luella's silence? I tried to stay unbiased, but I kept seeing
the gully with its wet leaves and flowing creek, the cool green
air tainted by the stink of bruised flesh and spilled blood. And
the limp beloved body, skin cooling in the night air, the last
echoes of a precious life swiftly ebbing. If the tables had been
turned and I'd been the one to find *my* daughter's body – would
I have acted differently?

I tasted blood, realised I'd bitten my thumbnail to the quick.
Fisting the gory mess out of sight, I stole a look at Luella.

She stood motionless in the tattered ribbons of light coming
through the blinds, gazing at nothing. A strand of hair had
escaped her beehive and glued itself to her cheek. Every time
she blinked, the strand quivered.

'Something's not adding up,' I thought aloud. 'You said you put the Winchester in the footwell, before you pushed the car in the water.'

'Yes.'

'But the newspaper report didn't mention finding a rifle.'

A soft intake of breath. 'Perhaps they decided not to disclose such a distressing fact.'

I steeled myself, knowing I was rushing across an invisible threshold but unable to pull back. 'Hobe told me that the gun Tony used on himself was a Winchester. He said it was Gurney's rifle, and that Tony stole it the night Glenda died. If it was the same one he used to kill his father, then what I can't understand is how it got from the footwell of the submerged Holden and back into Tony's possession twenty years later.'

Luella seemed frozen, as though the barest movement might splinter her careful control. When she finally spoke, her voice was eerie, an exhalation of sound in the stillness.

'Things get muddled over time. It might have been a different rifle, I can't recall.'

'But – '

'You know, I wouldn't have told you all this if Tony had still been alive . . . but he's gone now, and so is Glenda. There's nothing left for me. I won't mind if you decide to turn me in, Audrey. In fact, it'd be a relief not to have to hide anymore.'

I walked over to the window and peered through the slats. The glary daylight seemed artificial. I felt I'd endured a lifetime in this stuffy gloom, crushed beneath the weight of Luella's confession. And yet something told me she wasn't being entirely honest. I let the blind fall back.

'It's not my place to judge you,' I said. 'To be honest, I'd probably have done the same.'

Luella nodded, but she seemed distant again as though my reassurance was the least of her concerns. Tucking her hanky back in her bra, she trod awkwardly towards me. I felt a rush of dread, fearing that she meant to envelop me in a hug. After what we'd just shared I felt raw and exposed, on the brink of not coping.

To my relief she bypassed me and went to the window, re-adjusting the slats I'd left agape.

'You never know what you'll do, dear,' she whispered into the dusty stillness. 'Until you're right in the thick of it with your back against the wall and nowhere else to turn. You just never know.'

The first thing I noticed when I got home was the smell.

Stuffy and faintly putrid. I went through the house opening windows, hoping for a fresh breeze to gust it away, wondering if my imagination was going haywire after Luella's devastating confession. But the smell seemed to get stronger in the hall, and stronger still in my bedroom. I flung open more windows, but the odour lingered. Had something died in a bottom drawer? I scouted around, thinking maybe a mouse or a dried up gecko . . .

Then froze.

On the end of the bed sat my battered Minolta – the one I'd last seen bouncing into the bushes up at the settlers' hut. I did a mental backtrack. Had I retrieved the camera after all, and in my shocked state forgotten? Hell no. I could see it now, lying there in the grass, just a glimpse as I turned and ran. There'd been no time to grab it. Which meant . . .

He'd been here.

That would explain the mustiness, the smell.

I rushed through the house. My pro cameras and laptop were all still in my studio, my collection of valuable old lenses untouched. The stereo and TV sat unmolested in the lounge room; even the twenty dollar bill I'd placed on the table to fund Bronwyn's upcoming science project was right where I'd left it. Confused now, beginning to doubt myself, I ran from door to door, window to window, searching for forced entry – but there were no broken panes, no gouged woodwork, no jemmied door locks.

Returning to my bedroom, I stared at the Minolta. Picking it up, I removed it from the case. A crack speared across the face of the filter lens, and the lens cap was missing. Which was odd, because the cap should've been inside the case. I shook the case to make sure, and a square of paper fluttered out.

A Polaroid photograph.

One I knew well. I'd taken it five years ago when Bronwyn was six, a few months before her father walked out. It was a colour shot of her and Tony, grinning with insane happiness into the camera, their eyes alight. Tony had claimed it immediately, slipping it into his wallet, vowing he'd keep it there until the day he died. And judging by the concave photo paper and tattered edges, that's exactly what he'd done.

Until the day he died . . .

Dots began to join, firing off synaptic trails in my brain.

Tony had every reason to believe Cleve was dead. He'd shot him and then helped his mother dump the body in the dam. He'd made a partial confession to Danny Weingarten, knowing Danny would never tell. *I've done something bad*, he'd signed to Danny – and then the next morning got on a bus and never returned. For twenty years he'd stayed away, cutting all ties with his mother and the people he loved.

And yet, all along, he must have had his doubts. Why else would the discovery of Cleve's supposed remains prompt his return?

I searched the faded faces in the Polaroid – Bronwyn's round baby features and Tony's earnest smile. I searched until the image blurred, then shut my eyes and tried to piece it all together.

Tony's nightmares, his moodiness. His extended silences. There must have been an undercurrent of fear running through him all his adult life. That is, until he'd read about the discovery in the dam.

He would've wanted to see Luella, talk to her. He probably guessed she'd be feeling frightened and needed her son by her side . . . or maybe he'd wanted to align their stories in case the police opened an inquiry. He would have gone to William Road. He might have knocked for ages, nervous, planning in detail what he'd say to his mother after two decades.

But Luella was out, perhaps shopping in Brisbane.

Tony would have decided to wait. He'd kill a bit of time by hiking up the track to the gully . . . then further uphill to the old settlers' hut, a place that harboured happy childhood memories. And there, in the grassy glade on that glorious sun-filled, bird-bright afternoon, he had come face to face with the nightmare he'd just spent twenty years running away from.

I stared at the Polaroid pinched in my bloodless fingers.

Tony had promised to keep it in his wallet forever.

Something dark blossomed in my chest. Denial, perhaps. And crazily, like the echo of a faraway dream, a fragment from something Aylish had written drifted into my mind.

I used the washhouse key and let myself into the homestead, I do hope you won't be cross . . .

The Polaroid fluttered from my grasp. I rushed along the hall, through the kitchen, down the back stairs and into the laundry under the house. There was no rankness in the air, no sign that anyone other than Bronwyn or I had been here. It all looked so ordinary. The gleaming front-loader, the swept tiles, the roomy concrete basins, the line hung with washing. And Bronwyn's bike with its handlebar streamers and bright red seat, propped beneath the shelf she'd requisitioned for her silk-worm trays.

It took less than five minutes to find it – located midway along the door lintel, surrounded by an inch of dust. The clunky old key was mostly clean, as though it had recently been used. Apart from the heavy tarnish, it was a perfect match to the shiny, newly-cut keys Bronwyn and I used to let ourselves into the house.

I leaned against the doorframe, lightheaded.

Until now I'd assumed that the threat lay behind me.

Buried in the past, separated from us by an ocean of time. I'd assumed that we were immune to any real danger, by virtue of the simple fact that we existed in the here-and-now.

But as I stared at the key in my palm, feeling the cool air eddy around my ankles, a whisper echoed down the years, a warning.

Run as far and as fast as you can and don't look back . . .

And as the chill arms of new understanding wrapped around me, I saw that I'd opened a doorway, a portal into a dark and violent place – and thanks to my digging, thanks to my unquenchable curiosity, that doorway now yawned wide open.

25

My daughter's voice rose to a shriek. 'I'm not leaving Magpie Creek. You can't make me!'

We stood on the verandah. It was early evening, and Bronwyn still wore her school uniform. I tried not to look at her, tried not to notice the pain and accusation in her eyes. Instead, I clung to the rail and fixed my attention on the huge, purple-black thundercloud that hovered overhead.

'My mind's made up, Bron. I'm sorry.'

'But why, Mum . . . can't you just tell me why?'

'It's not working out for us here.'

'What do you mean?'

'It's just not.'

'Mum, I *can't* leave. What about Jade and Aunty Corey? What about Grandy? We can't just pack up and go as if they never existed.'

'Honey, I'm sorry. I really am. But we have to go.'

Bronwyn let out a ragged sigh. 'Mum, have I done something wrong?' Her voice had reached crying-pitch; she was hugging herself, kicking the toe of her sandal against the rail. I could smell her anguish, salty and bitter as tears.

My heart twisted, but I couldn't back down. 'It's not about anything you've done.'

'What, then?'

I studied her pinched face, suddenly afraid for her. I tried to smile, tried to inject some enthusiasm into my tone. 'We can sell this place for a bucket load now it's cleaned up, just think of the great apartment we can get, maybe something right on the beach – you'd like that wouldn't you? Looking out to sea, all those lights on the bay . . . we can pick up our old lives right where we left off.'

Bronwyn sprang away from the rail. 'What about my life here? Am I supposed to just forget it ever happened?'

'Of course not, but – '

'Well, I can't forget it, I won't! You go back to Melbourne if that's what you want, but I'm staying here. I'll go and live with Grandy, she won't mind. She'll be glad to have me.'

'Bron, there's no point arguing. We'll be driving back at the end of the week.'

She glared at me through her tears. 'You're jealous of Grandy, that's why you're doing this, isn't it? You're jealous! Just like you were jealous of Dad. That's why he stopped coming to see me. You drove him away with all your whingeing and nagging. He only ran to Carol to escape you . . . and now he's dead!'

She spun away and tore across the verandah, down the stairs and out into the rain. A moment later she'd vanished among the trees. It never occurred to me to grab an umbrella, or shoes, or even to just let her go. The Minolta incident was still fresh in my mind, and the possibility that we were no longer alone out here was enough to have me pounding down the steps after her.

She was perched on her cedar bench beneath the jacaranda, hugging her legs, her face pressed into her knees. Her narrow frame shook, her fingers made white-knuckled claws on her jeans.

I sat beside her, waiting for the crying to pass. Rain dripped on my head, skated under my collar and down my back. The dry earth had turned to mud, I could feel it squelching between my toes. Mosquitoes took advantage of the mobile feast we presented, nipping fingers and ankles, swarming up from under the bench in black clouds.

Bronwyn fumbled in her pocket for a hanky. 'No wonder Dad left. You're a total bitch sometimes. You make *me* want to leave, too.'

In the stormy gloom she was indistinct, a pale ghostlike figure, no longer my daughter but a figment from a dream. My heart flipped.

'Please don't say that – '

A thunderclap boomed overhead. The yard was lit by an X-ray flash so brilliant that every leaf, every blade of grass, every dazzling droplet of rain, was burned forever into my retinas. Bronwyn flinched. I reached for her in a gesture I hadn't used for years – smoothing my hand across her hair, letting it rest on the back of her head . . .

She jerked away, giving me a look that rivalled the icy downpour. 'I wish it was you who'd died, not Dad. I wish he was still here, and you weren't. I don't want to live with you any more, Mum. I hate you.'

Leaping up, she raced back towards the house.

Her hair was an ashy blur in the purplish light, and she ran half-hunched against the rain. I wanted to go after her and tell her that the hurt would pass, that one day she'd be able to think of her father without falling into the dreadful gaping hole of his absence. I wanted to tell her that everything would be all right, if only she'd curl up in my arms and let me soothe away her sorrows, the way I used to do when she was little –

The back door slammed and soft light fluttered in the kitchen. The storm must have caused a blackout. I could see the torch beam swivelling about, a blurred cone of luminosity that dimmed and brightened, bobbing from room to room before finally vanishing and plunging the house into blackness.

When the rain stopped, the garden erupted into a caco-phony of noise – bullfrogs, cicadas, the slap of raindrops on fleshy

leaves. The air turned clammy, the shadows beneath the jacaranda hummed with insects.

All I could hear were my daughter's angry words.

*You drove him away with your whingeing and nagging, and now
he's dead . . . I hate you. I hate you –*

I swallowed hard. Ridiculous that my throat was thick,
that my eyes stung, that a shadow had taken hold of my heart.
Leaning back against the jacaranda's sodden trunk, I rolled my
eyes upwards, hoping to lose myself in the sky. The storm was
clearing as suddenly as it had begun. One by one, the last of the
violet clouds drifted away. In their place appeared a timid scattering of stars. So small, they were barely more than luminous
pin-pricks; so few in number that the immensity of the sky
threatened to swamp them. Yet they continued to shine, a
handful of glitter cast across velvet, stubbornly pouring their
light over the earth even in the face of all that darkness.

'Bron? You're awfully quiet in there.'

I leaned my ear to her bedroom door, listening. 'Sweetheart,
are you awake?'

Over an hour had passed since our argument. I knew she'd
still be upset, which was why we needed to talk. Or rather, why
I needed to talk. To explain the real reason we were leaving, and
to trust that she'd understand.

After she ran back inside, I'd continued to sit beneath the
jacaranda. Observing the stars, and keeping watch on the house.
Drawing back together the pieces of myself that had fragmented
during the day's revelations.

I saw how deeply preoccupied I'd been with the past, obsessing
over dead people while neglecting the things that really mattered:
Bronwyn, my friends, the life unfolding *now*. I'd been using my
quest for Aylish's killer – and my compulsion to know the truth
about Glenda's death – as an excuse to avoid confronting the

knotted tangle of my own affairs. I'd expended so much energy sifting through the lives of people who were long lost . . . while my own life slipped irretrievably through my fingers.

Not any more, I promised. No more lies. No more hiding in the past.

'Bronny?'

I rapped softly on her door, and it swung open. Squinting through the shadows, I expected to see her lanky shape curled beneath the sheets . . . but the bed was neatly made, her school uniform abandoned on the floor. A hair ribbon dangled from the back of her chair, a strand of whiteness in the bruise-coloured gloom.

I went through the house, shining my flashlight into dark corners, calling. When the house proved as empty as her room, I hurried down the back stairs with my torch, searching her secret nooks around the garden. The last place I looked was the laundry. All bareness, just the silent concrete basins, a line strung with damp T-shirts, an empty peg basket, and the shelf with Bronwyn's silkworm trays.

But no bike.

I rushed upstairs to the kitchen, intending to check the house a second time. She knew better than to venture off without telling me first, but my palms had turned moist and I was teetering on the threshold of panic. It was dark outside, and I kept thinking about the Minolta on the end of my bed and Tony's old Polaroid tucked into the case, and the musty smell that had tainted the air.

The squatter had been here.

He'd used the laundry key and let himself into our house – and though he'd returned my camera and otherwise done no harm, his trespass had shaken me. I'd been planning to drive over to Corey's so we could spend the night there, and then sort out what to do in the morning when my head cleared. Only now . . .

A pink sticky note clung to the coffee maker.

Mum, I've gone to Grandy's, please don't come after me, I'll ring you when I'm ready to come home. I'm sorry I said I hate you, I don't really, I just need some time away.

Love, Bron.

I crumpled the note, already calculating. How long would it take her to ride to Luella's? An hour, forty minutes? How long had she already been gone?

I picked up the phone to dial Luella's number, but the connection was dead; the storm still rumbled in the distance, it must have shorted the line. Grabbing my car keys, I headed for the door, cursing myself for sitting under the jacaranda all this time, nursing my own private worries while Bronwyn was packing her carryall, writing her note, getting on her bike and heading off into the night.

God. She must have been so distressed. I imagined her now, riding along the dark road, gripping the handlebars against the potholed bitumen, her face streaked with tears, her skinny legs pedalling for all she was worth.

And *him* out there somewhere. Watching. Waiting . . .

I stopped dead.

Retracing my steps down the hall, I went into Samuel's room, retrieved the key from the wardrobe, unlocked the dressing table drawer.

And stared into the empty cavity.

Samuel's handgun was gone.

The quaking began in my stomach, worked its way up and outwards until my entire body was cold with sweat. Whoever had broken into my house had obviously searched the place after all. He'd found the dresser key and known what to look for.

Meanwhile, my daughter was riding her bicycle through the dark night, alone and unprotected as she pedalled towards her grandmother's house. The two images collided in my mind and filled me with a brew of emotions I'd never before experienced.

The raw urge to protect, to fight; to sacrifice anything to keep her safe.

In the kitchen I took Aylish's letters from my tote and jammed them in my back pocket. They were the real reason the squatter had been here. Not to return my camera, but to steal back the letters. The Minolta and the Polaroid were mere calling cards.

As I rushed to the door, the torch-beam flared and I glimpsed myself in the entryway mirror. My face was ashen, my expression fixed. Only my eyes betrayed what I was feeling. They were large and luminous, violently golden, almost feral.

Not a mouse after all.

Luella's house crouched in darkness beneath the bunya pine. Her LandCruiser sat in the driveway, but no glimmer of light seeped through any of her windows. The place looked empty, abandoned.

As I pulled onto the verge, a familiar object appeared in my headlight beam: Bronwyn's bike.

Cutting the motor, I dived out and ran towards the house. Taking the stairs two at a time, I hammered on Luella's front door. It swung open under the force of my knuckles, and I went in.

'Luella? Bron, are you here?'

The house was echoey and cool inside, a den of shadows. I noticed the same smell that had tainted my own house earlier that day – a hint of unwashed skin and nervous sweat, a trace of wood-smoke – and it followed me along the hallway.

Navigating by the moonlight that shone through a doorway at the far end, I found my way to the kitchen. I flicked a light switch several times but nothing happened. All I could hear was the wind in the trees outside, the distant grumble of thunder. The sunray clock ticked eerily, racing in time to my heart.

Hastening to the verandah doors, I located another light switch, but that failed too. Outside, the yard was sunk in darkness. An inky purple sky revolved around the axis of the old bunya pine, making cloud-shadows scurry over the roof of Luella's glasshouse. Moonlight shed tiger stripes on the lawn under the black fronds of the pandanus palm.

I tensed, checking over my shoulder. Hairs stood up on my arms. I sensed I was being watched. Movement in the doorway snagged the corner of my eye. Darkness closed back around the shape I thought I'd seen. Shadows reassembled into harmless emptiness. The doorway was vacant, but the after-image of the figure was locked to my retina.

'Luella? Is that you?'

I moved to the bench. Not wanting to take any chances, I slid Aylish's letters from my pocket and placed them silently into one of Luella's retro cannisters. Then I crept to the doorway, stood a moment to find my centre. I rocked forward, sending furtive glances up and down the hall. Holding my breath, struggling to hear above the roar of my pulse, I moved into the dimness.

The smell was stronger, the air in the hall was almost unbreathable.

Bypassing the bathroom, I elbowed into Luella's room but found it empty. Halfway along the hall I peered into the study with the blue wardrobe. Moonlight pierced the darkness, but that room was empty too. As was Tony's.

Glenda's room looked different. At first I thought it must be the dim light; the drapes had been dragged aside, the moon's face shone through the window, oily-bright on the iron security grille. Then my heart leapt.

Bronwyn lay on Glenda's bed, asleep on the coverlet, her fair hair arranged across the pillow in a silky fan around her head. She looked small and vulnerable, her thin arms draped across her chest, her face a smudge in the gloom. I rushed over, relief making me weak-kneed. Grabbing her arm, I gave her a shake.

'Bronny, it's Mum. Wake up, we're going home.'

She didn't stir, her eyelids didn't flutter. I bent to scoop her into my arms, detecting a faint chemical smell. A shockwave of fear went through me. What had Luella done to her? She was in a deep sleep. Had she been drugged?

The air was suddenly rank.

I heard a shuffle behind me. Loosening my grip on Bronwyn, I let her roll back on the bed. I registered a presence behind me in the dark, glimpsed a moonlit figure blurred in motion. Arm raised, it came at me swinging. I lurched out of the way and the first blow took me on the shoulder, knocking me sideways.

Throwing myself in front of the bed, I tried to shield my sleeping daughter. The next strike caught me on the side of the head. Shards of light exploded behind my eyes, blinding me. The room listed. My hands shot out, rubbery and useless. My body pitched forward, then buckled beneath me. I fought a wave of blackness, trying to twist out of its path, groping for my daughter, wedging myself between the bed and my attacker. Seeing for an instant the face illuminated by moonlight – a face I almost recognised, big and pale and nightmarish. A face I somehow understood I had reason to fear.

26

'Wake up! Please, Audrey . . . wake up – '

Blinking, I saw fluttering light. A candle. I was sitting on the floor in a darkened room. There were yellow roses on the wallpaper and ragged toys along the window seat – bears and a knitted ragdoll. Pop posters behind the door.

A face appeared before me, a woman's broad face, grey and clammy with sweat. The eye staring at me was wide and green. The other one was blackened shut. Her plump cheeks were smeared with what looked like blood.

'Luella? What . . .' I tried to sit forward. My eyes blurred and a wave of nausea swamped me. My head was pounding, but through the pain came glimmers of recall. A figure in the darkness. A rankness in the air. An arm swinging up, and lights exploding in my eyes. Then I remembered Bronwyn asleep on top of the covers, serene as an angel, her hair crimped over the pillow, her thin arms crossed on her chest.

My attention flew to the bed. It was empty.

Lurching up, I glared into the blood-smeared face of the woman beside me.

'Where is she . . . ?'

'I'm sorry, Audrey, I'm so terribly sorry . . .'

Awake now despite my ringing ears and double vision, despite the thunderous pounding in my head, I grabbed Luella's shoulders. 'For God's sake, Luella, where's my daughter?'

411

Luella was sobbing, but managed to choke out a single word. 'Taken.'

Terror flashed hot across my skin. The candle sputtered, sending timid washes of light up the walls, turning the yellow roses to gold. I got to my feet, fighting to control the dizzying roar in my head.

Luella clutched me with cold fingers. 'I tried to call the police, but the phone line's been cut. The cars too, neither of them working. The keys are in yours, but the motor won't start. It's a couple of hours into town by foot, and the closest neighbours are the Millers and they're just over an hour away. Oh Audrey, I'm afraid for her, terribly afraid!' Her voice broke on the last word and her panic infected me. My joints were frozen, I could barely draw breath. I kept getting flashes of my daughter on Glenda's bed, so still, so heavily drugged in sleep. I remembered the chemical smell lifting off her . . . and then the man I'd glimpsed in the doorway.

I forced myself to calm. 'Luella, you're not making sense. Slow down. I can't find her unless I know exactly what happened. So tell me slowly, from the beginning.'

Luella nodded. 'Bronwyn arrived about six o'clock. She was upset. She told me about your argument, and that you'd decided to leave Magpie Creek. I made her Milo and a sandwich, but before she'd taken a bite there was a knock on the door. She thought it must be you, so I told her I'd talk to you. Only there was no one there. I stepped outside to see if your car was parked in the drive, but it wasn't. I heard a sound and noticed this dreadful smell, then . . .'

Luella touched the back of her head, showed me the blood glistening wetly on her fingers. 'I came to my senses downstairs in the laundry. Gruffy woke me, he'd dug in under the door. I rushed up into the house, but Bronwyn was gone. I searched everywhere, found you lying here. And now she's been taken, and it's all my fault.'

I'd been pacing the room while she talked, going from the window to the door and back, only half-listening, trying to think. But now I took notice.

'What do you mean, your fault?'

She got to her feet, gripping my arm with cold fingers to steady herself. I could smell the coppery scent of blood lifting from her skin.

'I didn't tell you everything,' she said. 'The night Glenda died, after Tony shot his father ... later, at the dam, Tony thought he saw something.'

'What?'

'After disengaging the handbrake, we rolled the Holden down the slope until it gained its own momentum. Just as we released it, Tony let out a cry. He started running after it as it rattled down the embankment. I thought in his grief and shock that he intended to throw himself into the water. The car nose-dived into the dam and quickly began to sink, but Tony kept insisting he'd seen his father's eyes open. So we waited. Half an hour, maybe more. Watching for bubbles, signs of life. I kept my eyes on that spot for ever so long. But Cleve ... well, he never resurfaced.'

'But he could've survived?'

Luella let go my arm. 'It's possible.'

I felt myself sliding into hopeless panic. 'God. Bronwyn's out there with him.'

Shutting my eyes, I weighed up. No phones. And no cars. I couldn't waste time footing it into town, not when Bronwyn might still be nearby. The Millers were an hour. By then it'd be too late. I needed to act now.

'Go to the Millers,' I told Luella. 'Don't risk cutting through Thornwood, go via the road. Hobe'll know what to do.'

Luella stared. 'What about you?'

'I'm going after them.' I crossed the room, but as I reached the doorway a booming crack of sound shattered the night.

Gunshot.

Luella cried out. Her face turned slowly, like a sunflower tracking the hypnotic progress of the sun. My own gaze followed hers to the window, and together we stared at the moonlit landscape beyond. The hill behind the garden was dark, the dirt trail that wound up the embankment obscured by trees.

'The gully,' I whispered.

Running out to the kitchen, I retrieved the bundle of letters from the canister and returned it to my pocket. Then I flung open the back door and scanned the night. The moon shone between a convoy of purple stormclouds that made the sky writhe and roll in torment. The air was bitter with the smell of ozone, and the trees high on the hillside lashed from side to side like angry cats' tails.

Luella was at my elbow, jostling me in her shocked state. She slid a hard object into my palm. A bone-handled hunting knife. Small and heavy, its leather sheath old and cracked – but the blade was sturdy and well-oiled, wickedly sharp.

'It was my father's,' she said, peering into my face, her good eye watery with fear.

I clipped the knife to my belt and as I raced down the stairs, Luella's voice called softly from the darkness behind me.

'Do whatever you have to, Audrey. Just bring her safely home.'

The track winding along the embankment behind Luella's house was a tunnel of darkness. Cicadas screamed in the thick creepers that walled either side, shadows clung to the ironbarks, bats swerved and dived over my head.

As I ran, my thoughts turned crazy. What if I'd acted too hastily? What if Bronwyn wasn't up here at all, but instead was half-way to Brisbane with her abductor in a stolen car, or heading north to God knows where?

The gunshot I'd heard earlier still echoed in my head. I tried to tell myself it could have been anything – roo shooters, a farmer culling foxes, feral dog control – but no amount of reasoning changed the facts: my daughter was out there alone, and the man from the settlers' hut was armed.

The embankment widened, and ahead of me a broad shelf-like plateau of stone formed a natural bridge across the gully. The gorge was narrow here, its steep sides overgrown with black-thorn and prickly rock ferns, the trickle of creek water buried far below. When I reached the other side, the track veered left and led me downhill. A while later the ground evened out. I pushed through a break in the trees and emerged into the clearing.

It seemed smaller than I remembered. Silvery grass hemmed in by a perimeter of ironbarks, the tall curved stone at the centre looming like a grave marker. I cast about for evidence they'd been here – a trail trodden through the sward, or maybe a discarded scrap of clothing, but there was nothing. I approached the stone, listening over my ragged breathing for the sound of voices, for a muffled cry – but there was only the gentle drum of rain, the groan of branches, the crying wind. Overhead a boobook mewled, and from lower down the slope came the eerie thump of wallabies in the dark.

I approached the gully verge, in my panic treading too near the edge. A chunk of earth broke away and rubble spilled into the void. I stepped back. The ground appeared stable, but looking closer I saw it was a deadly trap. A flat rock shelf near the edge marked a section of earth around which a crack had formed in the soil, a zigzag fault line caused by years of drought and now carved deeper by the rain. One careless step and it would crumble away.

Moving along the verge, I found a more solid area of ground and looked over the side, dreading what I might see.

Far below, saplings grew from the steep walls, their slender trunks splashed by moonlight. Ferns trembled in the rain, and dead trees jutted like gangways over the chasm. All around were huge grey boulders, pushing from the soil and lending the appearance of stability, but that was an illusion; one misplaced step and the whole edge might cave in.

Another spear of lightning blazed overhead. In its flash I saw every leaf, every stone, every twist of deadwood, every rabbit hole and glittering spider's web as clearly as if in stark sunlight – an instant later it all plunged back to shadow.

Off in the distance, a branch crashed to the ground. I turned too quickly and my foot slipped, sending another shower of dirt and stones into the gully. As I hurried over to the boulder that sat at the clearing's centre, other sounds came to me – sly rustlings and stirrings in the undergrowth – as if someone was edging nearer, trying not to be heard.

My hands shook as I grappled Luella's hunting knife from its sheath. Aunt Morag used to say that it was pointless for a woman to carry a weapon because – in the event of an attack – it would most likely be wrested from her grip and used against her. Right then, dosed up as I was on adrenaline and terror, that old knife handle was melded to my palm. Nothing short of a nuclear blast could have prised it from me.

The moon drifted behind a cloud, plunging the clearing into near-blackness. In the sudden dark, my fears came to life. I saw another long-ago night in this clearing, a night I'd relived countless times in my imagination. Aylish had once stood where I was now standing, in the moon-shadow of the tall boulder. The darkness along the glade's leafy perimeter would have shifted, as it did now, and the shadows would have seemed to gather substance, change form, perhaps even morph into human shape.

Another thread of lightning pulled at the seams of the sky. The night tore open, and in the brief illumination I saw motion in the trees. The bushes at the outer edge of the glade trembled, as if disturbed by a breath of wind. The darkness quivered, fell apart, and reassembled. Then a lone shadow broke from the gloom and moved slowly across the glade towards me.

27

I recognised him at once.

Because, despite the shifting moonlight, despite the misty haze of rain, despite only having glimpsed him before now – the long passage of years following childhood had not changed Cleve Jarman so very much. Aylish's description of the boy still resonated in the man.

His hair was no longer bristly, but long and caught back in a ponytail, dull silver in the moonlight. His face was exactly as I'd conjured it in my mind's eye – the crease between his pale brows, the wide eyes brimming with unease, the whitish gleam of his skin. Now, though, he had a grungy beard, and wore a shapeless jacket and jeans. He was holding his right arm stiffly, straight at his side. I wondered if it was injured – then guessed that he was keeping something out of view . . . possibly Samuel's handgun.

'Hello, Audrey. Did you bring them?'

His voice shocked me. It was soft, cultured. Polite. At odds with his ragged, unkempt appearance.

With my free hand I drew the bundle of letters from my pocket and held it aloft, then hid them back out of sight.

'First I want to see her,' I bargained. 'I want to see that she's unharmed. Then you get your letters.'

'A fair trade.'

I waited for him to move. Waited for him to turn and shamble toward the uphill track, perhaps look back and beckon. But he continued to stand motionless in the shadows, watching me.

Had I misunderstood? A fair trade, he'd said. His letters in exchange for Bronwyn. So why was he lingering? Why weren't we going to her?

'Where is she?' I couldn't stop myself asking.

'Throw your knife to the side. Then we can talk.'

No need for a nuclear blast, after all; plain old garden-variety fear did the trick. I tossed the hunting knife into the shadows near the gully edge.

'I'll only hand over the letters when I see she's safe.'

'She's safe for now, you still have time. But first, there's something I want from you.'

'What . . . ?' I cringed at my eagerness, at the ragged desperation in my voice. 'What do you want?'

'You've read the letters, then?'

I nodded. In the back of my mind, his earlier words niggled. *She's safe for now, you still have time.* Time for what? What did he mean?

He trod closer. 'You're a seeker of the truth, aren't you, Audrey? I can sense it in you. You're driven by curiosity about the past – a passion I also share. But if you've read those letters, you only know *her* side of the story. Meanwhile mine remains untold.'

A sharp pain shot into my temple. I was struggling to grasp what he was saying. My heart had begun to beat erratically, my palms dripped with sweat. Understanding dawned. It wasn't going to be a simple exchange, after all. Cleve was toying with me, playing some sick game; a cat batting its claws at a frightened mouse.

'The police are on their way here, Cleve. If you don't take me to Bronwyn now, they'll find her. And you'll go to jail.'

Shadows danced over him as he ventured closer. 'That's what Glenda said. But there was no jail then, and there'll be no jail now. I cut the phone wires, Audrey. At Thornwood as well as William Road ... and there's no mobile coverage out here. Unless of course you sent an SOS via telepathy?'

'Luella went for help.'

'Then you'd better pray she takes her time.' Cleve's tone turned grim. 'If anyone interrupts us before we're done, then our sweet little Bronwyn is as good as dead.'

I faltered, lost my nerve. 'What have you done?'

'I've put her somewhere for safekeeping.'

'What do you mean?'

'She's my security. If you do as I say, she'll survive. But if you piss around and prattle on about cops or anyone going to jail or other such crap, then I'll stall. And if I stall, our sweet little girl will . . .' He drew his finger across his throat.

My skin went cold. A dozen images flooded in. My daughter crumpled on the floor of the settlers' hut, her blood leaking from a fatal gunshot wound; or lying on the gully bed, her body battered and broken by the fall; or slumped in some dark crevice, vomit drying on her chin as her heart slowed by degrees from a lethal dose.

'No cops,' I assured him, lifting my palms in a sort of shaky surrender. 'I'll do whatever you say, I just want her to be safe.'

Lightning flickered, but it was distant, its brightness fleeting. Cleve's face loomed with corpse-like pallor, then fell back to shadows. The purple twilight returned, but not before I'd registered the object he had, until now, been concealing. A wooden shaft that – though indistinct in the blotchy moonlight – was vivid in my mind's eye. Splintered and blackened, worn smooth by the years. I recalled the feel of it from the settlers' hut, the near-warmth of the old wood, the greasy patina. Blood, I'd realised later. Aylish's blood. Maybe Glenda's, too. Was Cleve now planning to add mine to the mix? And Bronwyn's?

Understanding gripped me with such great force that it caused a split between my inner and outer selves. I felt that time was shifting, changing shape and form. No longer running forward, but back. Back sixty years, when the creek had roared and the bellbirds chimed their calls, and another woman had stood in the shadow of a tall stone and trembled for her life.

I just knew.

For whatever deluded reason, Cleve meant to kill me.

I had a flash of Bronwyn that day in the kitchen, standing by the window, worry creasing her brow. 'If you died,' she'd said in a trembly little voice, 'what would happen to me?'

Now her words took on a disturbing new meaning. If I died or was otherwise immobilised, Cleve would no longer need her as security. Panic made me shut my eyes; again I saw his finger slicing his throat in silent warning. I clawed the panic away and measured my options.

I would fight, if I thought I had a chance. Or run, if I knew for certain I could get away. Run up to the settlers' hut to find my daughter, and then . . . then what? Cleve was in his seventies, but he had the body – and, I guessed, the strength – of a much younger man. He knew the surrounding bushland and he'd soon outflank me. And while I'd never used a knife before in self-defence, it was clear that Cleve had past experience wielding that axe handle. And, I reminded myself, he was armed.

I recalled something he'd said, and it made me realise what he wanted.

You only know her side of the story . . . while mine remains untold.

'You said we shared a passion for the past,' I said, fighting to steady the breathless wobble in my voice. 'You were talking about Aylish.'

'Yes.'

'You tended her grave. Left roses for her.'

'They were her favourite.'

'What happened to her? I mean . . . what *really* happened?'

He stepped nearer. 'You want to know about the night she died?'

I nodded.

His gaze drifted to the tall boulder with its fin-like curve and dots of pale lichen, but I sensed that his awareness of me had grown acute.

'That would've been March, 1946,' he said. 'Samuel had returned home from the war, thin and gaunt as a scarecrow. Later I learned that he and Aylish had made a bit of a scene in the street that morning, had a row. Samuel was brooding about it, and Dad wanted to cheer him up. So he invited Samuel over to our house for a few beers. Of course, a "few" turned into a few dozen. By eight o'clock that night they were maudlin, singing at the top of their lungs, reminiscing like a couple of old sailors. It was around that time my father called me in. He told me to take a message to Jacob Lutz over at Stump Hill Road. "Tell the unsociable old coot to get himself over here," my father said, "and make sure he brings a couple of flagons of his best brew."'

While Cleve was talking, I surreptitiously scanned the edge of the clearing. The gully was perhaps ten paces away. Along its verge, the soil was unstable. If I could keep Cleve's attention on the past, I might be able to lure him to the gully rim, to the loose rock shelf with its zigzag fracture and bed of crumbling earth.

Shifting my weight, I tested my theory by taking a half-step back.

Cleve moved into the space I'd created, and went on.

'I'd just turned fourteen. In my eyes, Samuel Riordan was a hero. After reading his letters, I felt I knew him and in a strange way felt close to him. I was reluctant to leave the party, but dutifully got on my bike and rode over to Stump Hill Road. I knocked for ages. Finally I gave up, but just as I was turning away Jacob answered the door groggy and dishevelled. The wireless was crackling away somewhere in the house, the static was deafening. Jacob must have fallen asleep, and he was as cross as a bucket of flies. He told me what I could do with my father's invitation, so I got back on my bike and started towards home.'

While he spoke, I took another half-step backwards.

Cleve moved distractedly after me. 'That's when I saw Aylish. Little Lulu was with her. They were walking up the track that led across the gully to Thornwood. It was late for Lulu to be out, and something told me Aylish was on her way to see Samuel. They used to meet right here at the gully before he went off to war. But that night, Samuel was drunk at my father's place . . . and in no fit state to be meeting anyone.'

'So *you* met her instead,' I prompted, inching a half-step nearer the gully.

Cleve remained where he was, absorbed in his story.

'I hurried after her, cutting through the wood yard and up into the trees, following close behind. Then Lulu ran away and Aylish panicked. I found her up here at the clearing – just as I found you tonight, Audrey. She was calling for her child, frantic with worry. I'd never seen her so wild . . . or so beautiful.' He sighed, and shook his head, shuffling into the gap between us. 'I only meant to talk to her. I only wanted to tell her that Mum missed little Lulu. We all missed her,' he added with bitterness. 'But Aylish refused to hear a word. She got angry, started accusing me of doing all these things. And then she said I'd scared little Lulu and made her run away into the bushes and now she was lost. She said other things too . . . cruel things. Things that deeply hurt me. I suppose that's when the greyness descended. I've no recollection of having moved, nor even that any time had passed between the fading of her shout and the silence that followed. When I finally blinked the sweat and tears from my eyes and looked down, the sight of what I'd done sickened me.'

Thunder cracked overhead and in the brilliant flash that followed, I clearly saw Cleve's face. It was twisted into a grotesque mask, streaked with rain or tears, I couldn't tell.

'I'm not a bad man,' he said, his words nearly swallowed by the rumbling thunder. 'I don't mean any harm. But I've been unwell. Even as a kid, I knew I wasn't quite right. Dad never noticed much, always too preoccupied with work. Mum saw me as a monster, I suppose. And Aylish – I thought she was different. Being an outsider like me, I thought she understood . . . but in the end, she was the same as everyone else.'

Cleve paused, and there was a part of me that hoped he wouldn't continue. It disturbed me that Aylish's story – the story I'd so craved to hear – was being told now, by *him*. I could already feel the toxic energy of his words seeping into my bloodstream, poisoning me . . . but I had to keep him talking.

'Just now, you said the greyness descended. What did you mean?'

A ragged sigh. Cleve trod nearer. 'It's hard to describe. An unpleasant feeling, as if your brain is swelling. There's a sickness in there, and it makes everything turn grey. Then . . .' He shrugged. 'Once it starts, I've no control over it. After that first time with Aylish, I convinced myself it wouldn't happen again. Years went by, and I felt certain the greyness was gone and that I'd be all right. I was happy, and it kept the sickness at bay.'

One of Glenda's diary entries flashed into my mind, that sunny Sunday morning she'd watched Cleve planting onions. Her account had been written with such fondness for the man she believed to be her father that it shot a bolt of pain into my heart.

'The greyness struck again, though, didn't it?'

Cleve stared across the moonlit glade towards me, his eyes like holes punched in pale clay. 'It was bad with Glenda. You can't imagine how bad. She was my little girl. She loved me, and I . . . well, I worshipped the ground she walked on.'

'What happened?'

'She found the letters.' A pause. 'Just like you did, snooping where she shouldn't. And like you, she took them and read them. Afterwards, she ran away. It was raining that night, so she sheltered in the hollow tree at the edge of Samuel's garden. I only wanted to talk, but she was confused about what she'd read in the letters. Angry too, I suppose. She said I'd go to jail, that the letters were proof. She said she'd tell Luella and then the whole town would know that it was me and not Samuel who'd killed her grandmother. Of course, we argued bitterly. So many bad words were said. The next thing I knew she was . . . she . . .'

As his words sank in I saw, in a blinding flash of hindsight, that the story I'd constructed about Glenda's death had been fundamentally flawed. I had assumed the letters she'd found were from Hobe Miller to her mother, which had sent me off on a wild goose chase after Hobe – when in fact they were Aylish's letters, the same ones I'd discovered in the settlers' hut. Letters which Cleve had stolen from the post office as a boy and kept among his hoardings in the shed . . . then re-stolen in a staged burglary a few years after his apparent death. Letters he'd killed for.

I slid my hand to my back pocket and touched cold wet fingers to the bundle. Some of the envelopes were blotched with dark stains, stains I had suspected were dried blood. Glenda's blood, I now knew.

Cleve palmed the wetness from his face.

'I kept checking for a pulse. Kept thinking I'd found one – then it would melt away beneath my fingertips. I remember running down the hill to Samuel's house at one stage, thinking I'd get a blanket to wrap her in. I stood down there in the garden for a while, praying that it was all a horrible nightmare, trying to shake myself awake. But when I climbed the hill again, there she was, lying in the dirt where I'd left her. I knelt and touched her face, told her I loved her – and that's when she spoke. It was nothing, a sigh . . . but my heart leapt. She was alive.

'Hoisting her into my arms, I ran towards home. Luella was training as a nurse, I reasoned that she'd know what to do.

I'd tell her Glenda had fallen, that there'd been a rockslide. Maybe Glenda would get amnesia and forget what I'd done, and we'd go back to being happy again.

'Of course,' he rasped, 'it wasn't to be. When I reached the gully I noticed something was missing. There was a stillness that hadn't been there before, a shadow where moments ago there'd been light. Her heart, you see. Her poor heart had stopped beating.'

For a moment there was just the rain and the hiss of windblown leaves. I was blinking back tears – tears of fright and rage and sorrow – and trying to grasp how a loving father could turn on his daughter with such devastating cruelty. Was love really so fickle? Or did Cleve use the word to describe some other emotion that had, in the end, only resembled love?

Cleve edged nearer. 'When I returned home, the house was empty. I went to the shed. Retrieved my old hunting rifle from its drawer and loaded up. Sat on a chair and rested my forehead on the muzzle. It would have been the easiest thing in the world to slide my finger past the trigger guard, put an end to the pain I was feeling . . . I can't recall how long I sat there, only that a noise alerted me – a nightjar calling through the darkness to its mate. Hours must have passed. I'd grown cold, my body ached. But my mind had cleared. I didn't want to die, so I'd just have to endure the horror of what I'd done. I unloaded the rifle and re-stowed it, then went about cleaning myself up.

'I'd only just begun to peel off my clothes when the shed door burst open. It was Tony. I told him to piss off . . . then saw he was armed. He had this old Winchester, lever action, .22 calibre. Christ knows where he got it. I remember thinking, Good thing the idiot boy has no idea about loading a firearm. Then I ate my words. Tony raised the rifle, aimed the bloody thing right at my face. "You hurt Glenda," he said. That's all. "You hurt Glenda." And then he pulled the trigger.'

Thunder clapped overhead, making me flinch. Cleve looked at the sky, then back at me. He frowned, as if he'd forgotten I was there.

'Little bastard,' he said quietly, wiping the rain out of his eyes. 'It took me twenty years, but I got him in the end.'

But he hadn't gotten Tony in the end. He'd gotten him much earlier, when Tony was a boy of fourteen. Cleve's violence had crippled Tony's spirit and condemned him to a life of nightmares, uncertainty and fear. Worse, Tony's own actions in the shed that night must have convinced him he'd inherited Cleve's violent nature. Was that why, all those years later when Bronwyn came along, Tony had withdrawn from her? Not because she resembled his dead sister . . . but because he feared what he might do to her?

'Tony was a good man,' I said, my heart starting to hammer as I inched nearer the gully edge. 'It's just a pity he didn't take better aim that night.'

Cleve nodded, shuffling after me. 'I've often thought the same thing. But the will to survive is a strong instinct, Audrey. No matter how miserable life gets, it's not always easy to give it up.'

'He found you at the hut, didn't he? You killed him to protect yourself – there was no greyness, no blanking out. You knew Tony would turn you in, and so you killed him in cold blood.'

'He took me by surprise,' Cleve said. 'I had no choice.'

Another fragment fell into place, one that had been niggling for a while. 'That rifle, the Winchester. It was the same gun Tony used on you twenty years ago, wasn't it? You went back to the Holden and retrieved it.'

'It was a shit of a thing, too,' Cleve snarled, 'always jamming up on account of having been submerged underwater for so long. You're right, I retrieved it, cleaned it up and kept it all those years – but I never planned to use it on Tony. I never thought about revenge. I just wanted to be left alone.'

My muscles were rigid, my body slick with rain and sweat. I felt grubby, dirty. I didn't want to hear any more of Cleve's sick rave, but we were only a couple of paces from the gully edge.

'I'd been out hunting,' Cleve went on. 'I'd just laid my catch on the chopping bench, when my old dog started barking. I whipped around in time to see Tony come around the side of the hut. He recognised me straight away despite the beard and rags I wore. He started backing away and I knew he meant to run, so I grabbed the rifle and went for him, managed to knock him out with the stock. In his pocket I found car keys and a wallet – and a Polaroid of him with a pretty little girl. I kept the photo, but put everything else back and went looking for his car, which I found at the William Road turnoff. I dragged him all the way, heavy bastard he was, too. I propped him in the driver's seat with his old friend the Winchester. And then I said goodbye.'

A bright thread of anger unfurled in me. I remembered the look on Bronwyn's face the day I sat her down and told her about her father's death, how she'd crumpled up and hidden behind her hands, tears leaking between her fingers, her thin shoulders shaking. For all his failings, Tony had been a decent man and a great dad, devoted to Bronwyn . . . until guilt and fear had finally driven him out of her life.

Cleve Jarman had a lot to answer for.

'How do you live with yourself,' I said, 'when you've caused so much devastation?'

Cleve made a sound in his throat. 'I never meant any harm. I told you, they provoked me. Aylish and Glenda – the things they said, horrible things. Threats and accusations. I felt betrayed. I loved them . . . but I came to hate them, too.'

His last few words were growled rather than spoken. I shivered. He was near enough for me to see the whitish threads of scar tissue on his craggy cheeks, and the glassy light in his eyes. I wondered how close he was to the greyness, to rage. To losing control.

I was a pace away from the gully edge. Near enough to the rock shelf and its loose bed of earth to see, from the corner of my eye, the dark zigzag of its deadly fault line. My palms were hot and moist, and an erratic beat throbbed in my temple as I backed towards it.

Cleve's face shone wet as he approached, the unwashed scent of him rank in the damp air. The arm he'd been holding by his side swung forward and the shank of wood – the axe handle – gleamed wetly in the moonlight. He put out his free hand.

'My letters now, Audrey.'

The rain had stopped. The moon had emerged from behind its barricade of clouds and drenched the clearing in yellow light.

'That wasn't the deal,' I said, my voice sharpened by fear. I'd known it would come to this, but my gut churned, I wasn't ready. 'You'll get them after I see my daughter.'

'There *was* no deal, Audrey. You were never in any position to bargain.'

He came at me without warning, the axe handle sweeping an arc as he lunged. I leapt backwards, intending to clear the eroded rock shelf and land on the solid section further along – but the weapon glanced off my shoulder. I stumbled, twisting away from the gully's crumbling edge, landing on my knees in the dirt. Cleve swung again, but I rolled sideways and the axe handle fell wide of its mark.

I got to my feet, panting in fear. I'd seen a glimmer, a moonlit shard lying a few feet away in the shadows. My knife. I dived for it, raking thought the dirt and clumps of grass, finally touching steel, and closed my fingers around it.

I saw the next blow coming but moved too slowly.

The club thudded against my ribs and the impact sent me reeling, the knife lost. Cleve lunged again. I cried out as the heavy wood connected with my hip. Pain shot up my spine, and my legs collapsed. As I rolled sideways, I felt the hardness of the knife under my back. Wriggling aside, I grabbed it and began to crawl, trying to gain a respite from Cleve's relentless blows. Somehow I got to my feet and about-faced just as he attacked.

My knife swept in a clumsy arc, but again fear slowed my reflexes.

Cleve circled just beyond my reach, easily evading the blade. Then he came back from a different angle. I tried to dodge, but stumbled and nearly fell, flinging out my arm at the last moment to fend off the blow. The club hit my forearm, the knife jolted from my fingers, and a tide of nauseating blackness rose up. My legs went to jelly, and I felt myself slide earthwards.

Cleve rushed at me again, this time swinging sideways. The long handle thudded into my thigh. I cried out, crumpling to my knees, throwing up my hands to protect my head. Another blow struck my shoulders and I buckled under the weight of pain. Cleve grunted and again the wood slammed into my ribs. The breath rushed out of me, and I hung suspended in an airless void. Curling into a ball, stunned by the ferocity of the pain, I was more terrified than I'd ever been before. My daughter was out there alone, defenceless in the night, and I was powerless to help her. I was going to die, and it was going to be very bad and this jagged nightmare place I now cowered in was only the beginning. I quaked with the horrible knowledge that history had got the better of me after all, that time had twisted back on itself, that I'd been here before . . .

I felt myself merge with Aylish. My ragged sobbing became hers, the thunder of my pulse beat a twin rhythm in her veins. And her anguish became mine. Her ribs were loose, her wrists and fingers disjointed, her thoughts hazing in and out of awareness. Blood filled her mouth, she was choking out cries, knowing no one would hear yet still clinging to hope . . . and then the darkness coming into her vision and the slow dawning that this was the end, and all she could do now was wait, curl into the shadows and wait for death to find her . . .

But I wasn't Aylish.

And I'd be damned if I was going to die like her.

Clawing myself out of the past, I got to my knees and scrambled across the muddy ground. A gleam of moonlight touched the knife blade and I reached for it, curling my fingers around its grip, holding fast.

Cleve approached and stood over me. His eyes were glassy, his lips flecked white with spit. Was he in the greyness now? Or was he fully aware, planning how best to finish me? I watched as if from a distance as his arm went back and the axe handle swung aloft.

This time I was ready. Twisting from the path of the oncoming club, I slashed out with my knife and caught Cleve across the fingers. He bellowed, his grip loosening. I dropped the knife, grabbed the axe handle with both hands and wrenched with all my strength, tearing it from Cleve's bleeding fingers. Then I flung it into the gully.

Cleve watched it arc silently and vanish in the blackness.

Turning to me, he slid his hand into his jacket pocket and drew out Samuel's revolver. Taking aim with both hands, he lined me up in his sights.

'Give me the letters, Audrey. Pass them over nice and slow.'

'Go to hell.'

'Come on, now. I'd hate to get more blood on them.'

Adrenaline surged. My hearing became acute. I heard, or at least imagined I heard, the loud snick as Cleve drew back the hammer; I heard the rasp of his palms as he adjusted his grip, the sandpapery slide of his finger as it eased past the guard and nestled against the curve of the trigger. I heard his intake of breath, and then the pause as he held the air in his lungs and prepared to fire.

My heart rate slowed. My brain shifted down a gear and sharpened focus. Here it was, the end I'd been fearing . . . and yet I was no longer afraid. Reaching around to my back pocket, I took out Aylish's letters and held them aloft.

'You want them?' I said, tearing the bundle free of its ribbon. 'Then get them yourself.' With a flick of my wrist, I threw the letters up and out over the gully. They didn't glide in a smooth arc and quietly vanish, as the axe handle had done . . . rather they burst apart and went every which way, the dusty paper whispering and fluttering like a horde of dying white moths, some snatched by the wind and carried a short way, some snared by branches, most settling like a sigh into the wet darkness.

Cleve cried out and took an involuntary step.

Right onto the loose rock shelf.

The ground shuddered, the unstable rock began to slide. He must have known what was coming because he reeled to face me, and fired. The shot went high, I felt it punch past me, but then somehow its dark force had me spinning, my legs going from under me, the ground rocketing up, and then I was lying at the gully edge, face-down, staring into the gaping cavity of raw exposed earth where a moment ago Cleve had been.

Gone.

He was gone.

The roaring in my head nearly carried me off, but I fought to stay present. It was over. Cleve was gone, fallen to his death. I should have felt relief, but there was just an empty ache. Bronwyn was lost out there, somewhere in the night, and Cleve's words haunted me: *You still have time.* How long ago had he said that? An hour? Forty minutes? What had he meant – time for what? Had that time now run out?

Blinking the moisture from my eyes, I found myself staring at a black shadow inches from my face. Slowly it took form and, as the haze lifted, I realised I was looking at Samuel's revolver. I reached out to take it –

A hand shot up from the darkness below the verge and clamped vicelike around my wrist. I cried out in fright and tried to yank free, twisting my arm and rolling sideways. The motion set off shockwaves of pain and nausea. My shoulder. It was burning and throbbing, the pain dull one moment, then the next it was gathering up around the joint in bright, stabbing, liquid shards.

Dimly I understood I'd been shot.

The fingers around my wrist, Cleve's fingers, tightened. I felt his weight dragging at me, pulling me towards the edge. I groped around but there was nothing to cling to, no anchor . . . just the crumbly soil and the loose stones, and the long descent into nothingness.

Looking down, I saw him. His fall had landed him on the trunk of a dead tree that jutted downwards from the gully wall. Its weathered surface was ridged and studded with broken branches, and it swayed precariously beneath Cleve's weight.

Again he dragged on my arm. With nothing to cling to, I went easily, writhing as I skidded over the crumbly edge and down the embankment. As I crashed onto the tree trunk, I collided with Cleve and threw him off balance. His feet went from under him and he lurched off the trunk and over the side, somehow maintaining his grip on my wrist. My shoulder joint wrenched under the force of his fall, and I yelled in pain.

Cleve dangled over the chasm, his free hand groping empty space. He found a toehold in a rock cleft, but the drop that yawned below was dizzying – the leafy treetops, the rocky creek bed invisible beyond. Soon, his weight would drag us both into the abyss, plunging us to the rocks that waited below. My body shook violently as I strained against his greater gravitational pull, but my strength was draining fast.

If he fell, I'd fall too.

'Tell me where she is,' I said hoarsely. 'I need to know she'll be all right.'

Cleve stared up at me, flecks of mud and sweat streaming into his hair, a bloody gash seeping near his ear. He was panting hard. Spit clung to the corners of his lips. His face was white with shock, the threadlike scars seeming to writhe over his clammy skin.

'Too much time has passed,' he said. 'You're too late.'

'Where is she!'

A solitary bellbird called. The bush around us was eerily tranquil. The only sounds were ragged gasps, and the groan of wood as the trunk strained under our collective burden.

'It's over,' Cleve said, and there was relief in his voice.

'For you maybe. Not for me.'

It was surprisingly easy to loosen my stranglehold on the tree. Unlocking my legs, I let my body go limp. Gravity did the rest. Cleve's weight dragged me along the trunk, and the short downward slither dislodged his toehold. He flailed and made a wild grab for me but I cringed away. My torso grazed along the trunk's corrugated bark, I felt the skin tear over my ribs, felt something dig hard into my belly. Then, in a brief giddying lurch, we slid another foot along the trunk towards the canopy of trees below. An instant before my body tore from the tree, I swung up my free arm and hooked onto a branch stump. Our forward motion ceased.

Cleve swung away from the gully wall. His face hollowed in shock, his fingers clawed the air. He looked up at me, menace shining from his eyes.

'You're coming with me, Audrey.'

Twisting my upper body, I wrenched my arm upwards, gritting my teeth against the shocking pain. Cleve's grasp slid over the junction of my thumb and I felt something in my wrist give, felt the nauseating crack of bone.

'In your dreams.'

'No, my dear,' Cleve said shakily, an odd little smile trembling on his lips. 'In yours . . .'

Then he shut his eyes and let his fingers splay apart. A cry went up – I think it was mine – as I stared wildly at the gap where, just a heartbeat ago, a man had been, but now . . . now . . .

Now I was alone.

28

The crunch of breaking branches, the tearing of leaves . . . the thud of falling rocks and earth, and the dizzying rush of a deadweight hurtling into the dark heart of the gully and onto the rocks below.

I tried to block it, tried to shut it out – feeling around for a memory, a dream, anything to escape into . . . but my senses only seemed to grow more keen. The air smelled of damp earth, crushed ferns, blood. The moist breeze left a sweaty slick on my skin. Leaves whispered, raindrops plopped on fleshy leaves, the distant babble of water drifted up from the creek bed.

Light as a leaf, I floated.

Then, something made me look up. On the far embankment, a figure stood in the shadows beneath an overhang of trees. A young woman. She wore a white dress and, though I couldn't see her face clearly from where I lay along the tree, it drifted into my mind's eye that she was uncommonly beautiful. I'd thought of her so often over the past months, I felt I knew her. And although the distance between us was a gulf of time and darkness, I thought for a moment that she knew me too. Lifting her hand in farewell, she turned and vanished into the trees.

I dashed a hand against my face, not sure if the wetness I found there was blood or tears.

When I regained myself, I tested my limbs one by one. I could move them all in a manner, apart from my left arm. I touched my shoulder, and the world overturned. When it righted itself, I gathered what remained of my strength, and – guided by the vision of my daughter's face – I began to climb.

Leaving the glade, I veered up the track that led to the settlers' hut. Rain was misting down again, and black clouds rolled across the moon's face. The night had seemed eternal, but I guessed that barely more than an hour had passed since I'd left Luella's.

I wore only bra and jeans. I'd ripped my T-shirt into a bandage and staunched the wound on my shoulder. Samuel's handgun, which I'd retrieved from the lip of the gully, was tucked snug into my belt against my back. One live round remained, and I prayed I'd have no occasion to use it.

Whenever I heard a noise – branches snapping in the rain, the eerie shriek of whip-birds startling from their nests – I found myself jerking around, examining the shadowy trees that now separated me from the gully, wondering. Had Cleve fallen, or had I only dreamt it? Was he somewhere out there, concealed by the stormy darkness . . . was he following?

His words haunted me.

You still have time.

As I forced my battered body up the hill, fear frayed at my nerves. I hadn't forgotten the gunshot that had shattered the night earlier. Again I worried that Bronwyn was crumpled on the hut floor, fatally wounded all this time, her life leaking out of her and vanishing between the cracks. The image was tearing me apart, doing my head in, sending a chemical spill of fear and adrenaline through my veins.

I reached the larger clearing and ran across the expanse of grass towards the hut. Bursting inside, I searched the dusty gloom. My heart dived. The place was too still, too silent. The narrow bed with its sunken mattress, the empty shelving, the table and chairs beneath the window . . . it was clear that no one had been here since that day I'd trekked up the hill with Danny. Going outside, I looked around the clearing. It was empty. The trees dripped water and the air was charged after the storm, but there was no sign that Bronwyn had even been here.

On the other side of the verandah garden I saw an oval shape, it looked like a mound of earth. I went over to it. The grass had been dug up, the soil smelled fresh and pungent, and it was muddy at the edges where rivulets of rainwater still trickled.

Something was buried there.

Again I thought of the gunshot we'd heard. Just one, punctuating the night with a single, violent report. And then I flashed on Bronwyn, riding along the dark road on her bike, her handlebar streamers whipping her thin hands, her hair flying behind.

Dropping to my knees, I began to claw away the wet soil. Mud went up my arms, my knees sank into the waterlogged ground, and I could hear a panicked sound nearby, a breathless sobbing that went on and on and wouldn't stop.

My fingertips met flesh.

Yielding. Soft. Still warm.

Raking the length of the motionless little body, I knew I must be dreaming, had to be dreaming. I wished I could wake up, straighten out my thoughts and make sense of what I was seeing –

Fur.

I gulped at the air, filling my lungs, trying to clear my head. The panicked sobbing dwindled, stopped. A rush of hot, almost painful relief. After a while the shattered fragments of the world gathered back around me, began to reassemble.

There in the moonlight lay Cleve's dog. It had seemed so large and fearsome the day it attacked me among the tea-trees.

Now I saw it was just a Jack Russell terrier, its small pudgy body limp and still, its white fur stained with mud.

Cleve had shot his little companion, perhaps anticipating his own demise at the gully ... or perhaps he'd done it as a warning for me. The rawness of my relief came back, but there was fear too ... If he'd done this to his faithful canine friend, then what might he have done to Bronwyn?

Pushing to my feet, I skirted the hut, calling her name. Wind-blown sheets of rain obscured the surrounding trees, veiling the distant hills behind a grey haze. The water tank at the rear of the hut was overflowing. Water babbled from its overflow pipe and onto the upended forty-four-gallon drum.

Think. You have to think.

Cleve had said she was his security, that he'd put her some-where for safekeeping. Had he lied, was she even at the hut? God, she could be anywhere ...

'Audrey – !'

A figure emerged from the trees and began to charge across the clearing towards me. In my dazed state, I felt an impossible glimmer of hope. Bronwyn? But of course it wasn't her. Through the grey curtain of rain I could see the figure's lofty height, the thickset shoulders. A man. And he was fast approaching. Who was it? Cleve? Had he survived his plunge into the gully?

Fumbling the old handgun from my belt, I gripped it in both hands and shouted a warning.

'Stop! Don't come any closer.'

He kept advancing.

Clicking back the hammer, I took aim. I re-screamed my warning, but the man didn't slow. The heavy thud of boots kept coming, splashing nearer, and my heart seemed to explode a little with every step.

I yelled again, but on he came, a blur in the dim clearing. My finger reflexed on the trigger. There was a powerful crack as the gun discharged. A flash, of lightning or memory or imagination,

I couldn't tell which, and in it I saw a face. Broad features framed by wild unruly hair, a full mouth, and dark eyes fixed on me in shock.

He pitched sideways, then went from view.

I raced after him. Careening around the side of the hut, I scanned the open expanse then fixed my attention on the verandah. No one there. I was about to whirl around when steely arms grabbed me from behind. I threw back my head and bucked against my attacker, my body exploding with fresh pain, barely registering the man's surprised grunt.

He shoved me forward at arm's length. A hand closed over my fingers and prised my weapon loose, tossed it onto the muddy ground out of reach. Then he swung me around to face him.

It took forever for my brain to stop spinning. Another eternity to comprehend. Rain dripped from his hair and his green eyes were wild, his face haggard pale as he looked at me. I'd never seen him angry before. At first I thought his anger was directed at me. A bruise bloomed on his forehead, a streak of blood smeared his brow; dimly I acknowledged it was my doing.

Danny took my face between his hands and searched it, then drew me close against him and held me firm in his arms. I hadn't known how cold I was until his heat engulfed me. Heat like a jolt of brightness that broke the spell of my terror. My good arm slid around him and I pressed near, as near as I could get. It had been so long, and my need for comfort was so great that I clung like a little girl, feeling the brittle walls of my protective shell finally crumble away.

We broke apart, but he stood near. Touching his fingertips to my swollen face, frowning at the blood-soaked wad tied to my shoulder, giving my cold fingers a squeeze.

'I can't find Bronwyn,' I said through chattering teeth.

Police are on their way.

'How?'

Luella walked to Hobe's. They telephoned police, then me.

'We might be too late.'

No, he signed sharply. *We'll find her.*

He took my hand and started towards the hut. I had a flash of the last time we were here, of our botched kiss at the rocky plateau, and then Danny showing me the buried water catchment built by the settlers, where he and Tony used to . . .

'Oh . . . God, no.'

I started running, splashing across the muddy ground towards the rear of the hut, Danny close behind. The underground tank was barely visible in the rain. Its low timber sides were water-blackened and raindrops danced on the circular cover, making it look like a wooden backyard swimming pool half submerged.

I grappled with the heavy plank lid, my wet fingers sliding uselessly across its splintered rim. Water was sloshing out from underneath the cover, had been for some time judging by the moat of water puddled at the base. This could only mean that the tank was full to the brim . . .

And Bronwyn was in there.

I was too late.

Danny was beside me, sliding the heavy lid across the tank's rim, wrenching it sideways until he was able to drag it off the top of the tank and heave it aside.

I stared down. Black water lapped the tank's circular inner wall. The smell of earth and sourness rose up, and my cry finally escaped.

Pale and ghostly, my daughter's upturned face floated on the surface. Water rippled against her cheeks and her milky hair spilled freely around her. She seemed to be clinging to the catchment wall – but she looked so ashen, so small and unmoving, that my heart stopped. The sight of her blurred before I had a chance to notice the vital signs: Was she breathing? Were her eyes open? Was she . . . was she even alive . . . ?

I was in the water, a cold shock in the dark, gulping dark mouthfuls. Bronwyn's skin was slippery as I pushed her upwards to Danny's reaching hands.

'Mum . . . ?'

Her voice came from another world. Shrill and tremulous, a faint spectral echo. I tried to catch it, tried to snare the threads of it so I could pull myself back to her, find her in the labyrinth of darkness which now engulfed me . . .

Danny wrapped her in his shirt then braced himself against the catchment wall and reached in again, gripping his fingers around mine, hauling me from the water. I felt solid ground beneath me, felt my daughter's shivering body in my arms.

'Oh, Mum – !'

Her body was wracked with sobs, her skin ice-cold. As I squeezed her tightly to me, she wound her arms around my neck and squeezed back. Hot tears scalded my face, mine or hers I couldn't tell. All I cared was that she was here with me now, breathing and alive, safe.

'Oh sweetheart, I'm so sorry, I'm so very sorry – '

'No, Mum.' Cold lips moved against my cheek, her breath warm. 'I'm the one who should be sorry. I shouldn't have said those things to you, I shouldn't have run away . . .' She pulled back suddenly, her eyes wide as she touched the side of my head with her icy fingertips. 'Your poor face. Oh Mum, it's all my fault . . . He said he was going to hurt you – '

I grasped her fingers, tried to warm them against my lips. 'It wasn't your fault, Bronny – do you understand? None of this was anything to do with you. He was a bad man, a damaged man, but he's gone now. You're safe . . . we're both safe.'

Bronwyn nodded, smoothing her fingers over the top of my head. Her face was streaked with filth, scratched in places, her eyes like saucers, the sapphire irises huge, nearly black. Tears spilled down her cheeks. Droplets of rainwater clung to her fair lashes.

'I know what he did,' she whispered, pressing her lips to my face. 'He told me. He killed Dad, didn't he?'

It chilled me to hear her speak so matter-of-factly – but then she'd always been the level-headed one, just as Tony had been. She started crying again, her eyes brimming like lakes, her gaze not moving from mine. One day I would tell her what I'd learned about Tony, and why he'd felt the need to withdraw from her life ... but not now. That would come later. Much later. Instead, I held her tight and near, didn't bother trying to talk away her tears, didn't bother trying to comfort her. I just let her cry, holding her silently until she was done.

Finally, she wiped her wrist across her eyes and – to my surprise – slid a motherly arm around my shoulders. Nestling close, she kissed the top of my head – the way I used to kiss hers a million years ago when she'd been a little girl.

She hugged me tight. 'We'll be all right now, won't we, Mum?'

'Yes, Bron,' I promised. 'Yes, we will.'

Looking over her shoulder, I found Danny watching us, his expression dark with emotion. He gave me the thumbs up sign, and I nodded. I tried to summon a smile, but my lips were trembling. The tears that had been wobbling in my eyes – it seemed for a lifetime – finally rolled over my lashes. We would, I knew. We would be all right.

I pulled my daughter closer and, just for that one precious moment, allowed myself to believe.

29

Leaves and sky. That was all I could see. I tried to turn my head to the side, but a great heaviness had settled on me. I'm asleep, I thought.

But no, my eyes were open. Otherwise how could I have seen the leaves and sky?

The bush crackled around me, waking up. It was pre-dawn, the cicadas were singing, and a bullfrog grumbled from some faraway muddy hollow.

Looking sideways, I saw a coil of long hair. My hair. For some reason the sight of it made my heart sink. The hair was tangled, littered with leaves and clots of earth. Strands of it were matted into clumps by a sticky dark substance, and a funny smell rose out of it. Towering over me was a boulder, its grey flanks dotted with lichen. Beyond the boulder curved the stony verge of a dirt track. Nearby, the ground was splashed with shadow, glimmering in patches as though something wet was spilt there.

Again, I tried to move. Nothing happened. I was lying on my back, my limbs twisted beneath me. My head rested on stones. All I felt was cold. Deep, bone-biting cold. I tried to raise a shiver, but my body wouldn't respond. It wasn't so much that I was uncomfortable. Rather, I felt disjointed, my bones loose

442

and no longer connected to me. I wanted to cry out, but even if I'd been able to muster a breath, I knew there'd be no one to hear –

I was wrong.

Footsteps approached. Then a man was kneeling beside me. Calloused fingers explored my face, grasped my shoulders, felt along my arms. His touch ran over me, every inch. I could feel the heat in his palms.

'Aylish,' he said. His face moved into view. His dear face. He was smiling. If I'd been able to move my lips I would have smiled back . . . and begged him to gather me into his arms, hold me hard against him, chase the cold with his own vital warmth.

He must have read my thoughts, because he lifted me as though gathering up a sleeping child. Then he bent his head and kissed me, his mouth just as I remembered it, warm and strong, lush with promise. My lips tingled. An ember flickered and burst into flame; my frozen body stirred. A delicate sensation: the knitting of bone, the flow of blood; the slow, delicious return of circulation through my limbs . . .

Samuel began to walk, but rather than going downhill in the direction of his father's old homestead, he went up. Along a ferny trail, between arching arms of bracken, around big boulders laced with lichen. Through a corridor of casuarinas whose weeping branches bowed and sighed in the breeze. Cool shadows gathered around us, while overhead the treetops shimmered in the sunlight. In between the leaves were bright coin-sized medallions of luminous blue sky.

Leaves and sky. Always leaves and sky.

'Samuel,' I whispered, 'where are we going?'

'To our secret place, of course.'

Of course.

He kissed me again, more tingles flooded me, more warmth. Then to my glad surprise he released me from his embrace and lowered me to my feet. I stood, a little wobbly at first, my limbs quivering, my head giddy-light, unsteady as a newborn foal. Yet when Samuel took my hand and led me up the trail, I fell in beside him, soon matching his long, confident strides.

While I walked, I breathed. Drinking in the spicy scent of yellow-buttons and eucalyptus, of bark and crushed leaves, savouring the darker aromas of earth and sap and stone.

With each breath I grew stronger.

The sky lightened. Dawn burst forth, making heaven seem close. I could hear the birds now, belling their dizzying song into the blue morning, a chorus of crystal notes that soared high and pure as the sky.

Bellbirds ... my bellbirds, their voices like stars, singing me home.

30

Audrey, March 2006

A perfect day dawned over the Lutheran churchyard. A pair of emerald-grey dollarbirds swooped from the branches of a nearby red gum and flashed across the sky. I wondered if they were the same ones I'd seen the day I'd come looking for Aylish's gravestone . . . and if they were, perhaps, not birds at all but guardians of a hidden world.

I shifted on the bench, cold in the shade despite the scorching sun. Three weeks had passed since that night at the gully. In that short span of time I'd tried to bend my mind away from the events that had nearly stolen my daughter from me. Which was no easy task; there were so many questions.

First the police, then the detectives. Then, with more ferocity than the other interrogators combined, the media. Who was he? they wanted to know. Was he a relative, a family friend? Why had he abducted my daughter, and was she coping in the aftermath? Did I plan to stay on at the property after my ordeal, or would I sell up and move?

I answered as best I could. My memory of that night was disjointed and nightmarish. Sleeping pills were keeping the dreams at bay, and Bronwyn and I had decided to simply put that night behind us and focus on the better times that we believed lay ahead. For her, it seemed to be working. For me . . . well, I knew it would take some time for the flashbacks to grow more infrequent and finally dwindle.

The discovery of Cleve's body in the gully, combined with my account of what I'd learnt, sped up the forensic investigation into the remains found in Cleve Jarman's submerged Holden. The body was that of a bushwalker who'd been reported missing in Toowoomba, a man in his twenties with a string of convictions for drug possession. Apparently he'd been 'bushwalking' to the remote highlands of the national park to tend his marijuana crop. That's how he'd encountered Cleve. There were no signs of physical trauma to the skeleton, and the police mentioned the possibility of strangulation or poison, but that particular detail was – like so many others now – buried forever in the impenetrable substrata of the past.

The police had retrieved the scattered letters from the dark spaces of the gully, where I'd thrown them during my struggle with Cleve. They'd made copies and returned the originals to me, though the sergeant later admitted that the events recounted in Aylish's letters wouldn't have been enough to lawfully convict Cleve of any crime – young Cleve might have stolen a possible weapon, but it didn't mean he'd used it. What had clinched the deal for them was the partial fingerprint they'd lifted from the Winchester found with Tony's body – Gurney Miller's old rifle, which Cleve had retrieved from the submerged Holden when he'd buckled his dope-growing stand-in into the driver's seat. The fingerprint was a perfect match to the man whose lifeless body they'd retrieved from the gully floor; the man the local sergeant had personally identified as Cleve Jarman.

'Hey kiddo, why the frown?'

The bench creaked as Corey settled beside me. She unburdened herself of an enormous bunch of gerberas, laying them next to my own bouquet of pink and white native daisies. She gave me a peck on the cheek and gently squeezed the fingers of my good hand.

'You're late,' I replied, ridiculously pleased to see her. Then handed her a bit of paper.

'What's this?' she cried. 'You've caught Danny's note-writing bug?' She held it up to her eyes, pretending to squint at my tiny scrawl as she read aloud. 'Corey and Eliza, BBQ at Thornwood, Saturday arvo, tofu snags provided.'

She nudged me with her elbow. 'Oh Audrey, I'm glad you've decided to stay. Danny and Jade are just so . . .' She sighed, rolling her eyes dreamily.

I laughed, then cursed as I hugged my ribs, and that set Corey off and then we were both giggling. A moment later she was serious again. 'So what's this present you said you had for me?'

Sliding two flat parcels from my tote, I placed them in her hands.

Corey unwrapped the first to find a book, *The Magic Pudding*, by Norman Lindsay. She gave me a curious look. 'I loved this as a kid, how did you know?'

'Open the other one.'

Inside the second parcel was another book, smaller, buckled and water-damaged. The stained cover, with its fluffy white kitten and blush roses, looked weatherworn in the sunlight.

Her smile faltered. 'What's this?'

'A diary,' I told her. 'I found it – or rather, Bronwyn found it – at Thornwood.'

She looked from me to the little journal and back at me, plainly mystified. Then her fingers were cracking open the cover, her eyes eagerly scanning the neat lines of cursive that inked the inner pages.

'Oh,' she said. 'Oh, Audrey.'

For a long time we sat silently. The raucous chatter of the dollarbirds echoed overhead. Gum leaves rustled in the balmy breeze, invading the air with their spicy green scent. Corey pored over the pages, not reading – that would come later – but touching the lines of water-blurred ink, shaking her head disbelievingly. Tears rained from her eyes, but the tremulous smile never left her lips.

At last she sighed and closed the diary, hugged it to her chest. 'Thank you, Audrey. You can't know what this means to me.'

'I think I can,' I confessed. 'Some parts will be difficult for you to read . . . but I think Glenda would have wanted you to have it.'

Corey's tear-streaked face was luminous. She mopped her eyes on her wrist and gave me a lopsided hug.

A shout from the graveyard had us both looking over.

Luella had brought along her grandfather's ancient Box Brownie and was calling for us to join them. Corey waved, but we continued to sit for the moment, happy to watch. Luella was bustling about trying to coordinate Jade and Bronwyn into some semblance of order so that she could take their photo. The girls were doing their wet hen routine – only this time they were being pursued by a swarm of exuberant kelpie puppies that seemed to want to be everywhere at once.

'Look at them,' Corey said with a laugh. 'Trust Hobe to find a way of offloading his excess puppies. None of us will get any rest from this day forward, mark my words. I hope Luella knows what she's getting herself into.'

I looked across the cemetery at Bronwyn's grandmother. She'd agreed to meet with Hobe later that afternoon. Her face glowed, and despite the bruises still lingering around her eye she looked relaxed and beautiful. Hard to believe that only yesterday she'd read her mother's stolen letters. Once, I'd have thought it right to keep them from her; right to protect her from the truth. But I remembered her face the night Bronwyn had been taken. Shock, at first; then the steely glint in her eyes as she'd pressed her father's hunting knife into my fingers, the quiet words that had carried so much command.

Do whatever you have to, Audrey. Just bring her safely home.

A delighted squeal drew my attention back to Bronwyn and Jade. They'd finally organised themselves into a tight huddle for the camera, only to scurry away again in shrieks as an oversized butterfly dive-bombed the armloads of roses they both held.

Corey stood up, still clutching the diary against her chest. 'Come on,' she said, helping me to my feet and collecting our bouquets. 'No point letting them have all the fun.'

She was right, of course.

After all, it was a glorious day. The sky was a cobalt-blue dome, the sun was deliciously hot, and the morning brimmed with promise.

It was Sunday, and we'd all brought flowers for Aylish.

Later, in the hushed bubble of my sunny studio, I rang Carol. She'd been following the news reports on the TV and in the papers, and the police had notified her about the ongoing inquiry into Tony's death. As the media was making such a meal of it all, I thought she deserved the simple truth.

I related my discovery of Glenda's diary and how it had helped me unravel the truth about her murder. And how that, in turn, had led me to discover what had really happened to Tony.

When I finished, she was weeping quietly.

'Thank you, Audrey,' she said through her tears. 'Tony was right about you.'

'Oh?'

'He used to say, and I quote, "Audrey's a girl in a million." Now I can see why.'

We hung up, and I sat in the stillness. The old house creaked. Outside, a pair of magpies warbled an intricate duet. For a while I trod water, engulfed by Carol's sorrow, and by my own. Then my mind stopped whirling. A feeling of relief folded around me, warm and soothing as bathwater. I shut my eyes, and in the semi-darkness behind my lids I saw the beautiful young woman I'd seen on the other side of the gully. She was smiling now. The late afternoon sun gleamed in her hair and burnished her skin, illuminating her as she turned and slipped between the trees, quickly vanishing into the light.

Epilogue

The world sleeps, the sky is at its darkest. My bedroom window is open and bare of curtains. Warm night air blows in, carrying the spicy perfume of gum leaves and roses. There are no neighbours for miles, no one to spy on us but possums and birds.

Soon, the sun will come and chase the night. Being woken by the diaphanous pre-dawn glow – that Aylish called the piccaninny light – is fast climbing to the top of my list of favourite things.

Most favourite of all is listening to the man beside me sleep.

I reach across the bed, and he's there. Large and warm, solidly real. I'm becoming accustomed to drifting off to the rhythm of his breath, held protected in his arms or pressed snug against his warm back. And when sleep finally comes, I take care to tiptoe through my dreams.

Silently, so as not to wake the dead.

He spoke to me again last night. One word, uttered so quietly I almost missed it.

'Love,' he said, and then his fingers curled around mine, tugging me to him, his arms wrapping me firm. His voice was gruff, lazy, pleasantly husky. Rusty, he claims, from a lifetime of neglect. In my view, if he only ever has the inclination to say one word in his life, then he's chosen the right one.

Acknowledgements

Writing a novel is never a solitary task, and I'd like to warmly thank the following people whose involvement made this one possible.

My agent, Selwa Anthony, for her valuable story input and writerly advice, as well as her steadfast belief in me over the years. Selwa, you are a treasured friend and role model – thank you with all my heart!

My publisher, Larissa Edwards, for her dedication and hard work, and the awesome crew at Simon and Schuster. My talented editors, whose insights helped me become a better writer: Selena Hanet-Hutchins, Drew Keys, Kate O'Donnell and Roberta Ivers.

Russell Taylor for being my rock, and for giving me his love, faith and support over many years. Sarah Clarke, Merrilyn Gray and Julian Davies for cheering me on. Dan Mitchell for giving me a home in the bush, and for his love and friendship and ongoing inspiration. Bet and Norm Mitchell for their kindness and hospitality, and for allowing me to pore over Norm's wonderful war memoirs.

Ian Irvine for being a fount of writerly knowledge and good sense; Josephine Pennicott for taking me under her wing. Megan Inwood for allowing me to borrow her daughter's name; Stuart Ruthven for insights about the Boonah region; and Hailey and Luke for reminding me that stories (and life) are supposed to be fun!

My mum, Jeanette, for inspiring my love of books, and for her wisdom and continuing faith in me; my dad, Bernie, for a lifetime of memorable stories and yarns; my sister Katie for her countless facials (to repair the wrinkles she gives me by making me laugh!); and my sister Sarah who's always been my staunchest fan – even when success seemed a remote and impossible dream.

My love and thanks to you all.

I would also like to acknowledge and thank the Ugarapul people of the Fassifern region of south-west Queensland, whose history inspired my references to Indigenous culture in *Thornwood House*.

Anna Romer

About the author

Anna Romer grew up in a family of book-lovers and yarn-tellers, which inspired her lifelong love affair with stories. A graphic artist by trade, she also spent many years travelling the globe stockpiling story material from the Australian outback, then Asia, New Zealand, Europe and America.

Her first novel, *Thornwood House*, reflects her fascination with forgotten diaries and letters, dark family secrets, rambling old houses, and love in its many guises – as well as her passion for the uniquely beautiful Australian landscape. Her second novel, *Lyrebird Hill*, was published in 2014.

When she's not writing (or falling in love with another book), Anna is an avid gardener, knitter, bushwalker and conservationist. She lives on a remote bush property in northern New South Wales.

If you enjoyed *Thornwood House*, you'll love *Beyond the Orchard*, Anna Romer's hotly anticipated third novel, coming to a bookstore near you in November 2016. Read on for a sneak peek at the first two chapters.

Restless Shadows

S uch a clever, golden-haired girl. Sandy freckles danced on her cheeks, and her watchful eyes were as dark as the wild kelp that grew beyond the shore.

'Found in a seashell,' the fisherman claimed.

The Queen clasped her hands to stop them trembling. A child washed up on the beach, all alone in the world, in need of a mother; and she, the Queen, with empty arms and a heart that ached to be filled.

1

With infinite care, he lifted her into his arms and staggered through the dark house, out into the garden. She weighed almost nothing, as though her living soul had been the only thing giving her substance.

Treading heavily across the grass, he went downhill towards the orchard, through the weeping mulberry trees she had loved. The sky was starless, the garden black with shadows. When he reached the dim leafy corner of the yard where the icehouse lurked unseen, he paused, breathless.

Drinking in the night air, he blinked to clear his eyes. He would not let his mind revisit what he had done. Later, in the dusty quiet of his room, among his books and familiar things, he would crumble. But not here, not now.

The trees around him blurred, the sea breeze blew icy on his cheeks. He pressed his lips to her forehead, wanting only comfort – but the chill in her skin, the clammy stickiness of sweat and blood, and the vague dark odour of death brought the realisation crashing down upon him.

He had lost her.

The linchpin that held the fragments of his world together, the singular ray of hope in his grey life; she was gone. He could only blame himself. He had tried to contain her in the prison of his love, but instead he had smothered her. He had wanted to keep her safe, protect her, give her the life he had envisaged for her, a good life. Instead, he had clipped her wings, stolen from her everything she held dear.

No one could know. If anyone asked, he would say she had moved on, gone back to her family. Returned to her old life, the life she had lived before him. The life he had always resented so bitterly –

A murmur drifted from the darkness. His heart kicked over. His breath became quick as he searched the pale smudge of her face in the moonlight. Shadows danced over her features, playing tricks with his mind. He prayed for a tiny sign – another murmur, a whisper of forgiveness, the faint utterance of his name. Not that he would have heard it; the booming pulse in his ears was deafening. Minutes ticked away. His ears and eyes began to ache, so keenly alert were they, but still he could not move. The sound came again, clearer this time. Hope ebbed away. It was not breath he had heard, not a whisper, merely the scratch of dry leaves along the brick path in the orchard.

Regathering her against him, he forced his numb legs to take one measured step after another. Slowly, he made his way through the darkness to the icehouse.

'You'll be safe now, my darling. I'll be here to watch over you always.'

The keys were in his pocket. He fumbled them out and then somehow forced them into the lock. The door creaked, opening into deeper dark. A gust of damp billowed out, and with it came the smell of earth and stone, of air undisturbed for many years. Air that would, as of this night forth, remain undisturbed for many more years to come.

2

Winter had arrived early. It was only five o'clock, and already the night sky had settled black over the city. Trams rattled past the old theatre, churning up a slipstream of chip wrappers and dust. The air smelled of diesel exhaust, and faintly of the ocean. As the streetlights blinked on along Dandenong Road, I hurried along the footpath towards the Astor Theatre. On the menu tonight was a Hitchcock double feature. *Rear Window* I had seen a thousand times, but *Rope* was new to me. Critics deemed it Hitchcock's masterpiece and I was abuzz to see it.

A short balding man with a shaggy beard stood near the stairs, gazing at his shoes. He wore jeans and a cardigan, and clutched a beaten old briefcase. The cold evening air had flushed his ears pink. I wanted to run to him, fling myself into his arms the way I'd done as a little girl, smother his round cheeks in kisses; instead, I trod silently up behind him and tapped him on the shoulder.

He whirled around and beamed, but then his face fell. 'Lucy, you look terrible.'

I gave him a quick hug. 'Thanks, Dad. It's great to see you, too.'

He peered into my face. 'Been getting enough sleep?'

'It's only jetlag. I'll be fine.'

463

'That's what you said days ago. How's Adam? He's arriving soon, isn't he?'

'Six weeks.' I gazed at the people swarming along the footpath around us; watchful for the one familiar face I most dreaded seeing.

'Missing him already, are we?' Dad said.

'Hmm,' I said noncommittally, and then nudged his arm as we shuffled forward in the queue. 'The place is packed. I hope we get good seats.'

'You sure you're okay?' Dad wanted to know.

'Stop fussing.' Regretting my sharpness, I tried to make amends. 'How's the new book?'

He brightened, wrestling a bundle of papers from his brief-case. 'Finally finished. I managed to turn a deaf ear to Wilma's nagging today and get the ending written. I hope you like it.'

'Wow, Dad.' Hitchcock and Adam both forgotten, I turned the manuscript over in my hands, marvelling at the weight of it. Suddenly I wanted to be at home, curled in my favourite chair, a pot of scalding tea by my side as I lost myself in the warped and wonderful world of my father's latest creation. 'Let me guess, Rumpelstiltskin?'

Dad nodded, latching his briefcase. 'I couldn't resist turning him into the love interest. He got a rum deal in the original; he helps a damsel in distress and then they weasel out of paying him.'

'He wanted their firstborn,' I pointed out.

Dad shook his head. 'A deal's a deal, Lucy. If you can't afford to lose, then don't gamble.'

'Trust you to tell the gritty side of the story.'

'The underdogs of the fairytale kingdom always get a bad rap. The so-called evil stepmothers and wicked witches, the trolls under the bridge – they were only doing what they thought was best. Why are baddies always so misunderstood?'

'Umm.' I bit back a smile. 'Because they're *bad*?'

Dad's round cheeks glowed. 'Luce, everyone's a hero in their own story. Even the crooks. They're all struggling to get along in life, find a measure of happiness, just like the next guy.'

I couldn't help smiling as we went up the Astor's wide front steps into the entry foyer. I had missed our talks. I'd only been back to Melbourne once in the past four years. London was on the other side of the world, and although Dad and I talked on the phone most weeks, the physical distance had brought back the hairline fractures in our closeness.

I hugged the parcel to my chest. 'It's good to be back.'

Dad gave my shoulder a gentle squeeze. 'Things aren't the same without you, kiddo. I'm glad you're here, but I know the next two months will fly. I wish you and Adam would move home.'

'London *is* home for Adam.'

'But not for you.'

'It is now,' I murmured, then instantly regretted how bleak my words had sounded. Dad seemed on the brink of commenting, but the queue progressed suddenly towards the ticket booth and, to my relief, the moment was lost.

Usually I would have been making the most of our father–daughter time. We could banter to our hearts' content, lose ourselves in the fantastical bizarro world we had created together. Things between us hadn't always been so sweet. We still skirted around certain topics but mostly we were stable, all thanks to Dad's stories. His publishers marketed his novellas for young adults, but he had fans of all ages, from five to ninety-five. He rewrote fairytales, turning the classics on their heads: a wicked Thumbelina who climbed into little boys' ears and drove them to evil deeds, a kindly Bluebeard who locked himself in the cellar to escape his overbearing wives, Red Riding Hood as a shape-shifting villain. I loved Dad's topsy-turvy world. My happiest moments were always those I spent bringing his twisted fairytales to life with pen and ink.

We had been a team for almost a decade, since I was seventeen. One day, cross with Dad after another of our rows, I had defaced one of his manuscripts with angry little sketches, which he later found. He'd begun to cackle; soon he was laughing full-belly.

'You caught it,' he marvelled, wiping his eyes. 'Damn it, Luce, you caught the ogre's expression exactly. Talk about comic! And look at the prince's feeble chin, it's perfect.'

A few weeks later, his publisher called, asking to see a folio of my work. I had sketches from my art class at school, and other doodles I'd done in my textbook margins. To my surprise, they loved them. When Dad's next book came out, his legion of young fans were overjoyed to discover it illustrated in full colour. That edition did so well the publisher commissioned me to illustrate the new print runs for all Dad's earlier books. Almost overnight, it seemed, my father and I had become a team. For the first time in years, we had common ground. The arguments petered out; our silences gave way to discussions about character sketches and colour palettes. Dad seemed to regard me through more appreciative eyes.

We bought our tickets and made our way up the grand staircase. We were early. The first film didn't start for twenty minutes. Still time to settle ourselves, grab a bite to eat and nab our favourite seats.

'Uh-oh,' Dad muttered as we reached the upstairs foyer. 'Here's trouble.'

I followed his gaze. At first, I didn't recognise the striking young man on the other side of the balustrade. He was standing with a group under the chandelier, and when he turned to acknowledge one of his companions, the light caught the side of his face.

My stomach knotted. Coby Roseblade had filled out in the past five years. His chronic skinniness was gone; he'd clearly been working out. The snug fabric of his pullover left just enough to the imagination to make any red-blooded girl's mouth water. He'd cropped his hair short, which accentuated his broad cheekbones and square jaw.

'What's he doing here?' Dad said.

I swallowed. 'No doubt he's come to see the double feature, like us.'

'I'm sorry, Luce. If I'd known he was a Hitchcock fan, I'd have suggested we do something else tonight. Want to leave?'

I shook my head. 'I was bound to run into him eventually. He wasn't the reason I left, you know.'

Dad didn't look convinced. 'You realise I'll have to go over and say hello.'

'It'd be rude not to.'

'You coming?'

'Actually –' I gazed around for a suitable excuse, and spied the queue of people at the kiosk. I dug out my wallet and forced a bright smile. 'I'll get us both a choc top before they run out.'

Dad looked back at me. His face softened. 'Since Wilma's not here to witness my depravity, you'd better grab a packet of chips as well.'

I stood in the kiosk queue for an eternity, fighting to control the butterflies swarming my ribcage, determined not to let my attention stray over to the group beneath the chandelier. My gaze didn't wander, but my thoughts did. The first time Coby Roseblade declared he wanted to marry me we'd been eight. He was a skinny freckle-faced boy, newly fostered and insecure, in need of a friend. I'd shrugged and told him, 'Sure, why not?' The second time he asked, four years ago, I'd been twenty-two. I'd made my feelings clear in the only way I'd known how: I packed my bags, and without explanation booked myself on the next flight to London.

I collected my chips and ice cream, relieved to see that my father had returned to our spot near the stairs. On my way back, a woman crossed my path. A tall, beautiful woman with sleek dark hair and the bluest eyes I'd ever seen. She stopped abruptly in front of me, taking only an instant to cover her shock with a smile.

'Hey, Lucy.'

My stomach flipped. 'Nina.'

She looked radiant. Her cheeks were rose-petal pink, her full lips stained dark red. She'd always been beautiful, but in the four years since I'd seen her she'd transformed into a goddess.

'I was hoping to run into you,' she said warmly. 'How long are you staying?'

'A couple of months. I'm housesitting for one of Dad's friends.'

Her dimples came out as she smiled. 'A soon-to-be married woman,' she said with a husky little laugh. 'Who would have thought?'

I found myself smiling back. 'Least of all me.'

'I'm dying to meet him. Adam, isn't it?'

I nodded. 'He'll be here at the end of July. Maybe we could all –'

'Oh, I'd love to!'

I took a breath, settling my flutters. 'How're things with Coby?'

Nina's lips quirked and she wrinkled her nose. On anyone else, the expression would have looked silly, but Nina Gilbert, my one-time best friend, managed to look even more adorable. 'We're great, never better. He's following Morgan's footsteps into uni, a history major; I'm really proud of him.' There was an uncomfortable beat, and then she leaned nearer and said softly, 'Is it too weird? You know, that Coby and I hooked up so soon after you left?'

'Maybe a little.' Then I sighed. 'Actually, it's not weird at all. Coby and I were never really together, remember. Besides, I was the one who ran off.'

She hesitated, nibbling her lip. Then, to my surprise, she brushed her fingers down my arm. 'He misses you, Lucy. So does Morgan.'

I tensed and drew back. A shadow crossed Nina's beautiful face, and she smiled with such sadness that it tore my heart. I hadn't meant to flinch away, to react so strongly to the mention of his name. Morgan, I thought bitterly. Coby's foster father. The man who'd come between us in the end. I felt a shiver coming on and rubbed my arms. Morgan's part in my sudden departure for London might have been unintentional, but it didn't make him any less to blame.

Suddenly, I wanted to tell Nina everything. The real reason I'd left, the real reason I'd stayed away for so long. The real reason I'd abandoned her and Coby, my two closest friends. I wanted to grab her by the hand and rush back out into the cold air of the street, and tell her the whole long sorry story.

'How are you?' I said instead.

Her smile was luminous. 'Really good. Amazing, in fact.' She moved her hand protectively to her midriff, and something made me glance down. She'd gained weight, I saw, taken a small step from the realm of voluptuous, into fleshier territory; but as I admired the sapphire blue vintage dress that clung to her hourglass figure, I noticed how the folds under the bodice gathered delicately over her belly . . . her rather swollen belly.

'Oh,' I blurted.

Nina blushed – not the sort of harsh veiny redness that afflicted me, but a pretty flush of colour that danced lightly on her perfect cheekbones. She bit her lips together, and then beamed.

'Yeah, who would have thought? Me having a baby, insane isn't it? A little girl,' she added with a hitch of excitement. Patting her bulge, she smiled warmly into my face. 'We couldn't be more thrilled. I'm so looking forward to holding her for the first time, can you imagine? And Coby's really stoked, he's –'

She caught herself, and pressed her lips into one of those smiles that said, *I've gone and put my foot in it, haven't I?*

'Coby always wanted kids,' I said quietly.

'Tons of them,' she agreed, widening her eyes. Then she added wistfully, 'Family equals security for him. Seven years in the foster system will do that to a person.'

'He'll make a great dad.'

Nina grasped my hand. 'Oh Luce, it's so good to see your face.'

This time I squeezed back. 'Yours, too.'

Then she grimaced. 'I really have to wee. Will you promise me something?'

'What?'

'Don't be a stranger. Come and visit. Please?'

'Sure.'

'Hey, Tuesday's curry night at our place, what do you say?'

'Sounds good. I've missed your curries.'

'Great! Come at six, we're early eaters. Lucy, it's amazing to see you. I can't wait to hear all about your adventures.' She dipped towards me, placed a butterfly-soft kiss on my cheek and then hurried away. Knots of people stepped aside for her, opened their little groups to allow her fleeting access, and then followed her with admiring glances.

A sticky trickle of melting ice cream leaked onto my hand. I headed back to where Dad and I had been standing near the balustrade. As I shuffled around the perimeter of a tightknit group, something made me look across the foyer towards the chandelier. Coby tilted his chin, a cautious acknowledgement. I lifted my hand in a wave, and then hurried back to Dad.

'You look peaky,' he said as I delivered his ice cream. 'How was Nina?'

'She's pregnant, actually.' My words came out stiffer than I'd intended. 'I guess it must have slipped your mind?'

Dad winced. 'Sorry about that, kiddo. I was scared you might jet off again if you knew.'

I sighed. 'It's okay, Dad. Coby and I were never really an item . . . He thought we were, but it wasn't that way with us. You know?'

'I know he had a hell of a time after you went AWOL. Morgan said he stayed in his room for six months brooding to Metallica.'

My cheeks burned. I felt hot and weak again. Tearing the cellophane off my ice cream, I cracked the hard chocolate topping with my teeth and devoured the cold sweetness in a couple of bites. The sugar hit revived me.

'Nina wants me to visit,' I told Dad.

'I think you should. She's missed you, you know.'

'She didn't waste any time jumping into Coby's bed.'

'A position you vacated rather swiftly, I recall.'

I busied myself crunching through the last of my cone.

Dad's eyes narrowed. 'What's with you tonight? You usually wait until the movie starts before you even take off the wrapper.'

Balling the cellophane, I glanced around for a bin. Dad took the rubbish from my sticky fingers and gave me his hanky.

I sighed. 'I was hungry.'

Dad scouted for a bin, and when he came back he said, 'You won't like hearing this, but I have to ask. Are you certain you're not rushing into this? Marriage, I mean. You're only twenty-six, you've got your whole life ahead of you.'

'What's brought this on?'

'You don't seem quite yourself. And it's not jetlag. Not getting cold feet, are you?'

'Adam's a really nice guy,' I reassured him, wiping my hands on his hanky and passing it back. 'I can't wait for you to meet him.'

Dad frowned. 'Hmm.'

I glanced towards the bright spot beneath the chandelier. Coby and Nina and their group of friends had moved along. My encounter with Nina had left me feeling as if I'd found something precious that had been lost, and now it was gone again.

I twisted the ring on my finger, the big square cut diamond warm from my skin. I was more like Coby than I cared to admit. I understood his hunger for security, but unlike him, I didn't crave a big family or marriage. I wanted a safe harbour, a place to drop anchor and drift quietly through life, knowing I was sheltered from any storms that blew my way. Adam, with his soft-spoken humour and gentle strength, was my harbour. There was no fiery passion between us, no tempest that might blow me off course, but rather a solid alliance built on loyalty and respect. For me, that was enough.

'Did I tell you about Morgan?' Dad said suddenly.

My shoulders slumped. 'Remind me again?'

'He and Gwen finally got divorced. They're still friends, although Gwen's living in Canberra now with her new partner. Funny,' Dad added wistfully, 'how things turn out, isn't it.'

'How do you mean?'

'Gwen and Morgan were always firm friends, but there was never any real spark between them.'

I wondered if he'd overheard my thoughts, and felt my defences prickle. 'What's so bad about that? Sparks are over-rated. They don't last.'

Ron looked at me. 'You used to light up when Morgan came into the room, you know.'

I shot him a warning glare. 'I was a kid.'

'Crazy, isn't it. Young Coby falling for you, when it was always his father you liked.'

'*Foster* father. And I didn't *like* him, it was just hero worship.'

Dad scratched his beard and smiled. 'You and Morgan always had a bond. As a kid, you thought the sun shone out of him. Then when you were older, I seem to remember a crush. These days you're barely on speaking terms with him. What happened?'

My words came out harsher than I'd intended. 'I grew up.'

'Did I tell you he's been helping Wilma at the historical society? He restored their photo collection, all those old prints from the war. Did a superb job. He blew up copies for your mother to put in the Red Cross auction, they were a huge hit.'

I clung to the moment's silence, and then said firmly, 'Wilma is not my mother.'

Dad's sighed. 'She'd really like to be, Luce.'

Pinching my top lip, I reminded myself for the millionth time that Dad was doing his best. My mother, Karen, had been his soul mate, his great love. Sixteen years had passed since we lost her, but it seemed like no time at all. Dad had fallen into a black depression after she died, his grief an entity in itself, a shadow-creature living right there in the house with us. I spent my early teenage years tiptoeing around my father, running and fetching to keep him happy, hiding in my room when rage and despair drove him to seek oblivion in the bottom of a wine cask. Years later, after the breakdown that sent him to Banksia House, Wilma came onto the scene and everything changed. We began to rub along as a family. Dad rediscovered his smile, and we found the common ground of his stories and my illustrations. Yet the shadow lingered, mostly ignored, a hairline thread of wariness still wedged firmly between us.

I took a deep breath. 'Can we not have this conversation right now?'

Dad had been studying me, his eyes betraying some of their old hollowness. 'Sorry, kiddo.'

'You were telling me about Morgan.'

Dad nodded. 'He's a professor now. A brilliant one, too. Hard to believe he started out as a skinny half-starved kid who didn't even finish high school.'

I stayed silent. I'd known Morgan since I was four. Dad met him at the university when Morgan was a down-and-out history student, and Dad a disillusioned lecturer. They'd recognised each other as kindred spirits, struck up a friendship, and had remained close over the years, through the hard times, and then as both their lives took turns for the better. Morgan had no family of his own – or so I'd assumed when he started coming back home with Dad for the holidays. He never spoke about his past, at least not to me. My mother took him under her wing and he became the son she'd always longed for.

The year I turned nine, Morgan announced he was getting married. My parents were beyond thrilled. They insisted he bring the lucky girl over for dinner. Gwen Larkin was another one of Dad's students. She was tall and willowy, as pale as a moonbeam, a staunch women's libber with a passion for saving the environment, the underdog, the downtrodden. She was everything I aspired to, and I might have been as smitten by her as everyone else was, but for one glaring flaw: she was about to marry the man I loved.

Dad looked at me. 'He's always had a soft spot for you, Lucy.'

'Who?'

Dad sighed. 'I hate it when you do that. You know perfectly well who I'm talking about.'

I narrowed my eyes and held up my hand, wiggling my fingers so my engagement ring – my very expensive diamond engagement ring – twinkled conspicuously. 'I'm already spoken for. Besides, Morgan's too old for me.'

'Ouch. You young people can be really cruel sometimes.'

I couldn't hold back a smile. 'Your choc top's melting.'

Dad examined his ice cream. Condensation bubbled over the hard chocolate coating, while threads of cream snaked over the back of his hand. Taking out his sticky hanky, he mopped the leaks thoughtfully.

'I just want you to be happy, kiddo.'

'I am happy.'

'Are you, Luce – really?'

I nodded.

Dad looked dubious. 'If you could have anything at all, what would it be?'

'You mean if I could rub a magic lamp?'

'Or wish on a star. Yeah.'

I blinked. That was no-brainer. I'd wish for a perfect body . . . ten million dollars . . . creative inspiration . . . a life that wasn't a shambles. Gosh, where to begin?

I tucked my diamond ring from sight. 'I've got everything I need,' I told my father crisply. 'What about you? What's your burning desire?'

He smiled wistfully. 'To hear my little girl laugh more often. It's such a pretty laugh. Not to mention how damn cute she sounds when she snorts.'

I swallowed. 'It's not like you to be sentimental.'

'I'm just getting the vibe that your life isn't as rosy as you want everyone to think. I mean, why are you here alone? You've half-blinded me with that diamond a dozen times, but the man himself is conspicuous in his absence. What's really going on, Luce?'

I couldn't meet his eyes. The air in the old theatre seemed suddenly stale, unbreathable. I gazed towards the stairwell, wanting to be out on the windy street, breathing the damp night air. Instead, I flashed back to the time *before*: before I ran away to London, before I stuffed things up so badly I could no longer bear to show my face. Before I turned my back on everyone I loved. Had I really thought that coming home would be easy?

Heat crept into my cheeks. My ears began to burn. I braced myself for Dad to continue prodding.

He must have sensed my defeat, because he said nothing more. A moment later, the gong sounded. The first feature was about to begin. I did a quick scan of the foyer and, satisfied my ex and my pregnant former best friend were nowhere in view, I linked arms with Dad and steered him towards the welcome darkness of the theatre.

*

Elegant golden curtains slid back from the screen and the film began. As the opening music flooded the auditorium, I settled back in the seat and retreated inside myself to mull over my father's words.

Gwen and Morgan were always firm friends, but there was never any real spark between them.

The divorce had been a long time coming, I mused. They had always been an on-again, off-again sort of couple. They had done their best to keep it amicable for Coby's sake, but he always seemed to get caught in the crossfire. As Nina said, family was everything to Coby.

The year I turned twenty-two, Morgan and Gwen separated, yet again. Coby had been devastated, and we began spending more time together. Not dating, at least not in my mind – just hanging out, listening to records, or walking for endless hours on the beach while Coby talked his parents' latest split out of his system. We grew closer, much closer than we'd ever been.

The night of my birthday party, Morgan had seemed distant. While I danced away the hours with Nina and Coby and our group of friends, I kept glimpsing him from the corner of my eye – talking to Dad and Wilma or replenishing the cooler, fixing a string of blown fairy lights. After my friends left, I found him alone in the garden. He was sitting in the shadows on an old timber bench, his back resting against the shed wall. His sandy hair was raked about, his face craggy with tiredness, dark circles under his eyes. He must have heard me approach, because he looked around and smiled.

'Who's this gorgeous creature?' he said with a wink. 'What have you done with my little Lucy?'

When I didn't say anything, he gave me an odd look. 'You okay, sport?'

'Dad's going to kill me,' I blurted.

Morgan cocked an eyebrow. 'What've you done?'

I sat beside him on the bench. I wore my usual jeans, Doc Martens on my feet, my dark hair loose around my shoulders. Nina had helped me choose a short dress to wear as a top, a glittery red sheath with spaghetti straps and low-cut neckline that made me look shapelier than I was. I let the lacy wrap fall away from my shoulders. The night was warm for November. The garden was mostly dark, except for the fairy lights that Wilma and I had strung from the trees earlier that day.

In the gloom, I saw – no, not *saw* exactly, rather, *felt* – Morgan's gaze linger on me. A slow, appreciative gaze that set my blood alight. Feather-soft, it took in my bare arms and danced its way across the skimpy neckline. It trailed up my throat and then, as warm as honey, settled for one intoxicating moment on my lips. When his eyes finally met mine, a shadow crossed his face. His jaw tightened. Then he tried to mask the tightness behind a smile.

'What have you done?' he asked again, only now his voice was strangely soft.

'I got a tattoo.' I lifted my shoulder for him to see. The design inked into my skin was still a little inflamed, but no longer sore. 'It's kind of a birthday present to myself. What do you think?'

Morgan looked at my shoulder and whistled. 'A little mermaid. She looks just like you.' He smiled and the garden seemed suddenly very dark, as though even the fairy lights had dimmed. The stars grew dull, the round face of the moon faded to a hazy thumbprint. Morgan, on the other hand, glowed.

'I love you,' I whispered. 'I always have, Morgan. Always will.'

His smile faltered. He tilted his head, as though uncertain he'd heard correctly.

I was possessed, I must have been. The heat he had ignited in me with his lingering, appreciative glance must have short-circuited the logical part of my brain. As though watching from a distance, I saw my hand float towards his face. I saw my fingers gently cup his cheek. I saw myself lean against him, my face turned upwards like a small pale sunflower in the dark garden, seeking the light. I watched my younger self with a mix of mortification and dread, as I slid my other arm around his neck and pressed my lips against his mouth –

'No!'

Jolting back to the dark cinema, I realised I'd spoken aloud. Not just spoken – I'd virtually yelled. My father shot me a startled look, but he then must have assumed a tense moment in the film had taken me off guard. He smiled indulgently and settled his attention back on the screen.

I sank into my seat. My cheeks burned. I thought of Coby and Nina, somewhere in the dark theatre, perhaps sitting nearby. They would have recognised my voice, known the shout had come from me. I imagined them casting each other sideways looks in the flickering gloom, Nina digging Coby with her elbow, the two of them laughing a little and rolling their eyes.

I sank lower, resigning myself to sit out the rest of the film in shame. Then, from somewhere behind me, a woman cried, 'Oh!'

The man on the other side of Dad jumped, and then gave a sheepish snort. A few people tittered.

'Bloody Hitchcock,' I heard Dad mutter. 'Nightmares all round, tonight.'

Exploring My Writing Process

For me, a novel begins a long time before I sit down to write. I always start a project with a new notebook. Over many months – or years – I fill it with photos, newspaper clippings, articles, and random scribblings. I make lists and timelines, draw maps, create detailed dossiers for my characters and build histories around them. I currently have about fifteen of these notebooks on the boil, each containing the raw ideas of a future novel.

As the bones of a story begin to emerge, I pick over my favourite themes – forbidden love, obsession, scandal and family secrets, and the lies we tell to each other and to ourselves. I never consciously try to work my themes into the storyline, but they are always brewing away under the surface, helping me to stay focused.

I also choose a fairytale that resonates with me, and think of ways I can weave it through the plot. In *Thornwood House* I played with the idea of Bluebeard, and his mysterious locked room which eventually tempted his wives to their deaths. The manifestation of this theme in the final story is very subtle, but it inspired the sense of curiosity and danger that I wanted to convey – both for the back bedroom of the house at Thornwood, and for the old settler's hut near the gully.

When I finish brainstorming, my pile of notes is thicker than a telephone directory. I rarely look at these notes again.

The story seeds have been planted; now it's time to let them germinate and grow in the dark garden of my subconscious.

Meanwhile, I dive into the research, which is another great way to peel open further layers of story.

My research involves a lot of travel to soak up scenery and get a feel for local people and families and their fascinating pasts. For *Thornwood House*, I needed to know what life was like in the Fassifern region of Queensland during the 1940s, and how a small rural community was impacted by the war. I studied old newspapers, maps and photographs, and explored the landmarks in my story, such as Boonah's historic Lutheran graveyard, and a spooky old settler's hut I discovered in a forgotten paddock.

I also read heaps of war correspondence, as well as wartime memoirs and diary entries. Mum gave me a bundle of airgraph letters that were sent to my grandmother during the Second World War. These letters documented a young pilot's longing for home, and made the war experience all the more personal for me.

By this stage I'm usually impatient to start the plotting process, which I really love. For me, there's nothing more enjoyable than sitting at my 'plotting table' with a thermos of tea, and assembling the skeleton of a new story.

I love making a mess with scraps of paper, jotting down ideas for scenes and plot points and possible twists, and then puzzling them all together like a huge unwieldy jigsaw. The plot is always organic; when I start drafting, the story flies off on tangents and I invariably write myself into a corner. Back I go to the plotting table and re-shuffle my paper scraps until the problem is solved, then I return to my embryonic story and redraft. This phase of the process goes on for many months, and is a mental and emotional rollercoaster ride!

Some scenes – endings in particular – are more difficult to write. I enter avoidance mode: gardening or knitting or brushing the dog, or collecting wildflower seeds for my various regeneration projects – meanwhile freaking out over the gaps in my story, worrying myself into a state of creative agitation. By the time I'm ready to write my most challenging scenes, I'm a mess . . . but that's good! Angst and chaos are part of the writing process, too, and are frequently the catalyst for better work.

Often I write to silence, but some scenes require that I work from a place of heightened emotion. If this is the case, on goes the music – Mumford and Sons, Will Oldham, Yma Sumac, Roky Erickson, Loreena McKennitt. For especially dark brooding scenes I play Espers, Six Organs of Admittance, PG Six, Nick Cave; for the ending I'll crank up Muse, maybe a few Metallica tracks, or some weird obscure 70s folk rock. At some stage during a critical scene I'll pull out Evanescence and have a great old cry.

Understandably, after all this intense focus, the story lines begin to blur; it becomes easy to overlook mistakes. One of the most exhilarating (and terrifying) parts of the process is handing over the novel draft to my agent and editors . . . and my eagle-eyed sister. They are the ghosts in the novel machine, and without them the story would be a shambles. An editor's job is to pick apart a story and then send it back for the writer to fix. If someone points out that part of the plotline or a character doesn't work, I gladly make the changes, knowing the story will be better for it. It's a daunting process, but my 'behind the scenes' team always gives me deeper understanding and insight – not just into the novel we're working on, but more importantly, into the craft of storytelling.

Another vital part of the process – especially after slogging towards deadlines – is clearing the brain fog. For me, this usually involves vanishing deep into the bush never to be heard from again . . . well, at least not until dinnertime! I'll swim in the river, or climb into the hills and daydream on a bed of wildflowers. When I finally return to the world with the peppery scent of yellow-buttons clinging to my clothes, my brain and body are fully recharged.

One of my favourite quotes comes from Joseph Campbell, who said, 'Follow your bliss.' For me, the process of creating a novel is very much about following the trail of ideas that I find most intriguing and inspiring . . . a strategy that works well for writing in general, and also for life.

                                                                Anna Romer